A TWISTED TALES NOVEL

SERPENT
IN
WHITE
NYLA K

Deep in the Empyrean forest… Nothing stays hidden.

We are The Principality, and our community is special. Some of us joined, some were born into it. But regardless of how we got here, we all serve *him*.

Our Head Priest is a wise and fearless leader. All-knowing, the secrets of our land are spoken to him through the air. We follow him willingly, worshipping the Earth as intended. While his brother lurks in the shadows...

But who *is* this King I can't stop watching, so captivating and beautiful? And who is the man with the snake eyes?
I must know more about them both...
I must peek beneath the cover.

Unearthing the truth brings me between a King and a Serpent, and the lust we share isn't the only unexpected gift. What is a young servant to do but follow his path?

I will seek answers in the woods of the mountain...

Where existence is not what it seems

To Special Agent Dale Cooper,

A true dreamer, in every lodge.

WE ARE THE PRINCIPALITY PLAYLIST

(Listen on Spotify)

The Promised Neverland – Rifti Beats
Come As You Are – Imaginary Future
Serpents – Sharon Van Etten
Come White – Marilyn Manson
Zombie – Miley Cyrus
Night Owls – Sleepermane, Cassio
Comedown (acoustic) – Bush
Closer – Boyce Avenue, Sarah Hyland
Young Blood – The Naked And Famous
Running To The Edge Of The World – Marilyn Manson
drugs – EDEN
t r a n s p a r e n t s o u l - WILLOW , Travis Barker
Disassociative – Marilyn Manson
Faded – Tyga, Lil Wayne
BITE – Troye Sivan
Comfortably Numb (acoustic live) – Staind
Bother – Stone Sour
Change (In the House of Flies) – Deftones
Coming of Age – Foster The People
I Don't Like The Drugs (But The Drugs Like Me) – Marilyn Manson
Mindreader – A Day To Remember
Control (acoustic) – Puddle Of Mudd
drowning – Eden Project
Think About U – Ryan Hemsworth, Joji
Nutshell (acoustic live) – Staind
Snuff – Slipknot
Feel Something – Jaymes Young
Tusk and Bone – Shaman's Harvest
Too Late – M83
A Forest – The Cure
Red Sky – Thrice
The Gift – Seether
Where Is My Mind? – Pixies
Bleed – Cold

Graveyard Girl – M83
Suicidal Dream – Silverchair
Rhiannon (Live 2005) – Stevie Nicks
Breathe Again – Pop Evil
Ghost (acoustic) – Badflower
I Always Wanna Die (Sometimes) – The 1975
Animal (stripped) – MISSIO
From Eden – Hozier
Hallelujah – Theory of a Deadman
In the Woods Somewhere - Hozier

FOREWORD

Welcome to the Expanse.

Just a quick note, to ensure you're prepared for what this story is.

This book is unlike anything I've written before. It's not *regular*, in any sense, and it doesn't necessarily fit into any typical tropes, as far as the romance molds go. If I had to label it, I'd call it somewhere in the realm of paranormal, though not quite. Maybe psychological or metaphysical.

In short, its message will depend on your interpretation.

Your mind must be open to understand the ways of this forest, and its inhabitants. In unearthing the truth behind what shapes us, there will be sensitive subjects. The world is not a pretty place.

If this thought makes you uneasy, please proceed with caution.

This story contains graphic depictions of certain elements imperative to the transformation of our characters. Some may consider them *dark*, but such is the way. There are also many different facets of relationships in this book. And they are not *typical* either.

Basically, if you're looking for a standard romance done the way it always has been, this book will not be for you. But if you're open to viewing sex, love, relationships and reality in ways that may make you uncomfortable, that may not fit how you usually perceive them, and if you're willing to accept the unique, queer, and curious for what it is, then step right up. We've been waiting for you.

Just remember while reading that this is a fictional story. And while some events could be triggering, every aspect is important to truly feel and understand what led us here.

Because deep in the Empyrean forest, things may not be as they seem to two-dimensional view.

CARPENTRY
BUILDING

LAKE
WILLOW

FISHERMAN'S
DOCK

MED
TRAILERS

GREENHOUSE

REGNUM HOUSING

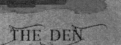

THE DEN

DOMESTIC
HOUSING

N

W THE EXPANSE E

S

THE OVERLOOK

THE CLEARING

SCHOOL TRAILERS

HUNTING SHACK

DRAKE'S CABIN

WHITE TRUMPET MOUNTAIN

TEMPLE

THE LAB

FARMLAND

THE FIELD OF INFLUENCE

*No sooner had it touched his tongue
than he heard a strange whispering
of little voices outside his window.*

The White Snake
Grimm's Fairy Tales

PROLOGUE

Human beings exist purely as pieces of a large puzzle; each one of our souls designed to fit the bigger picture. The greater *Expanse*.

As are we all made from the same components; blood and muscle and bone, flesh and hair. Built of organic chemistry, all creatures, equally.

As feet, hooves press into the soil, so hands, paws rush through the leaves or blades of grass. A whisper from the wind and the harmony of a babbling brook, from which we all breathe and take a drink.

You see, Earth operates like a machine, well-oiled and ever-moving. The constant turning over and over, day becoming night and night becoming day. Weeks turn to months, turn to years. Leaves fall, land freezes and thaws. Animals die.

People do.

And outside of it all, the spirit of a God so large, so powerful, we couldn't possibly comprehend Her. As we are a story in Earth's biography, so is Earth the chapter to a longer book.

Time and space are infinite.

I suppose such things could make us feel insignificant. But on the contrary… Each breath inhaled and exhaled moves the needle.

We are all a part of it. Wheels in motion, for something much bigger.

Everything is connected. Everything has a point.

Death. Rebirth. Transformation.

Ecdysis.

CHAPTER ONE

ABDIEL

Today is here, and today is special. Just like every other day. My mother taught me that, rest her soul.

She told me, when I was just a small boy, that each day is a blessing, and we should live our lives cherishing every single moment we are given.

She died when I was twelve, so did my father. They are with Mother now.

But death doesn't erase us. My parents live on, in me and in the works they left behind.

It's comforting to know that.

So I make today count, as I did yesterday; as I will tomorrow.

After my shower, I make an egg and bacon sandwich with honey, my favorite, and then I practice for tomorrow's reflection. I'm singing a new song, which is always a little nerve-racking. But Jordan knows it well, so I think we'll do fine.

Smiling, I slip on a t-shirt, then open my door, hopping down the steps of my trailer.

It's an addition, and I'm so grateful for it. I haven't earned my own trailer just yet; so instead, Paul and Gina agreed to help me get an addition to theirs, for some privacy. I'm nineteen now, and living in the same shared space as my guardians can get a bit… cramped. To say the least.

I would've liked to have had my addition when I was fifteen, but I grin and bear it. Paul and Gina are great, and they give me distance when I need it.

I'm not saying I love to be alone, but there are times when I cherish it. The quiet.

The... *solitude.*

At the thought, hairs stand on the back of my neck and my breath stops short. Glancing at my arms, I have goosebumps. I pull my lower lip between my teeth...

"Are you cold?" Gina's loud yet somehow raspy voice startles me out of my thoughts, and I jump. "It's warm today."

"No, no." I smile at her, closing the door to my trailer. "Not cold. It was just a breeze. Did you get the bread I left you?" I change the subject.

She squeezes my arm and tugs me to walk with her. "Yes, I most certainly did. You made that yourself?" I nod, humbly of course. "It's delicious. You must have gotten your mother's baking gene."

My smile widens at mention of my mother from her best friend.

Gina and her husband, Paul, took me in when my parents died. The four of them had been best friends for years, since Mom and Dad joined The Principality. My parents were young, but Gina and Paul are even younger. In their thirties with a nineteen-year-old...

Don't feel bad for them. They love me.

I was born on the Expanse. I've never been outside our territory, and in all honesty, I wouldn't want to. The Regnum is my family, the Expanse my home. Even if it took my parents...

I shake myself out of these thoughts. "Hopefully not my father's overcooking gene." I smirk at Gina, and she elbows me.

"I don't know how you eat your bacon like that. It's basically crumbles!"

"Better than having it still oinking at me," I tease, and she rolls her eyes. "Paul on hoe duty?"

She puffs out a breath. "Yea, and then he's pulling a double shift..."

I pause. "Training?" She nods, hesitantly. "Why are they ramping up security? Did something happen?"

Gina shrugs. "All we've heard is that this autumn's yield is the most ambitious anyone's seen in years. They're planning the harvest to outweigh what we're used to, and I guess that calls for an increase in the Tribe."

Interesting...

I've never considered joining the Tribe. Not that I have anything

3

against fighting to protect what's ours. I'd gladly lay down my life for The Principality, my family... Mother. But they never ask me. I've been a Domestic since I was a kid. I suppose my talents are better suited to serve *him*.

My stomach flips and I distract myself by feeding into our menial conversation. "Are we working together today?"

"Yes indeed, kiddo." Gina smiles while we walk, soil and rock crunching beneath our steps as we approach the Den. "We've got wash for a few hours before break." She doesn't miss my sigh. "But if you'd like, I suppose you could take meal prep."

My face lights up. "Yea?"

"Sure," she chuckles. "Why not? Seeing how excited you are about it, I'm not sure I could say no." She pinches my cheeks, and I brush her off.

My face heats a bit, eyes darting toward the giant cabin. "G, I'm not a kid anymore," I whine, sounding entirely like one in my petulance.

She holds up her hands. "Sorry. I know, you're a *man*. Speaking of which, have you seen Kinsey? I know she wanted to ask you to sit with her at the sermon tomorrow..."

I have to fight not to roll my eyes. "She didn't ask me." I can't help it if my response comes out short.

"Well, maybe you should ask her," Gina says in her prying-while-acting-like-I'm-not, motherly sort of way. I can't be mad at her for it. "I'm sure she'd love that."

I swallow. "Maybe I will."

Tugging her with me, I'm hoping for an end to this conversation. Kinsey is a nice girl. She's pretty, too. Or *fuckhot*, as Jordan would say. So I'm sure if I were going to date a girl, she'd be a good choice.

But she doesn't give me those feelings... You know, the tingly ones. *Aren't you supposed to get those for the person you want to date?*

I suppose that's why I've never had a relationship, of any kind. I'm waiting for something that may never come.

As we approach the giant, lavish cabin, known as the *Den*, my gut twists, and the goosebumps come back. I just pray Gina doesn't notice them this time...

The Den belongs to the Head Priest of The Principality... *Darian*. It's his home. The rest of us live in trailers, but don't take that to mean anything negative, because they're really nice.

4

But he's in charge. So he gets his own Den.

They built it shortly after The Principality first came to be, which was a few years before I was born. It's a two-floor mansion that sits on Lake Willow, made creatively of Maple and Douglas firs. There are eight bedrooms, six baths, an office, study, library, home gym, the most fantastic kitchen you could ever imagine, three fireplaces, and a... *lounge.*

I know, the lounge doesn't seem as interesting as I just made it sound, but I'll explain later.

The Den also has its own outdoor greenhouse, and an attached garage that could house at least five cars, not that it does. There are two cars inside, but more ATVs than anything else, which is how we get around the Expanse. We don't have paved roads, but trails, and we mostly use golf carts and four-wheelers to travel back and forth.

I've only been in a car once. Head Priest let me sit inside his Jeep when I was thirteen.

I swallow at the memory as Gina and I wander up the steps of the porch, smiling and waving at Layla and Timothy as they pass. We're relieving them of the early shift.

Approximately fifteen Domestics work here in the Den. We serve as *hands*, if you will, to the Head Priest, handling all the household chores, like cooking, cleaning, serving food; basically getting him whatever he needs.

And because the job requires us to be somewhat *on call*, our trailers are located on his land. Everyone else resides about a quarter-mile up the drive, between Lake Willow and White Trumpet Mountain; the main stretch of the Expanse. The rest of our territory is made up of farmland.

The Principality is self-sustained. We don't require anything from Outsiders, though we do have a lucrative import/export business, which I know next to nothing about. It's not my job to know about it. Actually, not many of the Regnum do. Business is handled by Drake...

The Alchemist.

He's Head Priest's brother. Well, they're not brothers by blood, but they grew up together, and formed The Principality almost twenty-five years ago.

Folklore has it that our Head Priest and his brother left behind a world of pain in their past lives and found solace here in the woods of the Pacific Northwest. They had nothing; no belongings or vanity, but they were able to survive on the providings of God; our Mother Earth, also known as *Mother*.

And from there on out, Mother spoke through them. She gave them shelter and food, tranquility for their souls, in exchange for a sacrifice of the modern world. They gladly gave up their connections to society, the evils of the *Outsiders*, who destroy our planet any way they can. Darian and Drake started a new community here in the woods, claimed a territory they named the *Expanse*.

And thus, The Principality was born.

The *Regnum*, our family, grew more and more over the years, though it remains small; about a thousand people. Our population fluctuates as babies are born, and the elderly pass away, but that's about it. No one leaves, and we rarely accept new strays.

To be honest, I'm not sure why not. But again, it's not my place to know.

As Gina and I get settled inside, I can feel myself sharpening. I'm always on alert inside the Den. I want to make sure I'm at the top of my game for *him*.

He doesn't require a lot... Meals prepped once weekly for quick breakfasts and lunches, though we cook and serve dinner each night for him and his wives.

Yes, the Head Priest has *wives*, plural. Five of them. *I don't want to talk about it right now...*

"Well, kid, get a move on." Gina taps me on the butt. "Timothy left a menu on the counter. You've got a lot of potatoes to peel."

Yay.

I love to cook, but the prep work sometimes feels daunting. Still, I do so without complaint, because I'm blessed to be here.

None of the jobs on the Expanse are particularly grueling, but I have empathy for Paul and the guys working on the farm. Tending to the land can be back-breaking work, especially when preparing for grow season. A majority of our crops grow in spring and summer, which is basically now, so they've been hustling for weeks. And at harvest time? Forget about it.

I'll just stick to peeling my potatoes.

Getting myself settled in this kitchen I know so well, I throw on an apron and begin my duties. The house is huge, yet still, at every noise I hear, my eyes dart up from my tasks on the off-chance I might catch a glimpse of him.

I know what you're thinking, but it's not like that. Sure, maybe my fascination with Head Priest has been intensifying over the last year or so, but it's no big deal.

I just... admire him. He's our King. A fearless leader who brought us all together in this great family, and gave us means beyond anything the outside world could provide. He teaches us to love and revere Mother. To appreciate Her and Her gifts, as well as to recognize the part we all play in the great transformation known as life.

Shut up.

Hours pass with me trying not to think about it, and next thing I know, it's break time. We have an hour to relax before we get started on dinner, and I use the opportunity to go catch up with Jordan.

He's my best friend. We grew up together, here. He's older than me by about four months, but according to everyone, we've been inseparable pretty much since birth. Truth be told, we couldn't be more different. Jordan is messy, and crass, and he spends a majority of his free time with his tongue down the throats of various girls. But I love him, regardless of his man-slutting ways.

Walking up the drive, toward Regnum housing, I tilt my face to the sky. My lips curl into a contented smile as rays of sunshine gleam across my face. It's a beautiful day. Colors are on full display, shades of green in the grass and leaves, yellow buttercups and purple irises sprinkled along the path.

Rushing of the creek's waters tickles my ears, the nearby birds singing their tunes, reminding me of tomorrow.

"Heyyy, what's up, you beautiful bastard?" My serene walk is interrupted by the booming voice of my best friend.

Jordan stomps over to me, disregarding the fact that he's shirtless and sweaty as he pulls me in for a hug.

"Dude! I have to go back to work in forty-five minutes," I gripe, but he just laughs it off. Typical Jordan.

"Oh, no. Wouldn't want to smell a little sweaty in front of your boss," he sneers, removing a joint from his back pocket.

"Uh, he's your boss, too," I remind him as he lights up and takes in a long drag before handing it out to me. But I shake my head. "Nah, I'm good. The sativa makes me jittery."

"I feel you, but I need it. We're hustling out there," Jordan says on an exhale of pungent smoke. I can tell from the smell it's the batch Barry harvested some samples of last week.

One hit and I couldn't sleep all night. *I'll pass.*

"They've really got you guys working hard, huh?" I ask, holding

7

out my arms to get them some rays.

"Yea, but it's worth it. Drake asked for me."

My brows shoot up. "He did?"

"Mhm." Jordan nods. "He must've seen how I've been busting my hump and decided it's time to recruit my awesome ass to the Tribe."

I scoff at his cockiness, but I can't help the contemplation painted across my face. Jordan's wanted to get into the Tribe since he was younger. He has a fighter's instinct, which would be good for them. Unfortunately, you don't choose to be in the Tribe. They have to choose you. Or more importantly, *Drake* does.

"Well, I hope you stay safe, brother." I pat his shoulder. "We've all heard the gunshots…"

He gives me a pointed look. "Training."

"Right." I narrow my gaze but decide to change the subject. "You ready for tomorrow?"

"Hell yea! I can't wait. We're gonna be drowning in pussy after this one." Jordan starts shimmying and poking me. I have to laugh.

"You're an idiot." I shove him away as he grins, taking in another drag.

"I've seen Kinsey on your nuts lately like a bad case of crabs." He blows the smoke in my face, and I cough, waving it away. "You hittin' that, baby boy?"

"No." I scrunch my face. "I'm not *hittin' that*. She's just a friend."

"Look, I say this with love, Abdiel." Jordan folds his arms over his chest, and I brace myself for *this* conversation again. "You need to get laid." I scoff and shake my head, but before I can even argue, he jumps back in. "You're putting way too much pressure on sex. Just do it and get it over with."

"I don't want to *just do it*, Jordan," I hum. He doesn't understand, and I know this argument is pointless. We've been having this conversation since we were fifteen, when he lost his virginity. "I want it to mean something."

"You sound like such a chick." He smirks. "You have to be in love, is that right?"

"No, I didn't say that." I squint at him. "It doesn't have to be about *love*, I just want to be like… I don't know, vibing on the person."

He gapes at me for a solid five seconds, and I can tell my words have gone completely over his head. But it's okay. I don't need Jordan to get it. I just need him to be a friend, which he is, because he says, "I feel you, brother," then winks and smacks me on the back.

He doesn't *feel me*, but it's fine. Again, totally unnecessary for me to plead my case as to why I don't spend my time chasing down every girl on the Expanse. The thing is, if he were smart, Jordan would take his time. There's a finite number of girls available to him here, after all.

I know I could fuck Kinsey, or any number of the girls who have been casually, or sometimes not-so-casually, flirting with me since I was like thirteen. But it's very much exactly as I told Jordan. I'm searching for something... And so far, I haven't found it.

At least, not in a way that could work well for me...

Jordan and I shoot the shit for a little while longer until it's time for us to head back to our respective jobs. I sneak in a quick bite in my trailer and then I'm back in the Den's kitchen with Gina, Perry, Cam, and Ryle, preparing dinner for Head Priest and his wives.

On the menu tonight is roasted corn casserole with smoked bacon, a vegetarian option for Lauris of course, fresh snap peas and my honey wheat bread I made the other day. Ryle has been helping me perfect my bread-baking skills for months, and I think I finally got it down. Only problem is, all the practicing left us with an abundance of leftovers, and now I have to give bread to everyone I come across.

By the time sun sets, dinner is ready, and the kitchen smells fantastic. My mouth is watering, and I can't wait to be done with clean-up so I can try some of this stuff for myself.

"Alright." Gina claps her hands together, looking anxiously over the table complete with seven place settings. "Everyone ready?"

We all glance at each other and nod, taking in a collective deep breath. We've been doing this for years, and yet there's always a brief moment of panic before showtime. Things don't typically go wrong, but that's because we don't allow them to.

For *him*, everything must be perfect.

Gina nods at all of us and grabs Perry, the two of them ascending the steps to fetch everyone for dinner. The rest of us take up position in the kitchen. Once they're all settled at the table with drinks, we'll plate their food to ensure it stays warm, then serve. It's a system, and it works.

But the surety of it doesn't stop my heart from racing beneath my ribs.

Only three minutes later, I hear footsteps, and muscles tense all over my body. The wives always come down before Head Priest. Tonight, I see waves of golden hair and long eyelashes first. *Kiara.*

She takes her seat and motions to Cam for a drink. *The impatient one.*

Next sneaks by a tiny little thing with a jet-black bob and giant blue eyes. *Emithel.* She sits as far away from Kiara as possible, nestling into her seat while tugging at the sleeves of her worn charcoal cardigan.

I'm distracted from the overall quietness of Emithel by the stark contrast of loudness brought on by the curvy brunette with lips painted blood red. Sashaying into the room, she falls gracefully into her usual seat at Kiara's side, giving her a smile that may seem genuine to some, though the rest of us know better.

Alissa. She might as well be wearing a sign that says *Watch out for this one.*

Making much less of a production of their entrances, in steps the tall, athletic one, *Lauris*, with the youngest, *Gem*, a freckled redhead who's always smiling, at her side.

And now all the wives are seated around the table, looking every bit as different from one another as they are. I'm not sure if that's what Head Priest was going for when he married them, being that he married them all around the same time. Within roughly a year of each other.

There's as much mystery surrounding our Head Priest's marriages as there is surrounding him in general. I think that's a part of what's so intriguing about him... We only know what he shows us, which isn't all that much. We're raised in The Principality with the understanding that Head Priest's personal matters are none of our concern.

We don't get to ask questions, and we certainly don't get answers.

My pulse is thumping as Gina and Perry slink back toward us, nodding briefly to signal that he's on his way. My hands are as clammy as ever, and I try jiggling them a bit to dry them off at my sides. I'll be expected to carry glasses in a moment, and I can't have them slipping out of my grip.

Heavy footsteps indicate his descension of the stairs, and all minute chatter from the wives is immediately silenced. Every eye in the room is on the staircase as our Head Priest finally makes his first appearance of the evening.

He moves with purpose, striding from the stairs toward the table, without so much as making eye contact. But it's nothing new. For all the anticipation of his arrival, he barely recognizes that none of us are breathing.

His large form approaches, oozing more confidence in his pinky than I could even begin to formulate in my whole body, presence taking up the entire room. He strides toward the table, and Cam hustles up to pull out his chair for him. He takes his seat promptly, running long fingers through his silky chestnut hair as Cam helps him scoot in before scuttling back to the rest of us.

It's so quiet you could hear a pin drop while we all stare, and Head Priest pays no mind whatsoever to the tension, lifting his gaze to Gina first.

"Red wine tonight, please," his rough voice booms through the silence.

And with that, dinner has begun. Chatter resumes amongst the girls, and we all move to get the usual drinks ready for the rest of them. It's as if the world goes on pause awaiting Darian King.

He moves time.

I can't help but glance around the corner at him from the kitchen, checking to see what shade his eyes are tonight.

Head Priest's eyes change color. It's the most interesting thing I've ever seen, thus proving once more that he was put here by Mother to lead us in transformation.

His gaze is stuck on the glass in his hand as Lauris talks to the side of his face. He doesn't appear to be paying much attention, and I can't tell from here if his irises are bright blue, gray, or black. Given his apparent contemplative mood, I'd be willing to guess they're on the darker side.

Darian is a stoic man. He's generally quiet, but he speaks to us when he needs to. He delivers his weekly sermons with power and conviction; with true faith thundering in his voice and his words. He makes his rounds too, checking on his people and operations. He's been known to laugh and smile, though it doesn't happen often, so when it does, it's coveted. And not only by me, though I'm beginning to think I might notice it more than most others.

Gina nudges me, reminding me to get it together and help with serving dinner. The next few minutes are spent bustling around. Getting drinks, and refills, plating food and serving it, then bowing our heads as Darian says grace.

Mother, we thank You endlessly for these gifts You've bestowed upon us. For this lovely meal, and the ingredients that have gone into it. To the animals who sacrificed their lives for our bounty, to the plants and minerals which nourish us...

We praise Your name for the soil, the seeds, the air and water needed to encompass us and our brethren of Your planet. Please continue to watch over us in transformation. Your will be done, always.

Amen.

And then they dig in. Talk continues amongst the wives, though Darian remains quiet, watching the red liquid swirl in his glass. I know what this means...

Only another day or two.

The thing is, I've been watching Head Priest for a while, and I've begun to notice more than just his infrequent smiles. The change in his eye color seems reflective of his actions; his behaviors. Specifically, his *solitude*.

Head Priest is all-knowing, and I'm not just saying that because I'm a bit enamored with him. It is said that secrets travel to him in the air. He is perpetually *aware* of everything that goes on within his Regnum, and across the Expanse overall.

Case in point, a few years back, Jordan's mother, Lucy, was diagnosed with an auto-immune disease. When she first found out, she was reluctant to tell anyone. She left the doctor and walked to the lake to sit by herself and reflect. Not five minutes later, Darian came out to greet her. And he *knew*.

He confronted her about her health issues and offered his full support. But he knew about her diagnosis, without her saying a word. Doctor Harriet confirmed she hadn't shared the information with him, swearing that it would go against the doctor code to do so. Plus, she wouldn't have even had time. It's a five-minute walk from the doctor's trailer to the lake.

And this is just one example of Head Priest's ability. He always knows every single thing that happens on his land, within his family.

And so it is believed that the secrets really do come to him through the air.

To expand, it's also known that every few days, Darian requires what is referred to as his *solitude*. He adjourns to a private lounge in his Den, a room which no one else uses but him, and he spends a few hours in there.

No one knows what he does during this *solitude*, but I think it's something of a ritual. And because I pay more attention than anyone else apparently, it seems that his eyes become dark, almost black when he's in need of his time. Then when he emerges from the lounge, they're bright… Grayish blue, almost like an overcast sky in the fall.

It's interesting, to say the least, but no one asks or talks about it, because we're not entitled to answers about such things.

Yet I'm curious. I'm not sure I've ever been this curious about anything in my life.

I'm *dying* to know what happens in the lounge.

"Who made this bread?" The brogue startles everyone, and we all freeze, faces turning and eyes darting in the direction of our Head Priest.

He's holding up a piece of my honey wheat, head cocked to the side as he stares back at us Domestics. My coworkers all shift to me, gaping in silence while my heart hurdles in my chest. I blink at Head Priest over wide, nervous eyes.

"I did," my voice scrapes, and I clear my throat. "I made it, sir."

Tension slinks through my limbs as I watch him, horrified that he's going to tell me it's disgusting or something. Not that he's ever done anything like that before, but I'm just so scared. I think I've only spoken with him directly three times in my whole life.

His tongue slides along his lower lip briefly. It's such a quick movement, but it roots me to the floor and sends a shiver through my stomach.

"It's delicious," he says, softly. A tone made of velvet.

And now I can see his eyes clearly as he stares back at me. *Dark blue, like the lake at night.*

"Thank you, Head Priest," I whisper, still all throaty and just trying not to shake.

His lips curl at one corner. It's the subtlest change in his face, but it makes me lightheaded.

The spell is broken when a loud bang comes from the front of the Den. I jump at the noise, eyes still locked on those of my Head Priest. He doesn't startle at all, his dark gaze remaining on mine for only a moment before slinking toward the entrance to the dining room, as a tall being with black hair stomps in.

The man pulls out a chair, rather loudly, and plops down at the empty place setting, which is always set for him, though he rarely shows up for dinner.

Letting out a loud breath, he looks around the room, then smirks. "Sorry I'm late."

"Drake. Lovely of you to join us," Darian addresses his brother with only a trace of reprimanding being swallowed up by humor and

13

fondness.

"Can't let you all miss me too much now, can I?" Drake releases his signature wicked grin, blinking over his peculiar eyes at Head Priest.

He turns a wink on Gem, and high-fives Emithel.

The conversation picks back up between the seven of them, and the Domestics retreat to the kitchen to start cleaning up. I move on autopilot, all the while replaying that look in my mind... That voice.

It's delicious.

I'm not a weirdo or anything. I know he was just complimenting me on the bread, compliments I've already received from ten people in the past two days. But for some reason, coming from him, it was like a great gift to be decoded.

I totally *seem* like a weirdo, I know. But I can't stop myself.

By the time everyone is having dessert and coffee, Darian stands, with Drake, and excuses them to talk business. I watch them go, my insides pleading to follow, though I know I can't. I'm not allowed to know what they're doing, if Head Priest is going for solitude now, and if so, what he's doing inside that room.

It's none of my business, and it kills me.

I'm not a nosy person either, I swear, but there's something about seeing the darkness in Darian's eyes, when he's in need of his *solitude*. And then seeing him the next day, eyes alit with crystalline blue-gray, clouds and wind. It's fascinating.

He's fascinating.

Once we're done with cleanup, us Domestics get to eat, and I was right; the casserole is delicious. As is my bread, but we already knew that. Head Priest said so.

It's delicious. A chill runs across my skin.

When my shift is over, I go to the nightly reflection. There's a massive fire pit built in the center of the giant circle that is Regnum housing, and everyone meets here at night to reflect on the day. It's a great time to catch up with the family, and once a week, Jordan and I will perform a song, which we'll be doing tomorrow.

Tonight, I'm keeping it low-key. Feeling a bit introspective, I suppose. I watch as my best friend cuddles up to a new girl. I smile when Gina and Paul nestle together at the end of a hard day's work. I force a smile when Kinsey waves at me from across the fire.

Searching, Mother. Just searching.

Leaving early, I sneak off to go home. And as I wander through the woods, back toward my trailer, I see the eyes of a serpent, glowing at me in the dark.

CHAPTER TWO

ABDIEL

Weekly sermons are one of my favorite things.
If I'm ever feeling down, maybe a little lost, I can always count on Head Priest's words to reaffirm my faith; in the plan, in Mother's gifts.

In a bigger picture and a higher power.

Walking into temple, however, my excitement is dampened as Kinsey grabs my arm.

"Hi, Abdiel!" She squeals in my ear while I cringe. "You look great." Her cheeks flush as she bites her lip, and I force myself to smile.

"Thanks, Kins. So do you."

Her face lights up, and I swallow, worrying I might've given the wrong impression with that completely innocuous response.

"I was hoping you'd… maybe… like to sit with me?" Kinsey asks, stuttering as she does.

It makes me feel guilty. Guilty for not finding her as attractive or interesting as she apparently finds me. Guilty for not wanting to sit with her as badly as she clearly wants me to. Guilty for all of the zeal inside me that has nothing to do with her.

I hate feeling guilty.

So I shove it away and use the manners that have been instilled in me since I was small, giving her another forced smile. "I'd love to."

She squeals again, thankfully quieter this time, and drags me inside the temple. We wave hello to our family as everyone gets seated. Usually, teenagers have a tendency to slink around in the back, but to my surprise, Kinsey tugs me up the aisle to the front row of seats. It's a mixed bag of feelings about it, since I do love sitting close, although I tend to stay away from the front. I like to avoid being seen or called upon by Head Priest during his sermons. It's too nerve-racking. I don't want to embarrass myself.

And yet here we are, front and damn center. My stomach is already churning away while we get settled, the doors behind us closing as, right on schedule, all noise comes to a halt.

Knowing he'll be here in just a moment has my pulse rapping. I can't help glancing around me to see if anyone else is having a similar reaction. Sure enough, everyone in the room looks equally eager to see him, to be enraptured by his presence and his thoughtful words. Still, I'm not sure any of these people are as *anxious* as I am.

When my head tilts left, I see Drake, sitting in the pew reserved for him and the wives. He's draped in white linen garb, his usual attire for sermons and special holidays. White, a symbol of cleansing and rebirth.

My eyes linger on his black hair, combed back messily, as if done with his fingers, or someone else's. Drake is another who loves to enjoy the company of many partners. It's not a big deal in the slightest, since free love is a belief of The Principality. We condone all types of relationships, and sex is celebrated, safely of course.

But aside from Head Priest, Drake is the most mysterious person on the Expanse, with his smoldering looks, high cheekbones and a jawline that could cut glass certainly contributing to the enigma. Tall with skin white like alabaster and a way about him that just *feels* sinful, even if you don't really *know* him, which I think none of us truly do.

And then there are the snake eyes. It's not an exaggeration either. His eyes are two different shades, dark, almost black with rings of amber yellow. They're probably hazel, but the way they look, like marbles, remind you of a snake's eyes. Which is fitting, since he's called the *Serpent*.

Always lurking in the shadows…

I'm startled when those strange eyes point in my direction. Drake is looking at me now; he's caught me staring at him. I gulp and quickly look away, though some force compels me to peek at him once more, only to find him still staring at me, smirking while he blinks slowly; studiously. *Like a snake.*

The hairs on my arms stand up straight, and I focus my vision on my lap, ignoring the strange sensation slinking around inside me.

17

Movement up at the podium distracts me, and my chin jerks as Head Priest saunters in, confident and poised, ready to address his Regnum. Warmth seeps into my veins.

"Good morning, family," he croons with a pleasant almost-smile on his chiseled face. "Are we all happy to be here?"

Everyone cheers, which brings on an actual smile. I can't help but grin along as I clap, since his is infectious. His charisma is unlike anything else, pairing with the way he looks...

Captivating.

I heard my mother say once when I was younger that Darian has *the face of a King.* At the time, I didn't know what she meant. But as I've grown up, and started watching Head Priest more and more, I have to agree.

He has the kinds of looks that are made to do more in this world. If he were an Outsider, I'm sure he'd be some kind of celebrity. He's not like Drake, with all those sharp angles. He has lines too, sure, but his look more like they were carved into him. Or rather, that *he* was carved. As if Mother made him out of stone and bronze, perfect symmetry and a natural glow. From his hair to his eyes, pointed nose, full lips, angled jawline always dusted in dark stubble, sitting atop a body so large, like Goliath, only calmer, more intelligent.

Beautiful, wise, and compelling. Everything a King should be.

I snap out of my daze to realize he's already started, and now I'm silently kicking myself for missing the beginning of his words.

"Seedlings are being birthed, new life implanted, a continuation to our glorious transformation is upon us," Darian says. "Our Mother has blessed us more than we can even begin to comprehend. But it's our job to try. To remain present for everything. To stay interconnected with one another and with ourselves. With Her."

He steps out from behind the podium and clasps his hands together, in thought. "How do you repay the ultimate sacrifice?"

Everyone remains quiet, knowing his questions are usually rhetorical, unless he decides to call on someone for participation.

"Some sacrifices are for our own benefit, yes?" He goes on. "For example, those tilling the fields. It's hard work, right? You put the burden on your bodies." He pauses, looking specifically to the farmers, all of whom are nodding along. "But do you not reap the benefits of the hard work? Grain for bread, hemp for clothing... hops for beer." He gives a small grin and a few people chuckle. "I just mean, these things aren't fully selfless. And that's okay. We're made

18

to receive when we give. It's all part of the circle of life."

He turns, pacing back again as he continues. "But for a *true* sacrifice, we must understand that there will be no benefit to us. We must be fully selfless. That is what our God has done for us. She has sacrificed herself so that we may live in her place, spreading good deeds and protecting Her at all costs."

He closes his eyes for a moment, breathing out slowly, fingers trailing his stubbled jaw. I shift in my seat, and when his eyes reopen, he looks in my direction. I stifle a gasp.

They're black.

His irises... They're darker now than they were last night. *Solitude is coming.*

I'm so intrigued that I can barely pay attention to what he says next. His words come in and out as my mind races. Thoughts swirl in my brain, images and wonderings, curiosity rippling through me until I can barely sit still.

My knee begins to bounce, and Kinsey reaches out, placing her hand on it. Immediately my movements cease, and I peer at her. She grins at me from the side as I glance back up to where Head Priest is speaking. He's talking about becoming one with the earth and giving ourselves fully to the power of rebirth.

"This is our sacrifice," he rasps, his dark eyes landing on me. I'm not sure, but I think he sees Kinsey's hand on my knee and his brow quirks; a slight movement as he blinks, right at me.

I can't swallow. My throat is closing up, and I wiggle subtly in an attempt to get her hand off me, but then he's back to pacing around casually, talking about unconditional love and devotion of spirit.

I'm so uncomfortable, I don't know what to do with myself. I suddenly feel very hot, and claustrophobic; like my thoughts and feelings are too big to fit inside my body.

Struggling to focus on Darian, I watch his long legs move when he walks, his large hands rubbing together when he pauses in thought. His lips formulating the words he speaks with clear diction and an even, mastering tone.

The way he speaks, like his presence in general, is entirely dazzling, which is why he's our Head Priest. I honestly can't take my eyes off him.

"Outside The Principality is a world that doesn't care to accept its reality. A dark, merciless possession of evil. Now, as we know, evil is a part of life. Without it, we wouldn't have good. That contrast is very important, my family. Seeing every side of every situation is a component of the ever-present give and take of the earth. Of our Mother."

Darian pauses, his eyes fixed left, where his brother sits with his wives. I witness a visible clench in his jaw, a momentary tension that draws me in. His chest seems to be moving more rapidly now, as he looks ahead in silence. My eyes dart to where Drake sits, and as usual, his face gives away nothing. But his head cocks to the side, eyes locked on his brother's. It looks like they're having some sort of conversation the rest of us can't hear.

And the hollowness in my chest gives way to even more of my eternal curiosity.

"Bad isn't always wrong," Darian whispers, almost as if he's not speaking in sermon anymore, but to himself. *Or to Drake.* "And the right decision is rarely the easiest." He shakes it off and breaks his staring contest with his brother to turn back to the rest of us. "Strength comes with facing difficulty. And making sacrifices."

At that, he ends the sermon, talking about tonight's reflection, and plans for the upcoming festival. *Summer Solstice is upon us.*

I let out a breath I hadn't realized I was holding in.

Once we're all dismissed, Kinsey and I stand up and chat with a few people. But my eyes remain on Head Priest the whole time. Usually after sermon, he'll come around and mingle with us, shaking hands and kissing babies, so to speak. But today, he seems on edge. He's lingering by Drake and the wives, and when I turn back from saying what's up to Jordan, he's gone.

Anyone else would think nothing of it, I suppose. But all I can see are those black irises...

All I can think is that the last time he went alone into his lounge was days ago.

Solitude.

"So, you wanna grab something to eat? Or maybe take a walk, or..." Kinsey rambles as we leave the temple, but I cut her off.

"I can't. Sorry, Kins, but I should really practice for tonight." I pat her on the shoulder, as platonically as I can.

"Oh... right. Sure!" She smiles wistfully, and I really hate how that look is making me feel. "Well, I'll see you tonight, then. Can't wait!"

"Yea. See you then," I mumble and stagger off, back toward my trailer.

I need to get my head on straight. I have work for a couple of hours before reflection tonight, and I should try to stay sharp. But even though I know these things, it doesn't stop me from floating around the rest of the day in my thoughts.

I go to work. Cleaning duty. And as I'm polishing the floors in the study, I find myself sneaking closer and closer to the forbidden door of Darian's lounge.

Really, it's just a room. We clean in there, so we know what's inside. It's nothing crazy. It's set up like a spare bedroom. And yet I'm still restless to step inside.

I know I shouldn't, but I'm like a curious kitten right now, pattering up to the door and twisting the handle. It's unlocked.

Checking over my shoulder, the coast is clear. It's quiet in the house, or at least on the first floor it is. Everyone's bedrooms are upstairs. This is the only room with a bed in it that's down here, which seems interesting to me. And as I slink inside, I'm even more intrigued at the fact that I think this bed is the same size as Darian's regular bed. It's huge, and it has those large canopy things surrounding it, tied back like drawn curtains.

Poking around, as silently as possible, I tug on a few drawers, which are locked. I observe a large painting on the wall. I'm sure I've seen it before, but I've never noticed how… *erotic* it is.

It's a man's body, naked, lying contorted into a rather compromising position. I swallow over my dry throat and turn away, looking out the window. The view of the lake from right here is breathtaking.

And then I notice something.

Hmm…

From where this window is located, one could theoretically look in from outside and see what's happening in here…

"Abdiel?" Gina's voice calls from the hall, and I flinch.

"Coming!"

Hustling out of the room, softly closing the door, I scamper back toward her, putting the position of the window to Head Priest's lounge out of my head as best I can.

For now.

21

The fire crackles, an easy sound trickling into the quiet that stretches right before we start.

A breath in, hold one second, and then Jordan's first chord strikes. The crowd of my family is silent, bopping to the music, listening closely and watching us with wide, attentive eyes.

I come in for the first verse, working my namesake.

We don't believe in last names in The Principality, but elders will usually give you a nickname as your surname, depending on what they decide makes you special; unique.

My name is Abdiel Harmony. And this is why.

Jordan strums me into the chorus of *Comedown* by Bush, and I see a few people singing along. We may not have much technology access, but the one thing we openly admit to cherishing from the outside world is music. Head Priest feels it's important to many aspects of life, and I would have to agree since, you know... *Harmony*.

I peek over at Jordan, and he grins back, singing backup to my second bridge. I love jamming with Jordan. Even more so, I love doing it by a fireside, surrounded by my family. It's such a chill vibe.

This here is Principality life at its finest. A cup of beer, a joint, and a good acoustic performance by the fire. This is what it's all about.

Tapping on my leg through the rhythm, I look up and almost fall backward.

He's here.

Head Priest is here, watching me. He's on the far side of the fire, grinning and giving little casual waves to people who acknowledge his presence, though refusing to speak and interrupt the performance. He's like that.

Respectful, sweet. Just a generally great guy.

Okay, focus.

I ignore the warmth flooding my limbs and keep singing. It must be from the fire, all this heat... *I'm fine.*

We finish up the song and everyone cheers. I smile politely, trying not to focus on Darian, though I can't stop peeking toward where he sits, Lauris at his side, grinning and sipping from her *Effortlessly Awesome* mug she uses for everything. And I can't help but fixate on the fact that they aren't holding hands or touching at all.

This isn't news. Head Priest doesn't do public displays of affection with his wives. Actually, he rarely interacts with them in any sort of way that would allude to romantic love, and I'm not the only one who notices that. He hangs out with them more like friends, and people have started to comment on it.

But that's a thought for another time. Right now, I'm being berated with cheers for an *encore*. Jordan and I share a look, and without any further discussion, he launches into one of our personal favorites. *Closer* by The Chainsmokers.

It's a ridiculous song for us to sing, but we kind of like that fact. Plus, the girls always get a kick out of it, and they all sing along, which is what they're doing right now. I can't help the little chuckle that slips through while I go in for the second bridge, gaze sliding across the fire once more.

Darian's dark eyes are shining right at me, and it almost chokes me up again. It's just such an intense stare. He appears casual enough, but then he's giving me this *look*. A look that no one else seems to be noticing, I might add, which appears to border on frustration. There's something desperately inquisitive in his eyes, and it's gripping at my heart from within my chest.

By the end of the song, I'm buzzing, but not from booze or weed, or even the adrenaline of singing in front of a crowd.

I'm high on those damn eyes.

The applause, cheers and whistles take a bit to die down, and Jordan's eating it up. I am too, but I'm still dazed. A few people come up to hug us and gush. But once the crowd parts, I find Darian and Lauris gone, and my stomach falls onto the floor.

It's such an odd reaction, I have no choice but to give it five minutes, then excuse myself for the night.

Heading back to my trailer, I'm kicking rocks and I'm not sure why. I had a great night. Jordan and I killed it, as we always do. And Head Priest showed up and apparently enjoyed the performance. I should be ecstatic, and I guess I am.

But I'm also confused.

I'm really not sure what these bizarre feelings are that I've been developing lately, but they're beginning to worry me.

It's not that I would care about being interested in men. And if I choose not to label my sexuality, that's fine, too. The Principality doesn't judge people based on race, gender, sexuality differences, anything like that. My confusion isn't about the sexuality aspect. It's not even necessarily about him being much older than me, which he is.

It's about the fact that I *can't* have a crush on the Head Priest. He's entirely unavailable, in many ways.

He's not ours to lust over. He belongs to Mother, and to his wives, and that's it.

Feeling only mildly defeated, I stomp up the steps into my trailer and lock the door behind me. I kick off my shoes, whip off my t-shirt, then step out of my pants, leaving things scattered everywhere as I head for the shower. I wash up quick, yet thorough, my brain rifling through the events of the day, and days past, wondering where the hell I went wrong, and how I became so fixated on a person I certainly shouldn't be.

After the shower, I crawl into bed, yawning and tugging the sheet up to my chin. Moonlight shines through my window, and rather than finding myself gazing up at it in awe, it's sort of pissing me off. Rolling onto my stomach, I cover my head with my pillow and close my eyes, trying to shove away the images of him from earlier.

His dark irises locked on me. That troubled expression I just couldn't read. Even now, I haven't the slightest clue what it meant.

His eyes are dark when he's in need of solitude. But what does that have to do with me?

I can't help but continue to wonder what he does in that room... alone. I've been wondering about it for a while. What I wouldn't give to be a fly on the wall...

And now, behind my eyes, I'm in a room I vaguely recognize...

My stomach flips as my pulse thrums. *The lounge.*

I'm visualizing it. Conjuring up this little fantasy in my imagination. I know it's wrong... I'm not supposed to be so curious about Head Priest's personal life, but I am. I'm imagining what he might do alone in this room...

He could be in the bed. That big, giant bed with the fancy canopy. He could be lying in it like I am now... Covered only by a sheet. And maybe it would be shockingly low on his waist.

Biting my lip, I imagine my eyes sliding against my will down the length of his *long* frame. Defined shoulders and chest, broad and sculpted, leading to abs that look like stones beneath what appears to be some very smooth skin... scattered in occasional ink.

I forgot about his tattoos...

I've seen him with his shirt off before, since we all go swimming at the lake in the summers and he's been known to join us. But I've never allowed myself to really *look*.

There's a V-shape in his pelvis, and it looks drawn on, pointing beneath the sheet. Where his hand is, too.

I gulp, my imagination concocting this visual of him, lying in that big bed, with his hand under the covers, moving. I think it's clear what he's doing in this fantasy, but I just can't believe I'm thinking this. I've never allowed myself to think these thoughts about him. But now that I'm doing it, I'm finding it very difficult to stop.

Picturing his fist going up and down, and up, and down. And *up...* and *down.*

"*Fuck,*" his voice whispers in my head, and my cock jerks between my legs.

My face is on fire as I meet his gaze. His eyes are almost obsidian, hooded, lids drooping in his clear state of ecstasy. They fall shut and his head leans back, a tasty-looking throat exposed, Adam's apple dipping as he swallows.

My mouth fills with saliva, and I swallow, too.

My lips part as if to speak, but I haven't the foggiest idea what I would say. I don't know how I'm here, or how this is happening, but I don't want to do anything that might make it stop.

The look of him like this... It's intoxicating.

I watch on with hungry eyes as his hand strokes in *long*, fluid motions beneath the sheet. With his movements, the sheet falls farther and farther down his muscled abdomen, and I'm desperate to see what's under there. It looks like he has... a lot of inches to work with in that hand.

"Do you do this to yourself, Abdiel?" Darian's voice calls to my imagination. "Would you do this for me?"

A short breath bursts from my lips, but I can't form words. My cock is so hard it has a pulse in my boxers; a throbbing, *aching* need. His eyes close again and he lets out a groan; the sexiest fucking sound I've ever heard in my life, even imaginary. I whimper, brushing my hand, nervously, down to my erection. As soon as I touch it, it jerks and I shudder.

"That's right," he whispers. "Just like that. I need it..."

"Fuck..." I cup myself over the fabric and rub, watching his big body squirm around in his fancy bed.

"You're so good," he pants, his hand beneath the sheet speeding up visibly while the other comes up to his chest. He pinches his nipple between his fingers and bites his lip to quiet himself.

"Oh my God." I can't stop myself from lunging at the bed, crawling over him quickly.

25

But just as I see his lazily erotic grin aimed right at me, our lips ready to crash together, he disappears and I awake from my little dream, sweating through the damn sheets.

My eyes open unwittingly, confirming that I'm in my own bed, alone. I whine out of frustration and run my fingers through my damp hair, grinding my hips into the mattress. My dick is as hard as a metal rod, jamming between my bed and my abs while I rock with need.

"I wish you were here..." I whisper to no one, reaching down to grab my cock. "I want to know how it feels."

Wrapping my fist around my erection, I close my eyes once more and remember the look of him, my Head Priest, naked in his bed. Only this time, I'm with him.

I'm sure in real life I wouldn't know what to do with a man like him if I had the chance, and I'm sure he wouldn't want me, a *man*, at all. But right now, in my imagination, he's mine.

I trail my mouth along his skin, feeling rough stubble beneath my lips. My cock leaks in my hand, tongue extending in my fantasy to taste him; like salt and male deliciousness. He smells that way, too.

Like strength, and power. Like a King.

"Touch me," I whisper in the dark, stroking my erection firmly, imagining sucking his pulse, and biting his shoulder. "Let me touch you..."

His fictional moans play on repeat in my mind like my favorite song while I jerk off, writhing in my bed. I imagine my hands traveling all over his large body, greedy fingers taking in the feel of his muscles, thick arms and thighs... big dick.

"I just know you have a big dick, my King," I breathe, fucking my fist harder and faster. "I want... I want it. I want to stroke it and... suck it."

I whimper at my own dirty words, desires I've never allowed myself to explore unleashed in the privacy of my bedroom. This... *This* is what I've been missing.

This is why I haven't been with anyone else. This is the feeling I've been searching for.

"I want to fuck you, Head Priest," I groan, as quietly as I can manage, though I think I'm about to burst. "Take my virginity. *Please...*"

God, it feels amazing. Jerking off has never been like this before. I can feel the building in my loins, like pressure bubbling up to the boiling point; top about to pop.

My hand is moving on its own, flashes behind my eyes of unbridled lust for the man I can't have. The man who's as forbidden as forbidden gets around here.

But that doesn't matter right now, because I'm about to...

"*Come...*" I growl, beating my dick so hard it hurts. "I'm gonna come, I'm gonna come... *Fuck.*"

My orgasm takes over and aching pulses shoot out all over my bed and my abs as I press my lips together to hold in my whimpers of bliss. I'm in a whirlpool of pleasure I've never felt before, the high lasting minutes longer than any climax I've ever experienced.

And when it's over, and I suck in a long breath, hold it and let it go, I realize I'm completely fucked.

I just jerked off to fantasies concocted around the Head Priest of The Principality.

Yea... I'm definitely going to Hell.

CHAPTER THREE

DARIAN

When I was small, my birth mother said something to me.

At the time, I didn't understand it. But as I grew up, after she died and I was left to the care of the state of Michigan, her former words bloomed in my mind, like a sunflower. Fast and *big*.

"Nothing happens by accident."

I'm sure you can understand my childhood confusion. I was only six when she said this to me, and I was eight when she died. But it wasn't until four years later, when I was twelve and landed with foster parents whom I believed would be my *forever* family, though they ended up becoming much more than that in my story, that it finally clicked.

I was born in Forest Park to a single mother who was a dope fiend. She died of an overdose when I was a child, and after that, I bounced in and out of various group homes until I was sent to live with the Lannisters.

The *Lannisters*, however, were not good people. But it was in their home, surrounded by sudden, unexpected torment and emotional plague, that I met him... My brother. *Drake.*

The events of the following years were what solidified my birth mom's words. As much as I would have loved to believe it at the time, none of those things happening to me occurred by *accident*. No coincidence, no happenstance or dumb luck.

Nothing happens by accident. Not even the worst kinds of pain

My life, my struggles and my redemption were planned out long before my mother got drunk and had a one-night stand with a stranger nine months prior to my arrival on this big, stark-raving mad planet. I'm only guessing this is what happened, since she never told me who my father was, other than a *mistake*.

Yet still, I was manifested as an idea before creation, in the large scope of the universe.

Sure, to an *Outsider*, I probably sound bat-shit crazy right now. And maybe that's part of it. Actually, I'm *sure* it is. The theoretically sane ideas of the world are typically recycled and plagiarized, in my opinion, anyway. You want real thoughts, you're gonna have to raise a few eyebrows.

I've continued on this path since I was a teenager, following my destiny alongside the one person I could never have survived without...

Glancing up across the dinner table, my eyes linger on the empty place setting. The chatter is lively tonight, and for some reason, it's irritating me. Well, I do know why. I know damn well...

"She said she wouldn't be that stupid yet there she goes again." Alissa's voice catches my ear, and my gaze darts diagonally across the table. "It's always a matter of time with her."

I roll my eyes. I really shouldn't do it. I'm the Head Priest, and Head Priests shouldn't roll their eyes, but I can't help it. She gossips too much. The rest of them don't participate often, I assume because they know I don't like it, but still. Alissa's judgmental ways could influence others in the Regnum, and we can't have that.

"Alissa," I snap, and her voice cuts out, face turning to mine with a purely guilty expression resting on it. "Is there something I should know about Jane? Something that could negatively affect The Principality?"

My wife gapes at me for a moment, as if stunned, and a bit confused by my question. She even looks to Lauris for a moment, who is sitting at my right, as usual.

"Don't look at Lauris. Look at me," I demand, quietly, though the bite is there, and I know she can feel it. "Answer my question."

"No, sir," Alissa squeaks, her reprimanded tone such a contrast to her typically loud persona.

"Good," I hum and lift my glass of wine. "Then let's keep the conversation productive, shall we?" I sip, eyeing her over the rim of the glass while she nods in acceptance.

I hear Lauris whisper *amen to that*, and I have to shoot her a quick look, though there's amusement dancing in my eyes. Those two aren't exactly besties, and I'm well aware it's all too satisfying to Lauris, and Gem and Emithel as well for that matter, when Alissa and Kiara are brought down a peg.

I sigh internally. My *wives*... all so different. You'd think the variety would give me some much-needed satisfaction, but it doesn't.

Speaking of satisfaction... I glance at the empty place setting once more.

I don't know why I'm surprised. Drake doesn't join us for dinner often, although he does show up when he knows I need him. Which is definitely now. Yet he's missing in action.

A movement catches my eye, and I glance up to find one of my Domestics shuffling in, balancing some plates of what appear to be blueberry cobbler on his forearm. *My favorite.*

I squint at him, watching his steps as he approaches the table and delivers dessert. Mine first, then he goes to Lauris, then Gem. He seems a bit more rigid than usual, and I don't know why, which of course is driving me insane. Normally, I would know. I could hear it, and his thoughts would give me solace. But right now, I only hear murmurs, like a heart's cadence, and the *unknown* sets my teeth on edge.

Without glancing my way, the boy darts back toward the kitchen, brushing his silky blonde curls away from his face. My gaze lingers, and I can't make it stop. Seeing him, seeing *anyone*, without knowing their truths brings on waves of my own insecurities.

I'm no King. I'm no Head Priest. I'm just a fraud.

A scared boy running barefoot through the woods.

I shake myself out of my thoughts and take another sip of my wine. It's cool, crisp, with notes of apple and honey. A great batch from Carlito, which will certainly do good this month. When I look up again, I catch the tail-end of the boy Domestic looking at me with those big, sparkly green eyes. Like jasper, minerals found in the earth. *Precious stones.*

I've known Abdiel Harmony since before he was Abdiel *Harmony*. I was there when he was born, actually. Well, not *there* there, but I came afterward to hold him, say a prayer, and congratulate his parents. I knew Jenny and Lars well. In fact, I adored them. Which is why it was so tragic when they passed...

I'm still not entirely sure I'm over it, and it's been seven years. Their little boy was shattered, naturally so, because they were good parents, unlike those Drake and I have known in our lifetimes.

Gina and Paul took Abdiel in, which was a blessing. I know they would have done so without me asking, but I felt a responsibility to the boy myself, what with some of the history... But despite that, I've always kept a special eye on him. From afar, of course. I hired him as my youngest Domestic when he was only fourteen, and he's since become a crucial member of the family.

I've come to rely on him, maybe unwittingly, and right now my frustrations are breaking me down. His eyes lock on mine, only for a split second, but I hear *nothing*. Then his dart to the floor as he continues bringing dessert plates to my wives, while my fist clenches under the table.

I can't deal with this right now. Where the fuck is Drake??

I endure more conversation with the five of them for the next fifteen minutes, remaining quietly pensive and not by choice, until we finish eating and adjourn to various parts of the house. Everyone goes their separate ways, and I decide to head into my lounge, likely in hopes Drake will show up.

He knows where to find me.

I saunter into the room and flop down onto the bed, covering my face with my hands. *Silence.* No echoed voices I've come to need. No hushed whispers of secret thoughts.

Nothing at all.

Scrubbing my eyes with my fingers, I let out a long breath. *Where are you, brother? Can you hear me?*

"I'm right here, needy. God."

I spring up, hands flying from my face to find the pale skin, dark hair, and unusual snake eyes I know so well. My brother from another mother, literally.

I smile, though trying hard to crush it. "I was waiting for you."

"Yea. I heard." He steps into the room, tinkering with things on all the dressers and shelves, as if he hasn't been in this room a zillion times in the last twenty-some-odd years. "What's wrong?"

I open my mouth to grunt that he knows damn well what's wrong, but before I can say anything, Kiara comes sauntering through the doorway with Alissa on her arm. She just walks in like *she* owns the place, brushing past Drake and taking a seat at the edge of the bed, with Alissa so close she's almost on her lap.

"Good evening, my Lord," Kiara whispers, well aware I hate it

31

when she calls me that, tucking her blonde hair behind her ear as she blinks at me.

"Can I help you?" I sit up and purposely try to put distance between us, though the girls aren't having it, leaning back on their elbows so they're almost lying next to me.

"You can," Alissa answers, her fingers walking up the bed, inching closer to my leg than I'd like them. "You know you can. But you won't, and it's making us sad."

She pouts, her lips looking even fuller than they already are. I'm sure many other men would be driven mad by the temptation of that mouth. But for me... Well, it's more complicated.

Yes, they're my wives. Yes, I married them, and yes, I'm sure I should be entertaining whatever salacious ideas they've been concocting together; my two wives who secretly despise one another, though they have a tendency to work together on a joint objective... Like getting their husband to fuck them.

But I can't. We've been married for three years, and I still can't make myself do it.

Why can't I? What's the big fucking deal? Just stick my dick inside any one of the five women I've dedicated myself to in holy matrimony long enough to make a baby and shut everyone up. It should be so easy. But again, for me, it's the most complicated thing a King could face.

"Why don't you show him what he's missing out on?" Drake's voice slithers, quite literally, at us from the corner, and we all glance up. "It could help your cause."

I glare at him, shooting a look he doesn't need spoken words to hear, and he smirks at me. *Evil motherfucker.*

But Kiara and Alissa appear enticed by this idea, and they waste no time at all touching each other, sensually running fingers through one another's hair, down arms, onto waists and such. Alissa, being the more assertive one, grabs Ki by the face and hauls her in for a kiss. Kiara returns it, though looking much more seductive with the slow build-up. Unlike Alissa, Kiara is a silent assassin. She's like Drake in that way. Quiet and calculating, but every bit as manipulative when she needs to be.

Drake is watching them kiss attentively, cocking his head to the side as Lissa's hands grip Ki's waist and tug her closer, Ki writhing into their little makeout session.

But I barely notice it. I'm too busy watching Drake in agony over

32

the damn *silence* in the room. It's suffocating. There are faint murmurs still, but I can't make out any actual words. *I hate this.*

I'm desperate.

Kiara crawls on top of Alissa, sliding the front of her top down to expose her breasts. Then she trails her lips down Alissa's neck, leaving a dull red from her lipstick all over Lissa's tits.

My eyes slink back to Drake, and he's already looking at me, his tongue gliding over his lower lip. My patience has worn out, frustrations bubbling over.

"Leave us," I bark at the girls, and they immediately pull apart, breathing heavily as they get up and do as I say, closing the door on their way out.

No surprises there. For all their errant behaviors, I'm still the goddamn King of this castle, and I'm not to be argued with.

Drake huffs a small chuckle, stepping over to the bar to pour himself a drink. "You seem on edge." He lifts the glass and swirls it before taking a small sip, eyes flickering at me. "In need of some... *solitude*, my King?"

My jaw goes tight. Any time he calls me that, it's laced with sarcasm. Drake is the only person in my Regnum who doesn't worship me, in a sense. And that's because he's basically my brother. He knows me unlike anyone else.

And I've always seen us as equals, too. I mean, all human beings are equals, I know that. But I'm also the leader of this community, and to a certain extent, I'm seen as a *King*, which is why I play the part.

But Drake and I... That's something different.

It makes me sad at times that no one other than my brother truly *knows* me. Being the Head Priest is a lonely calling, but it's one that chose me. I have to respect the wishes of Mother and care for her people as she has assigned me to.

Drake wanders over to the edge of the bed, and I crawl closer to where he stands, tilting my face upward.

"Give me a hit," I demand, and he raises a dark brow. I grit my teeth. "*Please.*"

He lurches over where I'm kneeling on the bed and leans up against the post. He slips a finger under my chin, tilting me even more, so that my throat is angled up to him. Then he slides his hand down, curling his fingers and holding right over my Adam's apple. I can't help but swallow, and it bobs beneath his palm.

I'm suddenly so much warmer, burning inside my clothes while he does that slow-blink at me. "Mmm... nah. Not in the mood. How about tomorrow?"

I growl out of frustration and back up, slapping his hand away from me.

"What do you mean *tomorrow*? I didn't ask you, Drake. It was an order. I need a goddamn hit. Now."

"And I said... tomorrow," he hisses.

My fingers rake through my hair, displaying my agony. It's no use hiding it from Drake. He already knows what I'm thinking.

"Why are you toying with me?" I rumble, chewing the inside of my cheek. "Just give me some now. I can take it without all the extra games, you know that."

He grins, a wide, evil-looking thing and leans over me until I have no choice but to back up. "Aww, brother... Where's the fun in that?"

I wish I could find it in myself to be repulsed, or angry about this shift in power. But I can't ignore the flutter in my stomach at his words.

And the anticipation he builds for me to get what I want; what I *need*.

Tomorrow.

The truth is, I wouldn't want Empyrean without the way Drake gives it to me. It's my superpower. My ultimate connection to Mother. But when it comes paired with a dose of my foster brother, it's like breaking my inner light free from chains, if only for a few hours. I really can't resist.

We've so woven ourselves up into something tangled beyond rationale, like a web of sensation and mind-altering completeness, that I can barely tell what's Empyrean and what's Drake anymore.

He *is* Empyrean. Empyrean is him.

And I think he likes that.

So Drake and I agree on tomorrow. I may or may not threaten him with death if he doesn't show up after dinner, and he laughs it off, but agrees. Then I go upstairs to try and get some sleep; to rest away my unease in the comfort of my master bedroom, which is different from my lounge. Sure, the lounge has a bed in it, but it's not typically used for sleeping like this room is.

With the moon glowing in through my skylight windows, it's not long before sleep steals me, and my mind is quiet. That is, until I'm awoken by a figure climbing into bed with me.

My eyes struggle to adjust to the lack of light, but when I take notice of the short black hair of the culprit, I sigh in realization.

"Em, what are you doing?" I whisper while she nestles up to me, pressing her breasts to my chest and whimpering at the contact. I swallow over guilt, doubt, and a myriad of other insecurities.

"I'm sorry, sir," she breathes on my clavicle before placing a soft kiss on my neck. "I know I'm not supposed to be doing this, but I... I need it." Her hands glide up the front of me, taking my hand and placing it on her waist. "I'm *aching*, my King."

Mother, why must you test me like this? Why must you make me feel worse than I already do?

"Em..." I sigh, shaking my head and taking my hand back. I pull away to look at her, but she won't stop kissing my neck.

I really would love to give her what she needs, but what she's begging for right now is a lost cause.

I've tried before. Believe me, I have. I've come as close as I ever will, and it nearly crippled me.

Taking Emithel's face in my hands, I force her to look at me. "I *can't*."

She looks less hurt and more sexually frustrated, which eases the guilt a bit. I'm not sure if any of my wives are actually in love with me, but they definitely want to fuck me, and I can't help them with either.

This was a mistake. I shake away the thought before it gets too loud.

"Lauris and I talk..." she murmurs, blinking her large blue eyes at me. "You've tried before."

"Foolish on my part." My tone is firm, to get my point across. She's just staring up at me and the silence is deafening. "Em, I'm not sure what to say. But you can't come into my bed like this. Do you understand?"

My wife furrows her brow, appearing as though she might want to keep trying, keep pushing for something. But eventually, she looks down and nods.

My thumb slides over her lower lip. "Thank you. And I'm..." The word gets caught in my throat. "Sorry. I'm sorry. I can understand what you're feeling, and I sympathize. Do whatever you need to do, just... be discreet."

"Like you are?" She gives me a pointed look.

I know she's not trying to call me out or anything. It's a delicate situation I'm desperately trying to dig my way out of, so rather than scolding her for the comment, I simply nod for her to get out of my bed, which she does, leaving quietly with her tail between her legs.

After that, you bet your ass I can't sleep. I'm wide awake, all night. Lying surrounded by secrets, lies, and waves of silence.

How the fuck am I going to fix this?

CHAPTER FOUR

ABDIEL

My thoughts are running away with me.

I've always been a bit of a dreamer. My mother used to call me her little free bird; head in the clouds with ideas big enough to soar on.

So I guess I've been like this since I was young, and now that I'm an adult, my daydreams have apparently become much more *lascivious* in nature.

The other night—the first time I've ever allowed myself to think sexual thoughts about Head Priest—I became unleashed. And now I can't stop.

I jerked off three times today alone, picturing him in my head, letting me touch him and taste him. I've never gotten off so damn much, and so damn *hard*, and it's driving me wild. I could barely look him in the eye last night at dinner.

But I did, for a split second, and I saw it. I *saw* how black his eyes were. I'd be willing to bet money he'll go into the lounge tonight for solitude. And I'm not just saying that because I'm *desperate* for it to be true myself.

Working so close to him all these years, I've picked up on the subtle nuances others haven't. I could tell from his mannerisms last night that he's on edge. He needs whatever he does when he's alone in that room.

And *I* need to know what that is, before I go completely insane from the curiosity.

I thought maybe it would happen last night, since he went into the lounge after dinner. But then Drake showed up, and Kiara and Alissa oo. Not very *solitary*. He left the room not thirty-minutes later. I practically had my ear to the wall listening.

The thing is, I know it's wrong to be prying for details. It's also an abuse of my position as a Domestic. I'm not invited into Head Priest's home to spy on him. I'm here to work.

But there's this need inside me… this burning fascination, like an ache that starts in my brain, then runs from behind my ribs, all the way down, deep into my loins. It takes over my entire body.

My mind is possessed with this yearning, and nothing shy of knowing what happens in that room will sate it.

I dreamt about him again last night. I dreamt I was watching him through a keyhole. He was in a bathtub for some reason, and he knew I was looking. He put on a bit of a show for me… washing and rubbing, his own fingertips dancing across his soapy wet skin while I gazed on with the widest eyes ever.

I woke up so hard I was tenting my sheets. My balls were practically vibrating. And when I came in my hand, it was *his* name on my tongue like a new favorite song.

Darian. My King.

God, yes.

I need to get a grip. This isn't right.

Those are the penances I'm repeating tonight as I prepare for dinner. We've roasted two chickens stuffed with lemons and fresh thyme from the garden. I made mashed potatoes and steamed some carrots. Focusing on the food will keep me distracted from the images floating around in my skull, and the way they want to make my dick hard, even here at work.

It's crazy. I haven't gotten this many erections since I first hit puberty. It's nuts that this is happening now, and all it took was a new fantasy to spur it on. Though, if I'm being completely honest, it's been a long time coming.

I never wanted to admit to myself that the reason I've been so fascinated with Head Priest is that I'm crushing on him hard. It's an inconvenience I don't need. Not to mention, it could never progress in any direction other than me being reprimanded and embarrassed beyond all reckoning.

I also don't really have anyone I could speak with about the potential of being gay. Like I said before, we don't do labels much in The Principality, which I've always liked and respected. But the default seems to be men with women. At least it is in the case of my friends. And I don't mind being different. Actually, I like it. But what I *don't* enjoy is being alone.

"Hey, kid. What's got you so torn up tonight?" Gina's voice breaks into my head, and I jerk. "You've been quiet since yesterday. Everything alright?"

I nod rapidly. "No, yea. I'm fine." She's not convinced, which isn't surprising after the way I just said that. "I'm just a little stressed. Overthinking and such…"

Gina stops what she's doing and pulls me aside. "Is this because Paul and I were asking you what you wanted for your future? Kiddo, I'm sorry. I wasn't trying to put pressure on you. It's just… Being a Domestic is great for now, but I want you thinking of something bigger. There are all sorts of jobs available on the Expanse, not just house and farm work. That's all I was trying to say."

"I know, Gina. I know." I rub her arm. "It's not that. You guys are great. You just got me thinking is all."

She observes me for a moment, still concerned, brows zipped up. But eventually, she straightens and nods, accepting my words, then brushes my hair back with her fingers.

"There are always classes you can take, too," she adds. "Maybe you could… talk to Drake."

I swallow like an instinct at mention of the Serpent. "Really? I wasn't sure you'd approve…"

"It's part of The Principality, Abdiel." She shrugs. "Could be worth looking into. Just to see what it's about."

I nod and end the conversation by tugging her back to the counter to finish dinner. And that whole thing certainly worked as a distraction, because I'm definitely not fantasizing about Head Priest anymore. Now I'm thinking about his brother…

There's a mass of mystery at the center of The Principality. We're open about a lot as a family, but there's also a lot they don't tell you as a kid growing up here. Things you stumble into learning as an adult.

Drake's operation is a big part of that. He oversees the import/export business for crops, sure, but he's also in charge of overseeing education, and chemical production. His title isn't *The Alchemist* for nothing. *Serpent* is something we sort of call him behind his back because of his creepy eyes and his odd behaviors, though I'm sure he knows about it.

Drake doesn't live in Regnum housing like the rest of us, nor does he reside in the Den with Head Priest and the wives. Drake has a small cabin near the top of White Trumpet Mountain, which is also where the lab is located. The Alchemist's lab is an enigma itself. We know there are chemists creating things for The Principality, like fuel and medicine. But all chemists are trained by Drake himself and sworn to secrecy. If they spill any details of what happens in the lab, they risk execution.

Yea. Like, actual *death* for talking.

Just another facet of life on the Expanse I've always been eager to learn more about, though I'm hesitant. I enjoy working as a Domestic, because I like to cook and serve. *I like being near him...*

But with all my friends either joining the Tribe or becoming farmers, it leaves me wondering what my future could hold. *And what could please this mischievous streak inside me?*

Dinnertime comes as it always does, and the process begins. The wives come down first, then Darian. Everyone gets drinks, then food. Salad and bread to start, then plates of farm fresh home cooking.

Us children of the Expanse have heard horror stories, from Head Priest and from strays, about food in the outside world, full of chemical additives, hormones and preservatives that can give you cancer or cause other disorders. I'm grateful to Mother every day that I've never had to experience it. Our food comes straight from the earth. We don't believe in chemical pesticides or engineering vegetables in the lab.

From what I understand, everything Drake does in his lab is completely natural. It's interesting... *Maybe I would like to learn about it.*

Drake's place setting stays empty, as usual, and Darian's eyes, black as coal, linger on it for most of the meal. The wives converse with one another, but Head Priest is quiet; tense. I can almost feel it every time I pass by him. His shoulders appear bunched, and he might even be clenching his jaw. I don't enjoy seeing him like this, but with my sympathy, restlessness is also building.

There's *no way* he won't be having solitude tonight. I think this is the longest he's ever gone without it. By my calculations, it's been at least five days.

He needs it. And as strange as it sounds, I need it, too.

The wives are barely finished with dessert when Darian excuses himself. And I can't help but notice he doesn't go upstairs...

I'm practically shaking with the urge to follow him. It's never been this strong before, and it takes every ounce of my strength to get through clearing the table and clean-up duty without darting across the Den to find out if he's in his lounge.

My mind is alive with thoughts as we finish up for the night. Eventually, just as everyone is leaving, I'm able to sneak off for just a moment, only to find the door to the lounge is closed. *He's in there, I just know it.*

Desperation claws at my throat while I leave the Den. I'm buzzing with adrenaline, and I can't go home right now. I just *can't* go back to another night of fantasies without first finding out what he does in there.

What gives his eyes return from black to the colors of the sky.

My face pivots left, then right as I check to make sure no one's around. The coast is clear in the quiet of the evening.

I tiptoe around the outside corner of the Den, in the opposite direction of Domestic housing, toward the lake. There's a group of trees off to the side, and I slink between them, keeping myself hidden in the shadows of the night as I creep to the windows on this side of the cabin. I pass the sitting room first, then the study, then the library, ducking to ensure no one sees me.

Finally, I arrive at the farthest window, the last on this side of the house. It's the lounge, and I *need* to see inside.

It's a bit higher than I can reach on my feet, so I make a quick, probably pretty stupid decision to climb up onto a shrub, resting my weight on the house to get a clear view into the room.

The curtains are drawn just enough for me to see inside.

My heart lodges in my throat. *There he is.*

Darian's in the room, just as I'd expected. He's alone, sitting on the bed. He looks stressed; I can see it from here. His knee is bouncing, and he keeps checking his watch over and over.

What is he waiting for?

My curiosity has taken a turn for the creepy at this point. I fully acknowledge that peeping into people's windows is wrong—and super weird—but I can't help it. This need to know has grown like a weed inside me, strangling the life out of my rational thought process.

I must lift the cover. I must know what's underneath.

A minute passes of nothing but my blood rushing in my ears, sweaty palms trying to grip the branches and the wood of the siding while I peer inside, suspended in time. Until eventually the door to the lounge opens slowly.

Darian's head springs up, and something like relief sweeps over

41

his face. My mouth falls in surprise.

It's Drake. I didn't expect him. *Don't tell me solitude isn't happening tonight...*

Disappointment sweeps through me for a moment as Drake steps into the room, then closes the door behind him. And he locks it.

My forehead creases while I watch, confused and hopeful. I can hear them vaguely through the window, muffled, though I'm still able to make out what they're saying. I'm so nervous, I have to hold my breath to ensure I can listen.

"I'm here for your *solitude*, your highness." Drake's tone is a bit sarcastic, yet he's giving Darian a knowing smirk.

I hear Head Priest sigh, "Thank God."

And my stomach clenches with my heart in uneasy expectation.

CHAPTER FIVE

DARIAN

I'm frantic as I unlock the nightstand drawer and take out my kit. Drake wanders over slowly and has a seat next to me on the bed, reaching into his pocket to pull out a small vial. My mouth actually waters at the sight of it. *God, it's been too long. How many days? Six?*

My fingers shake as I remove the rubber strap, then hand Drake the plastic pouch containing a fresh syringe. He takes his time opening it, sticking the needle into the vial and filling the syringe with clear liquid.

Attempting to steady my breathing, I wrap the thick elastic around my right bicep, just above the elbow. It quickly cuts off some circulation, the normally visible veins in my forearm popping.

I swallow, peeking up at Drake, who's staring at me.

"Relax. Jesus." He shakes his head. Clenching my jaw, I seethe at him silently, and he chuckles. "See for that, I have half a mind to make you sweat it out."

"Why do you like fucking with me so much?" I know the answer, but I still feel it necessary to ask.

"Because you're fun to fuck with," he rumbles, tapping my forearm with his fingers. "Always have been."

My body is so keyed up in anticipation of what he's going to do, the slightest touch of his skin on mine licks like flames. My mouth is as dry as a bone while I watch his eyes, gliding up and down my arm. He drags his fingers along the curve of my bicep and I shiver, my dick twitching in my pants.

"Plus…" He leans in closer until his lips are hovering over my mouth. "You're *mine* like this."

I've heard the words in his head a hundred times, but when he says it out loud, it still sends a rush through my heart. My pulse is thudding aggressively in my neck, echoing all throughout my body as he holds me still and pricks the needle into my skin.

A small breath bursts from my lips, my eyes locked on his face while he watches the needle in my vein. I glance down to see blood mix with the clear liquid in the syringe, and the moment it does, Drake presses down on the plunger to shoot.

As soon as the syringe is empty, I let go of the rubber. And I'm instantly hit with fuzzy warmth. Like my entire body is wrapped in a big, furry blanket while I lie in front of the fireplace.

Although I can't feel myself doing it, I lie back on the bed, grabbing Drake by the arm and tugging him with me. I vaguely see him tossing the syringe onto the floor as he crawls over me, caging me in with his arms on either side of my shoulders.

Colors twinkle and flash in my vision like a kaleidoscope, geometric shapes twisting around the room. I gaze up at Drake, and he down at me. Those snake eyes… they're comforting. I don't know what it is, but something so potentially scary looking doesn't scare me. Even if he is wicked, it's *right*.

He's supposed to be this way.

We're light and dark, him and me. Good and bad. Positive and negative.

The circle is complete.

Can you hear me, brother?

I answer him with my mind, *Yes.*

What am I thinking now?

A lazy smile takes over my face as my eyelids droop. I see the colors even brighter when my eyes are shut, my mind's eye wide open. A window made to show me it all.

I see many things… Shapes and creatures and feelings. I *see* emotions, each with their own color and symbol. Stars connect in my mind like constellations.

Focus, Darian.

You get so jealous when it's not all about you, I answer him through a slight chuckle.

Empyrean is me, brother. Never forget that.

I know it is.

So then tell me what I'm thinking...

Reopening my eyes to look up at him once more, I find him hungry. *Starved.*

I know he's the snake, but right now, he looks like a wolf ready to devour its prey. And I don't believe I've ever wanted anything more.

Do it, I tell him.

Do what, gorgeous? Even with his mouth closed, his voice is pure sex. It causes me to squirm beneath him. I'm so warm...

Use me. You know I want it. My hands travel up his waist, inside his shirt to feel smooth skin covering stones of muscle. I lick my lips. I'm so fucking needy right now, my cock is aching.

All the color just makes it that much more tempting. And hearing him like this... I can finally *hear* him again.

He abruptly grabs my hands to stop them, pinning them above my head. I gasp, but it sounds more like a moan, and he likes it. I know he likes it, because I can hear him thinking.

Mmm... You're right. I know you want it.

I blink. *You want it, too.*

He leans over me, extending his long tongue to trace my lips, thinking as he does, *You know I do... King.*

Writhing under him, the heat surrounding us is visible. A large, orange ball of fire swallowing us up on this bed. Drake's lips and tongue descend my jaw, and my neck, and the flames spread to the comforter, then the pillows.

He lets go of my hands enough to tug his shirt over his head. It catches fire too as he tosses it aside. Then he slides mine up my torso, much slower, fingers tracing the lines of me as he goes.

I love that you want me so badly...

His eyes come up to mine as I witness him swallow. *We only do this now.*

I know, I tell him, even though I hate it. But it's the truth.

Empyrean is us together as much as it is us apart. It's the only time we can be like this.

Drake removes my shirt completely, a scorching blaze igniting the bedposts as he goes for my pants, and I go for his.

What am I thinking now, your majesty? His lips curl wickedly. He looks goddamn beautiful when he smiles, but I try not to think it because I know it will only piss him off.

You're wondering if you should tie me...

Should I?

I don't care, just hold me down and fuck me. I'm panting, out of breath and arching up to him as he grinds into me. We shimmy out of our pants, and once in our boxers, he presses himself against my body. The contrast of his pale white skin on my much more bronzed complexion is a turn-on, although I'm not sure why.

We're brothers, though we look nothing alike, and I suppose this fact reminds me that no blood binds us. Still, our bond is one much deeper, and that's why we shouldn't be doing this. Among other reasons, of course.

You want my cock inside you, King Darian?

I groan at the feel of his erection, stiff and rubbing into my own. *God, I missed this.* It's only been a week, but it feels like an eternity when I'm stuck pretending.

I can be myself with you.

I know you can, beautiful brother. So let me take you for a ride.

Yes, yes. Please… Take me.

A growl leaves Drake's lips as they come down onto mine, fast and hard. His mouth assaults me, sucking all the oxygen from my lungs as he eats me alive, and I let him because I *love* it. I love the feeling of him. It's unlike anything I've ever experienced before.

Something dark works its way up, from the back corners of my mind. It makes me itch and attempt to wriggle free, but Drake holds me down.

Stay with me, he insists, lips sucking and tugging my own, teeth nipping in a way that isn't painful, but treasuring. *Don't let him take what's mine.*

A tear slips from the corner of my eye, pain escaping with it. Drake's hands come up to hold my jaw while he kisses me softer, sweeter, his tongue tasting the same as it has for years. *Like safety. Like protection. Like love…*

"Stop it, Darian," he growls out loud and runs a hand down to my throat, holding it hard, cutting off just the tiniest bit of air as a warning.

"I'm sorry…" I croak. I don't know why I said it out loud, because I am.

Mouths can lie, but thoughts are true.

I hate putting all this burden on Drake. I hate breaking the rules. I just want to feel good, like only he can make me.

His movements have slowed, and I feel him pulling away. It swarms me with panic as I slip my hand inside his boxers and fill my palm with him.

Come back to me, I plead, stroking slow, listening to him waging an internal war. I lean forward and kiss his neck, sucking his pulse while he groans.

I want to fill you up... His voice is dangerous inside, possessive. I know he has the potential to break me down, but I've never cared.

I always want it, no matter what.

"So do it," I breathe on his milky flesh, desperate to leave a mark on him.

Don't even think about it, he hisses, and I chuckle.

Stop me, then.

He sits up, and before I know what's happening, he's tearing my boxers off, then slithering out of his own. I can't help my gaze from sticking below his waist, at the incredibly impressive length of him. It's times like these, when I look in awe at him naked, that my sexuality is confirmed. There isn't a doubt in my mind.

This is my chemistry. I was made this way, of Mother. She made me perfect, exactly the way she wants me, and it would be a sin to go against that.

I'm faced with trials because of it. I always have been. I couldn't think that would change just because I left the outside world. And I'm fine with it. I must stay true to myself.

That said, I know what I'm doing here is wrong. But that doesn't stop it from feeling like the ultimate blessing from God.

It would seem as if Drake is barely paying attention to my rampant thoughts, because he's having a similar reaction to my body, which brings on a grin. We've seen each other naked a million times, and I still get him wiping away drool. I have to say, it makes me feel wonderful, especially because Drake sees a lot of people.

I don't ask. I can't know... It might kill me.

He crawls over me once more, pushing my thighs apart forcefully enough that I hum. Then he settles between them, thrusting his hips so that his balls are rubbing mine.

"It's not that I don't want..." He stops as his jaw clenches.

I gulp. "I know."

His eyes stay locked on mine as he reaches toward the nightstand, pulling a bottle from the drawer. He uncaps it and squeezes liquid onto his erection, stroking himself with it, then stroking me. My heart is jumping aggressively, lips shaking with need as I stare up at him. My brother.

My heart. My torment.

NYLA K

The bed is burning around us yet we're as still as stone, holding one another's gaze, eager enough to feel it before it's even happened.

Drake takes his erection in his right hand, while the left glides up my chest, brushing a nipple until I purr. He leans over me, kisses me once more, sucking my lower lip into his mouth while he nudges the bare head of his cock at the entrance of my ass.

Is this what you need, my King? He pushes ever-so-slightly, and I welcome him, gasping as the tip breaks through.

"God, yes…" I breathe into his mouth. *More.*

You want more, Head Priest? He shoves in another inch and I'm falling away from reality.

It burns, the sensation intense, but I love it. I could never get enough of this forbidden desire; this hunger from which I'll never have my fill.

"*Drake…* yes yes yes…" I pant while he pushes in more. *Good God, more.*

You love my cock in your tight ass, don't you, brother?

He flicks his hips once more and fills me, almost all the way. I groan out loud, unable to stop the sound because *holy fuck*, this is intense. It's marvelously dirty, and I need it.

He kisses me harder, taking my bottom lip between his teeth and biting me while he thrusts, balls deep. His bite breaks the skin and I taste the copper of my own blood flooding my mouth, his tongue lurching in to taste.

He's unhinged, desperate, sucking blood from the cut in my lip while he pulls his dick back and forces it in once more, driving so deep in me I'm seeing stars. His body weight forces me down, one hand curling around my throat, while the other grabs my thigh, holding my legs wrapped around his waist as he pumps every inch of himself into my body.

"Fuck me, you feel so good," he hisses, and my heart soars.

I need to hear him say those things. I want to be everything to him, just as he's everything to me.

I can't help wanting him this way. I always have.

But I can't have him, and it tears me apart inside.

So I just focus on his big dick tearing my ass apart, fucking me harder and harder, his pelvis slapping against me almost as loud as the bed frame knocking against the wall. My hands travel all over his body, feeling up his slim, defined surfaces, reaching around to squeeze his ass and pull him deeper.

48

SERPENT IN WHITE

"I love when you're this deep in me, Drake," I groan as quietly as I can manage. "I love when you make me come with no hands."

"Mmm... me too." He leans back a bit to watch my cock, bobbing on my abs, skin stretched almost shiny.

His dick is dragging along that spot deep inside me that feels like bliss realized, zapping my loins until my balls draw up tight. I'm about to explode already. I want to hold out, but I know there's no way. Drake won't have it.

He likes to watch me come first.

With his hand pressing on my throat and his hips bucking into me, stroking his long cock between my legs, I erupt.

My orgasm sweeps me up fast and I explode into a meteor shower, stardust shimmering all around us as my voice breaks.

"Fuck... Drake! Fuck fuck *fuuuuck...*" *Yes yes yes I'm coming... so... hard.*

Cum shoots out all over my abs, up to my chest while my brother keeps stroking, keeps pumping, watching my orgasm drench us. He reaches down and swirls his fingers through it, bringing them up to my lips.

My eyes stay with his while I lick up my own cum from his fingers, moaning at the taste.

It reminds me of the first time I tasted it... Tasted him.

He shudders and swipes more off my stomach, then licks it off himself.

You taste so fucking good. He hovers over me and kisses my lips, diving into me deep, bottoming out while he reaches his own climax. All I taste is him and me together, his need for me the best flavor on earth as he shoots off inside me, *deep.*

The feel of him pulsing in my ass is the hottest experience I can barely fathom. I hold his face to mine, keeping him as close as possible. And for minutes on end, we're just breathing each other in; his exhale to my inhale, and vice versa. We're one, just like we're made to be.

Though it can never last.

You're such a wondrous creature, I tell him.

His chest flutters, and I see the raw vulnerability in his snake eyes. They're so much more golden now than they usually are. This is the only time he's like this. Right after we're together. This is when I get him, and I always want it to last so much longer than it does. Because it can't. And I get that.

But it doesn't make it any less devastating.

You're...

"Mine," he finishes the thought out loud and kisses me once more, before pulling out and getting up.

I stay in bed, lying there while I watch him clean us up, as he always does. The colors are fading; still there, though not as vibrant. The shapes have gone, but I can still feel emotions in the room, thumping like the air has its own pulse.

The high from Empyrean lasts only about twenty-minutes. But that part's just for fun.

The power it gives will last days, and so right now, the voices are loud. Though the only one I hear is Drake's. This is how he likes it; why it's come to this...

I may be King, but Drake rules over the Field of Influence. He's *The Alchemist*, meaning Empyrean and everything about it belongs to him. And he certainly takes mass amounts of pleasure in being the one to supply it to me.

And for that reason, it's his power as much as it is mine.

Drake, my lovely snake-eyed brother, holds the key to my only lock.

CHAPTER SIX

DRAKE

I'm counting.

The thing about numbers is that they're a constant. They never change. Math doesn't, and neither does chemistry. Science is science, regardless of how you want to look at it. And numbers don't lie.

So in times of need, I count.

The flutters of his eyelashes on my chest when he blinks, one every seven seconds or so. The beats his heart jumps against my stomach. Eighty-two per minute. A *calm* pace.

He's relaxed, and it's good. I remember the first time I counted his pulse…

It wasn't such a good time.

But right now is a rapture. Shame it can't last.

I know it, he knows it. *Mother* does.

The unfortunate fact is that even though I thoroughly enjoy myself with my foster brother, we can never be more than a secret; a hidden fantasy fulfilled in the dark. With drugs in his veins, and in mine too, let's be honest… that's the only time we can do this.

And once the high fades, it's back to business as usual.

Darian stirs and I run my fingers along his back. He was listening to me just now. I hope I didn't upset him, even though it's just our truth. A truth he's well aware of, by the way.

That's the thing about Empyrean. There are no secrets. You must be prepared for complete and total honesty; openness to your fellow animals. Once the third eye is opened, it doesn't close, and keeping yourself cognizant of that is very important.

The first few times were a challenge. There are certain things I can't have Darian knowing, not yet anyway. I had to learn to block them from my thoughts, or to cover them up with other things, so he couldn't hear. It's worked so far, but I'm in a state of constant hiding.

Darian, on the other hand, hasn't perfected the skill of sequestering his subconscious. When he thinks, he thinks *loud*. His mind is wild and free, and I do love that about him. It's unfortunate he can't be that way in real life. Not completely.

I blame myself for his lack of self-confidence regarding his sexuality. After all, I've been the one telling him for years that it would be *wrong* for us to be together. That, paired with what happened to him when we were kids, I think has severely stunted his ability to see his proper path. And to really understand how perfect he is.

Let's be clear; I'm not saying him being with another man is wrong. I'm saying him being with *me* is wrong, because it is. But it's not about sexuality or being open with who you love...

It's about me being evil.

To put it plainly, I'm not a good person, and Darian is. He needs to be with someone who's equally good. Someone deserving of every wonderful thing about him.

And that's not me.

It's a scientific fact that every natural supply has a return. That light must be met with darkness. Darian isn't wrong in believing that. What he doesn't understand, however, is that Satan used a serpent to tempt Adam and Eve for a reason. And that's not to say I believe in the *Holy Bible* more than I believe in science. I don't.

But even in our consideration of the word of God, and our Mother Earth, the serpent is a symbol of death.

That's me.

I bring death wherever I go, and I'm almost sure I'm destined for some form of eternal pain. I refuse to let Darian get swept up in all that. He's far too important to me.

"Your thoughts are buzzing," he murmurs, pulling me tighter with his leg draped over mine. He likes to get all tangled up like this, I suspect because he knows I could flee at any moment. "Like radio static."

"Maybe my brain is scrambled." I grin, and he peers up at me, giving me a look like I'm an idiot. It makes me laugh.

A small smile tugs at his full lips, though it's clear he's trying to smother it as he crawls on top of me, straddling my hips. He's still naked, and it's active work not looking at all the places I want to touch, and taste.

I have to go.

"You're fighting too hard." He leans down and presses his lips to my jaw. "Just one more time... while I still have you."

"You don't have me." I keep my tone as firm as I can, resisting every urge to grab him by the waist and shove him down on my cock again.

He flinches but covers it up quick. "I know that. I'm just saying... it feels good. And no one will know."

He grinds his hardening erection into mine, and against every bit of animal inside me, I press my hands on his chest to push him back.

"That's not the point. We agreed..."

He sits back farther, jaw tight to sequester emotions I can hear as if he's screaming them in my face.

"No. We never agreed on anything like this. In fact, it was always about Empyrean, wasn't it, Drake?" His eyes are so light now. Even in the dimly lit room, they look like aquamarine, only with some gray thrown in. A stark contrast to the almost pitch black from thirty minutes ago. "So it actually makes no sense for us to hook up at all. You could just give me the vial and be on your way."

I sit up fast until we're nose to nose. He looks momentarily startled.

"First of all, you wouldn't know how to shoot yourself up if you tried, and you'd end up wasting it," I start. He opens his mouth to object, but I press my palm over it. "And second of all, the moment you stop needing me to turn you out, brother dearest, you let me know. This arrangement could be much more practical."

He appears wounded, as if I just shot him. And I don't feel any better about it myself.

But this is what I have to do... It's always been this way.

You're an asshole, he thinks, loud enough that it'll be echoing through my mind for the next three days.

I know.

I kiss the back of my hand covering his mouth, then I shift him off my lap and scramble off the bed. I have to leave, right now, before something bad happens. Before we say more stuff we don't mean, or before we keep thinking the stuff we really do.

I've known for a while that this is dangerous, this thing I do with Darian. He relies on Empyrean, though he doesn't need it. He experienced his Ecdysis long ago, and anything from this point on is just a means to an end. But I fear it's become more of him relying on *me* as well; on what I give him, more than the drugs.

Darian has needs only fulfilled by me. And I'm torn between wanting to always give in to him, and knowing I should steer clear, to protect him from my inevitable damnation.

"Don't…" His voice stops me, though it trails off after the first word.

I pause my hasty redressing and hang my head, back to him. *Don't turn around…* I tell myself.

But I do. I glance over my shoulder, and he's just kneeling on the bed, right where I left him, looking helpless. I hate seeing him like that, because he's the strongest person I know. He's the King of the Expanse.

But when he makes that face, it reminds me of all those years ago…

The day we ran and never looked back.

His eyes are wide, and he finishes his sentence with his lips sealed shut.

Don't go.

I shift away, tugging my shirt back on as I head for the door.

"I'll see you in a few days."

"Listen up, shrimp. Today's the day."

I look up from the pages of the comic book I'm reading and meet the eyes of my foster father.

Dan.

He sucks.

"What day?" I ask, eyes dropping back to my comic. I don't really want to talk to him, but I know if I don't it'll make him angry. So I play along with whatever he's trying to do in hopes it doesn't earn me a bruise.

"You're getting a new brother," he tells me, standing by the edge of my bed, looking down at me. "Hopefully, he's more useful than your sorry ass."

SERPENT IN WHITE

Oh please, Dickhead Dan. Do tell me more about how much of a disappointment I am to you.

But before I can even continue insulting him in my head, I focus on what he actually just said.

A brother? Really??

I've never had siblings before. I've kind of always wanted one. Someone to lessen the burden, and spend time with me when I'm alone, which is just about always.

Mom used to tell Dad she wanted to have another baby, but he'd laugh at her. One was one too many for him.

"Oh," I say, because I'm not sure what else I could. I'm a bit stunned.

Dan and Kara barely want me. Why would they want another foster kid?

"Kara's on her way home with him right now." He tilts his head at me. "And I want you on your best behavior, you little cretin. Got it?"

Anger bubbles inside me, but I nod anyway. I really hate this guy. I hate him so much, it makes me want to run far, far away.

Someday I will. I don't think I can wait until I'm eighteen. I can't do six more years in this hellhole. I just need to get a little bigger, save up some money, learn some more. I like school, but it's hard to concentrate knowing I have to come home to this.

Dan looks around, at my desk, piled high with books, my makeshift shelf I built out of some old crates stacked with comics, and he scoffs, shaking his head. "Make some space and bring the cot up from the basement. He'll have to sleep on that until we get him a bed."

He turns to leave the room, and I take a breath. But then he stops.

"You're a waste of a son, shrimp." He peers at me. "No wonder your father got himself sent to jail. To get away from you, I'm sure."

Then he leaves my bedroom. Leaves me staring at the door, fist tightened so hard at my side it's going numb.

My father didn't get sent to jail to get away from me. He got sent to jail because he was a drunk and he killed my mother. Strangled her to death when I was nine years old.

I found her...

My gaze goes far for a moment while I remember waking up to go to the bathroom, turning on the light to find dead eyes staring up at me from the floor.

Pasty face. Mouth open.

She'd been dead for hours.

I close my eyes and shake myself out of it. I've gotta get out of this place. Detroit is a pit of sorrow. That's all I've ever experienced here. The only place I've ever been truly happy was in the forest.

My parents took me camping once when I was little. We went to some place up near Flint; I don't remember what it was called. But we pitched a tent and cuddled up in sleeping bags. They made a fire, and we roasted marshmallows. It was fun.

And plus, I was too young to understand my dad's drinking or my mom's unhappiness. I was blissfully unaware of all the trouble in the world, and the impending destruction of my life.

It was just good.

Someday I'll go back to the woods.

I spend the next hour trying to get the damn cot upstairs. I'm only twelve and still sort of small for my age, so it's really difficult. Dan should be the one doing this, but he wouldn't. He just makes me do everything while he sits around, acting like a weirdo. That's why he calls me shrimp, *because I haven't had my growth spurt yet. But I will, I know it. I'll get tall, and strong.*

Hopefully strong enough to fight back.

I set the cot up in my room, across from my bed. Then I get clean sheets and blankets, making it up nice. There are no more pillows, so I give him mine. My new brother probably needs a pillow more than me.

I assume if he's coming here, it's because something fucked up happened. Life is shit. I wouldn't be surprised.

When Foster Mom Oblivious, I mean, Kara, *gets back, I dart out of my room to the top of the steps and peek down. And sure enough, in walks a kid who looks about my age, maybe a little bigger, with a backpack on, clutching a pillow to his chest. I blink slowly as they pass the stairs, Kara showing him around. Eventually they come upstairs, and I run back to my room, acting like I haven't been waiting anxiously to meet him.*

"And this will be your room," she tells him, bringing him inside. "You'll have to share. Drake, I'd like you to meet Darian. Darian, this is your new brother, Drake."

He turns his eyes on me and gapes at me for a moment. I look down at my lap, a knee-jerk reaction when people first see me. I know I'm a little different. My eyes are colored like marbles and kids at school call me a freak.

But when I look back up at Darian, he has this kind smile on. Then he waves at me.

"Hey," he says, pretty casually.

"Hey."

"Well, I'll leave you boys to get to know each other." Kara pats Darian on the back. "Dinner will be ready in about an hour."

She leaves the room, and he watches her go. As soon as she's audibly downstairs, he turns to me. "She seems alright."

"She's fine, I guess." I shrug. "Kind of stupid, if you ask me."

He laughs. It almost makes me smile, but then I remember I don't do that and put it away.

"Why is she stupid?"

"Because she's willingly married to that asshole." I nod toward the doorway.

"Dan?" He removes his backpack and sets it down on the cot.

"Yea. He's a prick."

"Wow. So you don't really like anyone, huh?" He glances at me in between pulling miscellaneous stuff out of his backpack.

I think about what he just asked me for a second. It's not that I don't like anyone, *it's just that I haven't met anyone worth liking yet.*

"I just don't like them," I mutter, plopping down onto my bed.

"What happened to your parents?" Darian asks, and I decide I like him.

I like him because he's talking to me. And asking about me. *No one ever does.*

"Mom's dead. Dad's in jail. He killed her," I answer, in my usual unfazed tone. "What about yours?"

"My mom's dead, too. She overdosed on drugs." He looks down at his shoes. "I never knew my dad."

"They're overrated," I tell him, and his eyes dart up to mine. "Parents."

"I was hoping Dan would be a good dad," he says softly, and you can really hear that hopefulness. I feel bad that he's striking out once again in the father department.

"I hate to break it to you, but he sucks." I flop backward on the bed and stare up at the cracks in the ceiling.

I hear Darian shuffling around for a few seconds, but I don't look up until he says, "Did you give me your pillow?"

I sit up on my elbows. "Yea. I didn't know you were gonna bring your own."

"Thanks." He grins, then stomps over to my bed, holding out his pillow. "Trade?"

I stare at him for a minute, wondering if he'll actually be a brother to me, or if he's just acting nice now, and once we get into school and he becomes more popular than me, he'll pretend I don't exist. I really hope not, because he seems cool.

He seems like he could be my brother.

I take the pillow from him and stuff it under my head. It has a different smell than mine, obviously because it's his. And as weird as it is, I kind of like it.

Darian, my brother...

I'll have to protect him. I almost don't have a choice.

CHAPTER SEVEN

ABDIEL

O*h God.*
Oh God, oh God holy crap.
What the fuck...
I blink and shake my head for the fiftieth time, climbing down from the bush I nearly fell out of a few minutes ago.

Watching that... Seeing what just happened in there.
Holy shit what the fuck?!

My hands are shaking, and it isn't until I get my feet on solid ground once more that I realize I haven't taken a breath in too long. I suck air in and hold, rubbing my face with my hands. When I close my eyes, I can still see it...

I can still see them. *Together.*

I shift on my feet, my erection solid and painful between my legs. I had to tuck it into the waistband of my pants. I would laugh if I wasn't still so... shocked.

That was the hottest thing I've ever seen in my entire life.

Head Priest, and The Alchemist... *fucking*.

So Darian and Drake fuck...? They're brothers...

I'm not sure how that makes it hotter, but my dick is leaking on my stomach.

I bite my lip. They're not brothers by blood or anything, so I suppose it isn't as *taboo* as one might think. But still... Head Priest is married. To women.

But what I just witnessed, the chemistry happening in that room. I've never seen anything like it, especially not between Darian and those five girls.

We're missing a key point here, though. I'm so focused on the incredibly hot sex, I almost forgot about the drugs. *That's right...*

Drake shot Darian up with something. *Maybe it was medicine?*

I've never seen someone react that way to getting a medical injection. His eyes nearly rolled back in his skull. His face flushed as he pulled Drake on top of him, gazing around the room like he was seeing things I most certainly couldn't see in there.

And then the two of them made this sort of eye contact. It was as if they were speaking without opening their mouths. I tried desperately to hear what they were saying inside the room, but they rarely spoke actual words. For the most part, they were silent, just staring at one another. In tune together; in sync.

It could be a brotherly bond of some kind. Or the bond of two lovers.

I'm not sure, but either way, I've never been so turned on in my life. My balls are aching and heavy, and I fear if I don't relieve this pressure soon, I might explode.

Rushing closer to the lake, I duck behind a large tree, which is far enough from the Den that I know no one will hear or see me. Plus, it's late, and no one's really out right now. People don't start staying out later until after solstice.

Leaning my back against the tree, I glance around one last time before pulling my cock out. It's *beyond* hard. The veins pulse when I wrap my fist around it and tug, my head falling back on the bark as I whimper. It already feels amazing.

Swallowing, my eyes droop shut as the sounds from inside the lounge echo in my brain. The gasps and grunts and pants of lust and pleasure. Of two *men* together...

I'd never seen it before tonight. I've never watched *any* two people fucking, let alone two men. I mean, I've certainly *heard* it before, men and women together that is. And I've seen Jordan hook up, since he does it constantly.

But two beautiful men... All hard lines and slopes of muscle. Stubbled jaws and hungry eyes and large hands... Big dicks.

"*Fuuuck...*" I whisper-moan, jerking harder and faster.

It only takes about three minutes before I'm soaking my hand.

I slap the other over my mouth to stop myself from crying out loud. The world twirls and the moon reflects off the lake as I come and come and *come*, picturing not one this time, but *two* people I shouldn't be fantasizing about.

As soon as I catch my breath once more, I look down at my cock, my hand covered in cum, which is also on the ground by my shoes, and I shake my head.

What's wrong with me? I just jerked off outside the Head Priest's home. I'm not sure what I'm doing anymore, but I need to get ahold of myself.

Tucking my dick away, I fix myself up and gaze out over the lake, its calm waters unmoving. Everything is at a standstill while I contemplate the state of these fantasies. Because now, I'm no longer just crushing on Head Priest, but also his brother.

The *Serpent* who seems so cold, so manipulative. So... unusual. He's a quietly unnerving person, although he's never personally done anything wrong to me, or to anyone I know. People on the Expanse love him, and he's a key part of business operations for The Principality; for our lifestyle.

But then we've all heard the rumors...

The gunshots.

The Alchemist runs the Tribe, and well, it's been said that they're trained to kill. Kill who, I'm not entirely sure. But the Expanse is a very private place. We haven't had intruders set foot within our territory a single time since I've been alive, and I'm glad for that fact. It makes me feel safe.

Still, I don't know what has to happen to keep it this way. I suppose the only person who does is Drake. The man I just watched inject something into our Head Priest and then fuck him so hard he was practically weeping.

It looked as if Darian had seen the face of God.

Who knows... maybe he did.

By the following afternoon, I've jerked off five more times, and as spent as my body is, I'm still desperate for more.

More information, more answers, more... of *them*.

I'm off today, which is good because I'm not sure I'd be able to walk around Head Priest, serving him food and drinks, all the while remembering what his face looks like while he's taking his brother's dick.

A shiver of elation runs through me.

I know it was wrong to spy on them. I'm not supposed to be doing any of the things I've been doing for the past week, but that doesn't stop me from wanting it. From acting on these fervent yearnings.

Maybe I'm a bad person.

Maybe I need to pray more.

Maybe I need to get laid.

It's like Jordan always says, I'm too wound up. Sex is obviously a great tool for relief, I saw it on Drake and Darian when they were done. Though it did look like Drake left in a bit of a hurry, and Darian didn't appear pleased by it.

I can't help wondering what's going on with them. I wonder if they're in love, or if Head Priest is going to leave his wives for his brother. I don't know how people in The Principality would feel about that...

Sure, everyone is accepting of love in all shapes and forms, but the Regnum has been clamoring for years about Darian impregnating one of his wives. They believe it's important for an heir to be born, just in case something happens to him.

I'm sick of hearing about it personally, so I can only imagine how Darian feels. I just don't think it's necessary for him to have a child if he doesn't want one, but I don't dare voice that opinion. A majority of the Regnum is on *team baby*, and they're relentless.

After what I witnessed last night, I finally understand why he's been avoiding it so hard. I feel for Darian now, more than ever. I wish he would just tell everyone the truth. I'm sure the secrets are weighing on him, and it can't feel good.

Deciding on taking a walk to clear my head, I step into my boots and leave the trailer. It's overcast today, though warm enough not to need a jacket. It's springtime on the Expanse, and everyone is bustling, preparing for a fruitful summer and a bountiful harvest.

Summer is the best time here. The weather is perfect, it rains a lot less than the rest of the year, and everyone is generally in high spirits. Mother blesses us all year round, but it's this season during which love is in abundance, in all forms.

Trudging along, I wave to a few people here and there. Most are working on chores, laundry being hung on clotheslines, flowers being tended to in the gardens. The children are having class outside today, and from what I can tell, they're learning about trees.

I remember those lessons. We're taught about nature right from the start, because the earth is everything. I recall reading for hours about different flowers, where they thrive and what they could be used for if needed. The ecosystems class was always interesting, but I preferred learning which plants you can eat. How to make certain ingredients and whatnot.

Now that I'm thinking about my future, after Paul and Gina started mentioning it a couple of months back, I'm thinking more about what I love to do. I enjoy singing and cooking. And as much as it isn't really a *career*, I do love to serve people. I think I just like to give, and to make people happy, though I'm not exactly sure if there's work in that...

My walk takes me through the trails, past housing and toward the mountain. I see the farmland coming up and I have to marvel at what we've built here. Fields and fields of crops, either being planted now, or already growing. The corn fields, which we turn into a maze for the kids after harvest, the berries and fruit, potatoes and grain. The barley, hops, and grapes for beer and wine.

It's not what I want to do with my life, but I admire the farmers. They keep this whole place going. Without them, we'd have nothing.

Once I've past the crops, I can see the base of the mountain up in the distance, which means I'm getting closer to the Field of Influence. I immediately spot two members of the Tribe, posted up for watch.

Lorn and Xander. They're dressed in combat boots, camo pants and jackets, with bandanas covering most of their faces. They're each straddling an ATV, with machine guns strapped over their shoulders.

As I saunter over to them, their conversation comes to a halt and they look up, on alert until they notice it's me.

"Hey, Harmony." Lorn tugs his mask down around his neck. "How's it goin, brother?"

"Hey, guys." I wander over, checking out their setup.

"Haven't seen you around these parts in a while," Xander says, leaving his mask up, dark eyes narrowed in my direction.

"Yea, I was just taking a walk," I explain. "It's my day off, so..."

"*Day off?*" Lorn huffs, pulling a cigarette out of his jacket and sticking it between his lips. "What's that like?"

Xander chuckles along as Lorn lights his cigarette and takes a drag.

"Hey, you guys know what you signed up for, right?" I grin, eyes unwittingly falling to the very large gun on his back.

"That's true." Xander nods. "Plus, the perks are worth it." He glances at Lorn, who grins a wide, devilish thing, taking another drag of his cigarette.

I stare at them for a moment, wondering what they're talking about. I'm sure they're well compensated for putting their lives on the line, working crazy hours, enduring all the training and the secrecy. The Tribe keeps us running too, but in a very different way.

"Um... is Drake around?" I ask, and the second the question leaves my lips, I immediately want to take it back.

Lorn and Xander go still. They gape at me like I've lost my mind for five full seconds, before Lorn mutters, "What do you want with the Serpent, Harmony?"

Well, you see, Lorn, I watched him fuck his brother last night, and now I really can't stop thinking about him.

"Paul and Gina suggested I talk to him," I answer as evenly as I can. "About classes..."

"Chelsea handles class registry." Xander squints at me again. "Unless... you thinkin' about the lab?"

"I don't really know..." I reply with more uncertainty in my tone than I can control. "It's just something I was considering."

The two of them share a look for a moment, then their eyes of trepidation come back to me, the tension between the three of us easily palpable.

"Well, there's a wait for The Alchemist." Lorn tosses his cigarette onto the ground and stomps it with precision. "As I'm sure you'd expect."

I nod. "Of course."

"But we'll let him know you stopped by." Xander glares. It's not a happy-looking expression, nor is it one that instills confidence in him doing what he says he will.

I'm not surprised, though. You don't just wander up to the Field and get invited into the lab to speak with The Alchemist. It's a process, I guess. And honestly, I didn't know I wanted to talk to him until I got here. *What would I even say?*

I've never spoken a word to Drake in my life. He makes me even more nervous than Head Priest does. But in his case, it's not because of fascination, or a crush. It's because he's the *Serpent*. A strange creature who lurks in the shadows. Who knows everything about you from a look and uses that knowledge to get what he needs.

That's the impression I get from Drake. He's smart, but not necessarily in a good way.

"Thanks, guys," I breathe, readying myself to walk away from whatever is happening here. "Good catching up. I hope to see you at reflection one of these nights."

"Yea, sounds like a plan, Harmony," Lorn says with a little wave, before tugging his mask back up. He's more pleasant than his colleague.

Xander just stares, watching me closely as I decide on my next move. I was going to hike the mountain a little. But the way the guys are watching me, now I'm not so sure it's a good idea.

We're entitled to the mountain. The Field of Influence and the lab areas are protected by the Tribe, and authorized personnel are the only ones allowed in. But the mountain isn't part of that.

That said, people avoid White Trumpet Mountain. There are things up there... things that Head Priest warns the Regnum from stumbling into. He says if you're going to go up there, make sure you're ready to face what you may find.

I've always wondered what that means. And my curiosity is close to piquing. I want to know what's up there, and why Drake lives there alone.

But then, that's where it happened...

I close my eyes for a moment and rub the back of my neck, where the hairs are standing straight. I can't go up there. I shouldn't.

Reopening my eyes, I turn away from the guys and walk back in the direction I came. I'm not doing this today. The mischief that burns inside me is one thing, but to willingly go wandering up a mountain where the bodies of my parents were found...

That's a part of my curiosity to be avoided.

CHAPTER EIGHT

DARIAN

I like being able to rely on people.
When I was a kid, I never could. Until I met Drake, that is.
I put a lot on him when we were younger, and I never meant to.
But he just bore the burden, and he did so without complaint. In fact, he seemed to want it.

We brought that with us into The Principality. He became my number two, my second in command. My Vice President, if you will. The underground controller of all the things I wouldn't be able to manage. I get the credit as the face of this whole thing, and Drake stays behind the scenes, operating.

I used to stop all the time and ask him if he wanted to be in the public more. After all, I have no problems giving credit where it's due. I don't like for people to worship me, because I'm no god. There's only one God, and She's the *only* One deserving of human worship.

I'm just a disciple of Her creation.

And I suppose that entitles me to some devotion. It took a while to get used to it, but I did. And now it's sort of necessary to keep things moving the way they need to here. But Drake doesn't like it.

For all the shit he gives me about being a *King*, he would sooner chop his own arm off than have people worshipping him; applauding for him. It makes him uncomfortable. Drake is every bit the *serpent* of his namesake. You never see a snake standing up in front of people and leading them. There's a reason for that.

Still, I *do* need him. I think I need him more than he needs me, which is an unfortunate power shift. And I have no choice but to deal

He threatens when he feels emotionally cornered, saying he could easily break off our arrangement. But I know he never will. He's a secret hero, like a vigilante; the one you'd never expect, and who would never admit to it if you asked him.

He's saved me many times, and I won't forget it.

Today was a good day. Seedlings are being transferred and planted, kids are about to break from school for solstice, new registration being organized by the teachers. My wives are planning events, and getting along doing so, for the most part.

And I can hear it all.

My relief is palpable by everyone. I think collectively the Expanse and everyone on it can breathe easier when I have my Empyrean. This land feels when I'm on edge, as much as I do. And when I can hear everything, as I should, it's just a generally better vibe in the woods.

I haven't seen Drake since the other night, which is common after we have *solitude* together. He always disappears for a few days, and I think it's so he can hide his thoughts from me. But who knows if that's true...

Maybe he feels ashamed.

I look out the window of my upstairs library. The sun will be setting soon, and we're in that sweet spot with dim light encompassing the trees, draping them in the silk of dusk. I can smell food cooking downstairs, and I'm sure we'll be called to dinner in minutes.

But for now, I'm just watching the lake. Remembering the first time...

We're tucked inside the tent, purposely trying to keep away from the walls, since it's pouring rain outside and we can't afford to let water in. We only have these two sleeping bags and the clothes on our backs.

"I'm sorry," I whisper in the dark, shivering as I stare at the back of his black head of hair. I feel so guilty for having him out here. It's only getting colder. We could die.

He spins in his sleeping bag to face me, those marble eyes shimmering in the dark.

"Are you cold?" He asks, rather than acknowledging my apology. I shake my head, but he gives me a look as if he knows I'm lying. Huffing, he unzips the sleeping bag and then reaches over to unzip mine. "Get closer," he says, firmly, like it's an order. "I don't want you getting sick."

I'm hesitant. I'm not sure what he expects me to do... Get into his sleeping bag with him? That's weird.

But I am cold. Freezing, actually. So I do what he says and inch closer, nestling up inside his open sleeping bag. I go to pull mine with me, but instead he yanks me even closer to him, until our bodies are practically smooshed together, then reaches over my waist and zips his shut. With me in it.

Both of us... inside together.

I swallow down my nerves, shivering for a different reason now.

"What are we...?" My voice dissolves as he locks me in place with a look laced with heat. He's so damn close to me, his face mere inches from mine.

My hand has nowhere to go, so I place it on his arm, which is still resting around my waist. I almost gasp. "Drake... you're freezing."

"I'm always cold." He shrugs. "The purpose of this is to keep you warm."

I scoff. "Yea, well... you're thinner than me."

"That doesn't matter," he grunts, hand running subtly up my back. "It's survival 101. Bodies create more heat when they're huddled together."

"Oh..." My voice is all breathy. It sounds stupid, but I can't help it.

We've never done this before... We've only ever touched like this one time. And we don't talk about that. Or at least we haven't since it happened...

I'm so tense, and I'm sure he can feel it, all my muscles bunched up as he rubs my back slowly, I'm guessing just to keep me warm, though my body is having an entirely different reaction. I rest my head on the pillow, tucking my face away so I don't have to look at him.

I'm embarrassed. I don't think he likes this the way I do. It makes me feel like a creep. But I have to appreciate him not calling me out on it. He never does.

"I don't want to hear you apologizing to me again, Darian." His voice rumbles into me, and my face pivots back up. "Do you understand?"

I'm speechless. I don't know what to say, so I just nod.

"You did nothing wrong," he goes on, his tone sure, and not to be argued with. "We left because we had to. I couldn't let you stay there for one more second. I won't ever let someone do that to you again. We're here because this is where we need to be. And we're gonna make it."

I gape up at him, my entire body flooding with warmth, at his *protectiveness, his love. I don't think I've ever felt it before. I've never had someone who would sacrifice everything to protect me. That's why we left...*

So he could keep me safe.

It should make me feel like a wuss. I mean, I'm fifteen, and I can fight. I have muscles, I play football. I can take care of myself.

But I didn't. None of that helped me when I needed it. That's why Drake was there. To get me out. And I like that. I like him feeling protective of me...

Because I think I would do just about anything for him.

"Okay," I speak, answering him.

Watching his eyes, I wish I knew what he was thinking. They're flickering between mine, his fingers still trailing my back. They go lower, and my body reacts. It takes me a second to register how hard my dick is. And heat rushes up my neck.

His powerful hand pulls me closer to him by my waist, and I hesitate.

"Closer," he whispers. "I need to keep you warm, dumbass."

I falter, shaking my head. I can't press my lower half into him... He'll feel my erection, and then he'll get freaked out. Because he's my brother, and he doesn't think of me that way. Even though we're not technically related, he's my best friend on earth, and I don't think he likes boys.

My jaw sets as he tugs me again, and this time I go, allowing him to meld our hips together. The moment my erection brushes his thigh, a wave of tingles sheets my skin. I gulp as my mouth fills with saliva. I'm so damn glad it's dark, because I'm sure I'm blushing like a total chick.

Even though all I want in the world is to look away, my eyes connect with his. I expect him to look disgusted, or angry. But he doesn't. He's giving me a look I can't read at all, and I just wish I could.

His hand, having previously halted its movements, picks back up again, rubbing me gently, flinching my dick against his waist.

And then something crazy happens. He hums.

A small, soft noise resounds from his chest, directly into mine. I'm not sure why, but the deranged part of me wants to believe it's because he likes the feeling of me, hardening against him.

I'm too busy watching his face, desperate to know what's running through his head to notice that his hand is shifting lower and lower, until it's resting right above my ass. I swallow my nerves, my throat as dry as a desert, prompting me to lick my lip.

His glowing eyes fall to my mouth, and my dick jerks even harder.

I can't even do this. I'm so afraid, of everything, and it's pissing me off.

I burrow my face into the pillow again to hide.

"Darian..." he mumbles.

"What...?"

"Are you okay?" His thumb is drawing circles on my lower back.

"Mhm."

"Are you afraid?" His voice is so deep. It's like mine, and I like that. I like guys' voices, because I like guys, and I don't want that to make him hate me.

"No, I'm not afraid," I grunt my lie into the pillow.

"Then why are you hiding?" This time his fingers slink around to the front, slipping underneath my sweatshirt. They're cold as they touch my abs, and I flinch.

"Your hands are freezing, too." I ignore his question, grumbling in a petulant tone.

He chuckles, and it's such a sweet sound, I have no choice but to lift my face again. Drake doesn't smile often. But when he does, it lights up the sky.

"Warm them up for me, then," he breathes, gaze zeroed in on my mouth once more.

I'm not imagining this. I know I'm not. Him looking at me and touching me this way has nothing to do with staying warm.

"How?" I ask, nervous that I'll interpret this wrong and get punched in the face. But in all honesty, if it hasn't happened yet...

Drake moves both of his hands in between us, and I make a decision. I take them into mine and hold them against my chest, in an attempt to warm them up, though the feeling of his long fingers on my chest, even through my clothes, is driving me insane. My nipples are hardened like pebbles, I can feel them, and my dick is weeping in my pants.

Drake moves his hips forward, just an inch, but it's enough friction on my erection for me to whimper.

He tugs one of his hands out of my grip and slides it up my neck, holding the side of my face. I'm frozen, I can't breathe or move or blink as he brings me closer.

"Drake..." I whisper, my lips trembling as his breath warms them.

"Don't stop me," he insists, close enough that I can feel his mouth move over mine.

I can't speak. I'm not sure what I would say even if I could, but my brain is scrambled and all I want in the entire world is what I think is about to happen.

He pulls my face to his, closing the gap between our lips and presses his to mine as fireworks pop behind my eyelids.

His kiss is everything Drake is not; hesitant, soft, curious. It's as if he's holding himself back, and I do love it, though part of me wishes he would just unleash on me.

We kiss slow for many agonizing seconds, and even though it's torture, this build-up, it's so damn sweet. This is my first time ever kissing a boy, and he's basically my brother. In the back of my mind, I know we shouldn't, but when he parts his lips, and I part mine, allowing his tongue to creep inside my mouth, I lose all rational thinking. Every hesitation disappears, and we become ravenous.

Drake groans into my mouth and I groan back, submitting to him like it's that easy, letting him suck my lips hard and explore my tongue with his. I can't even believe I was cold a few minutes ago, because now I'm burning up.

"Fuck..." he says when we finally tear apart to breathe, though the break doesn't stop him from touching me everywhere and rolling on top of me.

And even though I'm confused about what he might like, I'm very unconfused about what I like, so I drop my hand between us and rub his dick through his pants.

It's hard. It's so fucking hard, for me.

"I didn't know you would like this..." I pant, sounding like such a moron, though I can't help it. I've wanted this for a while, and I've never been able to have it outside of my thoughts.

"Neither did I," he hums, kissing my lips again, thrusting his hips forward to fill my palm with his clothed cock. "Have you done this before?"

I still, my movements coming to a halt as I gaze up at him, darkness flooding my thoughts. Terror washes over me, and my blinking becomes rapid, the fear trying to steal me though I don't want it to.

Drake seems to realize it right away, and he grabs my face in his hands. "Hey, Darian, stay with me, okay? Breathe for me. Please."

I nod and suck in a breath, holding onto it before letting it go, focusing on his face; his beautiful, concerned face. He's worried because of me.

I'm broken, and I'd almost forgotten about it for a minute there. Why we're out here... Why we left.

"You know I didn't mean him," he whispers, brushing my lower lip with his thumb. It's such a tender motion, the opposite of what I'd expect from someone as cold as my brother. And I love it. I want to be the only one who gets him like this. "He doesn't count, you know that, right?"

Chewing on my cheek, I look away, unsure. I don't think he should count as anything other than a monster, but what the fuck do I know? I'm just the dumbass who bought it for as long as I did...

"Look at me," Drake demands, and I do. "Just tell me this, Darian... Answer me truthfully. Do you like what you feel when I kiss you?"

My cock jerks between us, and my tongue swipes my lower lip. I miss the feeling of his mouth already, so I nod. "Yes."

"What about... when I touch you?" His voice goes softer, his right hand drifting slowly down my neck, over my chest and stomach, down to my crotch. His long fingers trace the shape of me through my pants and I groan a little, biting my lip as my cock flexes into his hand. "You like this?"

"Yes... so much." I squirm, blinking heavy lids up at him while he grins.

"Then these feelings have absolutely nothing to do with him, baby," he rasps, and my cock leaks at him calling me baby. *"He's just an unfortunate blip in your timeline. But we can erase him if you want..." He pauses, eyes widening just a bit. "I mean, you can."*

A smile tugs at my lips. "No, you had it right the first time."

He chuckles, leaning in to kiss me again.

And we kiss for a while, so long I hear birds chirping by the time we finally peel off each other.

That night was the start. The beginning of many nights spent kissing and touching, exploring in a tent, all alone in the wilderness.

That night was the start of everything.

I'm snapped out of my reverie when I hear someone coming closer. Not words, but thoughts.

It's Gina, and she's worried about someone seeming distracted... needs to open a new bottle of wine... she wonders what I'll want to drink tonight.

I blink and rub my face, ridding myself of that memory, for now.

It was right over there, by the lake I live on. Long before I had this home, or wives, or even a Regnum of people following me. The Principality wasn't even a thought...

We were just focusing on getting by. On figuring out how to live as two teenagers in the woods with no family to speak of, who ran away from pain to search for love.

I turn in my chair as Gina steps into the room, smiling at me. She motions to the door, and I'm already standing, walking over as she says, "Dinner."

I grin at her, well aware that she's here to get me for dinner, and also of every other thought currently running through her mind. We head to the stairs, and she follows me as I descend.

Turning over my shoulder, I ask, "You have any more of Ivan's honey ale?"

She looks momentarily stunned, but then nods and grins. "Sure. Feeling beer tonight?"

I chuckle as we make our ways to the dining table. "Definitely."

Cam pulls out my chair, and I have a seat, glancing up at my wives and the empty place setting for Drake. I give them a quick nod, and their conversation picks back up. I sometimes wish they knew they don't have to make such a production every time I enter a room, like I'm the damn Pope or something. I can already hear everything they're thinking anyway, so it doesn't much matter.

But then there's no way I would ever tell them that. The point of Empyrean, and the reason why I don't allow anyone else to know about it or its powers, is because I'm selfish. I *need* this control. I want to be able to hear people's thoughts because I never want to make the mistake again of thinking I know someone's intentions who is secretly lusting after something else entirely.

If there's a monster among us, I'll know about it. I'll never be caught naïve again.

All people have impure thoughts. It's a part of life and human nature, and this community isn't exempt from that. The difference here is that Ecdysis keeps us in tune with what Mother wants. And Empyrean helps me lead.

That's not to say we're perfect. No one is. *We all have our demons.*

Gina darts over to me, holding a bottle of the ale I was asking her about, and I bite my lip when I hear her thinking how she wishes I'd get my own damn drink for once. Sometimes it's really hard not to laugh out loud at the things people think, but I have years of experience in holding it in, not reacting, and most importantly of all, not taking it personally.

When Drake and I first started experimenting with Empyrean, we would be at each other's throats a lot. And there were times I had to step away after hearing a particularly unfriendly thought from one of my Regnum. But the thing is that if you're going to listen to something as personal as what goes on in someone else's head, you can't get mad, or be put-off about it.

After all, if they don't say it to your face, it means they don't want you to know about it. That has to stand for something.

I'm distracted from Gina and the ale she's pouring when I hear something new and startling, coming from a deep yet raspy source across the room. I take a sip from my drink to disguise myself while my eyes peer around suspiciously, and I listen...

How am I supposed to look at him without remembering...

My gaze slowly lifts.

The shape of him, the lust in his eyes and the flush in his cheeks as he laid there, legs spread with a huge dick pounding into his—

Ale sucks into my lungs with my breath, and I choke on it, coughing hysterically, almost dropping the glass onto the floor.

Catching it just in time, I place it down on the table while covering my mouth with a napkin, Cam and Gina rushing to my side.

"Sir, are you alright?" Gina pats my back gently, then barks at Abdiel to get me some water.

Abdiel. That's who was thinking those... *shocking* thoughts just now.

Gawking at the doorway, I catch my breath as the kid disappears into the kitchen and reemerges a moment later with a glass of water. He brings it to me, and when he's close, only a foot of space between us, I can *feel* his mind, buzzing like electricity.

I need to stop thinking about it...

I peer up at him.

Stop fantasizing, Abdiel, before you get a hard-on at work.

Swallowing, I reach for the glass of water, my voice grating out a, "Thank you."

His eyes are green, deep like moss, and they sparkle as his face reddens under my gaze before he turns away.

I wave Gina and Cam off, physically unable to stop watching Abdiel. Everyone goes back to what they were doing before my little choking fit, while my eyes narrow in the direction of my youngest

Domestic. *Did I hear that right? Was he thinking about me?*

It can't be. There's no way.

But if not, what would make him think those things while looking directly at me?

They begin bringing out our food, and I ignore all the other thoughts and voices in the room but one, singling out the mind of Abdiel Harmony. I need to know what he's thinking about me...

What he may have seen.

I heard his mind, referring to me taking a *huge dick*. And no one knows what Drake and I do together. Not one single person on the entire Expanse other than the two of us is aware of what happens during my solitude, not the Empyrean and definitely not the proper dicking I receive from my sexy serpent of a foster brother.

But Abdiel was thinking about it. *How?*

He seems to be avoiding me, unable to make eye contact, though eventually he has to bring me a plate of food, getting close and comfortable enough to let his guard down.

And I hear, *If I had a brother that hot, I'd most definitely let him...*

His thought is cut short when he sees me glaring at him. His eyes widen, and he turns away quick, rushing out of the room, while I sit there with my mouth open, flabbergasted.

He saw us.

He saw Drake and me. In the lounge. *But how??*

How would that even be possible? Was he *spying* on me?

Something like fury morphs quickly into flattery and then evaporates into an elated curiosity. I watch closely through the doorway to the kitchen as Abdiel busies himself with other tasks, I'm assuming so he doesn't have to come back in here. And I push food around on my plate, all the while observing the kid...

Seeing him, truly, for quite possibly the first time.

It's amazing how much he looks like his father. Masculine yet still quite... pretty. High cheekbones and that creamy even-toned skin, like Drake, only not as pale, with pink, plush lips that look like candy pillows you just want to bite. Curly honey blonde hair, just like his dad.

Lars was a stunning man, and clearly, the apple didn't fall far from the tree at all in this case.

I've never allowed myself to really look at Abdiel like this before, because of my history with his father, but also because he's so much younger than me. It wouldn't be right. Even if I had noticed how gorgeous he is, he was always too young. It would make me feel disgusting, like *him*, and so I've always forced myself not to acknowledge the boy.

But now, in this moment, especially after hearing his salacious thoughts, it's virtually impossible *not* to notice him; notice how much he's grown. He's not a boy anymore... He's a man.

A very, *very* attractive man.

I heard his thoughts, heard him thinking about me, and how watching Drake and I together turned him on. As angry as I should be at him for spying, I'm intrigued as hell now.

Did he see everything we did? Empyrean and all?

Is he curious? Does he have relationships with men?

The sudden thought of Abdiel being touched by someone else brings a sickening feeling to my gut, and I'm not sure why. I have no claim staked in him whatsoever. He's not mine, and for all I know, he could be involved with someone. Though I haven't noticed him with anyone...

I make a mental note to check up on this while I continue to watch him casually, sipping my drink and picking at my food.

Abdiel Harmony is a *man* now... A man who just became my most prized servant.

CHAPTER NINE

ABDIEL

The sky is a giant cloud of fire.

Smoke billows down to earth, but it's colorful. Purples and blues and pinks surround us while we laugh, and dance and sing.

Harmony.

Where are you, Abdiel?

A voice calls from somewhere, but I can't find it. All I see is colorful smoke and plants sprouting from the earth faster than I can blink.

What do you want to know, my servant?

Darian?

It's him, I know it is, but I don't see him anywhere. I can hear him, though.

Suddenly, the ground beneath my feet caves in and I'm falling. I scramble to grab onto dirt and roots as I tumble, but it's no use.

I'm falling falling falling while angels sing from above, blowing white trumpets.

This could be all for you, Abdiel.

Servant of God.

I scream as I fall into the abyss, the darkness below taking on the shape of two eyes.

The eyes of a serpent.

"Fuck!" I gasp, shooting up in bed, my heart hammering out of my chest.

Sweat lines my brow, and I wipe it away with the back of my hand as I cho~~se~~ for air, sucking in breaths. *That was crazy.*

What the hell was that dream?

My breathing finally evens out, and I rub my eyes. I shouldn't be surprised that I dreamt of them again, even in such a strange capacity. After the way Head Priest was looking at me at dinner tonight...

Staring at me in a way he never has before. The look in his crystal eyes...

It was as if he could *hear* what I was thinking.

I know that doesn't make sense, but I can't stop considering it. The way he and Drake were together, their connection while they were fucking. The way they gazed at each other, reading one another without speaking a word.

That was how Head Priest looked at me tonight. Like he knew my secrets. There was no barrier of my mind left. He was *inside* it.

I'm not sure how something like that would be possible, but the thought keeps coming back to me... Whatever the Serpent shot into his veins, it could hold the answers to my many questions.

At this point, my name might as well be Abdiel Curiosity, because I've never been so keen in my life. I've never been so *nosy*. My parents taught me it was rude. And especially when it comes to Head Priest, we were always taught not to ask about him.

He does what he does because he can. He's the *Head Priest*. It's an entitlement that comes with his seat.

But over the years, watching him from the sidelines, quietly observing him, I've developed quite the craving for more. Watching his *solitude* the other night solidified it.

I need answers. I need to see The Alchemist.

Interestingly enough, the next day, Lorn shows up at my trailer as I'm finishing breakfast.

Standing in the doorway, I offer to have him inside, but he declines.

"Not a social call, bud." He scrapes a palm over his shaved head. "I was sent to fetch you."

"To *fetch* me?" I lift a brow.

He grins, but shrugs. "Yea. You're needed in the lab."

Gulp. "What...?"

His voice goes quiet as he says, "He asked for you."

All my nerves are suddenly bunched up, the anxiety immediate. "He did..."

Lorn nods, then motions to his ATV, parked right by my trailer. "Let's go. He doesn't like to wait."

My mouth is just hanging open, and I probably look like an idiot, but there's nothing I can say or do right now. I'm speechless.

Drake sent for me?? Why? Is it just because I stopped by the Field?

This is incredibly worrisome, but I can't deny the mild excitement rushing through me as I step into my boots by the door and follow Lorn to his vehicle.

Hopping on the back of the ATV behind him, I wrap my arms loosely around his waist as he starts it up and pulls away. The trails for ATV and cart travel are off to the side, apart from the paths for foot traffic, so people don't get hurt. It's a one-way on the right side of housing, and the other way on the left.

We're traveling on the right side now, past the housing trailers, then the farmland. Lorn is whipping pretty fast, wind hitting my face every time I peer around him to check where we're going. Once we get to the entrance of the Field, he slows down but doesn't stop, saluting the other two guards on duty at the front as he pulls onto a trail.

We drive slowly up a path that cuts through the Field of Influence. It's a remarkable sight. I've never actually been in here before, though I've seen it from afar. It's only just been planted for the season, so all you see are little baby seedlings sprouting up. But still, it goes on forever. It looks like miles of them, although I'm not sure how much there actually is.

This is the part of The Principality not everyone knows about. I'm not even entirely sure what the purpose of the Field is, and why it's so heavily guarded, protected by the Tribe at all costs.

But I know what these plants are. And what they do...

We reach the end of the Field, then cut farther into the woods. We're traveling up the mountain now, approaching the lab. I can see it up in the distance, along with at least five visible soldiers, AK47's and M16's in hand.

I swallow my nerves as we pull up to the lab and Lorn parks. I hop off at his side, all eyes on me while we walk to the large metal door.

Lorn knocks on it hard, turning to me. "Well, this is where I leave you. I'll bring you back when you're done, just have someone radio me."

I nod as the door opens, and this dude from the Tribe named Jasper greets me. He brings me inside, walking me down a corridor. I can't help but peek over my shoulder at the door as it slams shut, hoping I haven't made some terrible mistake by coming here. Sure, these people are my family, but there's still an air of danger brushing through me at the unknown.

The inside of this building is unlike any other on the Expanse. It's a lab, so everything is clean, metal and stark white walls. Industrial doors with plexiglass windows, though I can't stop to observe inside. We're walking the hallway at a steady pace, and when we reach some double doors at the end, I see more people. They're in lab coats.

Chemists.

It's so interesting to me. I mean, I know these people, but I don't *really* know them. The chemists have separate housing too, just like us Domestics do, so they can be closer to the Field and the lab. Honestly, they don't join the rest of us too often, which I've always felt a little strange about. It's like they have their own little clique.

But that's their prerogative, I suppose.

At the double doors, Jasper pushes them open, then stands to the side, motioning for me to go first. I give him a look like I don't know where I'm going, but he just nods for me to walk, so I do.

My eyes widen as we enter a giant lab, full of metal machines and beakers and chemists bustling around. There aren't that many of them, but at least ten people in this room right now. It's huge.

I glance at Jasper again, and his eyes flick forward. "That door there."

I'm so nervous my hands are practically dripping with sweat as I walk across the platform toward a lone door with a sign on it that says *Do Not Enter.*

I'm trying not to focus much on what the chemists are doing, but they certainly seem busy. None of them are even paying attention to me. They're just rushing around, picking up gallons of chemicals, dumping things into machines, swirling stuff in beakers, weighing things on scales. There's a lot happening in here, and it's crazy overwhelming.

I get to the door and notice, below the big red sign, a smaller nameplate that reads *The Alchemist.*

Gulping over a throat dry and scratchy like sand, I shift to Jasper one last time. He's already back at the double doors, leaving. So I take a deep breath.

And I knock.

Hearing nothing for a second, I stand there, shifting my weight back and forth, contemplating what the hell I'm even doing here until finally the door opens.

And I'm met with snake eyes.

I don't see The Alchemist often. Really no one does, but still, he's around. I've known *of him* since I was a child, and yet we've never spoken actual words to one another. And every time I see his eyes, I'm always initially taken aback. Not because they're creepy, although some would say they are.

I honestly think they're sort of breathtaking. *I'm certainly without breath right now…*

"Abdiel Harmony." Drake's head cocks to the side, something smirk-adjacent on his lips, though I wouldn't categorize it as any type of smile I've ever seen. It's much more inquisitive, and even more alarming. He opens the door farther and steps to the side, motioning with his hand. "Please, do come in."

Watching him as he watches me, closely, I attempt to shake off my uncertainty and meander inside his office, if that's what this is, as he closes the door behind us. The room looks less like that of a lab, and more like a fancy therapist's office. He has a beautiful green leather couch up against the wall, two large wall-length bookcases filled with what look to be medical journals and chemistry books. I can't help but wander over to the shelves to check them out.

There are many science books, but he also has some fiction, some poetry, and even graphic novels. Quite the vast variety, which is appealing to me. I love to read. Always have.

"You like to read…" His voice slinks at my back, and I turn over my shoulder. It sounds like it was supposed to be a question, but it's not. And it's clear from his face that he already knows the answer.

Gaping at him for a moment, I've completely forgotten where I am and what he just asked me, because I have the distinct feeling that he's in my head right now. I'm not sure how or why I know, but after what happened with Darian last night, and then my dream…

I blink at him. *You can hear me, can't you?*

He slants his head again, blinking slowly at me, like a curious animal. Or like a snake, studying the mouse who just stepped into its office.

Finding my voice, I croak, "Yes. I like to read."

Our gazes remain locked, and I can *feel* the silence between us, like a fog. There's a conversation happening without words, and I've never been so intrigued by anything in my life.

Drake saunters to the couch, his movements graceful as he takes a seat and pats the cushion next to him. Getting close seems like the opposite of a good idea, but I can't help being drawn to his magnetic force, pulling me in without a choice. I drift over to the couch and sit down, keeping enough distance between us, though he shifts to face me and his knee brushes mine. I almost flinch, trying hard not to make it visible.

He's just watching me, and it's so peculiar, I have to look away out of sheer insecurity.

My eyes roll over the rest of the room, taking in its comforts and decor. The desk and chairs, all handcrafted by our carpenters. A table of various plants and flowers. Art hanging on the walls, paintings and sketches. I recognize the style of a couple.

"Did Emithel do those?" My chin tilts to a collection of three small oil paintings depicting different trees before turning to face Drake once more.

He nods, barely a movement at all, still just watching me. I don't know what he wants, or why he brought me here, but it couldn't possibly just be so he could stare at me in silence like this. And I'm at a disadvantage because being this close to him is reminding me of what I saw in the lounge the other night...

His body, long and slender yet defined with slopes of muscle; strength in a different form. His scattered tattoos, sort of like my own, little pictures here and there, telling an individual story that comes together in flesh. Jet black hair, hanging in his eyes while he filled our Head Priest, pushed and pulled between his legs, animalistic grunts fleeing his pink lips...

"I guess you heard I was interested in classes..." I jump in with words before I accidentally blurt out something perverse.

I need him to stop staring at me like that. And I'd like to know why I'm here.

He says nothing, just keeps giving me this *look* with his snake eyes, glaring as if he's part angry, part fascinated.

"I've been thinking lately about what I want to do," I keep talking, blathering to fill the silence, "And I thought maybe something in the sciences. It might be worth looking into—"

"Cut the act, Abdiel," he interrupts me, tone sharp, yet still somehow smooth, like a blade. "We both know why you're here. Is there something you want to say to me?"

I gawk at him with wide eyes. I don't know what to say, or if I could even make words right now.

Does he know…?

"Yes, I know what you were just thinking, Abdiel Harmony," he seethes, abruptly grabbing me by the shirt and hauling me up to his face, until I can feel his breath over my lips. I'm startled fast, my heart jackhammering in my chest. "Now, I'll ask you again… What do you have to say for yourself?"

My lips shiver through the words, "Okay, yes. I saw you. I saw you and… your brother. Head Priest." I'm shaking so hard he can probably feel it, and I desperately want to look away from those penetrating eyes, but I can't. I'm stuck. "I'm sorry. It was wrong."

"Yes, it fucking was," he growls.

"It was. I shouldn't have done it," I breathe unsteadily through my nerves. Not the time, I know, but my dick is as solid as stone right now.

"Then why did you?" He leans over me more, and I try to back up until we're almost horizontal on the couch.

"I…" I can't answer. I don't know how to. And I don't know what to do with my hands.

My arms are just lying limp at my sides, so I place both of my palms on his chest. I'm not sure why… Maybe to keep him back. Or maybe to touch him. I have no clue.

Either way, he doesn't like it, and he releases my shirt, grabbing my wrists in his hands, pinning them down at my sides while he leans in closer, visibly clenching his jaw.

"I was curious." My voice trembles with the rest of my body. "I was desperate to find out what Head Priest does in that room. The solitude… I had to know."

He glares at me, fire burning in his eyes, swirls of deep brown and amber, like molasses and honey. Then he sucks in a breath, eyelids drooping in a slow blink as his right hand circles my left wrist, thumb pressing hard into my pulse point.

"So you watched everything, did you, young servant?" He hovers over me, holding me down in such a way that I'm not even sure is against my will.

I mean, I know it *should* be. But having him on top of me like this, this much older, admittedly a bit terrifying man… It's turning me on like crazy.

"Yes," I gulp on a raspy breath as his hips press forward into mine, just a bit. Just enough for me to whimper a little. I can't help it. It just came out. "Yes, I watched."

"And you liked it…" he whispers, gripping my wrist hard enough that I might have bruises. My cock thumps in my pants.

"Yes, I really liked it," I gasp, and he hums.

"You touched yourself afterward, didn't you?" He lurches in, eyes locked on mine.

I hesitate, and his eyes narrow. "Yes. I did."

Heat spreads up my neck onto my cheeks at admitting something like that to him. I don't even know him. This is the first real interaction we've ever had, and he's on top of me, cracking open my head like an egg to let the yoke of my thoughts run out.

"Don't be embarrassed, young servant," he croons. "I like to watch sometimes, too."

"How do you keep doing that?" I grunt up at him, wanting to lift my hips to grind my erection on him a little.

I know it's ridiculous. That's the last thing I should be thinking, but I can't stop…

And now he's grinning at me, a wicked curve of his lips as his pupils dilate.

"You can hear my thoughts." I blink at him in fascination.

He pauses for a moment, before grinding his hips into me, giving me that friction I was just pleading for in my mind. "I can."

"How is that possible?" I ask on a moan. "Does it have something to do with what you injected into Head Priest?"

"You'll have to be specific, kid." He moves his lips down to my ear. "I injected him with two things that night." He extends his tongue to my earlobe, and I shiver so hard, it's like I'm convulsing.

God, this is hot. Why am I letting him do this?? I don't even know him…

He's just such a sexual being. His voice, his look, the dangerous charm and all of his erotic qualities. They make him irresistible. He's seduction personified.

"The drugs…" I murmur. "What are they?"

"Wouldn't you like to know," he sing-songs, teasing me with his voice and his tongue in my ear.

I'm vibrating. I'm so keyed up right now, the slightest brush might set me off.

"I would. Please," I beg, and he pulls back to look down at me, tilting his head in that way I'm beginning to realize he does often, when he's studying you. "I want to try it."

The little smirk disappears from his face as he stares at me. He lets go of my wrists, and it isn't until he does that I realize how tightly he was holding them. I'm getting blood back into my hands, like a scant rush.

"You don't know what you're even asking, do you?" He lifts a brow.

"Then show me." I lean up on my elbows. "I want to try what makes him... feel like that."

"*I* make him feel like that," he growls, barely audibly. I gape up at him, bemused, and he closes his eyes, taking a breath. When he reopens them, he's back to examining me. "You want to experience Empyrean, Abdiel Harmony?"

A small voice of worry in the back of my mind warns me against it... everything I'm considering. But my curiosity snuffs it out as I nod. "Yes. Please."

The smirk tugs at the curve of his lips once more and his hand slides up my torso, fingers grazing my throat. "You'll be fun to play with, little mouse."

My heart leaps behind my ribs as he hops off me and slithers over to his desk. I sit up, nervous energy rippling through my limbs as I watch him open a drawer and take out a vial, the same one he had for Head Priest the other day. Then he removes a plastic package and opens it, revealing a fresh syringe.

I swallow hard. I've never had an injection before. I don't mind needles, since I get tattooed, and acupuncture on occasion. But being injected with an unknown substance is a totally different thing.

Drake trots back over and sits down next to me, crowding me on the couch so that our legs are touching. "Don't be scared, little mouse," he whispers in my ear. "I won't hurt you."

He sticks the needle inside the vial and sucks up all the clear liquid.

"What's in that stuff? Is it safe?"

"I made it." He grins at me. "So, yes. It's definitely safe." I show him a nervous look and he hums, "Trust me. I wouldn't give it to the most important person in my life if it weren't." *Darian.* "Yes. Darian," he speaks my thought and my head spins. "Now, lift up your sleeve and wrap your left hand around your right bicep, just above the elbow. Like this."

He shows me by cuffing my arm with his hand, and I can't ignore the sparks I feel at his touch. My eyes slowly lift to his, and he licks his lip. My breathing shallows.

"Stop giving me those eyes, little mouse, or I'll have to eat you," he rumbles by my face.

Nothing has ever sounded as good as that. He chuckles. *Stop listening to me.*

"It's harder than you think." He smirks. "You'll see in a second. Behave, and do as I say."

Wrapping my hand around my bicep above my elbow, I squeeze and look up at him for some confirmation that I'm doing it right.

"Tighter," he instructs, pressing on the pump of the syringe until some liquid shoots out. "Let me see those pretty veins."

Shivering at his words, I do as he says, squeezing even harder, watching the veins in my forearm pop more than they usually do. He inspects them, then taps one with his fingers before inching the needle to my skin.

"Breathe, little mouse," he says over my lips, and I'm so focused on his mouth I don't even notice that he's stuck the thing into me.

At the pinch, I glance down at my arm, watching blood mix with the fluid before he pumps it inside my vein.

Once the syringe is empty, he removes it and whispers, "Let go, Abdiel."

As I release my arm, the air around me shimmers and thumps instantly. My head darts around as I watch it... The air.

I can *see* the *air,* moving like waves, colors snapping all around my body.

"Fuck..." I breathe, and I hear a small chuckle from Drake, but I can't even focus on that. Molecules are sprouting from the oxygen, taking shape in front of my eyes. I reach up to touch one, popping it like a bubble with my finger. Then I do the next one, and the next, huffing a laugh in awe. "Are you seeing this?"

"Pretty cool, huh?" It isn't until he speaks that I realize he's touching me. His hand is on my thigh and his face is inching closer to my neck. *Now you're mine, too.*

I just heard him say that, even though his lips weren't moving. I heard it in his brusque, bold voice.

My head pivots to look at him. The colors everywhere are so

bright, a rainbow splashing across my vision. But his skin is pale white, such a contrast to the black of his hair.

His lips are almost red like blood, and they're right at my neck, as if he's drinking it from me. My cock is standing firm between my legs, trying to break free from my pants while every object in the room dances around us.

What is this? I think, and he looks up at me.

Welcome to Empyrean, little mouse.

Empyrean. That's what this is. I feel it all around me.

I feel the light and the dark. I feel each breath as it leaves my body. And I *see* everything.

I see who I am. I see my part, here on this planet. I've just come to this realization, and it's so beautiful I could cry.

Drake's hand touches my chest, and I look at him. *Can you feel it?*

Yes, I tell him, grabbing at his jaw. *I love it.*

Unwittingly, I pull his mouth to mine, but he hesitates. I can feel his resistance, and I hear something, something I don't think he wanted me to hear. *He's unsure.*

I stammer for a moment, twitching away. "Oh... I'm sorry. You and Darian... I shouldn't have..."

"No. It's not that," he rumbles, his eyes etched in seriousness. I'm trying to hear his thoughts, but it's suddenly all fuzzy. Like static. "You don't know what you're doing, Abdiel Harmony. I'm not what you think..."

"What does that mean?" I ask, eyes flicking to the books as they open up on the shelves, pages flipping and flipping.

This is just Empyrean. Do you understand?

I gawk at him, blinking.

It won't be anything more.

I think I understand what he's saying, but it's hard to focus on his words when I can hear so much; feel so much.

It's so strange, all of this. I have this bizarre urge to cling to him, and I have no idea why. Again, I don't know him. But in this moment, I feel like I do.

Your first instinct is right, little mouse. You don't know me.

I scoot closer to him, running my hand up his chest. *But I want to.*

His lips twist. *So eager.* He walks his fingers along my thigh. *Are you a virgin, Abdiel?*

I swallow hard, desperately trying to hold back my thoughts, though it's no use. His grin goes wide, and he reaches for the zipper on my jeans.

"W-what are you doing?" I stutter out loud, forgetting myself as little zaps of colored lightning dance around where he's unbuttoning and unzipping my pants.

Let's play. I know you want to.

My breaths become unsteady again as he tugs my jeans down just a bit, enough that my erection is visible through my boxer briefs. *What am I doing? What's going on?*

Don't overthink it, his mind whispers in between rampant thoughts that bring heat to my face.

I can hear him thinking of things he wants to do to me, and it's overwhelming. But also hot as fuck. I can barely contain my movements as I go for his pants.

I want to kiss you, I think as I unzip his, reaching my eager fingers inside enough to brush his cock. It's hard, and big. So much bigger up close.

I can't be anyone's first kiss, little mouse. You understand, don't you?

I really don't, but I choose to ignore the rejection bubbling inside me and settle on how turned on I am. I've never fooled around with anyone before, and here I am, with a grown ass man I barely know, touching and thinking of ways I can make him feel good.

You're so innocent. He presses a hand on my chest, pushing me backward on the couch and crawling over me. *I shouldn't be corrupting you like this.*

I want to be corrupted, I plead, yanking at his shirt to take it off him. He lets me, reluctantly, though he gives me a look.

Only this much. He removes my shirt and tugs my jeans down farther so that the full shape of my erection is visible. Then he does the same with his own pants. I can't stop staring at the outline of his dick through his boxers. It looks massive.

And apparently, he's thinking similar things about mine. I can hear him.

Look at your strapping young body... He runs a large hand over my erection, and I groan. I've never been touched by anyone but myself. It's amazing. *You're so big, Abdiel. I bet you taste sweet, like honey.*

I whimper, shaky fingers reaching out to touch him. *I want... I want...*

You don't know what you want yet, do you? He chuckles, pressing his hips forward. *This is all so new for you, isn't it?*

I nod, sinking my teeth into my lower lip as I gaze up at him with hooded eyes, color waves crashing all around us.

Your lips look so soft. One day you'll learn how to suck, little mouse. I whine out a raspy noise, and his hand comes up to my throat. *But not yet.*

I want to. I can, I swear. You can teach me… please.

He growls and leans over me, rippling his hips into me as he drags his clothed erection over mine. *Teach you to what?*

My head is fluffy, everything hot enough that I'm sticking to the couch. I reach around to hold his back as I whimper, "To suck your dick."

We both groan at my words, at my complete and utter lack of sexual experience, which seems to be a major turn-on for this man who I believe is almost forty. I'm in a frenzy over how aroused I am. This guy is gorgeous; seriously hot as *fuck*. He's older, and he wants me. I almost can't believe it.

A small frisson of guilt slips in through the back of my mind, and for some odd reason, I see Darian.

I see his face; I see him that night in the lounge as I watched through the window. I see him in my dreams…

Why do I feel like I'm betraying him right now? It doesn't make any sense.

But when my eyes come up to Drake, he's giving me a similar look. Severely unsure.

But he keeps moving his hips, keeps pushing his cock into mine, rubbing them together, slow yet firmly enough that the friction closes my eyes, a purr escaping my lips.

This feels so… good.

"Abdiel Harmony," he whispers my name, hands running all over my chest, thumbs circling my nipples, sending a zap to my balls. "You're a temptation I don't need…"

I'm sorry, I think without thinking, and he pinches me. I gasp, reopening my eyes. He just pinched my nipple. It hurt, but it felt more good than bad.

"Don't apologize to me, little mouse," he grunts, rutting into me over and over. "Ever."

I groan, unable to think as I look down to watch. The heads of both of our dicks are popping out of our boxers, and Drake pauses, yanking the fabric down farther; mine, then his, until our cocks are fully exposed. About the same length, though he's a bit paler than me, and my dick has shimmery liquid coming from the tip.

He grazes my erection with his, and I moan, biting my lip to keep quiet.

Fuck yes... I hear from his deep, rumbling mind as we move together. Then he grabs both of our dicks in his hand and jerks them, together.

God, that's amazing. Oh yes, more. More more more.

"Greedy little thing, aren't you?" He rasps, breathless like pure sex in my ears.

His hand is moving frantically, fist just barely able to close around our girth. It feels insane, my cock moving against his. Being jerked by a hand that isn't mine. The feel of his balls brushing on my own is winding me up like a rubber band.

Moving my hips with him, I writhe beneath his weight as he straddles my legs, holding himself up with one hand on my chest, while the other strokes our cocks furiously. I'm bending, about to snap.

You gonna come for me, baby? He aims his snake eyes on me, and they hold my gaze, the fire I saw in them before now burning visibly, a wild inferno.

"Yes..." I pant, pushing up and up and *up*. "I'm gonna..."

"Be a good servant and *come* when you're called."

A cry fleas my lips as I let go, the most intense orgasm I've ever felt washing over me. My dick aches out pulses of cum, all over his hand and my abs.

My breathing is erratic, and all the colors are blooming into flowers around the room. We're in a garden.

Good boy, baby. You're making me come like the sweet thing you are.

I watch hungrily as his dick erupts right after mine, cum jetting from the head of his big cock, squirting up to my chest. When he's done, he drags the tip up and down mine, swiping our cum together, coating our cocks with it.

It's beyond dirty, unlike anything I've ever experienced, or ever thought I would experience for my first sexual encounter. Fucking *mesmerizing*.

Feeling the flush in my cheeks, I gaze up at him, and him down at me. He blinks a few times, and the static is back in his head. I can't hear anything he's thinking right now. It stitches my brows together.

I think he notices, because he hops off me and saunters over to his desk, grabbing a towel to clean me up. Propping up on my elbows, I watch him as he does, a silent air of regret surrounding him. I feel it, weighing down the air. *Suffocating.*

I don't want to be something he regrets. And I definitely didn't want my first sexual experience to be tainted like this.

I didn't even get to kiss him...

"Thanks for stopping by, Abdiel Harmony," he blurts out, having already redressed. He hands me my shirt.

I feel like such an idiot. A total booty call, if that's even what this would be. *Is that why he called me here? He wanted to hook up with me and then kick me out?*

He keeps blinking at me, his forehead lined. I have no idea what that look means, and I can't even hear his thoughts. It's beyond frustrating.

The colors are fading, and things are going back to normal, though I still hear voices. Just not from Drake.

Pulling my pants up, I tug my shirt over my head, running stressed fingers through my hair.

"I'm—"

"I told you *not* to apologize," he cuts me off.

"Right..." I shake my head as I walk to the door. "I guess I'll just ask Chelsea about classes, then." I glance back at him one last time, and he nods.

"She'll get you set up."

Biting the inside of my cheek, I pull the door open, muttering a weakened, "Thanks, Serpent," as I wander back out into the lab.

Before I close the door, I hear, *Be good, little mouse.*

CHAPTER TEN

ABDIEL

I decide to walk back from the lab, rather than calling Lorn for a ride. And none of the guards seem to oppose, all of them just staring at me as I slink away from the Field, radiating awkward humiliation.

Of course, they don't know anything about that, but I can hear their thoughts, and it's crazy overwhelming.

I'm jerking left and right at every noise, every idea spoken without a word uttered. This is baffling to me, though I don't have time to stop and feel insecure about how all my friends from the Tribe are watching me leave and suspecting I just got shot down in some sense by The Alchemist.

It has me wondering how many people he does this with… At first, I thought it was just something he did with Head Priest. And I actually allowed myself to feel *special*, as if he was bringing me into their inner circle.

But after being dismissed like that, after he came and then immediately regretted doing so with *me*, I have to assume this is his thing. He gives people drugs, makes them feel like they're one with God, takes advantage of their openness by messing around with them, and then sends them away.

I don't know, maybe not, but I'm just a little lost right now.

Yet, despite that, as I walk through the Field in the direction of home, I can't ignore this awareness inside me. The vibrant colors and speculative designs seem to have faded for the most part, but the *feeling* is still there.

I have such a sense of my own mortality in this moment, and it isn't anywhere near as scary as one might think. I know my purpose. I'm fulfilled because as small and insignificant as one human life may seem, I'm a part of the great transformation of life.

I'm a piece of the puzzle. *Me*. Abdiel Harmony.

I wonder if my parents ever felt this...

I wish I could see them now.

Turning over my shoulder, I look back toward the mountain. Something happened to them up there, and it killed them. It's still a mystery to this day. Or at least, it *was*.

One day I'll go up there and find the truth. It's my duty.

I hear Mother telling me so.

Seek solace in the mountain, young servant.

For now, I wander back toward Regnum housing, past the farmland, admiring the work of our people. Marveling at the beauty of the earth, of *our* territory. I truly hope Head Priest knows how grateful we are to be here with him. How much he's done for us by allowing us here.

Guilt sweeps through my insides fast like a crashing wave at high tide.

I fooled around with his brother. My Head Priest; the man I've admired since I was a young boy. The man I've grown to love and need, as less than a god, maybe less than a father, but more than just a regular man.

And the thing is that I can't tell if I'm guilty for having my first sexual experience with his brother, someone who's supposed to be his... or for not having it with *him*.

I'm so confused, but I barely have time to reflect on it, my inner turmoil cut short by all the voices. They're so loud as I approach housing, I have a strong urge to cover my ears.

I hear so many things... Complaints, worries, joys, ideas. It's all around me, swirling up through the air like a twister. *How do Darian and Drake deal with this??*

Focusing on my steps, I try not to listen in on things I feel I shouldn't be hearing. A woman, angry with her husband for paying her less attention than the girl they've both been sleeping with together. My eyes dart right. The husband, feeling jealous of that same girl's endless attention on his wife.

It's like a soap opera in this place. Who knew?

Passing by students finishing up their lessons, most of their thoughts are on schoolwork, either worried or confident, both ends of the spectrum. And then there are those who are thinking about other things entirely. Friends, family, and vanity.

It's astonishing how much I can hear.

As I approach my trailer, I decide to pass it. There's no sense in going home right now. I can't squander this sort of gift sitting around the house. So I keep walking.

I walk for hours, all over the Expanse, just listening. Hearing it *all*.

It feels very intrusive, and morally, I must say, I'm not sure if listening to someone's thoughts is right. Maybe for Head Priest, but not for me. Who am I, after all?

I don't know that this drug was designed for recreational use. Sure, the high was a rebirth of sorts, and the way I feel now… There's really no way to describe it. I'm *awake*.

But the first part seems to last only minutes, and now I'm left with this ability. I understand more now about why Head Priest becomes so edgy after a while. I'm guessing when the power wears off, he feels hopeless.

I have no clue what *I'm* meant to do with this… *Or why the Serpent allowed me this experience.*

I'm wandering around for hours, until the sun sets, and darkness washes over the Expanse. I find myself coming back toward the Den, and even though I'm not working today, I can't seem to stay away. Dinner will be done soon.

I wonder what they're having… I hope Head Priest likes it.

I decide to go in and at least say *hi* to Gina. I have nothing else to do right now, and I'm sort of hungry. Maybe she'll hook me up with leftovers.

As I enter the Den, I'm met with the sounds of people moving around, typical after-dinner cleanup. Swinging through the doorway to the kitchen, I hear Gina first, though she isn't speaking. She's worrying about Paul, and how hard he's been working lately. It brings a knot to my stomach. I don't enjoy hearing her worry. She's such a strong person on the outside.

Then I hear Cam. He's jealous of Ryle, and the attention he always gets for his cooking. Cam seems bitter, but beneath the frustration I hear insecurity. I want to pat him on the back and let him know it'll be alright. Someday he'll find his genuine purpose. But I can't do that… Because he can't know I'm listening.

I hear Perry as he's coming in from cleaning the table, thinking about how hot Kiara is. His thoughts are rather perverse, and it has me blushing as a grin sweeps over my face.

Wow, this is crazy. How do they listen to people without it affecting them?

Then I remember how Head Priest glared at me yesterday, and it brings warmth to my chest. He was affected by my thoughts… if even just a little.

Gina turns to face me as I'm shaking away Perry's thoughts about various places on Kiara's body he'd like to put his dick. "Hey, kid. What are you doing here on your day off?"

"I was just out for a walk." I pull up a grin for her. "Figured I'd stop by and see what you guys made."

Gina shakes her head through a chuckle, then she nudges a plate across the counter in my direction. "Ryle made some delicious spiced fish."

"This isn't yours?" I ask, already digging into the plate while she smirks.

"You're good to go, hippo. The rest of us ate."

She calls me *hippo* sometimes because I'm always hungry. Apparently, *Outside* there's a game where four hippos try to eat as many balls as they can, and whoever gets the most wins. It sounds ridiculous, but Gina says she used to play it when she was little.

I smile at her with my eyes while digging into the fish. We have an abundance of trout that stick to the north side of the lake, and they're delicious in many preparations. *Gotta love the fisherman.*

I have an early memory of my dad taking me fishing, but after he passed I never went again.

The food is scrumptious, and I clear the plate in all of two minutes while they finish cleaning. Gina cracks open a bottle of ale, then hands me one. I hear her thinking about how much she loves me, and it startles me for a moment. My heart is overflowing with so many things, it takes me a minute to get past it.

But I do, swigging a large gulp of the delicious drink. "I don't deserve this. I didn't even work today."

"I'm sure you were working in some fashion." Gina smiles. *He's such a good kid. His parents would be proud.*

I swallow, blinking at her as I take another big sip.

Would my parents be proud, though? I've been spying on Head Priest, seeking out his brother for drugs… Having my first sexual experience ever as a dirty little secret.

I don't exactly feel *good* in this moment.

95

But still, I show Gina a kind smile and squeeze her shoulder, finishing the ale before heading for the doorway closest to the bathroom. "See you at reflection tonight?"

"We'll be there if Paul isn't too exhausted," she answers, and I nod at her as I leave the room.

Voices assault my ears from every direction, most of them female, which must mean the wives are around somewhere. That's the part that's tripping me up; that I hear people even when they're not standing directly in front of me, and I can't get a handle on where they're coming from.

Ignoring it, I use the restroom near the gym, and when I come out, I swing around the corner and bump right into a giant wall of muscle.

Abdiel, I hear my name in a cavernous voice.

My eyes lift, and I recoil under a deepening blue gaze. *Darian. Head Priest. Shit...*

"Uh, I'm sorry," I stutter, trying to back up, though the wall is right behind me.

"Don't be." Something of a grin tugs at his lips. And it's while he's staring at me that I take in what he's wearing...

Fitted gray sweatpants. That's about it.

My teeth move uncontrollably over my lower lip as my eyes follow the wide plane of his chest, curves and divots, glistening with a bit of sweat. He must have been working out in the gym...

He pushes silky hair away from his forehead with his fingers. "I hope I didn't get you sweaty..." My eyes spring back up to his, finding him watching my mouth closely. *I bet that lip tastes like candy...*

Swallowing fiercely, I grip the wall behind me to keep from falling backward.

He just thought that... about *me.* I heard him. *He wants to taste* my *lip...?*

Head Priest's eyes narrow, and his expression turns dark. I'm just standing here shivering beneath his gaze like a waterfall of cool rushing water. The way he's looking at me is overwhelming. I can barely breathe.

Can you hear me, Abdiel? He lifts a brow, inching in closer until only a foot of space separates us.

My back is sealed to the wall as I gape up at him over an inch or two separating us in height, though it's his presence which is overpowering. He's taking all the air out of the hallway.

My lips part, but I can't form words. Of course, since he mentioned it, now my mind is flashing back to Drake shooting me up with his drugs a few hours ago. I'm not sure if I should be revealing everything to him in my mind, but then I'd have no idea how not to.

Head Priest swallows, Adam's apple dipping in his throat, a movement my eyes have to stick to because it's quite captivating. Then he takes in a deep breath.

You've tried Empyrean, haven't you, my servant?

I begin to stammer, and he reaches out, placing a hand on my shoulder. I'm sure it's supposed to calm me down, but all it's doing is making me tingly everywhere.

No need to be worried, he tells me without parting his lips. *It's fascinating, isn't it?*

I nod uncontrollably. *Yes, Head Priest.*

His mouth twists into a small smile, and a breath puffs from between his lips. *So cute.*

My hands are shaking. *Me? I'm cute? Is he... flirting with me??*

Please, call me Darian. He blinks. His eyes aren't as crystalline as they were yesterday, though it's still a miraculous color, having deepened into a shade similar to the blueberries we harvest.

"I-I don't..." My head wobbles, not knowing what to say or do.

I'm uncomfortable, because we've never really talked much. Yet here we are now, chatting telepathically in the hallway of his home while he's half-naked and sweaty.

I might pass out.

His grin widens still. *It's okay. I'm just a person, Abdiel. A servant, like you.*

His hand trails off my arm as I stand frozen, and he watches me, reading me. I'm so nervous he's going to hear my impure thoughts about him; that he'll pick up on my little crush. My entire body is flushed, and I feel like my clothes might disintegrate right off my flesh.

Because I'm sure he can hear *everything* I'm thinking, he backs up an inch, then stretches his arms behind his back, eyeing me while swiping at his bottom lip with his tongue, an act I just know I'll be seeing in my dreams for the foreseeable future.

"Would you like to come for a walk with me?" His tone is casual enough, though now I'm even more stunned.

"Um... me?" It's the stupidest possible response, but I can't help it. He turns me into a giant ball of smitten jelly.

This time his laugh is a more prominent, dimples appearing on his cheeks. It makes him look much younger, although it's still obvious there's an age difference between us. A pretty decent one at that.

"Yes, Abdiel. *You*." He folds his arms over his chest. "Please? It would be rude to deny my invitation, would it not?"

Considering his words, I nod hesitantly. "Probably…"

"Okay, then. It's settled."

Before I can even ask him where we're going, he wanders away. I'm still stuck to the wall as he turns over his shoulder and croons, "Come now, young servant."

And my body betrays all other hesitations to follow him like a puppy. I power walk to catch up, falling in step behind him as he stalks toward the back door. He opens it and we saunter out into the calm breeze of this lovely late spring evening, making our way to the lake I'm guessing, since that's the direction he's headed.

Once we're outside, he slows his pace to a stroll, and I walk beside him, the quiet between us not as quiet as it would seem. I can hear things happening in his mind, and I'm awestruck, because it's such a fascinating place to be; inside the brain of our Head Priest.

His thoughts aren't necessarily profound; he's thanking Mother for this gorgeous night, for the lake, and the plants and trees which give us oxygen. He's gazing up at the stars and wondering who else could be doing so at this very moment.

He's wondering about me… Specifically, why Drake gave me Empyrean, but also how it makes me feel. If I understand what it means for my own subconscious. If I experienced…

"What's *Ecdysis*?" I ask out loud, and he glances at me as we approach the lake.

Darian says nothing for a moment while we keep walking, right up to the bank. Once we're on the shore, he turns to face me, and I do the same. He gazes into my eyes, a breeze giving me a shiver as goosebumps sheet my skin. His eyes fall to my arms, observing them, hairs standing up, before they come back to mine.

"It's your rebirth, Abdiel," he finally responds in a lush brogue that graces me with even more chills. "Ecdysis is technically molting, in a sense. You remember what that means, right?"

I think for only a moment before I nod. "When a bug loses its exoskeleton?"

He grins. "Yea. Only ecdysis is more for reptiles. Snakes…" His voice trails for a moment before he continues. "It's a personal transformation we must all go through in order to find our true selves."

His words dance in the air between us as I watch his irises, glittering cerulean in this light.

"There are things we find in nature that Mother uses to guide us," he tells me, stepping out of his shoes. I peer down, brow furrowed, wondering why he's now barefoot, but I ignore it because his words are more important. "The white trumpets are one of those things."

I blink at him. "So that's what the Field is for? Making Empyrean?"

He cocks his head. "That's simplifying it. But in a way, yes. The Alchemist has created many variations. The Empyrean you and I have taken is what brings us closest to Mother. It is sacred, Abdiel. You must not squander it."

My throat slides in uncertainty. *How will I know if I've squandered it? I don't mean to...*

Darian huffs another one of his almost-chuckles. "I can already tell you haven't, Abdiel. Your transformation is a work in progress, sure. But you're getting there. I have faith in you."

My lips part, but I don't know what to say. I'm simply amazed at this man. He's so wise. A perfect leader.

"I'm not perfect, my servant," he sighs. "No one is. Now, shall we go for a swim?"

My forehead creases. "When... *right now??*"

The smile of our Head Priest seems to be ever-present tonight. "You're curious yet hesitant, Abdiel Harmony. Like a cat. I like cats. They're mystifying creatures."

Without saying anything else, he shoves his sweatpants down and kicks them off his feet.

And every ounce of breath leaves my lungs in one fell swoop.

Oh my God, he's naked. He's naked, right here, in front of me.

I struggle hard with not allowing my eyes to drift as his head tilts at me and he leans in. I'm still not breathing.

"I'm going to get into the water now, young servant," he whispers, close enough that I can smell him, like cloves and wood and the earth. Like a *man*; a large, strong, important one. A *King*. "It's a beautiful night. We should enjoy it."

And then he waltzes away from me, a few long strides, fully naked, all the muscles in his back flexing as he moves. I can't even keep myself from watching his ass; full and round and so damn plump, it reminds me of a piece of fruit I want to sink my teeth into.

"You know I can hear you from here, Abdiel." He peeks over his shoulder at me. Then he winks.

That's so embarrassing, holy hell.

But he simply chuckles, my cheeks flushing deep as he steps into the water, walking in up to his waist before diving beneath the crisp surface. He's gone for a moment, leaving nothing but ripples, until his head pops up, looking extraordinarily beautiful all wet. Like a merman, or something out of a mythological fantasy.

He aims his chiseled face in my direction and pins me with a look. *Come to me, my servant.*

I'm crazy nervous, my adrenaline jacked up so much my limbs are vibrating. But I can't deny my King. I never could.

So I remove my shirt, then my boots, and finally my pants and boxers, stripping completely naked out in the open. The urge to cover up is hefty, but Darian isn't looking. He's swimming around in the lake, graceful and gorgeous. Sensual in his prowess. *Enticing.*

Darting over to the water, I wade in quickly, unable to keep from looking over my shoulders. I'm unsure of what someone might say if they saw us, but it could be difficult to explain.

The wet ground is squishy beneath my toes as I sink deeper into the water until I'm up to my shoulders. It's warm, not as warm as it will be in peak summer, but not bad. Refreshing, and even if I were cold, I couldn't think about that right now. I'm too busy gazing after my Head Priest as he swims back and forth, going farther out, then coming back to me.

He must swim often, because his body is that of someone who does; evenly defined, from his arms and shoulders, to his chest and abs, to his ass and legs. I remember drooling over him when I watched that night in the lounge.

He and Drake have different bodies. Both strong in their own ways, though Drake is taller and made of cut-up lines, whereas Darian is thicker, broader and resembling a warrior.

I shake myself out of my thoughts as he swims closer to me, stopping with only a foot between us. He's giving me an intense look, and I can hear him inquiring about things, so I dunk myself beneath the water to avoid the inevitable explanation. I'm not sure if water stops the telekinetic properties of Empyrean, but I'll try anything right now. I can't stand making a fool of myself in front of him.

When I come back up, I wipe the water from my eyes to find him still right there. Still staring.

"You watched us the other night," he speaks the words I was

dreading. "No sense dancing around it, Abdiel."

Fumbling, my mouth begins to spill. "I'm *so* sorry, Head Priest. I don't know why I did it... it was a mistake. Please don't be angry with me. I messed up, and I'm very sorry..."

He wades in closer, just an inch, though I feel his nearness, and it shuts me right up. "There is one part of what you've just said that isn't quite true. Isn't there, my young servant?" I swallow as I stand gawking at him, my wet hair sticking to my face. "You *do* know why you did it."

"I... I wasn't..."

"Tell me the truth, Abdiel." He moves in closer still, crowding me, and this time there's no wall behind me to hold me in place. Yet I don't back away. "Tell me why you watched us."

The silence stretches as I work up the nerve to tell him the truth. The water around us is practically still we're moving so little.

Deciding to think it so I don't have to physically say the words, my mind admits, *I was curious about you, Head Priest.*

Curious how, my servant?

I was... desperate to know what you did in the lounge...

Why?

I waver for a moment. *Because I... I...*

Tell me now, Abdiel.

I close my eyes and gulp, reopening them slowly to lock our gazes. *Because you... hypnotize me.*

A droplet of water tumbles over the peak of his upper lip. I almost *need* to lick it off.

Darian sucks in a quiet breath. *And? What did you think of what you saw...?*

He moves in even closer, now only a few measly inches separating our bodies. His warmth graces me through the water, the shadowed outline of his colossal frame advancing on mine. My face tilts to his, all the smooth lines dripping wet, stubbled jawline so sharp it could make me bleed.

My thoughts are speaking for themselves, but even so, I can't help but think, *You are the most beautiful thing I've ever seen.*

Rather than a visible swooning, his jaw sets, tense and clenching as his eyes darken and burn in my direction. It feels like he wants to come closer to me, even without listening to his thoughts. I physically *feel* the draw between us like a current. But I know he won't do it.

We're out in the open. If anyone were to see, we could get in serious trouble. It must look suspicious already, with him this close, though a bystander might not know we're skinny dipping.

Darian moves another inch until we're so close to touching, a deep breath might meld us together. His hand swims beneath the surface of the water, sending ripples past my arm without actually touching, while his eyes stick to mine.

He does it again, this time his hand moving lower, closer to my waist. My cock fills rapidly, and I back up as an instinct, afraid he'll feel it. Reading my thoughts, he lets out a soft groan, lashes fluttering as he runs his own hand over his chest.

I wish I could touch you... I hear, and it almost knocks me down.

Swallowing all the excess saliva in my mouth, I hum. *I really want that.*

My beautiful young servant... Such a sweet temptation.

A small gasp flees my lips as my cock thickens more, and like an instinct, my hand runs down to grip it. The memory of Drake calling me a *temptation* earlier flickers through my mind, and Darian gives me a momentary look of confusion. But it's swept away by the lust I find shimmering in his eyes as he watches me.

We're so close, it'd be the easiest thing in the world to wrap myself around him. And truthfully, it's all I want.

He runs his own hands along his flesh again, the moonlight bathing him in an illustrious glow as his fingertips dance on places I'm dying to explore.

"You're more of a temptation yourself than I think you realize, sir."

"Fuck," he groans, head falling forward, almost onto my shoulder, until his breaths are lingering on my skin. "Do you know how good that sounds coming from those lips?" He lifts his face, eyes set on my mouth.

"M-my lips?" They're trembling as my cock throbs in my palm.

"They're irresistible." He leans in, his mouth practically hovering over mine as he thinks very un-King-like things about my lips.

My balls are drawn up already... I fear I might come if he moves near me one more time.

And of course, he knows that. His hand moves down to his own erection, and I'm frustrated that it's too dark to see into the water right now. But I feel him stroking it slowly.

"We shouldn't be doing this..." he growls, eyes falling shut as his body sways in the water before me. "Someone could see."

SERPENT IN WHITE

"I know," I murmur, hating that I can't have what my body is craving down to my marrow.

Darian reopens his eyes, and then his hand appears on my lower back, pulling me into him for just a moment. Our hardened cocks brush together in the water, the curves of his pectoral muscles on mine as his peaked nipples graze my skin until I whimper.

He whispers in my ear, "You're a gift, young servant. One I don't deserve."

Then, before I can curl myself around him and never let go, he dives under the water.

I spin around and around looking for him, but I've lost him.

When he finally resurfaces, he's swimming away, toward the shore. He wades out of the water, walking up the bank and redressing fast. Glancing back at me, his irises are alit in sorrow. The only words echoing through his mind are *I'm sorry.*

I tilt my head to wet my hair once more before I get out, thinking back to what happened today with Drake. And now this...

I don't know what I'm doing in my love life, but it's obvious I'm going after the wrong people. I feel like such a joke.

I wait for Darian to be back in his clothes and walking away before I come out of the water. Rushing to my own clothes, I dress quickly, trying desperately not to watch him leave. But I can't help it...

My eyes are on him as he wanders toward the Den, peering back at me one last time with something on his face I can't read, speaking a thought I cannot hear.

Wearing an expression that will surely haunt my dreams.

CHAPTER ELEVEN

DARIAN

It's too quiet.

I'm making my rounds, spending the day walking the Expanse and checking on everyone. Not something I like to do when my Empyrean has worn off because I have to rely on my family telling me the truth, which people are often hesitant to do, especially with someone *above* them.

It's human nature to lie. Anyone who says they don't lie is lying. The pertinent factor being, of course, that there are variations of lies. To simply say *lying is bad* is a broad and unfair assessment.

As with everything else in this glorious existence, things are not black and white. We live within a wide prism of color; endless possibilities for every single situation.

It's as fascinating as it is overwhelming.

So when I ask the farmers why we seem to be missing at least three barrels of our barley yield, and they tell me bugs got to it, when in fact it was the fault of Henry for not securing the lids, leaving it exposed to rain and causing it to mold, which I was able to learn from their thoughts, I have to give them the benefit of the doubt.

Of course, I make note of all these things, and if the lies accumulate, there will be repercussions. But in a case like that, it's not a life-or-death situation. The farmers lied to protect one another, which is something only human beings do, and it's an impressive quality.

Unfortunately, though, *right now*, I can't hear as much as I want to, and it's stressing me out. Drake was supposed to come by last night and he blew me off. I wish I was surprised by it, but it's happened so many times over the years, I can't waste time letting it bother me anymore.

The thing that's bothering me the most on this lovely, if not slightly overcast day, are my own thoughts, and more so my recollections.

What happened with Abdiel the other night was a mind-fuck on many levels. Mainly because he could *hear me*. It shocked the shit out of me when I heard him, listening to me listening to him. I couldn't believe it at first, but then I heard him thinking, remembering being with Drake, and Drake injecting him with Empyrean.

Startling myself as well, my first reaction wasn't anger or jealousy, more so confusion and intrigue. I've been thinking more and more about Abdiel Harmony, since the night I overheard his lascivious thoughts about me and my brother. I couldn't stop wondering how he knew, what he'd done, and why.

I came to the conclusion, which was verified when he confessed, that he must have spied on us. And when he admitted he was *desperate* to know what I do in the lounge, it sort of spurred on even more erotic musings for my youngest servant.

One of my best friends' son... I really shouldn't be thinking about Abdiel as much as I have been, but I can't stop. Especially after what happened in the lake.

He reacts to me in such a way that brings fever to the blood in my veins. He looks at me like I'm a god, flushes and stutters when I'm near him, and damn if it doesn't make my dick harder than I know what to do with.

There's nothing in the world quite like innocence wrapped around mischievous carnal lust.

The lake was a lapse in judgement on my part, but one that I can't fully state with confidence I won't make again. Anyone could have seen us out there, and while we weren't necessarily doing anything, I felt his erection on my own, and for the briefest moment I almost fell beneath the surface to give him what very well might have been his first time entering a man's mouth.

Bad bad bad.

What would that say about me? Abdiel is half my age. He's my servant, and let's not forget, which none of my Regnum will let me, I'm *married*.

The only slight reprieve I take with no Empyrean is that I don't have to listen to everyone's thoughts on my inability to procreate. It's nonstop lately, mostly from the operators of our *government*, if you could call it that, which I'm not sure I would. They're the planners, and apparently, a large part of planning the future of The Principality relies on me giving it an heir.

It's clear to me now that I fucked up when I married multiple women. It just gives me more opportunity for failure in reproduction. But at the time, when I married—Lauris first, then Kiara, then Alissa and Gem at once, and finally Emithel, within only eight months of one another—I thought I could force myself to do it. I *thought* I could fuck them, just as much as would be needed to make a baby.

That was the original plan... Not a very good one, I can admit.

Because the more time has passed, the more time I spend denying my true self and my internal nature, the more I come to terms with the realization that I *can't* do it.

I don't have it in me to fuck someone I'm not attracted to just to get them pregnant, and even trying, even *thinking* of trying, makes me feel sick.

Not sick as in *repulsed*, but more like, ashamed. Ashamed of the even mild desire to go against my biology. My *soul*.

God, our *Mother* made me the way I am. She built me, and I'm perfect in the form She sculpted, regardless of what old texts may say, or what the human body is made to do through procreation. I can't force myself into a mold for the sake of pleasing other people and keeping my name going.

I *won't*.

But I'm also nervous about how this will look. What will happen when they find out I can't give them a natural heir? What would that mean?

I won't give up rule of The Principality. It's mine. This entire block of the transformation that Drake and I carved out, it's ours and it's important.

I knew going into this that I could never fall in romantic love with a woman. But when we first started, I held different ideas about what I could endure for the sake of my people.

It's times like these, when my Empyrean has worn off and my insecurities are riddling my mind, that I think things I know I shouldn't. Irrational fears and paranoia...

What if they want him to replace me?

Drake fucks women. He likes to, and I won't deny that I harbor a lot of jealousy over it. Not because I wish I fucked women, but because I wish he only fucked me...

But that's a nerve to strike another time.

Drake doesn't see gender as something that should prohibit sexual desire. He fucks who he wants to fuck, which means in theory, he could get someone pregnant. Though he has no desire to reproduce, something he's been telling me since we were young. But still… if the Regnum were to find out I couldn't do it, would they look to my brother?

He wouldn't want it, but I suppose that could change.

I always thought I was the one person who could hold him, if only for a few moments. Empyrean was ours, and it kept us together, even though I know he says he could never be in a relationship, and we can never be something because we're brothers. Despite all of it, we were still *connected*.

But then he gave it to Abdiel, and ever since I found out, it's left me wondering who else he's done this with…

What sorts of things is he keeping from me? Is that why he's controlling when I can have Empyrean?

He's using it to manipulate me, that much is clear. But with Abdiel, he crossed a line.

My blood is rushing in my ears as I think about it. It's been on my mind since I left the lake the other night… when I heard Abdiel thinking about Drake.

I know Abdiel isn't *mine*. I mean, he's my servant, but that's it. But if I find out Drake fucked him, it might just nick my heart a little. *Okay, maybe a lot.*

I care greatly for Abdiel, as the son of my late best friend, yes, but also more than that. I know I shouldn't. I know it's wrong, and outside of my rage for the unknown of what Drake may or may not be doing to fuck with me, I'm now filled with dread over how I can't seem to stop lusting after the wrong people.

I have five wives I'm not attracted to, not even slightly, although they're lovely women. But the only people I want are a servant who's twenty years younger than me, whose father was a very close and often very *intimate* friend, and my own foster brother.

I'm fucked. What kind of leader am I??

My emotions are going haywire, and I decide to cut the rest of my day short and go find Drake. I'm wound up tight right now, tense and bordering on irate by the time I get to the Field. Chances are I'll find my brother in his lab. It's a safe bet since this is where he spends most of his time. Here and up the mountain.

107

As I stomp to the entrance path, the patrolmen, who are shooting the shit and smoking cigarettes, notice me and startle. They drop their butts onto the ground and straighten as I approach, acting like I'm a damn military sergeant. It would be comical if I weren't so damn frustrated.

"Head Priest," one of them—Lorn, I can tell by his eyes—says.

"At ease, boys." I smirk. "Can one of you take me up to the lab, please?"

"Yes, sir. Right away." Lorn gets settled on his ATV, and I hop onto the back as he starts it up.

He pulls away from his friend and we begin up the path through the Field, heading toward the lab. It's only about three minutes going as fast as he does, and once we're there, the guards let me right in; no questions, no words.

It's good. It means I can surprise brother dearest.

"I'll wait for you here, Head Priest," Lorn says as I approach the giant door to the lab.

Turning over my shoulder, I tell him, "I might be awhile."

"That's fine, sir. I don't mind waiting."

He's a good one.

I shoot him a wink and then I'm inside, wandering the long hallway leading us to the inner laboratory. I don't come in here all that often, since Drake typically takes the reins on this operation. But every time I do, I'm always amazed at how much it feels like him in here.

Drake has loved science since we were kids. While I was playing football and trying to act like I wasn't checking out my teammates, he was reading and studying. Becoming a *master* at all things knowledge. It would have gotten him picked on in school if kids weren't so scared of him. And then once I moved in with his foster family, no one would dare say a word about my brother. They would answer to my fists. A few of them did.

Moving through the double doors, I wave off the soldiers who are practically escorting me and saunter up to Drake's office. I knock on the door and wait, gaze flinging all around as I watch the chemistry happening in here, wishing I could hear *anything* other than what everyone else hears.

The door tugs open, and of course Drake already knows it's me, since I'm sure he heard me coming. He smirks and steps aside without a word, motioning for me to come in, which I do without hesitation. I barge right inside, brushing past him in my anger as he closes and locks the door behind us.

"So... to what do I owe the pleasure of your impromptu visit?" Drake inches toward me, his ever-present smugness bringing my blood to a boil.

No pleasantries. "Abdiel Harmony." My face, and my thoughts, say everything that doesn't leave my mouth.

The smirk stays planted on his lips, though his gaze narrows in my direction, and it's *enraging* me that I can't hear him right now.

He straightens up. "What about him?"

"Don't play stupid with me, Drake. It's not you." My jaw tenses. "You gave him Empyrean. What the fuck is that about?"

Drake shrugs while I fume silently. "He came to me. I'm sure you know by now that he watched us..." He pauses, and I give him a slight nod. "Well, he saw it and he was curious." He stops again to run his thumb along his lower lip. "Apparently, he's curious about a lot of things."

Red splashes my vision. I stalk up to my brother quick, pushing him until his back slams into the door as I hold my forearm to his throat.

"Did you fuck him??" I growl in his face, close enough that I witness his pupils dilate.

"Calm down, *your majesty.*" He shoots his own flames of fury at me through his swirling eyes. "You don't own anyone other than your five, remember?"

I surge closer to his face until I'm hovering over him, even with his couple of inches on me in height.

"I'll ask you again, Drake. And this will be the last time. Did. You. *Fuck*. Him?" I'm vibrating with the heat of wrath and jealousy; so many intense things I can't control whipping through my body.

He still takes a moment to answer me. "No. Is that what you want to hear?"

"Is it true?" I seethe at him, and he has the nerve to laugh.

"Yes. It's true. I didn't fuck him." I relax my hold just a bit, until he says, "I made him come, though."

I smack the door right next to his head with a roar. "I swear to God, Drake..."

"Why are you so jealous?" He angles his face in closer until his lips brush mine when he speaks. I swallow hard. "Is he your new pet, King Darian?"

"Why would you give him Empyrean?" I ask my own question, jittering in anger. "What are you playing at?"

"I'm guessing you've already picked up on this," he speaks softly, "But Abdiel Harmony is special. He came to me in need of Ecdysis, Darian. You remember what that's like…"

There's truth in his words, but still, the thought of him with Abdiel is driving me absolutely purely *insane* with envious rage. I'm not even sure for whom. Maybe both.

Drake's tongue lurches out to brush my lower lip, and my eyelids flutter. "Why are you so mad…?"

"You know why," I snarl at him, pressing harder into this throat with my arm until he grunts. But he shivers all the same. Grinding my hips into his, I feel the rigid shape of him that makes me weak. "You like this don't you? Controlling me… *manipulating* me."

He sighs an eager sound that throbs my cock. "I've always loved controlling you, brother. You know that."

I watch his eyes closely, the marbled brown and gold like polished stones. So many things from our collective pasts live in those eyes. It's impossible for me to hate him, even when I know I should.

But at the same time, he's playing too much, with my emotions and my needs. He knows it isn't right, but he does it anyway.

"I want to know exactly what you did with Abdiel," I demand, pressing into him harder. He chuckles breathlessly. "I'm serious, Drake. Don't fuck with me."

"I gave him Empyrean," he croaks beneath the pressure of my arm in his windpipe. "He reacted… the same way you do. He needed it, Darian, so I gave it to him. It wasn't much… I just touched him. He's a virgin, you know… So needy, it's delicious."

I hate that my cock is hard right now because I want to detest what he's saying. And I want to punch him in the face. *Wouldn't be the first time.*

But more than anything, I'm thinking of Abdiel… Sweet, innocent Abdiel, at the hands of my wicked foster brother.

"Don't be so cruel with your thoughts, your highness." He smirks and licks my lip again, this time giving it a little nip that my cock reacts to, way more than I'd like it to. "You should have told me Abdiel was yours. I'm not a mind-reader."

His smile goes wide and devilish, and I want to bash it off his face because of how goddamn good it looks.

"You're being insubordinate," I growl and quickly shove him to his knees, wasting no time unbuttoning and unzipping my pants. "I'm gonna need some retribution for your obstinance."

He looks up at me with the slightest bit of that confidence wavering, and I love it all too much. There's a constant power struggle between us, but it's not often that I demand him to obey me. Only when the emotions bubble over, and surprisingly enough he doesn't fight me on it. Well, not *totally*.

I open my pants and take my dick out, wasting no time pressing the head up to his mouth. His eyes stay on mine, the rage at having to submit to me being swallowed up by his own arousal as he parts his lips hesitantly. Too slow for my liking, and I shove my cock into his mouth swiftly, bringing a grunt out of him. Grabbing the back of his head, I fist his hair, stuffing my dick down his throat until he gags.

It's not as rough as it seems. I know he likes it, as evidence from his own hand rubbing himself over his pants while he sucks and sucks, going harder for me the way I like. My eyes roll back as his tongue sweeps underneath my erection where it throbs in his mouth.

Puffs of air escape him in between my thrusts, my shaft sliding in and out of his warm, wet mouth while I take the pleasure he's giving up, willingly, though I had to drag it out of him. He's so stingy with his affections, and I fucking loathe it.

It's like he wants me to hate him, and I don't know why.

Drake brings his hand up to my balls and tugs on them while he sucks, driving me absolutely mad. From the sensation, yes, but also from seeing him like this...

It reminds me of when we were younger, and still figuring out what we liked. Drake has always been the more dominant one, the more demanding one. It's a rare occasion when I get him on his knees and the sight of it alone is usually enough to bring me to the bursting point.

I keep pushing and pulling, his spit dribbling while I fuck his mouth, surging deeper into his throat, forcing him to swallow on me. The tightening is mind-blowing, and I groan, head dropping back for a moment. His hand is on my nuts, massaging and squeezing, before it slinks between the crack of my ass until I'm trembling.

Gaze aimed down at him, I watch his flushed face as he brings his hand front, holding my cock in his fist while sticking his index and middle fingers out. My breathing shallows, our eyes locked, as he glides his fingers into his mouth, with my dick, sucking to get them wet. The anticipation in me is sizzling.

Once his fingers are lubed as much as they can be, he removes

111

them, still sucking my cock while his hand slinks between my thighs, tugging my boxers down a little more so he can get better access to my ass. I bite my lip, slowing my movements enough for him to press his index finger up to my rim, circling it for only a moment before shoving it inside.

I whimper a hoarse noise at the intrusion, burning from lack of proper lube, though I welcome it, relaxing enough to let him in farther. He pushes it *deeper*, swirling to hit my prostate until my eyes roll back.

Typical Drake... Has to be in charge. I'd love to believe it's about making me feel good. And as I look down at him while he's fingering my asshole and sucking my cock like a fiend, I can fool myself into thinking he does these things for me. He wants to make me as happy as I want to make him.

But it's probably smoke in mirrors; this game he plays.

The thought has me grinding my teeth, forcing my cock deeper and deeper into his throat, holding his head steady so he has nowhere to go. He adds a second finger, using them to ride my ass hard, almost painfully so, but I'd be lying if I said I didn't love it.

"I need you to feel this, Drake," I hiss above him between clenched teeth, his eyes sharpening, watering from the slight suffocation; inches of dick fucking his throat, hitting a wall, but not stopping. "Feel what I can do to you."

His dark lashes flutter, the crazed lust bringing him up to an edge he so rarely lets himself approach. His left hand frantically undoes his own pants, pulling his dick out to jerk himself rough.

"Feel that I can own you just as hard as you can own me." My voice grinds like sandpaper as my fingers twist in his inky black hair. "Even *harder*, brother. You need to know..."

Grunts are escaping him while I push, leaning my upper body on the door, angling so I can ride his mouth. He adds a third finger into my ass, and I purr, the burn pulling me closer to an inferno of a climax, yearning in my balls, ready to erupt.

Our eyes meld while I impart my decree to my brother on his knees. "I want you to feel me for *hours* afterward, like I do with you. I never want you to forget, Drake, my lovely Serpent, who your fucking *King* is."

His eyes roll back in his skull as he groans, swallowing on my dick while he strokes his own erection harder and harder, beating it until he snaps. His cheeks hollow and he sucks me fierce while cum shoots

112

out of his erection. I watch in fascination, his cries of pleasure muffled by my cock in his mouth.

Never once does he stop sucking me, though his movements have slowed, and now he's almost worshipping it, humming while he drags the orgasm right out of me with his soft lips and that long, wicked tongue.

His fingers stay knuckle deep in my ass as he peers up at me, snake eyes sparkling, begging me to come in his mouth.

So I do... Almost on command.

My balls seize, and my dick jerks and pulses, streams of cum pouring down his throat while I groan out hushed sounds, whispers of praise to every perfect inch of him that does these perfect things to me.

"You like drinking my cum?" My voice scrapes through trembling lips while he swallows me, nodding and sucking, and *God*, this is so fucking toxic, but so delicious, I would never be able to stop. "Swallow me, baby... Every drop, like you're supposed to."

My eyes close, and I just breathe, in and out, fast and harsh as the world spins and pleasure racks my loins. I stay in his mouth for a while after I'm done coming, and he lets me. He tugs his fingers out of my ass, and I slip mine beneath his chin, watching him lick and suck off my spent cock, cleaning me up.

Finally tucking my dick away, I drop to my knees before him. His eyes widen a bit from his post-coital daze as I take his hand in mine and bring it to my mouth, licking up his cum. He makes a low growling noise, which I silence with my lips, kissing him slow and warm, slipping my tongue inside. He flicks it with his own as we taste each other, together and always better that way. That's what I want him to know...

I just want him to remember what he promised me all those years ago.

We pull apart just enough to breathe, his hands on me and mine on him.

And then he whispers over my lips, "Let's get high, baby."

CHAPTER TWELVE

DRAKE

Darian is just staring off into space. It would worry me, if I weren't sort of doing the exact same thing. The only difference is that he's staring at my plants and I'm staring at him.

We just shot up. I did some too, since it's been a while and it felt like something I needed after what just happened.

Him storming in, thoughts ablazing. His jealousy, his anger, his possessiveness.

I shouldn't like it, but I do, and it's a problem. Not to mention, my plan of trying to get him to realize he doesn't need Empyrean anymore to access his gifts backfired. Maybe I gave in too easily, who knows. I'm sure the thing with Abdiel didn't help.

I sort of knew it wasn't a good idea while I was doing it. But as cliché as it sounds, it really did just happen.

He *saw us*. The jig was up at that point. And it's not like I've ever given Empyrean to anyone else before… I'm not that much of a narcissistic asshole.

Abdiel Harmony coming into my office was an unplanned gift; one that I couldn't refuse. I'd never interacted with the kid before that day, but I would have to be deaf and blind not to notice him. He's the kind of man who can make even the straightest of arrows bend, and ultimately snap.

And for every lingering glance I've given Abdiel over the years, against his knowledge, Darian has downright *gawked*. Metaphorically so, because my brother is a good man, and he would never wantonly check out a minor. Still, Abdiel's been a man for at least a couple of years now… visibly.

Darian is also good at hiding his true desires from the Regnum. Not that he needs to, but there's a certain level of politics involved in reigning over the Expanse that we never anticipated when we started The Principality. Him admitting he doesn't want to have children is hard enough. Imagine the confusion he'd be met with if he revealed his desire for a Domestic half his age… The son of his former secret fling.

I knew Darian had an interest in Abdiel, and I seduced him anyway. But despite what Darian thinks, I didn't do it intentionally. The kid's innocence drew me in, beyond anything I've ever experienced before. It worries me, which is exactly why I'm going to avoid him at all costs, especially now that I know how Darian feels about it.

All that said, I can't seem to forget how hearing Abdiel's thoughts brought me to my damn knees, like only one other person ever has before.

The person sitting across from me, on the floor of my office. Propped against the couch, staring at my plants like they're doing something exceptionally interesting.

"Is that…" his voice bursts from his lips, quiet and gradual like a puff of smoke. I can *see* it. *I fuckin love this shit.* "Is that a hybrid?"

Blinking at him, I force away the internal gushing over how damn smart he is. I hate myself for having to play down how much I adore all these qualities he possesses. But it's better this way. It has to be.

I nod to his question. "It's lavender aloe."

He glances at me, sincere curiosity and fascination shimmering in his eyes, which are back to their bright sky-blue. A humble grin sweeps over my lips as I peek at the plant.

"I'm surprised it started flowering like that. It actually looks way prettier than I thought it would. But apparently, Lamiales can bond with Asparagales under proper conditions. I had to keep it in the eco-garden for a while, but now it's just about ready to test." He shows me a little smile I have to look away from, rubbing the back of my neck as I mutter, "I'm excited about it."

"I can tell," he rumbles, giving me a look that quite literally says, *It's the best blessing of my life to know you, baby.* But then he clears his throat and shakes it away as fast as my uncomfortable hesitations can creep into my mind. "What will you use it for? Topical stuff?"

I nod. "Yea, definitely. But more specifically, I think it could be a great supplement for metabolic issues. It can regulate blood sugar, too…"

"For Donna and Jim," he finishes my thought, regarding at least two of our diabetic family members. I nod again. "Wow, Drake. That's amazing."

I scoff away his praise. "It still needs to be tested. It might not do anything…"

"Or it might," he says with all the confidence of a King. My eyes lift back to his. "Manifest that shit."

I can't help but grin, and he returns it. He sits up straight, and for a second, he looks like he might crawl over to me. I blur out my desperate desire for him to do it, and unfortunately it works, because he stands up and stretches his arms.

"I guess I'm out," he sighs as I stand, too. He glances at the floor. *Sorry for bursting in on your day like that…*

You were pretty worked up, I tell him in my head, and his eyes spring. "So… Abdiel Harmony?"

"He watched us." He blinks at me.

"Yea…"

"You were right to give him Empyrean," he admits. "He needs Ecdysis. It was time."

My head bobs, because it's true. I knew it the moment Abdiel set foot in my office. The spying, his obsessive thoughts I've overheard about Darian, the uncertainty about his parents' deaths and what his life stands for…

The kid was searching, and Mother led him directly to us. What it means, I still have no idea. But we're not always meant to understand the plan. Just to follow it and have faith. The answers will come.

For some reason, my lips part to ask Darian if he's interested in Abdiel… *romantically.* But I slap them shut and redirect my thoughts because what the fuck is that going to accomplish? Darian's in charge, and we're not a thing. None of this needs to be discussed or thought about.

He swallows visibly, then does this little shrug, turning toward the door to leave. My muscles are tensing as he unlocks it and grabs the handle. But before he turns it, he looks at me over his shoulder.

You should come for dinner more often. His eyes shimmer. *Gem and Lauris miss you.*

I smirk at him. *Do they?*

He chuckles and shakes his head, opening the door to leave. "Later, bro."

I watch him walk away for far too long. Even after I know he's halfway back to the Den, I'm still standing in the exact same spot.

Later.

Darian gets home later than usual.

I know he had football practice after school, but still. When I hear him stomping upstairs, I glance at the clock, and it's almost eight-thirty.

He missed dinner.

I'm on my bed, reading, when he bursts into the room and immediately flings his backpack into the corner. My eyebrow lifts as he starts kicking his shit everywhere, practically fuming.

Normally I find his messiness funny, because I'm overly neat and I think it's cool to have a brother who's my best friend and so very different from me. It annoyed me at first, but at this point we've been sharing a room for over two years, and I'm used to being the one who cleans up after both of us. I'm fine with it.

Though right now it's not amusing, because clearly, something's bothering him. It's alarming how much his mood affects mine. I was fine until he stepped into the room, and now I'm crazy tense.

"Everything okay there, champ?" I ask, eyeing him carefully as he yanks the dresser drawer open forcefully, damn near ripping the whole thing out.

"Great," he grunts, removing some clean clothes.

"Well, that's a fuckin lie," I huff, and he finally looks at me. "Practice didn't go well?"

He sucks in an audible breath, then lets it out slowly, raking his fingers through his damp hair the color of cinnamon. "Not really."

I sit up straighter. "What happened?"

"I was distracted as fuck," he admits quietly, as if I really give a fuck about football and would judge him on something like that. "I fumbled twice. Got my ass tackled more times than I could count. Coach wasn't pleased."

"So? It's just practice. Not like it was a game." I give him a look

117

like this should be obvious.

"*That's not the point, Drake.*" *He shakes his head.* "*We're playing the 'cudas next week. I need to be on top of my game, and I can't fucking focus.*" *He slams the drawer shut hard enough that all the shit on top of the dresser rattles around.*

"*Why can't you focus?*" *I tilt my head.* "*What's wrong? Maybe I can help.*"

"*You can't,*" *he says dismissively, tugging his t-shirt over his head.* "*I've got it under control.*"

He tosses the shirt, which lands nowhere near the hamper, but I can't even be bothered by it because I'm too busy staring at the bruises on his ribcage. They're shaped like fingerprints...

He slips a new shirt on, cutting off my line of sight, but the image is burned into my brain. Putting my book down, I scoot off the bed and stand up, watching him closely.

"*You have* what *under control, Darian?*" *My tone is firm, enough that his eyes widen at me.*

He's frozen for only a second before he brushes me off. "*Nothing. Just... my life. My problems. I'm fine, Drake. It was just a bad day.*"

Eyeing him, I ask, "*Are you sure?*"

"*Yea,*" *he answers too fast, nodding too much.* "*I just... I'm sorry I missed dinner. I hope Dan wasn't pissed.*"

My eyes narrow. "*Who gives a fuck about that asshole...*"

He blinks, his brows pulling together in such a vulnerable expression, he looks like he could break down at any moment. "*Yea...*"

I step closer to him. "*Darian, please... Tell me you're okay. Just...*" *I stop to work out my thoughts. I don't know anything. I have no evidence of anything at all, and this is the first time I'm noticing it. But now that it's in my head, it won't leave.* "*If something's wrong, you have to promise to tell me, okay?*"

His Adam's apple dipping in his throat catches my peripheral, but I can't stop watching his face. He looks distraught. He's not fine, despite what he says. Far from it.

Please, God...

Let me be wrong.

My mind sifts through an inventory of things that never clicked until right now.

How much attention Dan pays him.

The occasional bruises in strange places, even for a football

118

player.

The alone time…

When I was younger, it made me jealous; the fact that my foster father spent his time with the new addition to the family rather than me. I always hated Dan, but still… He's the closest thing we have to a dad.

When Darian arrived, he was bigger than me. He's interested in sports, and I'm not. Dan clearly loves him and hates me. I made my peace with it over the past couple years. And as I grew up, got taller and bigger, gained some confidence in myself and one amazing brother, I stopped giving a fuck what that asshole thinks.

But Darian is different. He's been searching for a father his entire life. He's desperate for one.

If that fucking scumbag took advantage of him, I swear to God…

"I will," Darian breathes, blinking his ocean eyes at me.

"Promise." It should be a question, but it comes out more like a demand.

He nods, hesitantly. "I promise. But you have to promise something to me…"

"Anything," I whisper, sounding way less manly than I'd like to.

"Promise you'll never leave me…" he pleads. He clears his throat, glancing at the floor for just a moment before his eyes are back with me. "Promise you'll always be my brother, no matter what happens."

I have the strongest urge I'll never understand to hug him in this moment, and it confuses me down to my core. My mind spins and whips up the need inside me, making sure I believe it's just compassion and empathy for my brother, though deep in a strange corner of my heart, I don't think that's all it is.

Instead of holding him like I want to when I shouldn't, I just extend my hand, pinky out, and murmur, "I promise."

The first bit of relief I've seen since he got home flashes in his eyes, his lips twisting only a little as he reaches out, curling his pinky around mine.

We pinky swear on it, and that's it. It's done.

I've made a promise I have no intention of breaking, ever.

Despite anything that may come to us in the future, he's my brother. I'll never leave him, and I won't deny the need to end any lives for him. He's that important, after all.

Darian is heart and home. The first ones I've ever had.

CHAPTER THIRTEEN

DARIAN

I'm carrying a mixture of emotions as I come downstairs for dinner.

I'm eager to see Abdiel, though I know I shouldn't be. I'm nervous that I upset him when I left him in the lake the other night. And then there's my awareness of the fact that he messed around with my brother.

Every time I think about it, my teeth set, my fists clench, and I just want to hit something. And even having such a reaction is baffling to me.

Abdiel isn't mine at all. He's just my Domestic, and a young, sweet member of my family. I can't understand why I'm suddenly so drawn to him…

It's like ever since I found out that he watched Drake fuck me, and how he reacted to it, I haven't been able to get him out of my brain. He's taken up residency in my mind, and honestly, nothing, not even Drake, or the constant reminder that I'm already married, has been able to kick him out.

Confusing, but in an unexpectedly good way. The kind of way that feels like a kaleidoscope of butterflies fluttering up my esophagus; one of those uncomfortable tickles that triggers dopamine to your brain, whether you want it to or not.

It's something I've only ever *truly* felt for one other person.

The second I set foot in the dining room, I'm listening for Abdiel. I don't hear him right away, and disappointment sweeps through me as I consider that he might not be working tonight.

But just as I'm settling into the idea of another dinner staring at

Abdiel. He's humming.

I take my seat at the table, paying no mind to anyone or anything other than the sound coming from the kitchen. I can tell right away that it's Abdiel's voice. Such a distinctly beautiful sound, captivating me even from the next room. It's very faint, but I can hear it better because of Empyrean. I can't actually tell if he's really humming or doing so in his mind.

Either way, I think I recognize the song.

Definitely *Pink Floyd,* though I'm unsure of which one...

They begin bringing us drinks, and I can see Abdiel through the doorway, darting back and forth as he plates the food. I'm trying not to be obvious in my obsessive watching, but I'm simply fascinated by him now. The way he moves, the sounds of his thoughts...

I wonder if he captivated Drake the same way he's captivated me.
The thought squeezes my fist beneath the table.

We get some bread, and I say a prayer over the meal, followed by gazpacho that smells amazing, though I'm having a hard time concentrating because Abdiel *still* hasn't come into the room.

Finally, *finally*, he saunters over with my plate of dinner, eyes on anything but me as he approaches, setting it down in front of me. My gaze slides up him while he leans over to deliver my food, ogling the slope of his neck, the line of his throat, his sharp jaw and those pillowed lips. My cock stirs as his eyes finally meet mine, his cheeks turning subtly pink, as he undoubtedly heard what I was thinking about him.

Our eyes stay locked, for just a moment, though it feels like hours, and I hear him, only for me...

I've been thinking about you, too.

My breathing shallows, and he tugs his lower lips between his teeth, bringing a delicious ache to my balls. I shift in my seat, and he clears his throat, flushing up a storm as he scurries off, leaving me to stew in the sexual tension we've somehow managed to create together. I don't know where it came from, or how it got here, but it's burning me where I sit.

We all dig into our food and Lauris is talking to me about something solstice festival related, though I'm barely paying attention. I feel bad, and I know I shouldn't ignore her, but I can't help it. Every time Abdiel comes into the room, he flashes me with these little looks, innocently fluttering his long eyelashes, licking that tasty-looking lip, cheeks visibly blushing through his creamy complexion.

I'm fucking enamored. And as he's refilling drinks around the table, he's all I can hear.

Sexy... He's so damn sexy. God, stop thinking this, Abdiel. He can hear you. But I can't help it... I haven't stopped remembering what he looked like in that lake. His beautiful body, his warmth and his strength and the way his voice sounds in my head. I just wish I could... I wish we could...

Abdiel, please, I growl at him with my mind, and he flinches, almost dropping the pitcher in his hand as he gapes across the table at me. *You're driving me crazy.*

I'm sorry... He swipes his lip with his tongue, then stalks away, mentally scolding himself.

I don't want him to feel bad, but I can't help the grin that forms uncontrollably on my face as I chuckle and shake my head, gaze falling to my lap in hopes of disguising it. The boy seems smitten, and it's making *me* feel smitten.

This is crazy. *I'm* crazy. I shouldn't be entertaining this at all. I don't really know the kid, and there are so many reasons why we shouldn't be flirting, but I can't help it. His innocence really turns me on more than I ever thought it could.

Drake said he's a virgin. I don't want to think about how he knows that, but the more I'm observing Abdiel, the more inclined I am to believe it. *I wonder if he's ever even been kissed properly...*

I haven't, his voice startles me out of my thoughts, and I look up to see him trying to cover up a smirk, pouring water for Lauris at my side. I struggle to remain subtle as my eyes slide up to his, brow lifting with my intrigue.

His thoughts tell me, *I've never been kissed... at all.* Then he bites that damn lip again, and I'm going out of my mind.

How on Earth is that possible, my precious young servant? I lift my drink and take a slow sip, eyeing him over the rim of the glass. *I could eat you alive.* And then I suck my lip between my teeth, giving him a taste of his own medicine. I can practically hear him shivering.

Abdiel's paying so much attention to my mouth and so little attention to what he's doing that it's Lauris's startled shriek which brings us both back to reality when we realize he's overflowing her water glass.

"Oh, shit. I'm so sorry!" Abdiel stutters as Lauris backs up to prevent the water soaking the table from rushing onto her lap. "Let me clean that up for you."

Kiara and Gem are giggling, and I have to cover my mouth with my hand to stop from having a chuckle myself. *He's so damn cute. The poor thing, all flustered.*

Abdiel rushes back over, Gina right behind him, both of them hustling to clean up the water.

"Don't worry about it," I tell them in an easy tone while I scoot over and tug Lauris's chair closer to me. "No harm."

Abdiel gives me a grateful look framed by permanently pink cheeks, and I can't help but wink at him.

Please... He whines in his mind. *This night has been embarrassing enough as it is.*

I chuckle to myself as they retreat to the kitchen, and we finish eating. I'm barely aware of what I'm putting in my mouth, though it's certainly delicious. Chicken and wild rice with fresh salad. *I wonder if Abdiel made it...* He's a great cook, that I know about him.

Once we're done with a dessert of hazelnut gelato, another favorite, I excuse myself from the table. I go to freshen up, which results in me pacing around my bedroom for fifteen minutes. The desire burning inside me to spend more time with the kid is undeniable. I hate denying myself. And I have to do it all the damn time.

Denying myself has become an unfortunate presence in my life, and I despise it. I don't want to do it anymore.

I deserve happiness, don't I? Shouldn't I be allowed to spend time with someone interesting? To have a nice evening that doesn't revolve around mind games or faking...

If Abdiel wants to spend time with me too, well then who am I to say no?

Making a snap decision, I leave my bedroom and head back downstairs. Listening closely to the sounds in the kitchen, I can tell they're about done cleaning up. And all my wives have long since adjourned to wherever they're spending the rest of the night.

So maybe this could work...

I wait in the study until I hear Abdiel going into the restroom, and when he comes out, I reach around the corner and grab him by the arm, pulling him quickly with me back into the study.

The look on his face is priceless. Nothing but nervous at first, until he realizes it's me. And then I can hear his elation, glad that I haven't gone to bed or forgotten about him. It floods me with heated excitement.

Pushing him into the corner so I know we won't be seen, I crowd him and he looks up at me, swallowing visibly.

"Hi." I cage him in with my arms on either side of his waist.

"Head Priest... h-hi." His deep irises the color of evergreens glisten at me as he melds himself into the wall behind him.

"Pretty sure I told you to call me Darian," I rumble, and he huffs a small chuckle. "Are you almost finished with your shift?"

He nods slowly, radiating uncertainty. I don't want him to be so nervous around me, but at the same time it stiffens my dick beyond belief.

Keeping my eyes on his, I whisper, "I was thinking... if you're not busy tonight, I would like to see you."

His face freezes in dazed wonder as he gapes at me, silent for a full five seconds before he finally croaks, "You would?"

"Yes, young servant." I lean in closer, brushing his ear with my lips until he shudders. "If you were to show up at the lounge in a few minutes undetected, you could come into the room."

He hums quietly, resting his head into me. It takes every ounce of my strength to pull away. But I have to. We can't do this out in the open. If anyone sees, it could ruin everything.

I back up a bit, trailing my hand down his side briefly. "I hope to see you soon, Abdiel."

His lips part, but nothing comes out. Even his mind seems to be blank, nothing but disbelief bouncing around. It makes me smile. Then I tap him on the chin and turn to leave, heading toward the lounge to wait for him.

When I get inside, I let out a long, rough breath. Wandering to the table by the window, I pour myself a glass of brown liquor, sipping to calm my nerves. Staring out at the lake, at least ten minutes pass while I drain the glass and pour another. Everything that happened by that lake... all the recollections swirling as I remind myself to go slow. I need to keep my wits about me, but I also need to relax. I'm actually shaking.

I have no idea what I'm doing, but I haven't been this excited in a while. Still, I can't let my anticipation ruin my time with the kid. I don't want to push him...

Maybe he won't even want to come. Maybe I'm being an aggressive creep, like—

My thoughts are cut off by a knock on the door. I close my eyes, grinning in relief as I rush to answer it.

This could be a giant mistake... One there's no possible way I could stop myself from making.

ABDIEL

Breathe, Abdiel. Just... breathe...

I'm not sure I've ever been this nervous. Not during any of the thousands of dinners I've spent serving him, not the first time I sang at reflection, not even when I had to speak at my parents' funeral.

Certainly not when I went to the lab the other day.

I was nervous then, sure. But this is a completely different beast of burden. I can barely stop my hands from shaking long enough to knock on the door.

I still manage it, and keep reminding myself to breathe as I listen to his heavy footfalls on the other side, his thoughts becoming clearer as he approaches.

And then I hear something that gives me solace.

He's nervous, too.

That thought allows me to breathe easier as the door opens a crack, my Head Priest peering through, his blue-gray eyes glittering right at me. They hold me captive, almost long enough to overlook the fact that he must have taken more Empyrean recently, though he hasn't been back in for solitude... Not to my knowledge, anyway.

"Come in," he hums, sneaking me inside in a stealth manner, checking that there's no one around before closing and locking the door behind me.

Swallowing hard, I take him in, trying not to be obvious, especially since I know he hears everything rolling around in my mind. I'm getting used to it, though. I'm getting used to him always being able to hear me.

Right now, for example, he definitely knows that I'm admiring how *big* he is. I'm not a short person. I'm six feet tall, but Darian must be at least six-two. Not quite as tall as Drake, but still, he certainly has the bulk of muscle in his favor.

I know he works out a lot. Even if I didn't know it, it would be obvious from how *wide* his arms and shoulders are. I remember all the lines and sinews of his chest and abs, visions burned into my brain… Clusters of muscle I'd love to drag my tongue through. The images in my head have me drooling.

I want to see him naked again.

I blink myself out of my reflections at the look he's giving me. He has some stress in his brow, and I can't really tell why. His thoughts are mixing up in his listening to mine, apart from something that sticks out about him not wanting to be like *him*… Someone from his past…

Who's him?

He doesn't answer me, not with his mouth or his mind. Instead, he turns and wanders over to the bed, having a seat on the edge. I glance around the room for a moment, remembering what I saw happen in here only last week.

The night that changed my view of everything.

"They steer the course of our lives," Darian rumbles, and my eyes fling in his direction once more. He's seated with his hands folded on his lap. "Each and every one." Narrowing my gaze at him, I wonder what he's referring to, but he explains right away. "Our decisions, Abdiel. Our choices, and the footsteps we plant on the path the universe devises."

It's strange, a few days ago I might not have had a clue what these words mean. But now…

Now, with Empyrean lingering in my blood, the Ecdysis birthing a new Abdiel, I nod along. I *see* what he's saying, as if a new door in my mind has been opened.

It makes him smile, tiny and faint, yet deliciously beautiful and tender all the same.

"So," he sighs, leaning back a bit on the bed, propping on his elbows while he stares at me, "What would you like to talk about?"

Confusion ripples as I blink. "Talk?"

His tongue swipes his lower lip. "Or is there some other reason you're here, my servant?"

"I um… I thought you wanted to see me," I mutter with very little confidence. I wish I could find my backbone, but I can't seem to be anything but timid around him.

My entire life has passed watching this man from afar; admiring him as if he truly were my *King*. And now here I am, in a private room with him… Door closed and locked.

We've been flirting, and at dinner I heard his thoughts, about wanting to kiss me, to taste me. I had to adjust my erection multiple times.

And now he just wants to talk?

Darian chuckles, shaking his head. "So eager, young servant. I wanted to see you so we could talk..." My stomach drops in disappointment, until he continues, "About that kiss you say you've never received."

"Oh," the word gusts from between my lips.

Head Priest's brow lifts, and his mind growls at me, *Come here, Abdiel.*

My pulse is rapping like crazy inside me as I go to him, like I have no choice whatsoever. And maybe I don't. Maybe this course was set for me, since the beginning of time; the plan already arranged.

Go to the man you want undeniably, unequivocally, irrevocably. It's where you need to be, Abdiel. Right here, right now.

When I reach the edge of the bed, I tilt my chin to look down at him, palms sweaty and dick as stiff as marble.

Closer, he commands, his pupils even darker now, compared to the brightness of his irises.

Taking a leap of faith that it's what he wants, I kneel on the bed and crawl over him, my arms caging his hips. The look on his face is mirroring his hungry thoughts, which are of course reflecting my own. Yet he backs up.

He crawls away from me.

Rejected, I can't help the wounded tone of my thoughts, fragile ego taking a hit that hurts. But Darian doesn't look pissed or creeped out, or upset. He doesn't look unsure at all. His eyes are beaming with a playful need that keeps me crawling after him. Chasing him, because it's what he wants.

I lunge for him, but he backs up again, scooting away from me on the bed while a youthful chuckle escapes him. I'm unable to stop myself from grinning wickedly as I grab his calf to keep him in place. His pupils dilate visibly as I climb on top of him, straddling his hips.

"Abdiel," he hums my name breathlessly, hitting me right in the junk. It's the sexiest sound ever invented when he says my name.

I part my lips, ready to call him *Head Priest*, but I remember his request and whisper, "Darian," going for his wrists, pinning them at his sides. Interestingly enough, just like Drake did to me the other day.

"What are you going to do with me now that you've caught me, young servant?" He licks his lips, the wall of muscle that is his chest fluttering through his breaths.

I'm trembling with excitement. "You lured me here with the promise of my first kiss." I lean over him, inching in while he squirms beneath me, such a big, thick beast of a man, yet I have him trapped at my mercy. *God, what a turn-on.*

"Is that what you want?" His voice vibrates into me like a deep bass.

I nod, slow and sure. "Only if you want to give it to me..."

Drake's words come back to me. *I can't be anyone's first kiss...*

"Of course, I do," Darian says like the purr of a jungle cat. But I'm still holding him down. I'm sure he could break free from my grip, but I think he wants it like this. I lean in closer, until my lips are hovering over his and he actually gasps. It's a faint sound, but it flinches my cock against his through our clothes. "Kiss me, servant boy. Take what you want me to give."

I don't even think. For the first time with us, all hesitation is gone as I lower my mouth to his, pressing our lips together softly, yet firm enough that he grunts. One touch, one noise, and my cock is weeping in my pants.

Holy fuck...

Parting my lips over his lower, I suck it into my mouth, gently at first, but when he whimpers, I lose my damn mind. My hands leave his wrists and come up to his face, holding his jaw and his throat, kissing him like I have the slightest idea how, which I don't.

But it doesn't matter because he seems to be crumbling beneath me. My King... *He loves what I'm doing.*

"I do," he whispers into my mouth, grabbing my waist hard enough to startle me, pulling me so close we're practically one body. "*More.* God, give me more more more..."

My tongue slides into his mouth, licking his, tasting him, like scotch and hazelnut. He's my dream flavor. Our lips work on one another, his owning the fuck out of me, even though I'm on top and I started this. He's kissing me back, and it's so sweet, so erotic; leisurely laps and nips and sucks.

I honestly never imagined that my first kiss would be with a boy, let alone a *man.* Let alone the Head Priest of The Principality.

Get out of your head and fucking kiss me harder, Abdiel. Bruise my lips, baby.

"Fuck..." I pant and give him everything I have, tasting his power and dominance and making it my own.

He wants me to overpower him. I can hear his thoughts, and while I never considered myself *dominant*, for him I want to be. I want to ravage him; tear him to pieces and put him back together again.

I want to do to him what Drake has done to both of us.

"My gorgeous, delicious servant." His voice is hoarse with arousal as his hands sink to my lower back. "Can I touch you?"

"Please." My blood is rushing, mainly below my waist. I can feel it throbbing into my cock, hardening fast, until it's trying to snake out of my jeans. "*Please* touch me."

"God, you're so precious," he growls. "So fucking delicious. I could feast on you all day and night and still never be full." His large hands glide down to cup my ass, hard, and I mewl like a kitten.

His stubble burns the flesh around my lips, swimming my head into a frenzy of lust. His mouth is warm and wet, and his little gasps and moans slipping between my lips taste like him; a sweet and fiery flavor, like cinnamon candy.

He breaks our kiss to rasp, "Touch me," squeezing my ass in two large handfuls.

So I do. My hands slink down his chest and abs, slipping inside his shirt. Curious fingers graze the line above his pants, soft skin and the hair of his happy trail disappearing into them. I trace it, feeling him quaver at my touch.

"Abdiel." His tone is almost tortured in his need. "I want so much from you."

"You can have anything, my King," I tell him in between sucking on his lips with fervor.

"You don't know what you're saying, baby." One of his hands slides up my back, fingers combing through my hair, stopping the merciless kisses so that our eyes can connect, deep green meeting topaz. "I don't want to take from you what you wouldn't give up willingly."

"I am giving it." I try to reassure him, though I probably seem just like the horny teenager I am, grinding my aching cock on his crotch, salivating over his delicious mouth and everything I want to do to it. "I'll give you all of me. Any part you want."

His lashes flutter and he groans quietly, giving me access to his neck I've dreamt of biting and sucking purple. I use the opportunity to drag my lips over his jaw, down the slope to his throat, grazing his Adam's apple with my tongue until it moves with his swallow.

"Fuck me…" He pushes me down on his erection by my lower back.

"Is that a request?" I grin, and he peers at me, amusement hard to miss even beneath those lids hooded with fervent desire.

"Have you ever done that?" He lifts a cocky brow, and I can hear in his mind that he knows I haven't.

"Doesn't matter," I rumble. "I know you want it. I can hear you, remember?"

"Of course I want it," he breathes. "But, Abdiel, it's… I need you to be sure."

"I'm sure. I have been for a long time," I tell him with more certainty than words could ever convey. "There's a reason I haven't done it yet."

"Mmm… and what's that, beautiful?" He croons to me, rich and possessive yet so needy, for *me*. I can't believe it.

Moving my lips to his ear, I whisper, "I was… I was waiting for you."

Fuck, he growls loud in his mind and abruptly flips me onto my back, pinning me to the mattress as his lips come for mine. He kisses me fierce, deep, forcefully treasuring. Exactly how I always imagined he would kiss, only better. Because this isn't a dream. It's not a fantasy anymore…

This is *real*. His hands are all over my chest and my waist, tugging at my clothes while his teeth tug my lips, hard enough that I might bleed, but I don't care. Not one bit. I need this.

I need you…

My hands are racked with nervous trembles as they move over his chest, feeling the solid muscles there, curves of his pectorals making me hard, unlike anything I could have imagined. Then down to the stones of his abs, wavering just a moment before I get to where his big dick pushes against his pants.

"You're teasing me, love." The lazy grin in his voice would be audible even if I couldn't feel it on my mouth.

My palm covers his erection and we both groan. "You're so *hard*."

"That's all you." He moves his lips to my neck.

I shudder. "*I* make you this hard?"

"Mhmm… You're addicting, sweet Abdiel."

Mmm… I love the sound of that.

I rub him a little more, feeling him flex into my palm. I can't believe this is happening… I'm finally getting what I've always wanted. I'm finally doing what I've put off for so long because I didn't want it with anyone else.

And my waiting has paid off. This is *euphoric.*

I never want it to stop.

And then there's a knock at the door. It startles me enough that I jump, heart lodging in my throat. But Darian doesn't seem fazed by it.

"Ignore them," he grumbles, sucking my pulse while his hand goes for my erection. My eyes fall closed, then dart back open when the knocking happens again, louder this time.

"Go away," Darian snarls at the door, a chill zipping up my spine and simultaneously zapping me in the balls.

God, he's fucking sexy.

"Sir, it's uh… it's an emergency," Cam's voice stutters from behind the door. "Drake's calling for you. It sounds serious."

Darian pauses and then sighs in defeat, head dropping forward onto my chest. "Motherfucker."

I can't help the grin that hijacks my puffy lips. He lifts, grinning back at me, a sexy little chuckle escaping him as he kisses me once more, this time so soft and sweet I'm swooning all over the place.

"I suppose I must go attend to this…" He sounds endlessly upset about it, and I have no choice but to lean up and kiss away his worry.

"Of course you do. You're a good leader. The best."

He gives me a look, his hand resting over my heart for a beat before he sits up and scoots off of me. He crawls off the bed and tries to compose himself, turning back to me while I sit up, doing the same.

"Will you still be here when I return?" He looks so hopeful.

I'm dying to say yes, but I'm not sure that's wise. What would I do anyway? Sleep in here? Sneak out in the morning like some kind of secret tryst?

That doesn't sound like fun, although I'm sure what could happen when he returns would be.

Darian runs his fingers through his hair. "Wait two minutes after Cam and I go, then you can sneak out the back door. If you wish…"

I feel the hopelessness on my face as I stare up at him. He understands my reservations, and his thoughts are nothing but sympathetic. *So perfect… Such a good man.*

His head shakes as he walks to the door, but I jump up from the bed to stop him just before he can open it. I pull his arm until he spins around, his face etched in uncertainty. I'm feeling it myself. I don't know what to do with these feelings… I'm not sure what to do about *us*.

But that doesn't change how badly I need him, which is what I try to convey with my kiss, my lips caressing his, slowly drawing out hushed pants and sighs. His large hands come up my chest, then my neck, and he holds my jaw, kissing me deeply; such a profound feeling I can't believe I went nineteen years without experiencing it.

I told you… I was waiting for you, my King.

I think I've been waiting for you, too… Prince Abdiel.

CHAPTER FOURTEEN

DRAKE

It's gotten a bit chilly tonight, not entirely peculiar since it isn't technically summer yet. But the sharp breeze is bringing everything into perspective.

Glancing down at the lifeless form on the ground, my vision swims with memories.

When I lift my hands, I see blood on them. But when I blink, it's gone.

I didn't do this… There's no way.

Did I?

Pulling the small pipe out of my back pocket, I light it with the old familiar Zippo I've had for twenty-five years. The American flag on it is all worn out and chipped. I like it.

Sucking smoke into my lungs, I hold it. I hold on to it as long as I can until I physically can't anymore, breathing the rest into the air. Lights twist and dissolve before my eyes, colors and shapes dipping into my vision. The forest is humming, and I kneel next to the body, head tilting, waiting for some answers.

I'll find them, one way or another.

The whirring sound of an ATV engine grows nearer, and my stomach flips. *Darian's almost here.*

I wonder what he'll make of all this as I reach out and poke the body. It's not fully cold yet, despite the drop in temperature. *This happened recently.*

For a moment, just a split second, the man's head turns and his eyes connect with mine. They're all red, possibly popped vessels or

You're the one, he says to my mind, and I flinch. *You've caused this.*

It's the only way.

The ATV pulls up a few feet away and I shake my head, blinking hard as I pocket my pipe. When I reopen my eyes, the man's face is back in the dirt. Where it belongs.

Darian stomps over to me while I stand, then turns over his shoulder to Jasper who drove him here and barks, "Perimeter."

Jasper nods. "Yes, sir." Then he hops back on the ATV, driving off to go converge with the rest of the Tribe and do a perimeter check.

The fact is that we don't know this person. He isn't part of the Regnum, meaning he snuck onto the Expanse. And then got himself killed.

"What do you think?" Darian asks me, out loud for some reason, which I find interesting. As if he doesn't already know what I'm thinking.

"My guess would be... ballsy hiker who decided to go for a mountain outside of the travel guides," I tell him, leaving out a few key points he already knows.

"That's it?" He leers at me, and I shrug.

"What else do you want me to say?" I squint at him. He seems strange right now, and I can't put my finger on it.

"Alright, then. Just take care of it and make sure no one finds out," he grumbles, fidgeting in place.

"I'm sorry." I fold my arms over my chest, facing him. "Did I *disrupt* you with this unexpected dead body on our mountain?"

He glares at me, jaw tightening visibly. "I was busy."

"With what?"

"Is it your business?" He bites, and it's then that I notice his lips... all pink and puffy. His hair looks run-through by fingers, too.

Maybe his own... or maybe someone else's.

My brow lifts as I study the look on his face. He's having trouble making eye contact, and it's obvious he's forcing himself not to think about something... to hide it from me.

"I'm sorry, I'm just..." he breathes, rubbing his jaw with his fingers. "I'm worried. This is the third body this year. Second who isn't one of our own..."

"It's the balance, Darian—"

"I told you to stop with that shit," he barks at me, quietly. "I won't accept that."

"You have no choice," I tell him with certainty. "I've been studying this for years. I think I know a little more than you."

"We get it, Drake. You're a genius," he rumbles, and it makes me smirk. But my gut twists at the flush in his cheeks... It was like that when he got here.

He was with someone tonight.

Was it Abdiel?

Darian's eyes dart to mine, and he gives me a severe look. *Don't.*

"There's something else." I change the subject on an exhale. "Come."

We walk the trail, a path leading to a secret spot between the lab and my cabin. I pull out my walkie. "Lorn. Burn the body."

Lorn radios back the *ten-four* as Darian and I walk in silence. The chill in the air brushes my skin, telling me things.

The forest whispers on this mountain, and using the white trumpets is the only thing that helps me understand what it wants. Darian is in denial about it, but I know the truth.

There's a gateway up here. An opening.

We keep walking for a half-mile to the small shack, and as I open the door for Darian, his eyes turn reprimanding. I sigh and give him a shrug, to which he shakes his head, stepping inside as I close the door behind us.

This hunting shack is really just a decoy. There isn't much inside, extra tools and some farming equipment, but its actual purpose is beneath the false floorboards. I move them aside and take out my keys, opening the trapdoor and motioning for Darian to climb down first. He doesn't look pleased as he descends the steep stone steps into our manmade dungeon, with me right behind.

It's much colder down here, obviously, and I catch Darian tugging his coat tighter around himself as he walks toward the cells. There are only three of them. We've never needed more. Actually, we've only ever used two at a time.

Things work out well for us here on the Expanse, the reasoning two-fold. The surface reason is Darian. He's a dedicated, kind, and diplomatic leader. The people love and respect him. They even idolize him in a sense, so we have few problems with the Regnum breaking any rules of our society.

But beneath all of that *poster for The Principality* shit is the real reason why things work out here, and that's me.

Me and my guys, the Tribe, who work tirelessly to protect this place and these people at all costs, keeping any and all defectors out of public knowledge. I'm a big proponent of what the people don't know won't hurt them. Secrets are a part of life, and I've accumulated quite the collection.

I designed the dungeon a few months into us forming The Principality. I was convinced that at some point we might need to lock someone up, and as much as Darian hated the idea, and has continued to fight me on it for decades, I was right.

Case in point, the worthless sack of shit we're staring at right now, lying in a puddle of his own blood and piss. Darian gives me the side-eye, though it's nothing compared to the angry tone I'm getting from his thoughts.

Where did he come from?

I shrug. *Not sure. But Xander caught him in the Field.*

Darian's face turns to mine. *He was trying to steal the seedlings? They're just babies.*

I know, I chuckle in my mind, shaking my head. *What a moron.*

Darian faces the prisoner once more. *Or maybe he planned to clone them.*

He doesn't strike me as a master grower.

So you think someone sent him? Darian sounds worried. I hate it, and it makes me want to mash this asshole's face with my fist some more until he stops breathing from his thieving lungs.

That's what I'm trying to find out…

"Drake," he sighs, his crystal eyes sparkling at me, lighting up the darkness. "You don't have to."

"See, that's where you're wrong, brother," I say with conviction. "I'm the one."

Darian swallows, the sight of his Adam's apple bobbing giving me some thoughts I immediately push away.

He was with someone tonight… And I don't know how that makes me feel.

"Hey… please… let me out," the prisoner gurgles, crawling up to the bars that separate us. "I'll tell you whatever you want to know, please."

"I know you will," I growl at him, then turn back to Darian. "I'm sorry I interrupted your night."

He gives me a guilty look that cuts me so deep, I immediately storm away from him, leaving the dark, dreary place I created, the piece of shit I'm going to kill later, and my brother… The only person

SERPENT IN WHITE

I would stop at absolutely nothing to protect.

Even if it means damning myself in the process.

"Darian," I whisper in the dark, my breathing ragged and my movements jittery as I shake him where he sleeps. "Get up. We have to go."

"Huh?" His sleepy voice croaks at me as he rolls over in my bed, rubbing his eyes open. They're still red-rimmed from crying himself to sleep.

I stayed in my bed next to him for a while, just watching over him, my protective gaze never once leaving my brother while he sniffled and shuddered. He tried for a while to act hard; unaffected, like a man thinks he should. But we're still only teenagers. He's fifteen... He can only be so sturdy while he's bent and crippled and warped before he eventually cracks.

That's what happened earlier, and I convinced him to sleep in my bed, so I could make sure he was alright and keep him safe. From him, sure, but also from himself. I'm not sure if Darian would ever harm himself, but tonight I saw something in his eyes I'd definitely never seen before.

He looked broken. Guilty when he shouldn't be, torn up when he's the last person on Earth who deserves to hurt this way.

It created a hatred in me so strong, there was no way it could be avoided. So I waited for him to fall asleep. And then I did what I had to do.

And now we have to go.

"You gotta get up." I keep shaking him because he's still half asleep. "I packed a bag for you. We have to go. Now."

"Go where?" He asks, eyes widening more, now appearing beyond worried. He sits up, his shirtless chest catching my attention for a moment.

I blink it away and grab his hoodie off the floor, tossing it at him. "Get dressed. We need to leave. We can't stay here anymore. I won't let you stay here for one more second, Darian."

He gapes at me for a beat in stunned silence before slipping his long arms into the hoodie and zipping it up. "We can't just leave, Drake. What about school? What about—"

"I don't give a fuck about any of that," I bark, keeping my voice down, mainly because it's shaking and I don't want him to know that. "We can't stay, Dar. Let's go. I'm getting you out of here."

"Where would we even go?" Trepidation still lines his tone, though he's getting up now, crawling off the bed to step into his sweatpants.

"I have a few ideas," I tell him, stuffing some remaining items into my backpack before moving the desk aside to locate my cash stash. "But first thing's first... We need to bounce."

Pulling out the little pouch, I open it up and count the bills quickly, doing math in my head.

"Jesus, Drake," Darian huffs. "How much money is that? Where did you get it?"

"It's about eight grand," I grumble in frustration. We definitely need more, but there's nothing I can do about that now. "I've been saving since I was little. Squirreling away." Stealing from the foster dipshits. And others.

"That's awesome!" Darian gasps. "Let's get a hotel! Ooh, maybe one with a pool and a Jacuzzi!"

My face pivots in his direction and the sheer look of excitement on his formerly devastated face is enough to bring all the warmth to my chest.

I smirk and shake my head. "Let's just go. Hurry up. Put your shoes on."

Darian does what I ask without any further question or argument. We clear out our necessities, and I hustle him out of the bedroom as quietly as possible, practically pushing him toward the stairs. His face goes instinctively to their bedroom, but I keep shoving him so he can't look that way.

Once we're downstairs, I grab us as many bottles of water and Gatorade as I can, raiding the cabinets for snacks I can fit into a spare bag.

"What if they find out...?" Darian's nervously shaky voice catches my attention. I turn, finding him practically hugging himself inward, eyes locked on the staircase. "It'll just make it worse..."

"No," I snap at him, and his eyes fling to mine. "Never again, Darian. I told you. Never fucking again. That's why we're leaving,

and that's why we have to do it right now."

He takes a deep breath and nods.

And then we leave. We sneak out the backdoor, cutting in between houses, avoiding the roads. Kara's working the overnight shift, but she'll be home in a couple of hours. Once she gets home, all hell will break loose.

We need to be far away from here by then.

We take the QLine to the bus station, where I buy us tickets to as far as we can get; Denver.

"Denver?" Darian hums while we stand outside, waiting for the next bus, which doesn't leave for another hour. We're cutting it close, but it's shady enough around here that I think we'll be able to get onto the bus with no one being any the wiser. It's a risk, which is why I keep my hood up the entire time, and urge Darian to do the same. "What's in Denver?"

"I don't know." I shrug. "Mountains."

"You and your mountains," he chuckles. It's amazing to see him smiling. He's so damn strong, I can't believe it.

"Maybe we won't stay in Denver, but it's just... nowhere near here. And that's where we need to go. Fucking away from this shithole."

Darian nods, though I can see the pain in his eyes as he angles his chin to the ground. I pull a pack of cigarettes out of my pocket and stick two in my mouth, lighting them both at once, and handing one to him. He doesn't really smoke much, since he's all athletic and shit, but he needs it right now.

He takes it and we smoke in silence for a few minutes. My mind is so busy running through a plan, forcing away the memories of what happened tonight that I almost miss it.

A little sniffle. But it catches my ear, and I tense.

"Hey." I move up to Darian, crowding him so he has to look at me. "Don't worry. It's fine. You're safe now."

He's fucking shivering so hard I can hear his teeth chattering, his hands shaking so bad he drops the cigarette on the ground. He sputters for air, and I toss my cigarette, grabbing him quick. Wrapping my arms around him, I hold him tightly while he breaks the fuck down.

"Darian, breathe," I whisper, my hand cupping the back of his head. "He can't get to you again. I promise. I swear on my life, he'll never hurt you again."

"H-how do you kn-know?" He buries his face in my neck, tears soaking my flesh. *"You can't p-promise that, Drake."*

"Yes… I can." My voice comes out firm; certain. His face lifts, our eyes meeting and sticking together, unable to break the bond no matter how hard I feel like I should look away.

His bottom lip is all pouty, and I can see it quivering, which brings my attention to the fact that I'm watching his mouth now, not his eyes.

I swallow hard as a strange sensation slinks around in the pit of my stomach. I've felt it before when looking at Darian… Seeing him change, or come out of the bathroom in a towel. I always assumed it was discomfort. Because I shouldn't be looking at a guy like that, especially not my foster brother. My best friend.

But now it doesn't feel like a sickness as much as it feels like the cure.

Darian licks his lip. I'm still holding him, molding his strong body to mine, and I don't think we should be doing this… We shouldn't be touching like this.

"Dar, I'm sorry…" I whisper. *"I should let go…"*

"I-I don't…" He doesn't finish his sentence, though I can almost hear him saying, I don't want you to.

But eventually, we pull apart. He goes to the bathroom to fix himself up, then we chain-smoke more cigarettes until the bus comes.

Once on board, we get settled in the back, preparing for our roughly twenty-hour journey. This bus will take us to Kansas City, then we have to transfer, which could be dangerous. Hopefully not.

I refuse to let Darian know I'm worried. I don't need to add any more stress to his plate.

But I'm torn. I don't know if I should tell him what I did, or if I should leave him in the dark. Like plausible deniability.

Darian falls asleep fast while my mind races, his head propped on my shoulder. I take a small throw blanket out of my bag and drape it over him. A guy gives us a look as he walks past to the bathroom shaking his head, and I glare at him, silently warning him to look somewhere else before I end his miserable homophobic existence.

This world is a disgusting place. I barely even want to stay in this country. Maybe we can go somewhere farther, like Norway, or Scotland or some shit. Somewhere better.

My head flops back against the seat. It's futile. This entire planet is bullshit. The amount of damage humanity does is staggering. No animals kill each other more than the human race. I guess I would *know…*

Capitalism and war, famine and pollution, rape and murder, child abuse and sex trafficking.

I don't want to be a part of it anymore. I wish we could go somewhere else entirely. A different planet or universe…

Eventually, I fall asleep, clutching Darian on one side, hand gripping my knife on the other.

Someone must be watching out for us because we get to Denver with no issues.

Unfortunately, though, Darian has slipped into some kind of depression, and I'm desperate to get him out of it. I thought the best idea, the best way to stretch our funds as long as possible would be to get a tent and camp out. It's still pretty chilly, but summer will be here in a couple of months. We can make it. I know we can.

But when I float the idea to Darian, he's sort of unresponsive. We've been in a diner for the past two hours, nursing our sodas while I read a map and figure out the easiest way to get us to the sporting goods store, then to an off-the-grid camping area.

"Dar, I know you miss school and the football team, but trust me when I tell you it has to be like this. At least for now," I mumble at him, watching his face as he zones out.

"It's not that," he grunts, tearing the wrapper from his straw into a million pieces. "I don't care about football. It was just something to help me feel normal."

I gulp. "Being normal is overrated. And stupid." He scoffs. "All the best people are freaks."

A small smile tugs at his lips, but he pushes it away, finally glancing up at me. "You know I actually convinced myself that I liked it? I mean, I think I kind of did…" His voice trails, and he shakes it off. "And the first thing I thought when you told me we were leaving was that I was gonna miss him." He breathes out hard and closes his eyes for a second. "How fuckin pathetic is that?"

"You're not pathetic, Darian. He is," I growl from across the table. "He's a fucking perverted scumbag who manipulated you and

made you feel like it was right. The way you reacted, that wasn't your—"

"Just stop," he cuts me off, rubbing his eyes hard. "Can we get out of here? The smell of greasy food is making me nauseous."

I stare at him for a moment, despondent and unsure of what I could do to help him. I just want to fix him, and I have no idea how.

I suppose first thing's first. "Okay." I nod and signal the waitress for the check.

But then an idea pops up. Checking the map and the tourist guides, I grin to myself.

This is perfect.

We pay and leave the diner, taking a cab to our new destination. One pit stop before the mountain...

When we arrive, Darian's glum face morphs into one more bemused. "What is this?"

We both step out of the cab, and I grin. "The fanciest hotel I could find that would take cash. And yes, they have an indoor pool and a Jacuzzi."

Darian's face lights up, and he turns to purse his lips at me. "I know you're just trying to cheer me up."

"Is it working?" I smirk, and he laughs.

"Yea. Definitely."

We check into our hotel room for the night. It's nothing too extravagant, but certainly nicer than anywhere either of us have ever been. The Jacuzzi is actually in the room. Apparently, all the suites come with one. Only problem is that they only had single rooms available, so we'll be sharing a bed. It shouldn't be a big deal, since we're brothers, but for some reason it's all I can think about for the rest of the afternoon.

That is, until I see how amped Darian is to chill by the pool. We spend all day in there, alternating between driving people crazy doing cannonballs you're not supposed to do, and lounging in the chairs set up around the pool. By the time we come up to the room again, we're all wrinkly. But Darian still wants to use the Jacuzzi.

I opt out, because while it claims to fit four people, it seems a little more intimate than I'm prepared for. Darian goes in and closes the door, and even though I know he's had a great day and has been smiling nonstop, I'm still on edge. I can't stop worrying about him, and eventually, I forgo trying to read and knock on the bathroom door.

SERPENT IN WHITE

"Dar?" I put my ear up to it. "You okay?"

"Yea... I think." His voice sounds small and insecure, which is so unlike him, it only serves to trouble me more.

"Can I come in?" I ask, not wanting to intrude on his alone time, but I can't help feeling like I need to watch over him every second.

"Sure," he grumbles.

Opening the door, I step inside the room, my eyes falling to where he's propped in the Jacuzzi tub. They widen immediately, and I slap my hands over them.

"Jesus, Darian! You're naked!"

He laughs out loud. "Uh, yea. What did you expect, I was gonna wear my boxers in the damn hot tub?"

"What the hell, dude?? I saw your dick," I mumble, fidgeting where I stand because now the image won't leave my brain.

"I didn't ask you to come in," he points out.

"I wanted to make sure you're alright," I admit. "I just want to be here for you."

"You are here for me, Drake," he says, and I peek between my fingers to look at his face. "You're the only one who is. You're all I have..."

Swallowing my emotions, I'm struggling not to feel like a total chick, though I can't help it right now. "You're all I have, too."

We're quiet for a moment, some strange tension building in the air, suffocating me as if the walls of the bathroom are closing in, until he says, "Can you hand me a towel? I would just get out, but apparently, you don't like looking at my dick."

I force a laugh that feels harder to get out than it should and hand him the towel, leaving him alone in the bathroom.

By the time he gets dressed, I've ordered a pizza and picked it up from the lobby. Darian is sitting on the bed in his sweats and t-shirt, chestnut hair damp and tousled around. It has me grinding my jaw for unknown reasons while I serve us up some food. We eat in silence, watching bad TV, and by midnight, he's passed out next to me.

I'm trying to keep as much distance between us as possible, but Darian sleeps sprawled out, taking up the whole damn bed. As I lie flat on my back, I keep my arms at my sides. And despite how loud my thoughts are, I eventually manage to fall into an uneasy sleep.

I wake up stiflingly hot in the dark. The clock across the room reads three-fifteen to my groggy eyes, and when I go to kick the blankets away from me to get some air, I realize it's not a blanket

143

covering me at all.

It's my foster brother.

And not only is he wrapped around me in his sleep, but he's sort of grinding his hips against mine. It takes only another moment for my fuzzy brain to acknowledge the hard shape he's pushing into me, dragging in long, fluid strokes while he breathes out sharp breaths on my chest.

His hand is resting dangerously close to my crotch, my own erection so hard it's visible through my sweats. Gulping down my shame, I look over his face to find his eyes closed, lips parted just a bit. He's clearly sleeping, having a dream about someone else.

I'm sure it has nothing to do with me, but then that idea stabs me in the chest like a sharp blade between my ribs. He could be dreaming about a girl from school... Maybe he has a girlfriend and he just never told me.

Though the more I think about it, the more it dawns on me that Darian has never mentioned a girl to me before, ever. Even when I've remarked on girls we know, or celebrities I wouldn't mind sticking my dick in, he always just laughs along and gives me that admonishing Darian headshake.

My mind is floating around all these things while he pants and writhes into me...

Maybe he's just shy.

Or maybe he likes guys...

A memory comes back, something I never thought about until right now.

From school. I met up with Darian after practice, and I remember the smile he gave one of his teammates. His eyes lingered on the guy as he turned away...

My mouth is suddenly dry as a bone.

Darian's gay.

Not that it matters. I wouldn't judge him either way. Even though I'm straight...

I'm totally straight. Right?

The problem, though, is that my dick is beyond hard right now. It's like a rock.

This could just be a morning wood type situation... But something about that thought doesn't feel right. And now my entire life since puberty is flashing before my eyes.

I developed later than most of the guys we know. I was fourteen when I shot up to almost six feet, and then I still didn't stop until pretty much this year. While everyone else has been thinking and talking about sex for years, for me it only just started.

So maybe I don't know what I like... Maybe I could like guys, too.

In this moment, for sure, the feeling of Darian pressing his hard dick into me is euphoric, in an uncomfortable kind of way.

And then I remember something he started saying earlier, in the diner.

I convinced myself I liked it. I sort of did...

He thought he liked what that asshole did to him... That prick probably justified what he was doing, making Darian think he enjoyed it because his body responded.

Is that what I'm doing now??

No no no. We're not like that. He's my brother and my best friend. I need to stop him. Wake him up before something bad happens.

I try to roll away, but there's no room, and I end up rolling right off the bed. And unfortunately, we're so tangled that Darian comes with me, landing on top of me on the floor.

"Fuck," I grunt, breathlessly because he sort of hit my balls a little with the fall. They're aching something fierce now.

Darian blinks himself awake and looks around. "What the hell happened?? Why are we on the floor?"

"Um, we must have... fallen." I can't help sounding like an idiot. My face is warm as fuck, and it doesn't look good. My cock is still hard, and so is his. They're just resting together like old pals.

Darian notices fast and backs up. And when he does, his erection drags on mine, and it feels so fucking good I can't help the little gasp that flees my lips.

He looks startled, glancing between us at our dicks, then back up to my flushing face. And rather than moving away or looking horrified, he does something completely unexpected.

He does it again.

A pleasure unlike anything I've experienced before, with someone other than my hand, rushes through my loins, and I bite my lip to keep in any more embarrassing sounds. His eyes are twinkling down at me, his lips looking especially full and pouty while his tongue swipes the bottom.

He presses his hips into mine, and this time we both groan, quietly, watching one another without saying a word. My entire body is balmy. Burning hot, in fact. So much so that I'm sweating through my clothes, but I can't stop myself from rutting upward to get more of whatever this incredible friction is.

I never thought another hard dick rubbing mine would feel so good, but it's delicious. I don't want to stop.

That is, until Darian leans forward, and for one brief, terrifying moment I think he might kiss me. And the thing is, even though I know it's probably a bad idea, and it scares the shit out of me, my eyes close, and I await the feeling of those soft lips on mine.

But it doesn't happen. Instead, he nestles his face in my neck and shivers. "I can't... I can't stop thinking about it."

I already know what he's talking about. He doesn't need to elaborate.

My heart, regardless of how black and blue, how diseased it is in my chest, is still breaking for my brother as I wrap my arms around him, holding him tight.

"I'm sorry..." he whispers, and I just squeeze him tighter, silently telling him to shut the fuck up.

No apologies. Ever.

We lie on the floor for hours, until sun peeks through the curtains of our hotel suite, just breathing, my hands brushing his back, combing through his hair. Comforting him, trying desperately to put him back together with the love that asshole stole.

After a while, he whispers, "I read about this lake in a magazine once... in Washington state. It's by a mountain." His voice holds a certain amount of wonder I hope will always be there when he speaks. "It looked like magic." He lifts his face to peek down at me. "We should go there. You can have your mountain, and I can have the lake. We can go there and forget about everything else. We can start a new life."

Gazing up at him, my fingers slip down to his chest, feeling his heart beat calmly beneath them. I count each one, each thump of his pulse until it's time for me to nod.

"Let's go."

CHAPTER FIFTEEN

ABDIEL

Something has been growing inside me.
It started out in my head, like an idea or the beginning of a thought. A small bud, not yet having been exposed to the proper elements to sprout.

But the more time has passed, the further these feelings have taken me, whatever this new sensation is has spread to my heart where it's taken up roots. And now it's almost as if my spirit is in the process of an awakening. That curiosity which used to worry me… there's a reason for it.

There's a reason for everything.

These are my musings during this week's sermon. Darian talks about purpose, each of us finding our true meaning in life and how we can be our best selves for Mother. My eyes are on him the entire time, which isn't unusual, since everyone else's are, too. But when his occasionally find me, sitting next to an ambitious Kinsey, who again keeps trying to hold my hand, there's something shimmering and intense buried within the blue.

He's smart. He makes sure not to let his gaze linger on me. But still, there were one or two little smirks that graced his full lips and sent flutters to my stomach. I had to shift and look away before my cheeks flushed like a smitten little girl.

And then I peeked in Drake's direction, where he sat beside Lauris, as usual. And the look on his face was one much more eagerly ravenous.

Dark and mystifying.

The problem with it all is that I can't hear their thoughts. I can't hear *anyone's*. My Empyrean seems to have worn off, and it's driving me a little crazy. It's like they introduced me to this whole new world, gave me a taste of the most delicious fruit ever, and then ripped it from my mouth mid-chew.

It's frustrating, but I can't be bothered with that right now. I'm too busy trying to get some space between Kinsey and me as I wait for Head Priest to come our way. He's making his rounds, talking to the Regnum after his sermon, and I want to say hello.

It's completely innocent, I swear.

It has nothing to do with the fact that I haven't stopped thinking about the way his lips feel, the way he tastes, the little grunts and gasps that escape him when he's drunk with lust, for *me*.

For two days since our unnecessarily brief romp in the lounge, all I've thought about is what might happen the next time I saw him. I resented working the day shift, the entire time impatiently looking forward to today; his sermon *and* dinner service tonight.

I'm so excited, and anxious, I'm vibrating out of my skin.

Peering left, I see Darian coming my way. Our eyes meet for a moment, and it's incredible how casual he comes off because I'm practically melting into a puddle of angst and hopefulness on the floor, and nothing's even happened yet.

He saunters up to me, an easy curve to his lips I just want to suck like a lollipop.

"Abdiel." His deep voice gives me the shivers, before his eyes dart right and his smile becomes more polite and less secretly rapacious. "Kinsey. Good to see you both."

"Lovely sermon, Head Priest," Kinsey flutters, leaning into my side. I inch away from her again and Darian subtly lifts a brow.

"Very entertaining," I add, then flinch at my poor choice of words.

Darian's grin widens, though he's clearly trying to suppress it. "I'm glad to have *entertained* you." His eyes twinkle right at me, and I feel like we're the only two people on the planet. "I aim for nothing less."

"I loved what you said about resonating in our feelings," Kinsey chirps, breaking the little spell between Darian and me. He looks at her again and nods along while she blathers, "I've always thought having bad feelings was bad. Or like, when I'm upset, I don't want to be, you know? So I wait for it to go away…"

I've completely tuned out what Kinsey is saying, focusing on the slopes of Darian's lips, the slightest crease in the bottom, like a pillow of temptation just waiting to be kissed raw. When he tugs it briefly between his teeth, I snap out of my trance, eyes slinking back to his, where his gaze narrows just enough. I wish I could hear what he's thinking...

Probably admonishing me for staring at his mouth in front of everyone, while Kinsey is rambling on and on to him. *Great, and now I'm blushing.*

"Very insightful, Kinsey," Darian replies when she finally comes up for air. Then he turns back to me. "What did you think about it, Abdiel? Have you been resonating in your feelings?"

The way he's looking at me, it's virtually impossible not to feel like I have a spotlight shining in my face, but not in a bad way. He's just so present, he makes you want to spill your guts to him. Not to mention, he's looking at me like he's remembering the exact cadence of my breaths while he kissed and touched me. The shape of my erection as it grew for him, and no one else.

Well, let's see. Have I been resonating in my feelings?? What feelings, my King...? My pure desperation for another taste of your mouth? My ever-present ache when I think about your strong hands caressing my flesh...?

While I can't hear him, he can certainly still hear me, and my thoughts seem to be making small stress-cracks in his composure. He clears his throat, jaw tensing just a bit, though his eyes are alit with need.

"Yes, Head Priest," I whisper, his eyes dropping to my mouth for one brief moment. "Resonating... a lot."

Darian parts his lips as if to say something, but before he can, a tall, unmistakable form with jet-black hair and swirling eyes steps up to our little group, placing a large hand on Darian's shoulder, hard enough that he flinches.

"Great sermon today, brother," Drake's cool voice slithers beside Darian's ear, and he straightens, the amusement falling from his lips, though he's clearly trying to remain aloof.

Then Drake's eyes move to me, and I swallow hard, remembering that same large hand stroking our cocks together. He quirks a brow in my direction, and I have no choice but to force my gaze to my shoes before I combust where I stand.

"Hello, Abdiel Harmony," Drake speaks calmly, a baritone of erotic sound.

It zips a chill up my spine, and while I'd prefer not to look at him again, I have to be polite and act normal, since Kinsey's here watching this entire interaction go down.

My eyes connect with his for the first time since I left his office that day, dripping in sexual gratification coated with shame, and I murmur, "Hi."

"Lovely to see you again." Drake's eyes skate the length of my body, subtly enough that Kinsey probably doesn't notice. But Darian definitely does.

And there's a moment of sheer wrath in the Head Priest's eyes, which he turns on his brother. Drake simply winks at him, and Darian appears to be seething.

My throat is so dry I can barely swallow. *This is so awkward.*

"Well, we should be heading off." Darian's repose returns as he forces a smile for Kinsey. Then he aims his shimmering gaze on mine once more. "I'll see you at dinner tonight, young servant."

I'm unable to keep the needy smile off my face as I nod, watching Drake's eyes sizzle while they both wander away. And I can finally *breathe* again.

Peeking at Kinsey, I hope she won't remark on the obvious tension.

She simply locks her arm with mine. "The Alchemist... wow. I don't think I've ever heard his voice before. It's uber sexy."

I can do nothing more than chuckle and shake my head as we leave the temple, heading back toward housing.

Yes… it certainly is.

I'm pleased to be able to cook tonight, and not just because I want to impress my crush.

I love cooking. It relaxes me. I know we've established that I live to serve and make people happy, but I also truly enjoy creating things made to nourish my family. Cooking is taking the ingredients, gifts from Mother, and turning them into something exquisite and fully necessary.

In thinking about my future, of course my love of cooking came up first. But there isn't exactly a career to be made of that on the

Expanse. I suppose I could be Head Priest's personal chef, but that's only assuming nothing ever happens again between us, a brutally devastating thought.

And one I don't think will be accurate, since the moment he sets foot into the dining room tonight, his eyes are on me and no one else. As forbidden as it is for us to keep this going, I can't ignore the elation that simmers in my blood at the thought of capturing the most unattainable man of all.

Head Priest of The Principality, Darian King, wants *me*. It's almost unbelievable.

A second round of drinks are poured, salads finished and spirits lively as I bring out the first plate of dinner to Darian. Setting it in front of him, I'm ready to scurry away quick, in an attempt to hide my nerves, but his voice stops me where I stand.

"What do we have tonight?"

When I turn my eyes on his, he's wearing a look of interest, waiting patiently to hear what I'm serving him.

Swallowing to help steady my rapping pulse, I stand up straight. "It's a roast pork loin with blueberry balsamic glaze and um... asparagus." My voice trails under the intensity of his gaze.

"Mmm... sounds delicious." His brow lifts. "And what's this?" He motions to the side I forgot to mention.

"Quinoa." I blink at his beautiful, attentive face. "With raisins and fresh goat cheese."

Darian looks wildly impressed. "And you made all of this, young servant?"

"Yes." I nod, then correct myself. "Yes, sir."

"That's marvelous." He grins, just for me. It lights up the world around me. "I can't wait to taste it."

"Enjoy," I whisper, unable to keep from tugging my lower lip between my teeth.

A slam interrupts my swooning and everyone's eyes dart in the direction of the doorway as Drake saunters in, oozing his usual confident indifference, as if he's not fifteen minutes late and disrupting Head Priest's dinner service. He plops down in his seat, a wide smile forming on his lips, aimed right at me and his brother.

"Drake," Darian croons, amusement written on his face, though his eyes are narrowed rather suspiciously. "I didn't expect you tonight."

"Well, you told me to come by for dinner." He shrugs, still smiling eerily at Head Priest, before his eyes flick right. "Apparently, Gem and Lauris miss me."

"Oh yea, we miss you like a yeast infection," Lauris sneers and Drake bursts out laughing while Gem gasps, throwing her hands over her mouth to hide her giggles.

"It's a lasting impression," Drake sighs, then turns his gaze up to me. "I'll take it." *Wink.*

I look away and hustle out of the room. And he watches me go. I can *feel* his eyes on my back.

Once I'm in the kitchen, I take a moment to breathe before plating Drake's food. I can't help noticing the look Gina's giving me, which I try desperately to ignore while I focus on steadying my hands before I drop something.

Sucking in some more air, I let it out slowly and carry Drake's plate to him. Setting it down in front of him, I linger just enough to hear the conversation without being obvious in my eavesdropping. *If the Empyrean was still working, I could hear them two rooms away.*

"Drake, we saw fire coming from the mountain the other night," Emithel's small, feminine voice breaks through the rest of the dinner noise. "What was it?"

Drake looks at Darian, Darian at Drake. And for a moment they share a telepathic conversation I'm just dying to hear.

I don't know why I'm suddenly desperate to be involved in whatever business these two are attending to. I'm feeling a myriad of new things, for both of them.

The curiosity, yes, that's a given. But also protectiveness, jealousy, a desire to help them if they need it. I'm not sure what I could ever do to help Head Priest and The Alchemist, but I'd love to try... if they would let me.

"It was just a fire." Drake gives Emithel one of his looks. I barely know him at all, but I'm beginning to decode certain looks of his, and this one has a gaslighting vibe.

I have no idea what you're talking about. You must be crazy. That sort of thing.

Emithel glances down at her plate, and Gem reaches out to rub her back.

"Everything is fine, Em," Darian adds, reassuring her, with his words, but mostly his tone and the look in his eyes. She immediately seems to relax beneath his gaze.

Wow, he's good.

"You know, sometimes we have to burn things up there, to keep it from spreading around housing or the crops," Drake says, scooping a bite onto his fork. "It's contained. No worries."

"Oh yea?" Lauris raises her brows in Drake's direction, and he narrows his peculiar serpent-gaze. "What about the gunshots?"

"Excuse me?" He practically hisses at her, dropping his fork.

"Alright," Darian barks, quietly yet commanding enough that everyone immediately goes still. "That's quite enough of this conversation. We've talked about this, Lauris." He aims a darkening gaze at her, which says he's not to be argued with. "The gunshots are training practice for the Tribe. The fires are to get rid of excess debris and animal remains we can't use." He folds his hands on the table and sits back, looking around at the rest of them slowly. "Any more questions?"

Everyone is silent for what feels like minutes, before they all shake their heads and agree, whispering, *no, sir,* like kids who were just scolded by Daddy. It's as fascinating as it is arousing, and I feel like I'm going to burst by the time dinner is over.

Slinking out of the room, I lean up against the wall, my head spinning.

The rest of the meal goes in a much lighter direction, the conversation staying casual as Drake laughs with Darian and teases the girls. He doesn't come around often, but when he does, it's like a very important piece of the equation is set back in. While an often tense presence, one that works to stir people up on occasion, Drake seems comfortable anywhere that Darian is.

As much as Drake isolates himself, living miles away from the rest of us, up on the mountain, keeping his distance from the Regnum other than the Tribe and his chemists, it's still clear he enjoys being with the family. I'm interested in his dynamic with Darian. They appear to have such a deep love for one another... It's hard to comprehend why they wouldn't want to make it more.

I doubt people would really disapprove that much. And even if they did, would it be a big deal? I mean, I can't imagine a world I'd want to live in where people don't approve of who I love, out in the open.

Once everyone's done eating, Darian excuses himself, and Drake stays at the table, though his eyes follow his brother, lingering on the direction he disappeared into. The wives get up and mull about, going to the sitting room for drinks, or upstairs to their rooms. Drake gets up last, and he wanders to the hallway between the dining room, which leads to the rest of the house.

As I'm cleaning up, I can see him watching me from the hall. No one else seems to notice him, or they don't care. But it's very distracting; him just watching me, *staring* with those rippled eyes. The fact that I can't hear what he's thinking stresses me out more and more as I clean, until eventually I can't take it anymore.

When we're finished, about to dig into our own dinner, which is usually my favorite part of the night, I excuse myself to go to the restroom, though I'm really going to find Drake. I wander the corridor, looking into each room, but I can't find him anywhere. I'm about to give up and head back for dinner when I hear a whisper from the study. A *psst* I'm sure is meant for me.

Stepping into the room, I find Drake standing there with a glass of liquor, sipping slowly, eyeing me over the rim.

"Hey there, little mouse," he says on a breath, like he's been expecting me. *Was he watching me looking for him?*

"Hi." I wander farther into the room, making sure to keep my distance. I don't know why I'm still so wary around him, but he makes me crazy nervous, in a very different way from Darian. The silence between us stretches until I decide to speak just to fill it. "I'm glad you came to dinner tonight."

"Are you?" He cocks a brow, swirling the liquor in his glass, around and around and *around*... It's hypnotizing.

Blinking hard, I shake myself out of it. "Yea. It seems everyone was happy to have you join."

He lets out a little scoff, eyes falling away. "It sure seems that way, doesn't it?"

"Well, yea," I reply with sincerity, and they dart back up to mine. "They set a place for you every night."

"I know," he mumbles, almost petulantly.

I squint at him. "Then why don't you show up more?"

His jaw clenches as he sets his glass down, stalking up to me, so fast I back into the wall. "You certainly have a lot of advice to give, little mouse."

He towers over me, leaning in so close I can smell the scotch on his breath, and the rest of him... sweet and sort of musky, like fire and the evergreens that surround us.

"I just call it like I see it." I puff my chest a bit.

I'm not sure where I'm getting any of this confidence, but I think he loves the cat-and-mouse game, and I don't want to play into whatever he's doing, especially if he plans to put me between him and Darian.

I refuse to do that. I won't be a wedge between anyone.

That said, I'm dying to see Darian again tonight, and I'm also stiffening up in my pants from the current closeness of his brother, so who the hell knows what I'm doing anymore.

"Well... you don't call it like you *hear* it, hmm?" He grins, inching over my lips. "You can't hear me right now... And it's driving you *crazy*."

His tongue lashes out to catch my lip, and I shiver, pulling away. The last thing I need is Darian walking in right now, thinking I chose the Serpent and his mind games over my King.

"You could fix that, couldn't you?" I burn him with a fiery glare. He shrugs. "Give me more Empyrean."

He eyes me for a moment, sliding his index finger up my chest, then throat, tipping my chin upward before humming, "Mmm... nah. I'm good."

"You're an asshole," I seethe, jerking away from him again, this time walking away.

"Never claimed I wasn't." He follows behind me. "Where are you going, little mouse? It was just getting fun."

"I'm going to find Darian," I mutter, leaving the study and heading in the lounge's direction to see if he's there. "You just admitted you have nothing for me... Nothing but games."

"I never said I had *nothing* for you," he rasps, and I stop walking, turning over my shoulder. "I suppose you could have more Empyrean..." I face him fully, folding my arms over my chest. "But I can't just give it to you."

I pause for a moment, my confidence wavering. "What would you want for it...?"

He reaches out and wraps his long fingers around my forearm, tugging me closer to him. I have no choice but to go. My body just moves to him, on its own, like an instinct.

He places his hands on my hips, holding me close, almost as if we're slow dancing. My gaze darts around, nervous that someone will see.

"Remember what we were talking about in my office?" He tilts his face down to my ear. "You wanted to give me something... Wanted me to teach you..."

My dick stirs significantly between us. I'm afraid he might feel it.

I wanted him to teach me how to suck dick...

I can't help but whimper, leaning into him. "I can't now."

"And why is that, little mouse?" His breath warms my ear, and my cock jerks again.

I answer him with only one word... "Darian."

Drake pulls back and his eyes become much more severe. There's heat in them, sure, but it's momentarily doused with rage. It sort of scares the shit out of me.

But before I can try to duck away and run for my life, he sucks in a quiet breath, letting it out slowly, a new, much more wicked grin covering his lips. "What if we go see if brother dearest wants to play, too?"

My heart stops. *Seriously, I think I died for a second.*

I'm just staring up at him blankly, half expecting him to laugh it off as a joke. But he doesn't. He's fully serious, I can see it painted on his face.

As hard as my dick is at the idea of being with both of them, I shake my head a little. "I'm not sure he would want that..."

"You think you know what my brother wants more than I do?" He growls in my face, bringing the fear back again.

I'm about to shit myself. This dude is terrifying.

"N-no," I stutter. "I just meant, I'm not sure how... that would work."

"Well, little mouse." He smirks, grabbing me by the arm, hard enough that I might have bruises. "Why don't we go find out, hm?"

I can't even speak because he's dragging me up the hall toward the door to the lounge. He knocks, a quick *tap tap tap* with his pale knuckles, all the while watching me closely, no doubt reading my every thought. And this time, it doesn't feel sexy. I'm on high alert.

My dick is still hard, though. Make no mistake about it... I think the fear is turning me on even more, which is alarming. *I might have some serious problems.*

Darian answers the door, seeing Drake first, raising a curious brow. Until his eyes drop to me. And then he looks partially excited, partially enraged. It's a strange combination, but if anyone could pull it off, it would be him.

"I brought dessert." Drake lets go of my arm and brushes past Darian into the room, making a beeline for the crystal decanter on the desk.

Leaving him, my gaze comes up to Darian, who pulls me into the room, closing and locking the door fast.

"Abdiel," he breathes my name, sounding like he's relieved to see me. It gives my chest some serious burn. "I'm so happy to see you." He shows me a small smile, but it disappears fast, his angry glare bouncing over to Drake quickly. "What, uh... What are you two doing together?"

"We're not doing anything together." My words jump. "I was asking him about Empyrean, and he brought me to you. I mean, I wanted to see you." Pausing to collect my thoughts, my cheeks heat beneath his gaze. "Of course, I've been dying to see you."

Darian's lips curve and part, enough for me to see his tongue touch his top teeth. He leans in closer, cupping my jaw with his strong hand. "Have you been *dying* to see me, young prince?"

I nod slowly, losing all cognizance as his mouth eases over mine. His lips capture my lower, sucking in a gentle kiss that has me going cross-eyed. I purr into his mouth, and he groans back, pressing his tongue in to meet mine. *I missed this...*

I fucking *missed this* so bad I barely even realized how much until right in this moment, with him giving me life through his kiss. Breathing a rebirth into my lungs.

Darian pulls away while I'm still clutching his shirt, clearing his throat and heaving in a breath. When my eyes reopen, I witness him glance over at Drake, who's leaning up against the desk, sipping his drink and glaring at us.

Right now, I don't know that his thoughts would be entirely positive.

"You two are so sweet together," he says, like a gun shooting a fuzzy bullet. I don't know whether to feel wounded or complimented.

Darian moves farther into the room, and I sort of follow him, though not trying to come off as the eager puppy I feel like. "Drake... what kind of nonsense are you trying to pull here? Because whatever it is, I'd prefer if you left Abdiel out of it."

"I'm not pulling anything, your highness." Drake smirks. "The boy wants more Empyrean. I can't just *give* it to him... If I don't do that for you, I certainly won't be doing it for this kid I barely know."

"You knew me enough to put your hand on my dick," I mumble, and when they both turn their fiery glares at me, I press my lips together and glance at my shoes. *Whoops. That just came out.*

"No, actually... the kid has a point." Drake sets down his glass and steps closer to the bed that separates us. "We've all entered into this sort of... web together. Like it or not, the three of us here in this room are the only people on the planet who have used Empyrean. That binds us, you know it does." His eyes are on Darian.

I peek at Darian, and although he looks like he wants to argue it, he concedes, his head doing a brief nod.

"Okay, so then what would you suggest?" Darian sighs. "I can't deny someone's Ecdysis, especially once it's already started."

"Such a diplomatic king." Drake grins, his eyes shimmering at his brother before they snap to me. "Mother has given him to us for his sexual awakening."

"She did?" I burst into their conversation, even though it's about me. I should definitely have a say.

Drake is giving me those eyes, so I turn to Darian, knowing Drake could just be fucking with me. But if Darian agrees, then I know it's legit.

He exhales and nods again. "You told me you were..." His eyes dart to Drake for a moment before he lowers his voice. "*Waiting* for me. I believe it could be a sign from Mother that you wound up here with me." Drake clears his throat, to which Darian rolls his eyes. "With *us*."

I don't know what to think about this. But because my hormones are raging, the first thing out of my mouth is, "So what would we do... together?"

Apparently, that's Drake's cue, and he waltzes over to the bed, taking a seat on the edge. His eyes are on his brother for the most part, but then he peers at me and licks his lip. "Come here, little mouse."

I can't help but give my Head Priest a quick peek before I make a move. He doesn't speak a word, but his eyes seem to say, *go ahead*, though I can't be entirely certain. Which reminds me...

I step over to where Drake is seated, and looking down at him, I ask, "May I have Empyrean first?"

Drake reaches for my hand, linking our fingers gently to give me a hard yank, causing me to stumble forward. The fastest reaction I have is to straddle his hips on the bed, which must be what he wanted because he holds onto my lower back to keep me there.

"Not until after." He takes hold of my jaw, tugging my face to his. "Remember how desperately you wanted to kiss me that day in my office?"

Swallowing a hard lump of guilt, I tilt in Darian's direction. I really don't like the look on his face. He seems hurt, and I need to let him know I always wanted him to be my first kiss. But Drake pulls me back to him.

"I'll tell you when to look at your King," he murmurs. "For now, I asked you a question."

Hesitantly, I nod. "Yes, I remember."

"Well, now I want it," he says with his eyes on my mouth. "You've had your first kiss with my brother, and now I want my taste."

Watching his face, I realize I want it, too. Even if it feels disloyal to Darian, I can't help my attraction to Drake. It's not the same, but it's there; its own beast.

Leaning in closer to his lips, I hear a soft gasp. I feel it dancing over my lips, and it gives me a surge of confidence. Draping my fingers around the nape of his neck, they slide up into his silky black hair, shorter at the sides and longer on top.

"Are you *desperate* for it?" I purr, and he grins, a motion which tastes uncharacteristically sweet.

"I've only ever been desperate for one person," he rumbles, and I notice his eyes go to his brother. But then he takes my face in his hands and kisses me, abruptly and hungrily, yet somehow soft all the same. I groan, to which he croons in my mouth, "You might be the only exception to that fact, little mouse."

Drake kisses so differently than Darian. Harder and wilder, yes, but also, there's a dedication in his kiss. As if he's figuring out the best way to do it, to ensure I'm kissed properly. Licking my lip before offering a small bite, allowing my tongue to graze his first, dipping his head to the opposite direction of mine.

He's a technical kisser, and I can't help how utterly hypnotic it is. My head is spinning.

Leaning back on the bed, he lies down and brings me with him, our kisses dousing the surrounding air with heat. His hand runs gently down my back, voyaging a trail to reach my ass. But he doesn't stop. In fact, his hand slips right inside my pants.

"Alright that's enough," Darian growls, his voice startling me.

I jump, pulling back in guilt, though when I glance down at Drake's face, for once he isn't smirking. He looks turned the fuck on and almost awestruck. *For me...*

"I never agreed to sit back and watch this," Darian snarls from right behind me, the vibration of his jealousy hitting my back. It sends a chill over my skin and blood pumping to my cock.

"I never said you had to *sit back and watch this*." Drake lifts my shirt up. I follow his lead and take it off, tossing it. I can hear Darian hum from behind me, so I lean back, just a bit, until I feel him, strong and urgent, pressing into me.

"My sweet, innocent prince," he whispers in my ear, his fingers gliding around to my front, tracing the lines of my pectoral muscles. "You don't have to do anything you don't want to… you realize that, right?"

"Stop projecting, brother." Drake runs his hands up my abs until their fingers meet in the middle, locking together over me. "You want to play with us both, don't you, little mouse?"

"Yes," the word rushes out. "So badly."

"Good." Drake aims his hooded eyes behind me. "Will you please undress him, your majesty?"

I feel Darian's pause of trepidation, but he gives up with a hum. "With pleasure."

Darian's hands travel down to the waist of my jeans, where he unbuttons and unzips, all the while skimming his lips on the nape of my neck. It feels so good already, I can't focus on anything other than the sensation.

So when Drake tugs me forward and kisses my lips, I'm startled at first. But I sink back into kissing him right away, because it feels phenomenal.

While we kiss, Darian removes my boots, then he tugs my pants off, with my boxers, until I'm stark naked lying on top of The Alchemist with his tongue in my mouth.

I'm insecure as hell, even though I'm comfortable with my body. I'm a humble guy, but I know my body looks good, and I like liking that fact. But still, right now, with both of them fully dressed and me fully naked, I feel a flush of humility creeping all over me.

"Abdiel," Darian breathes in my ear, kneeling with his crotch on my ass, hovering over me on the bed so that I'm sandwiched between him and Drake, "You have a beautiful body." He nips my earlobe until I gasp in Drake's mouth. "Absolutely perfectly *delicious*."

"Do you want us to get undressed with you, little mouse?" Drake whispers in between kisses, almost as if he physically can't stop for one second. It's mesmerizing, especially after the rejection I felt in his office when he wouldn't kiss me.

"God, yes." I shiver when Darian's lips trail my shoulders, dropping kisses all over my bare back.

Drake looks behind me again, which means he's looking at Darian.

I feel Darian removing his shirt, then his pants, and turn over my shoulder to watch, impatient because I need to see this. I've yet to get a close-up look at his dick and it haunts my dreams. In a good way.

Darian chuckles. "Eager, my prince?" I nod, overzealously. "Then you do it."

Crawling off Drake, I turn, sitting with my ass between his parted thighs while I finish unzipping Darian's pants, pushing them, with his boxers, down over his impressive length.

Seriously, seeing it up close and personal like this is a completely different story. It's *massive*. Probably the same length as Drake's, though certainly thicker, with a fat, shiny head like a crown of flesh I want nothing more than to lick and lick while he whimpers my name.

"Fuck, Abdiel..." Darian reaches for my hair. "You are *killing* me with your thoughts..."

"Uh, yea," Drake rasps from behind me, tugging off his own shirt. "Me, too. My dick is going to break, it's smashing so hard in these pants."

I turn over my shoulder to Drake. "Then take him out so we can play."

Drake's eyes light up as he looks at Darian. And they both say, "You created a monster," at the same time, which makes me laugh.

Drake shimmies out from under me and removes his pants while I gaze up at Darian, standing before me like the King he is. He slopes down to grab my face, kissing me slow and sweet. Feeling Drake behind me, his erection pressing into my lower back, I purr into Darian's mouth.

This is insane. Up until a couple weeks ago, I never even thought I was interested in men sexually. And now I'm with two of them, at the same time. And I'm nervous about what this could mean, yet my excitement is raw and fierce. I want desperately whatever pleasure the three of us can make together.

"You're not taking his virginity," Darian growls in my mouth, breaking our kiss to glare at his brother over my shoulder.

"Calm down, King." Drake reaches around me to hold Darian's face. "I can't be anyone's first... again." I witness Darian swallowing. "That said, he's a virgin. He won't know his preferred position until he tries them all."

Electricity ripples through me. From what I saw when I spied that day, I know Darian loves to be fucked. That much is clear. And I would really love to be the one fucking him.

But then... *would I want to be fucked by Drake? What would that be like?*

"Abdiel," Drake rumbles. "We need to focus, or I won't be able to help what I do to you."

"Sorry..." I whisper, liking the sound of that more than I probably should.

"Drake..." Darian calls softly, "His cock looks so damn mouthwatering." Glancing up at him, I realize his eyes are stuck on my dick, and he's practically drooling.

Drake presses his lips to my ear. "Would you like to try our King's mouth? He has a God-given talent for sucking dick, and that's definitely not an insult."

I'm quaking, my heart hammering in my chest as Darian falls to his knees, pushing my thighs apart. "B-but... I want to try next."

Drake licks the shell of my ear while our Head Priest runs his hands up my thighs, possessively, eyeing my cock like he's about to devour it. "Mmm... little mouse, I want to stuff both of our juicy cocks in your throat at once."

"Fuck..." My head drops back to lean on Drake while Darian bows to me, swirling his warm, wet tongue over the tip of my dick. "*Fuuuck...*" I whine, my erection pulsing between Darian's parted lips.

"God, you taste so good, my prince," Darian breathes, sucking again until my toes curl. "I need more of that delicious cum, baby."

"I'm not gonna last..." I whimper, and Drake chuckles in my ear, holding me close to him from behind, cupping my pecs and circling my nipples with his fingers.

"No, you won't." He grinds his erection even harder into my back. "I told you, he's good. Even when trying to hold out, he gets me off in like five minutes. Been practicing on me for years..."

"Fuck you, Serpent," Darian huffs in between licking lines up and down my erection.

Drake snickers again while Darian sinks his plush lips over my cock, taking me slow and deep until my crown hits the back of his throat. He doesn't even gag.

"Lord have mercy," I whisper uncontrollably, reaching behind me to grab Drake's dick, because I have to do *something*.

"Mmm... You are a needy thing." Drake thrusts into my fist. But then he backs away, leaving me going out of my mind from the feeling of Head Priest's mouth on my cock. "Let us worship you first, little mouse."

He moves around to my side and tugs my face to his, sewing deep passion with his kiss while Darian's cheeks hollow and he sucks me good. I can't get over the feeling. It's unlike anything I could have dreamt up; his warm tongue cradling the underside of my cock while his mouth fucks me, taking me so deep my balls tap on his chin.

I know I've been blessed. My dick isn't short by any means, yet Darian is throating it like it's no big deal. It's miraculous.

At the same time, Drake moves his kisses down my jaw and neck, hands caressing everywhere while his soft lips find my nipple. He sucks it between them, and I jerk, my cock flinching in Darian's mouth until he groans. The vibration feels fantastic. Drake flicks my nipple with his tongue, now pebbled and wet with his saliva, then nips it, causing my hips to buck, surging my dick deeper.

"Throat that big virgin cock, Dar," Drake snarls in that wickedly erotic tone of his, trailing his lips over to my other nipple. Darian moans on my dick again, and my eyes roll back in my skull out of pure euphoria.

These two are like sex machines. I'm so close to coming already...

Drake worships my nipples, licking all over my chest, tracing the curves of muscle with his tongue, sucking and biting everywhere until my flesh is damp with sweat, my eyelids wanting to droop, though I force them open. I can't miss the sight of Darian's sumptuous mane of hair, head bobbing between my legs while he sucks me silly.

Drake moves his mouth lower, kissing down my abs, nipping the V-shaped muscles in my pelvis, slithering until he's on his knees next to his brother.

Darian pops off my dick and turns his eyes on Drake, the sparkling crystal beneath lazy lids drunk with lust. Drake moves in slowly, pressing his lips to his brother's, kissing slow, gentle. It's such a sexy thing to watch, the two of them with all their history, kissing sensually with my erection standing up right by their faces. I can't help but hold both of their heads, one in each palm while they make out, panting and practically climbing on each other.

When they pull apart, my dick is leaking, hungry for either of them, or both. They gaze at each other for a moment before turning their fiery eyes on my erection. And then they move in, simultaneously, mirroring one another as their lips lower to my cock. Their tongues swirl on the head, coming together, lapping it like candy while my eyes fall shut.

"*Fuck...* oh my *God...*" I'm shaking. My balls are already drawn up so tight I could erupt in their faces at any second.

"I think he likes it," Drake growls, and Darian nods, their eyes staying together while they lick and lick and lick, coming in to suck my head at the same time, practically kissing with my dick in the middle.

It's unbelievable. There's no way this is my first time getting a blowjob... with these two manifested fantasies. I must have died and gone to heaven.

They keep going, keep sucking me, together and then separate. Darian will take me deep in his throat while Drake licks lines around the base, and then Drake will suck me into his mouth while Darian kisses my balls.

I'm shivering as my climax approaches, gasps and pants bursting from my lips while my head spins.

"Come for us, Abdiel," Drake commands. I watch closely as they jerk each other off while sucking me, Darian's fist around Drake's erection and Drake's palm cradling Darian's. "We want to taste you."

"Come in my mouth, sweet prince," Darian releases a hoarse command, then slides down to suck me vigorously while Drake drops his face into his brother's lap, sucking Darian until he cries on my cock.

It's the hottest thing I could ever imagine, and it immediately sets me off. My orgasm flows into Darian's throat, and Drake comes up to catch the tail end, Darian forcing himself away so Drake can suck out the rest, which he does. It physically feels like he's *pulling* the cum out of my cock.

I'm trying to keep my voice down, but it's hard when I'm experiencing a pleasure unrivaled by anything I could have dreamt up. My moans revolve between the walls, breathlessly singing praises for them both while my chest flutters, not enough air in the room.

"Mmm... delicious." Drake pulls Darian to his lips, and they kiss with my cum in their mouths while I gasp for air.

I'm all fuzzy, sweat-kissed skin buzzing and lips quivering as they crawl back up onto the bed next to me. They each hold me on one side, kissing my neck and jaw and shoulders all over.

"How was that, my precious prince?" Darian pulls my lips to his, kissing me sweetly while Drake sucks on my pulse.

"I never... I can't... *fuck...*" I croak, and they both chuckle.

"Sounds like he had fun," Drake rumbles.

And everything about them, their deep voices, their hot bodies and beautiful features, their similarities and differences and just how fucking amazing it feels, this apparent sexual awakening, gives me a second wind.

I sit up and run my hand down to Darian's erection, reaching my other hand out for Drake's. "I want to try. Please... You said I could."

They share a look. But I'm too impatient, and I want so much. I feel like I could do this all night, and all day. Forever.

I want so much more.

"Prince Abdiel." Darian runs his fingers through my hair. "You want to make me and my brother come?"

"Yes." I nod. "I want to try... sucking dick." My face flushes crimson. I can't believe I'm saying these words.

But apparently, they like it because they both groan, Darian shuddering with his hands all over me, Drake with his own erection in his fist.

Darian slants his head toward Drake. "Lean over his lap and take his dick in your mouth."

I do as he says, no hesitation, moving my mouth to Drake's long cock, pale pink with a blushed round tip. It's very pretty. I like looking at it, and so I press a kiss on the head. Drake shivers.

"*Yes*, little mouse..." he grunts, holding my jaw. "You like to tease with those pouty lips, don't you?"

Peeking up at him, I keep our eyes connected while I suck on the head, tasting the salt of his arousal. I really love it, and it fuels me to take more, sliding my mouth over his inches, the way they did to me.

I feel like a wanton sex creature, and it's driving me wild; having these two much older men enjoy me like this...

Because deep down, in my most honest place, I feel kind of like a slut, and I like it.

Maybe because I know I'm not. But acting like one in this moment, in the privacy of this room, gives me the most thrilling sense of power. *They're mine. Both of them, even if only in secret.*

Sucking harder on Drake's big cock, I take it slow, trying to go as steadily as I can with him lurching into the back of my throat. It taps, and I gag a little, but Drake seems to like it because his eyes close and he groans. Darian rubs my ass and thighs, grinding his length into me, the feeling of which sets me ablaze.

My watering eyes stay on Drake's while I suck him, deeper still, struggling to breathe in between gobbling him as best I can. The look he's giving me is enough to fill my erection once more, thickening it between my legs. Writhing into the bed while I bob, I gaze up at his snake eyes, filled with flames of need, strands of dark hair hanging in his face while he bites his lip.

"Take him before I fucking come down his throat," Drake growls to his brother, pulling away from my desperate suction.

Blinking up at him, he turns me around to face Darian. My breathing is heavy, pulse thudding so hard I can hear blood rushing in my ears. I'm barely even aware of what's happening, I'm frenzied with lust. High on it.

"Hi, beautiful prince." Darian trails his fingers along my jaw, kissing my lower lip softly before pushing my face down. "Give me those sweet lips. Please, baby."

"Darian," I whimper, kissing down the cut-up lines of his abs and his *V* before latching onto the fat head of his cock.

"Oh my *God...* his mouth is perfect," Darian groans, fingers threading in my hair.

"Right?" Drake's voice is hoarse as he bends over my back, pressing kisses down my spine.

Wasting no time taking Darian into my mouth, I suck hard, hollowing my cheeks and giving him everything I have. Treasuring his cock, going slow and doing him sensually because I just love it so much.

I've dreamt about this, and I want to make him feel every ounce of pleasure he deserves.

My eyes stay on his, as they did with Drake, and he bites his lip, guiding my mouth with his hand in my hair, gently tugging with enough pain to throb my erection. My jaw is sore from his thickness, saliva dribbling from my mouth because I don't have time to swallow. But it works well like this.

I'm amazed at how fast this is coming to me. I'm just doing what they did to me, or at least trying, and as hard as it is to stay focused, I love watching them come apart for me.

Darian is crumbling; my King. The Head Priest is falling the fuck apart because of *my* mouth.

Since I can't tell him the dirty things I want to, because my mouth is occupied, I tell him in my mind, knowing he'll hear. *I want to drink your cum, my King. I want to make you feel so good... I want to suck on your big cock all day every day... Please, Darian. Come in my mouth.*

"Abdiel… fuck fuck *fuck*… You're driving me insane." His lashes flutter, eyes falling shut.

"The virgin's thoughts are crazier than mine," Drake purrs from behind me, and it occurs to me that I can feel his warm breath on my ass.

I pause for a moment, with his lips on my cheeks, pressing gentle kisses all over my flesh. Then he takes my ass in his hands and spreads me open.

My eyes widen as I gape up at Darian with his cock nudging the back of my throat. He lets out a soft, sexy chuckle, hand gripping my neck.

"You wanna feel something really nice, Prince Gorgeous?" His eyes flit from mine to his brother, whose mouth is now *in* my ass.

Dead serious. Drake's lips are sneaking into my crack. And then I feel a long swipe of his tongue… over my asshole.

Groaning out loud on Darian's cock, my eyes droop while I try to focus on sucking, but it's such a foreign feeling. It tickles, but like… in a *very* good way.

"Sweet sweet virgin ass," Drake mumbles into me from behind, licking and sucking my hole, pushing his tongue in. *God, his tongue is so long…* "Relax your muscles so I can stick it all in, little mouse."

I try to relax, slurping on Darian's thickness while a tongue slides into my ass.

"Ummff…" I slump forward, unable to hold myself up anymore. But Darian keeps me in place, thrusting his cock in and out of my lips, alternating between watching me and what his brother is doing.

Drake's tongue feathers again and again, sliding down to the space in between my ass and balls, really just eating me alive until more cum leaks from my cock onto the bed.

I'm swept up into a cloud of the naughtiest, filthiest pleasure I could ever imagine. I can barely feel anything but mischievous needy greediness; a yearning that turns me into a sexual plaything.

Wrapping my fist around Darian's balls, I tug on them while he fucks my mouth, and Drake eats my ass.

"I'm gonna come, my prince," Darian gasps, our eyes meeting while he keeps himself deep in my throat. "Swallow my cum, *please*, baby…"

I nod, preparing to take his load in my mouth. And when he snaps, he groans the sexiest noise I've ever heard, stroking my face while his huge dick pulses out salty liquid. There's a lot. It fills my mouth, and

167

I swallow and swallow, sucking him at the same time to get as much as possible.

Because he's my King, and this is how I bow to him.

While Darian is coming in my mouth, purring my name over and over, Drake is plunging his tongue into my asshole, while jerking himself off. I can hear it, *feel* it.

"Abdiel," Darian breathes, lifting me off his cock and shifting me. "It's Drake's turn."

"Yes... please." My voice is gone, raspy as hell, but it doesn't matter. I spin back to face Drake, angling over him to take his dick in my mouth again.

I suck him gently while he pushes up to me, thrusting and thrusting, only a few times before he grunts, "Fuck, shit... I'm coming. Drink me down, baby."

More cum bursts into my mouth, and I swallow it. It's a lot and some spills over my lip. But I keep sucking for him, taking it all.

And somehow, without anything else touching my cock, I have another orgasm. Groaning on Drake's dick, cum shoots out onto the bed, all over my abs.

By the time Drake pulls me off him, I have no idea where I am anymore. I could be on another planet for all I know; somewhere far from here, cruising the solar system.

My mind is a blizzard of static. I can't feel my limbs. I feel nothing but endless peace.

I've been used up like a slutty little servant. Like a sexy toy, made to get my masters off. And I've never been happier, never felt more complete in all my existence.

When I come to, all the lights are out in the lounge and I'm lying in the big bed, beneath the softest comforter I've ever felt. My eyelids flutter, and I nuzzle into some warm skin which smells fantastic. I know right away that it's Darian. His skin is so soft, covering hard muscles where my head rests on his wide chest, moving up and down with calm breaths.

I lift my face to find him asleep. Shifting, I turn, looking around for Drake. I spot him across the room, dressed and smoking what appears to be a rolled joint. I blink at him, and he just stares, watching us in the studious way he does with those snake eyes.

"You should come to bed," I speak quietly, knowing it's not really my place to request such a thing.

But we've gone through something together, the three of us. I don't like the idea of him just leaving…

He's quiet for a moment, his eyes momentarily severe, though he blinks slowly and exhales, visibly dropping his shield, just enough. "I don't think I can…"

"Of course, you can," I tell him. "I would like for you to be here. And I know he would," I refer to Darian.

Drake puts the joint out by squeezing it between his fingers. I gape at him as he wanders over to the bed, relief swimming through me at the idea that he might come to sleep with us. It's such an interesting notion…

I want to be with Darian. Now that we've been through what we have, I can admit to myself that I've been in love with him for a while. But after tonight, I don't think we would ever make sense without Drake. And that's a problem.

Because Drake seems to be the most emotionally distant person ever.

I know Darian is madly in love with him. Being with them together like this, seeing them together that night I watched… It's clear. It will never go away. And I have my own feelings for Drake, separate from what I feel for Darian.

It's complex and confusing, and I'm instantly wondering what the hell I've gotten myself into.

Drake sits on the edge of the bed and removes a vial from his pocket. Gulping, I realize what's happening as he reaches into the drawer of the nightstand, pulling out a packaged syringe.

He's giving me Empyrean. Because I asked for it…

He thinks this is all he's good for? Like a drug pusher?

"I don't need it," I assure him. "I would rather you just stay."

He narrows his gaze at me. "That doesn't even make sense."

"Yes, it does," I argue. "This isn't all you are, Drake."

He blinks, then purses his lips, opening up the needle, sticking it into the vial. He goes through the process, this time squeezing my bicep himself with his left hand while his right injects me.

All the breath leaves my lungs while the drugs enter my veins. And once he lets go of my arm, I'm seeing things much differently.

Drake is Empyrean… whether he wants to be or not.

CHAPTER SIXTEEN

DARIAN

When I blink myself awake, I feel like I've been asleep for three years.

My body is in slow motion, head all fuzzed over, warmth surrounding me like a bubble of protection from everything negative there is or ever was.

Seriously, I don't think I've ever slept as well as I did last night. And when I tilt my chin, I realize why.

Abdiel Harmony… My nineteen-year-old Domestic, is curled around me, head resting comfortably on my chest, dirty blonde curls tousled all over the place while his eyelids flutter. Watching him closely, everything from last night comes back to me, and I instinctively look around, as if expecting to find Drake on my other side… where he should be.

But that thought is ridiculous. Drake hasn't slept with me in twenty years, since before everything…

Pushing away the memories, I focus on Abdiel, resting peacefully. He must have knocked out too, exhausted and sated from what we did. What we most certainly were not *supposed* to do, though it felt as easy as breathing.

His breaths are tickling my flesh. Actually, I think he's drooling a little, which makes me smile. And in this moment, gazing over the lines of his face, his long lashes, the pointed slope of his nose, his pillowed lips and carved jawline, leading down to his naked frame of all slim, cut-up muscles, soft skin and occasional scattered ink, I can think of nothing other than how purely *beautiful* he is.

Inside and out, yes, but he just looks like he was made to be my

Prince. A prince I never thought I could have…

I've spent so many years chasing Drake, while simultaneously pushing away my wives, dodging the expectations of the Regnum, that I seem to have forgotten what happiness is. In hiding myself, I think I forgot how it feels to be in love…

I know it's crazy to consider being in love with Abdiel already. But I *have* known him for nineteen years. I've always loved him as a part of my family, but now I'm seeing him for who he's become. A gorgeous specimen of a man; a curious being with lust in his eyes and devotion in his fingertips.

Abdiel wants me, I know he does. He probably wants Drake, too. I know I do.

This whole thing is immensely complicated, but I can't deny how badly I'm dying to see where it goes.

Abdiel shifts on me, bringing my attention to his thigh draped over my legs, morning erection brushing my own. It prompts a hum from within my chest, which has his eyes fluttering open. He glances up at me, then closes them once more, a contented smile covering his puffy lips.

He stretches out, like a kitten who just awoke from a particularly grueling nap, and I discover a need inside myself, another thing I never really knew I could experience…

I want him like this all the time. I *need* to keep him, take care of him; to cherish him.

I need more nights with him, burning through the sheets, and more mornings with him gazing up at me like he is right now. Flushed and starry-eyed.

Mine. My Prince.

Abdiel's throat moves as he swallows, blinking his sleep-eyes awake, hand resting on my abs, fingers tracing the lines.

"Good morning," he whispers, sounding uncertain, in his voice and his head. He heard what I was thinking…

"Good morning, my sweet Prince." I sift my fingers gently through his mussed hair. "You've slept well?"

He nods, timid thoughts racing in his mind. "Yes, sir."

I huff, a grin pulling at my mouth as I cup his jaw. "Abdiel, I think we're past the point of coy, are we not? I've had your dick in my throat. You can call me by my name."

He lets out a little whimper of a noise that registers in my groin, and it clearly does the same to him because his dick flinches against my own.

God, that feels divine.

Doesn't it? My thumb grazes his lower lip.

Last night was... the best night of my life, Abdiel's thoughts are loud regarding last night. He can't believe it, and yet he has to. Because he would sooner die than find out it was all a dream.

"It was very much a reality, baby." My hand slides down his throat, tracing his chest and shoulders because I physically can't stop touching him. "When did Drake give you more Empyrean?"

He breaks our gaze for just a moment, looking down at my chest while he remembers Drake leaving last night. In his thoughts, he's feeling rejected. And I need to put a stop to it.

"Don't be upset, my prince." I tug his eyes back to mine by his chin. "This is what Drake does. He cares, I know it for a fact, but he can't make himself stay. He thinks it's his own curse..."

"I heard it last night," he agrees. "He thinks his only purpose is to give you Empyrean. That's fucked up."

I have to smirk at his candor. I love that he's finally warming up around me. I want him to be himself. "It is, baby. I know it hurts at first, but trust me when I tell you I've been dealing with this for a long time. It has to be this way."

Abdiel doesn't seem to agree with this part, but he won't voice it out loud. Not that it matters, but if he wants to keep his thoughts to himself on this, who am I to stop him? After all, I know better.

Drake and I have been fucking since we were teenagers, and I've been in love with him the whole time. I'd like to think he's felt the same, but I can never be sure. He's a pro at talking himself out of things, and for whatever reason, he believes he isn't worthy of love.

Once we formed The Principality, it became even more of a problem for us to be together. The Regnum would never understand. It would hurt our credibility and only serve to make people feel cheated.

This is the conversation we've been having for almost twenty-five years. It will never change.

Thankfully, Abdiel decides to change the subject. "I'm still a little stunned that I'm here with you right now..." He squirms into me, long cock grazing my own in the perfect way, his balls resting on top of mine. I mean, *God... I want to wake up with him like this all the time.*

"I know it's complicated," I tell him, rolling to face him better. "But last night was the best night of my life too, my prince."

He places his hand flat on my chest, feeling my heart thud beneath his palm. "Will you tell me about your wives...? What's going on there?"

There's so much curiosity in his mossy green eyes; so much desire for the truth, but not just because he's inquisitive. He wants to listen to me and see if he can help. It's a wondrous thought to hear in his head.

"It was a marriage of convenience that has become incredibly inconvenient," I admit, gliding a hand down his back. "For many years, I was a bachelor, and it was fine. And then eventually people in the high seats began to ask questions. They wanted to plan for the future, and they wanted insurance that The Principality would be given to someone when I pass on. Of course, I don't plan on dying until I'm old, but that's not any of our decisions to make."

Abdiel shudders, and I narrow my gaze at him. "I don't want to think about it... What life would look like without you." He shakes his head, putting an adorably stubborn foot down. "No."

A laugh creeps from within my throat. "You're probably the cutest thing that's ever happened to me."

A flush graces his cheeks, and I can't fucking stop myself from pulling his lips to mine. We both hum out the satisfaction from such a slow, simple kiss that somehow has our cocks thickening up even more together.

I pull away and clear my throat. "So that was how the marriages happened. I thought I could do it... I really thought I could just fake it, long enough to make a baby and shut everyone up. But the more I thought about it, the worse it felt inside." Abdiel shows me sympathy in those evergreen eyes. "I'm not attracted to women." I shrug. "I'm just not, and furthermore, I don't even think I want kids. It seems like such an abstract concept in my mind. A baby that I'm made to look after and take care of? I can't even picture it."

I sort of can... His mind tells me, though he doesn't speak it. I give him a pointed look, and he grins.

"But regardless, now I'm in it," I sigh, flopping my head onto the pillow. "And I'm not sure how I can get out."

"I'm sure people would understand." His voice rumbles, low and sexy, even when we're talking about serious matters it's the hottest damn sound I've ever heard. I think I could get off just listening to him talk. He smirks and swats my chest. "I'm trying to be serious. Stop thinking about my hot voice."

I laugh out loud. "Sorry not sorry. It's like sex for my ears. Will you sing to me, please... Abdiel *Harmony*?" I lean in to place a gentle kiss on his jaw, trailing my lips down his neck.

He trembles, but determined to fight it, keeps talking. "I was *saying*, I think you should tell people the truth. What's the worst that could happen? They might be a little shocked at first, but people adapt. They'll get over it, and I'm not just saying this because now I'm personally invested."

I chuckle while licking and sucking his pulse. "Are you, my prince? Invested?"

He nods. "I don't want you to have to hide. Especially... where I'm concerned. Or Drake." I pause my slow seduction of his neck region and glance up at him. His thoughts go a bit jittery with insecurity and his mouth starts to run. "Not that I'm pushing for anything serious... Or that I want you to tell people about us. I'm fine with whatever, I just think, you know, it would be best for you to—"

I stop his rambling with a kiss, a soft one meant to let him know how special he is to me already. I know we just started whatever this is, but I think he could really be something to me. And I think I could be something to him...

"Why do you think I've been calling you my prince, Abdiel?" I whisper over his mouth, eyes opening gradually to watch his lips quiver. "I told you last night, it's no coincidence that you're here with me. Nothing happens by accident."

"So then," he starts, opening his eyes to pin me with a firm look, "All the more reason for you to be honest with the Regnum. If that's really what you want..." He swallows visibly. "This."

I can't stop the doubt slinking around inside me. I don't want it to be there, but it is. For all the successes we share in The Principality, half the time I still feel like that same lost boy... struggling to find himself in the woods.

"They'll be disappointed, Abdiel. I've wasted so much of so many people's time." My jaw clenches. His fingers comb through my hair, and I let my eyelids fall for a moment, savoring the feeling of someone being here for me.

I hadn't noticed how much I've needed this. I lost it a while ago with Drake, and I've been letting it devastate me for so long. Because outside of him, I have no one. No one who knows the real me, who can help carry this burden.

I would love to help, my King.

SERPENT IN WHITE

My eyes fling open, locking on his irises of endless green. *You are a true blessing, my beautiful prince.*

I lean in to kiss him again, but he pulls away. "Can I freshen up?"

I can't help but grin. "Bathroom's over there." I nod my head in its direction, and Abdiel plants a quick peck on my chin before scrambling out of bed. Chuckling, I roll onto my back, watching him strut, naked and unashamed, toward the bathroom. His innocence is something I truly adore, but I can't ignore how amazing it is to watch his confidence grow.

He goes into the bathroom and closes the door. Then after about a minute, he reemerges, peeking at me from across the room. "Toothbrush?"

Biting my lip, I scoot out of bed, striding toward him, loving the appreciation in his eyes as he watches me. In the bathroom, I pull out a spare toothbrush from the vanity, handing it to him with a wink. He looks excited as I pick up my own toothbrush, squeezing on some toothpaste before handing the tube to him to do the same.

We brush side by side, stealing glances at one another every few seconds like we're doing a sort of erotic dance, or some version of foreplay. Really, I just like that I can hear him, and he can hear me. It feels like with Drake, only easier, which is what I've always dreamt of having. A *relationship*.

Someone to love… openly.

I spit and rinse, shifting to face Abdiel while leaning up on the counter. "You wanted to brush your teeth so we can make out, didn't you?"

He does the same, facing me and crossing his arms over his chest. We're both still fully naked, and I love it all too much. His body is perfection.

"What would make you think that?"

"Um, your thoughts, young prince." I grab him by the waist, pulling him in closer, our dicks touching as we both shiver. "You're new to Empyrean, so you're practically screaming at me."

He laughs, palms on my chest. "I'm sorry… how else am I supposed to think?"

"I'm not complaining. I like it." My mouth inches over his. "I like hearing how badly you want me."

"Mmm… I do want you. So bad." His minty breath warms my lips.

"The feeling is mutual, baby."

I kiss him harder this time, pushing my tongue into his mouth while his twirls around mine and we suck at each other like ravenous animals. I lift him up onto the counter and wedge myself between his legs, nearly dying over those blushed cheeks and the little gasps that flee him when he's turned on and needy, for *me*.

With my hands drifting down his abs, then his pelvis, I slowly cherish the feel of his hard planes and soft skin, reaching his erection, full and thick, stretching up to his navel.

"I thought…" he whimpers in between us mauling each other. "Last night, I thought we would…"

"Fuck?" I growl into his mouth, and he purrs, his dick jumping in my hand. My fist moves up and down it in leisurely strokes, yanking him closer to me so I can push my hips forward and jerk our cocks together.

"Yes…" He mewls, strong hands gripping my shoulders, caressing the flesh of my chest and my back… down to my ass. "I want to fuck you." This time I whimper. "Or I want you to fuck me, whatever you want. I don't even care, I just need it."

"I *love* getting fucked, Abdiel," I tell him, and he groans, head falling forward to rest on my shoulder while I grind us together like it's my job. "Having a cock deep inside me is unlike anything I've ever experienced, and I *desperately* want yours." I pull his face back to mine so I can look into his eyes. "I want you inside me, my prince."

Abdiel becomes frantic, kissing me wild, hands everywhere, breathing unsteady. Pulling off my mouth, he pleads, "Let's do it now."

I chuckle, swooning over his ardor. "It should be special, baby. It's your virginity. And plus, I'm sure you'll want to try getting fucked also… to see if you like it."

Drake said that last night, Abdiel thinks. "Is Drake the only person you've been with?"

His question catches me off-guard, and I freeze, my mouth hanging open as I gape at him. He immediately backtracks.

"I'm sorry. That's none of my business." He shakes his head. "I shouldn't have asked. Forget about it. I'm so sorry."

"Abdiel." I take his face in my hands. "Stop apologizing. I don't want you to fear me, baby. I want you to feel comfortable enough to ask me things…"

Guilt gnaws at me inside, despite what I just said, and I focus on blurring my thoughts, sending them as far away as possible. Just for now…

I know someday I'll need to tell him the truth, about the other two people I've been with. The one I wanted… and the one I didn't.

Abdiel nods at my words. "You're perfect." He kisses me softly, and I'm melting inside. "I wish we didn't have to hide."

Great. More guilt. "Me too, baby. I'm so sorry I've dragged you into this…"

"Please," he scoffs, grinning. "I've had a crush on you for years. You're not dragging me into anything I haven't been willingly dreaming about since basically as soon as I hit puberty."

Swarms of rampant delight overrun the guilt. I've never felt anything like this… Maybe once. A long time ago…

We spend the next two hours kissing and touching. *Everywhere.*

On the bathroom counter, on the floor, in the shower, in the bed… No spot on Abdiel Harmony is left untouched, no area ignored by the exploration of my kisses.

We don't go further than sucking and jerking, because I was serious when I said that losing his virginity is special. I don't want it to happen rushed while we're watching the clock, wondering when someone will knock and remind me it's time to get up and be a leader.

The first one comes at nine-thirty, which is already hours after I would normally get up. Typically, people know not to bother me when I feel like sleeping in, but even this is excessive. They might just be checking to make sure I'm not dead.

I bark at them through the door that I'll be out shortly. And then an hour later, they knock again.

"Dammit," I croak, my voice hoarse from all the hushed whispers and growls I've been giving the kid since last night. "I guess I need to get up."

"You've been *getting up* all right," Abdiel rasps from where he's straddling me on the bed, my head nearly hanging off. He's still grazing my chest with his lips, but his movements are slowed and lazy from all the activities.

A seductive laugh rumbles from inside me while I hold his ass in my hands, loving the feeling, of him and of this. Us, together. Doing things we shouldn't be doing and not giving a good God damn what anyone would say.

Though I suppose I'm still a coward. We're in the privacy of this room, with the door locked. Would I have the guts to walk out there, holding his hand? Could I tell my wives I want a divorce because I'm gay and I'm falling in love with my servant?

I know none of them would care. They're not in love with me, and they all have their own side arrangements, too. It's not them I'm worried about. It's everyone else…

"Stop worrying." Abdiel kisses the corner of my mouth. "This just started. Let's enjoy it. We can figure out the serious later."

"You're very wise, Prince Harmony." I grin, kissing his lips *more more more* until another knock on the door finally pulls us apart.

We get up and get dressed, agreeing that Abdiel will stay in the room for a few minutes after I leave, then sneak out the way he did last time. I search his face and thoughts for any unease regarding this arrangement, but I can't find it. I have to take him at his truth that he's not upset with me for not having the balls to throw caution to the wind for him.

I want to… But he's right. This just started. We can at least see where it goes first, before getting bogged down in the future.

"Will I see you at dinner tonight?" I ask, clutching him like my lifeline I can't possibly let go of. And much to my own shock and awe, he's doing the exact same thing.

"I'll be here." He nods with his face buried in the crook of my neck, sniffing me like he's committing my scent to memory.

Like we won't see each other in a few hours. *But actually… that sounds like a good idea. I'm gonna do it, too.* Taking in a deep whiff of his scent, I'm crumbling. He smells masculine yet sweet, like amber and honey. Like an autumn day, falling leaves and crisp air. I'm obsessed.

"Are you cooking?" I lean up against the door with one hand in his hair and the other on his lower back.

He shakes his head. "Not tonight. You'll have to settle with Ryle."

"Mmm… shame. I love eating your food." He chuckles, launching my heart up into the sky like a bird.

"Ryle's food is great, you know it."

"I'm not kidding, Abdiel. You're a phenomenal cook." I whisper in his ear, "You're exceptionally talented, baby. I hope you know that."

"Okay, you need to leave before I fall to my knees again," he mumbles, and I laugh.

I kiss him one, two, three more times before we finally pry ourselves apart and I leave the room.

The second I step out into the hallway, I take a deep breath, closing my eyes and letting it out slowly. My fingers brush over my lips, raw and swollen from all the kisses. I savor the feelings, just as I savor the tightness in my chest…

I think I'm in love.

"Sleep well, sir?"

A voice startles me out of my reverie, enough that I jump and glare at the culprit. It's just Perry, standing there looking at me like everything is normal. Which it isn't… Because I'm in love with a Domestic half my age, and I spent all night and all morning doing very un-straight things with him, some of which involved my brother.

But to Perry, I just slept until almost eleven, which is also not normal. Still, I need to respond to him and act like nothing out of the ordinary happened. So I straighten up and stretch my arms behind my back.

"Yes, thank you. I needed a sleep-in day."

"I'm sure." Perry grins. I narrow my gaze at him. "Because of all the stress… with the upcoming solstice festival."

Letting out a quiet breath, I nod. "Right. Yes… the festival. Speaking of that, let's go find Lauris and get to work."

"Very good, sir," Perry agrees, and we wander off.

It takes all my strength not to turn over my shoulder, to glance back at the room where I just left the newest piece of my heart.

It's been a few hours, and I'm pleased with how much we've gotten done. Although I was late, and the girls started without me.

We've been planning our annual summer solstice festival for a couple of weeks now, and everything is set to go off without a hitch. Solstice is in ten days and we're ahead of schedule, which pleases me.

Festivals are a big part of The Principality. We like to celebrate as a family, though we don't follow the traditional holidays of the outside world. It was something Drake and I agreed upon when we first started. Why celebrate Hallmark holidays that revolve around vanity when we can celebrate the seasons' blessings from Mother?

Summer solstice is probably the most popular, though the harvest festival is the biggest. A majority of our family truly love summer, and solstice is the kick-off of everyone's favorite time of year. We also have a winter solstice party, complete with an exchange of gifts. We wanted to keep the values of Christmas, gratefulness and giving, without the same confused religious aspects. And then there's the budding festival, like a mix between Valentine's Day and Easter, or as close as you'd get here. We just did that one a couple of months ago. It celebrates the end of the winter months.

Lauris always takes the reins on planning the festivals. Gem and Emithel love helping her with it, and Kiara and Alissa tend to steer clear, though I'm usually able to wrangle their assistance with menial tasks. I like everyone to feel included, and I think everyone should pitch in.

"Alright. This is good," Lauris says, making notes on her list, crossing things off and adding new items to address. "Ryle will prepare the food. Though, do we really want to put all of that on him? It's a lot…"

Without even thinking, my voice bursts, "Abdiel should do it."

Lauris and Gem stare at me, and I try incredibly hard to keep a straight face. Not the face of someone who just unintentionally brought up the name of his secret lover he hasn't been able to stop thinking about in three hours and thirty-six minutes.

"Abdiel? Really?" Lauris asks. "Isn't he a little young?"

"He's not that young," I grumble. *Projecting. You're projecting.* "And besides, he's an excellent cook. You can't deny that."

"He's right," Emithel murmurs while sketching the lake in her notepad. "Last night's dinner was incredible."

"It was," Gem swoons at the memory of the delectable food Abdiel made last night. "And he's, like, really cute."

She giggles but stops short when her eyes meet mine. I'm glowering, and I hadn't even realized it.

"That has nothing to do with it." I fold my hands on the table. "He's talented enough. Have him work sous chef to Ryle if you like. But give him at least two menu items of his own."

Lauris squints at me for a moment but straightens up quick and nods. "You heard the King."

I wink at her, and she grins, jotting down information on the meals we'll require. Everything else is taken care of. Drake will have Lorn and a couple others from the Tribe string up those cool twinkly lights everyone loves, Gina will help secure flowers and decor. Cam will handle games for the kids, and Perry will make sure we're stocked on party favors for the adults.

As a family, we know how to have fun. I personally think when used recreationally, drugs and alcohol can be very helpful. The tricky part is not relying on it. We don't have many issues with addiction here, but I'm not really the best to ask about that since my brother injects me with drugs once a week to keep me from losing my shit.

I just have to hope I'm not leading by example on this one topic, though Empyrean is completely safe. Drake makes it, and I trust him with my life. I think we're fine since no one knows I do it. It's Drake's and my little secret.

Well, Abdiel's now, too.

This leads me to think about Abdiel's process of Ecdysis. Now that I've been away from him for a few hours, and the dust has settled on what we've done together so far, I find myself really hoping to Mother I haven't pressured him into anything.

I know it feels different for me, and frankly, it feels different for him too, since I can hear his thoughts. But he's so much younger and just experiencing a new mind-altering thing for the first time. It's had me worrying nonstop since the night in the lake.

I can't be like *him*... If I ever do anything even remotely as abhorrent as what he did to me, I'd chop my own dick off. The troubling fact that I still think about it all time, and I'm almost forty, makes me feel like more of a failure than anything else. *Why aren't I strong enough?*

Why can't I let it go?

I decide to leave the girls before dinner and take a walk by the lake. The whole time, my mind seems to be lingering in the past. I wish it wasn't, but there's no helping it. Sometimes when I come out here, I remember too much. I do believe the past shapes us, and we all know I believe things happen for a reason. But that doesn't mean we should dwell on it.

Yet I can't not, especially around this lake.

The trees sway with me, with my memories. Birds hum familiar tunes, and the wind whips ripples across the surface of the water in shapes that remind me of years ago.

I'm not necessarily *troubled*, no more than I usually am. Just... unearthed. Torn up.

Exposed.

As I'm walking back, the sun is setting, meaning they'll likely start dinner soon. The flutters in my stomach at the thought of seeing Abdiel again give me comfort paired with distress. I can't believe I've fallen so quickly for the kid…

What would his father think…?

The uneasy thought is cut short when I see him. *Abdiel.*

He's over by the side of the Den, between Domestic housing and the path to the front door. A small smile grazes my lips but disappears quickly when I see him pacing. He looks unsettled. And he's speaking to someone.

As I grow nearer, I can see around the corner. See who he's talking to.

I stop in my tracks and blink.

It's Drake.

Tilting my head, I watch them, Drake with his arms folded across his chest while he looks over Abdiel, listening to him intently while Abdiel apparently spills his guts. I worry my lower lip with my teeth.

What has him so upset? And why would he tell Drake and not me?

I calm my racing pulse and attempt to listen to them. I'm several yards away, but I can still make out what they're talking about based on their thoughts, carrying much louder than voices.

I just can't shake these feelings anymore… I think this is part of my Ecdysis, Drake. My rebirth…

Drake simply stares back at him, his brain full of fuzz. He does that… keeps us at a distance, so we can't hear him unless he wants us to. First me, and now Abdiel.

But my prince keeps going. *I need to know. I can't put it off any longer.*

I swallow, my heart thumping in my chest as he stops his pacing in front of my brother.

I'm going up the mountain. I have to find out what happened to my parents.

A chill runs over me, so hard my limbs tremor. And a deeply-set worry plagues my insides as I watch Drake nod. Then shrug. Then nod again, as if he has no possible response for the boy.

I tug at my hair, hard enough that it stings. *Drake wouldn't let Abdiel go up there alone… would he?*

Stepping forward, I prepare to walk fast over to them, to interject. But then I pause once more when Abdiel launches himself at Drake, throwing his arms around his neck and burying his face in Drake's sternum.

Drake stands frozen for a moment, arms dangling at his sides. His brow furrows in unease, and I hear a flash break through… weak thoughts growing stronger as he tentatively wraps his arms around Abdiel's waist.

There there, little mouse. I have you.

CHAPTER SEVENTEEN

DARIAN

"**O**h my God…" I whimper, eyes closed, head pressed back into the pillow.

"That's my name, don't wear it out," Drake croons through an audible smirk, dragging his lips over my throat while he pulls, then pushes in deeper.

The burn below my waist is so intense, I'm afraid I might pass out. And every time his cock pushes on a certain spot inside me, I see stars.

"You're so annoying," I huff a laugh that turns into a moan when he thrusts again, holding my ass tight in his hand, hips rippling against me, slow and steady.

I'm fucking sweating, this is so good. And yes, it's summer, and we're inside our new trailer we bought last year, which turns into a sweatbox from June to September. Especially when we're doing bad things together.

"You love it." He licks a line over my Adam's apple, biting my chin before going for my lips.

"I do… I fucking love… fuck, I love your cock in me." I'm clinging to him like a vine, holding him as close to me as humanly possible.

I want him deeper than deep. I want him to live inside me forever, that's how utterly amazing it feels.

"I love my cock in you," he repeats my words on my mouth, picking up the pace.

His hips move faster and harder as he fucks me into oblivion, our tiny bed creaking, the whole damn trailer rocking with his pumps. Drake holds my face, kissing me, groaning in my mouth while harsh breaths escape me into his, my moans mixing up in cries of ecstasy for

SERPENT IN WHITE

Every time we do this it's better than the time before. It took a while for me to warm up to it, after everything that happened. But Drake didn't mind. He was just there for me, in whatever ways I needed him. As a friend, a brother, or on occasion something like a boyfriend, only not really. It's hard to explain, but we've been living out here for almost two years, and so far, it's working.

I wasn't sure in the beginning... That first year was tough, but we made it through.

Together.

Eight months ago, I couldn't take it anymore. We'd done just about everything else two men could do to each other, within reason of course. Everything but this, which I'd been afraid of for too long.

I woke him up in the middle of the night, pleading with him to fuck me. To erase him *from my history and be my first.*

Drake was wary initially, because he didn't want to scare me or hurt me. But it's Drake. I love him, I trust him, and just thinking about him makes me rock hard.

He eagerly obliged. He lost his virginity to me, and as far as I'm concerned, he took mine. That first time doesn't count. It was the first time I'd consented to being fucked, and so it was my first time. With Drake... my foster brother.

And we've been humping like gay rabbits ever since.

"I'm gonna fucking come," I whine, wrapping my legs around him to keep him as deep as fucking possible.

"Come for me, beautiful," he growls, a command if I've ever heard one, and it sets me off.

My dick aches out stream after stream, all over the both of us while I gasp and groan, tingles sheeting my entire body.

"Come with me, baby," I croak, out of breath and hoarse, holding his face before mine so I can look at him while he has an orgasm. For me.

He's so damn sexy sometimes I can't stand it.

"Anything for you." He shivers, the telltale sign he's about to burst.

And then he takes my lower lip between his, sucking and biting, crying out nonsense into my mouth while his long, beautiful cock swells up inside me, releasing a climax that fills me up. It's the best feeling on earth, knowing I've driven him to this.

That he does this with only me. Only I *make him feel this way.*
Mine.

Drake comes down slowly, kissing my lips and my jaw and my neck, while I lazily trail my fingers up and down his back, touching his muscles, up his neck to the shaved sides of his hair. I remember when I did it for him… when we cut each other's hair.

It's been just us for so long out here. I'm not complaining, but sometimes I wonder what's going on outside this little bubble of safety and undying happiness.

"I wish I knew what you were thinking," Drake whispers, nuzzling behind my ear.

"It wouldn't be hard to guess," I murmur. He picks himself up, gazing down at me for a moment. "What?" I ask when he says nothing for a solid minute, just staring.

"Nothing," he answers definitively and presses a chaste kiss on my chin. "I'm going to make you dinner."

He pulls out of me, slowly, though it still feels strange enough to make me grunt. Then he gets up, grinning at me over his shoulder before grabbing a cloth to clean me up.

We take a quick shower, then head outside to build a fire and get ready for dinner.

I'm sort of amazed at what we've done out here in only two years. We've grown a small garden, built a hunting shack where we skin animals we've killed. I'm decent, but Drake has shot a couple of deer for us so far, which according to him makes him a master hunter. He tried hanging the antlers of the buck on the wall inside our trailer and it fell down and almost maimed me.

I can laugh about it now, but at the time I was pissed.

We have a small boat too, which we use for fishing. We're basically like two Davey Crockett's, or some shit. We live off the land, and the land has been good to us.

To be honest, I don't miss anything about the outside world. We have a cell phone, but the service out here is shit and we rarely use it. We use our battery-powered radio more, for music and CD's. The way we see it, if we could make it through that first winter without freezing to death or eating each other, there's nothing we can't do.

We're invincible, and more important than that… we're exactly where we're supposed to be.

We make occasional runs, not necessarily into the nearest town, but to a cabin a few miles south of here. There's a guy who lives there, Chet, who trades with us. If there's stuff we want or need, like books, medicine, or clothes, he'll get them for us and trade. It's amazing.

Getting back to the roots of civilization. No money, no taxes, no goddamn capitalism.

We're like frontier men, and it's the best kind of bliss.

Drake and I have marked out spots on the land based on how far we get before seeing other people. We joke around and call it our territory. I know it doesn't really belong to us, but that doesn't matter. Out here, we make the rules.

As far as we're concerned, these woods are ours.

I get the fire going while Drake grabs us some leftover venison. I'm setting up plates and forks as he starts shouting at me from inside the trailer.

"Dude, please come out here so I can actually hear what you're trying to ask me," I bark, lips curling into an amused grin as I shake my head.

He pokes his head out of the trailer door. "I'm asking if you want corn or tomatoes, or both, deaf ass."

I chuckle and look up at him, ready to answer when I see him glaring over my head, eyes narrowing at something behind me. Turning quickly over my shoulder, I make out the form of what looks like a man, wandering through the woods a few yards out.

I glance back at Drake, and he already has his shotgun in his hand, stomping down the steps.

"Drake, chill!" I whisper-shout, jumping up and scurrying over to him.

"I'm not going to shoot him," he huffs, eyes locked on the figure. "I'm just being cautious."

"Why would you assume he's here to attack us?" I stand in front of him, blocking him as he tries to maneuver around me. "It's just a hiker, Drake. It happens."

"Yea, not often," he grumbles. "He's on our land. I won't let anyone threaten my family."

My family. Meaning me.

Swoon.

I push away the warmth at his protectiveness and straighten up. "He's hiking. At least wait until he actually threatens us before breaking out the shotgun."

"If I wait for him to threaten us, then it's already too late," he grunts, aiming the scope toward the hiker. "I'd move if I were you."

I sigh and step out of the way, distracting myself with cooking dinner, while Drake watches the hiker. He says it's a man, probably in his late twenties, and he seems to be alone. He watches him as long as he can until the guy disappears out of sight.

"Will you come eat now?" I mutter at him when he finally puts the gun down. "It's cold."

"I'll warm you up." He grins, plopping down next to me on the log we turned into a bench, slinking his arm around my waist and pulling me closer to bite my earlobe.

"I meant the food, asshole." I smother my smirk and shift through the chills he's giving me.

"Ohhh, right. The food," he hums in my ear, almost more arousing than him biting and sucking on it.

I shove him, and he laughs, digging into his food while I just watch him, because I already finished eating, while he was busy protecting *us.*

The sun sets, and it's dark all around, the only light from the crescent moon and the glowing embers of a dull fire. I'm roasting a marshmallow I probably won't eat while Drake talks about some plants he's been studying in the books he got from Chet. He says they can do a lot for the human body, but mainly they can be made into psychedelics, which he's sort of fascinated by.

Drake's been mentioning this for a while. He was always a science nerd, for as long as I've known him, but in the last two years, he's been studying chemistry and botany more and more. He tries to teach me, but I'm more interested in reading fiction, or learning about history and the social sciences.

Even though we're no longer a part of society, so to speak, we still understand how important education is. I've been reading up on sociology, because I think it's very interesting how a society comes to be. But Drake is all about biology and chemistry. He talks about wanting to grow more, and we both agree that if we could build a greenhouse of some kind, it would be hugely beneficial to us in the long run. We could make our own supplies, our own medicine.

I enjoy thinking about the future, but I don't bring it up to Drake often. He likes to focus on the moment, and I agree with that. But I also don't think it hurts to plan, especially since we're becoming self-sustaining and we need to be prepared for storms in winter, floods, poor crop harvests, stuff like that.

"I was thinking of going up the mountain," he murmurs, fingers grazing up and down my thigh. "I want to go farther... See what I can see."

188

SERPENT IN WHITE

"You think that's safe?" My eyes are stuck on the flaming marshmallow as it singes into a black ball.

"We'll never know until we try, right?" He leans into my side.

I turn my face to look at him, the glow illuminating his pale skin and sharp lines. I still remember when I first met him, how small he was. He sprouted up like crazy as a teenager, and now he's huge, his presence even more overpowering. Those eyes, marbled in color, could be potentially startling, but I love them. They're different, which is what Drake is. He's one of a kind.

"Right," I whisper, inching closer to his face. His eyes drop to my lips, fingers slinking up my thigh, closer to where I'm hardening up quick.

A twig snaps to our right, and we jump, heads springing in the sound's direction to see a man.

The same man from earlier.

"Hi. Sorry to burst in on you like this." The man gives us a kind smile, his eyes falling, maybe to observe how close we're sitting.

Drake's hand leaps off my leg. Seriously, I don't think anything has ever moved so fast. I peek at him, watching his jaw clench as he scoots away from me, eyes narrowed on our new friend.

"Who the fuck are you?" Drake grunts, and I see his left hand reaching for the shotgun at his side.

The man catches on and lifts his hands. "I mean you no harm. My name is Pete. I'm out here to hike and camp, and I saw you guys. Figured I'd introduce myself since I haven't seen anyone else in days."

Drake is eyeing the guy as if he's an intruder, studying him with squinted eyes, likely trying to determine if he can be trusted.

So I decide to give the man a smile. Might as well play good cop bad cop. The dude's right, after all. We rarely see other people around here, which is why it's come to feel like our own little solitary woodland haven. But there are still people out there, and good ones at that.

Drake doesn't trust anyone, and I suppose I shouldn't either. But I'm inherently positive, and I like to give people the benefit of the doubt. Drake would call it stupid, or naïve.

I like to see it as hopeful.

"I'm Darian," I introduce myself. "This is my brother, Drake."

The man's forehead creases for just a moment before he smiles back. "Nice to meet you bo—"

189

"You're on our land," Drake hisses, fingers still curling around his gun. "That's why you haven't seen anyone else around here. It's ours."

I glance at my brother like he's lost his mind. Sure, we like to claim this land is ours, but technically, it's not. We don't have any sort of property rights over it, and we certainly can't willfully shoot someone for trespassing.

Pete appears partially nervous, but also intrigued as he nods, palms still facing us like he's being held at gunpoint, which he almost is by my crazy brother. "I'm sorry. I didn't know. I'll leave if you want..."

"Don't be silly." I nudge Drake with my elbow until he finally takes an audible breath, and a much-needed blink. "You can hang out for a bit if you want. We've got marshmallows."

I grin, and Pete smiles back, though his wary eyes stay on my brother for a moment. Drake releases the gun and does this subtle nod that I can tell means, I guess you can sit.

Pete takes off his backpack, sitting down on a stump by the fire. "Thanks. I really appreciate it. Like I said, I've been out here for a bit, and I haven't seen anyone else. Which is kind of the whole reason I came out here in the first place, I suppose."

"Us, too," I tell him, shaking my burnt-to-hell black blob into the fire and grabbing a new marshmallow out of the bag, stuffing it onto the stick and handing it to Pete. "We came out here to get away from all the bullshit, but it's definitely cool to meet a fellow camper."

Pete chuckles, taking the stick and aiming the marshmallow into the fire. I feel Drake shifting farther away from me, and I peer at him for a moment, wondering what exactly his issue is all of a sudden.

"How long have you guys been out here?" Pete asks, sounding friendly, rather than prying. Still, I'm hesitant to give away details of our lives or situation. We don't know this guy.

"It's been a while," I say through a kind smile, while still conveying the need for privacy.

"Well, I'm jealous of that trailer. The thing looks awesome." He observes our home. "All I've got is a one-person tent."

"Trust me, that was us until only a few months ago. The trailer was a necessity, though. Working plumbing and shower? Yes, please."

Pete laughs. "Yea, bathing in the lake is cool for a while, but I can't imagine it in winter."

"It sucks," Drake rumbles, leaning forward with his curious eyes on our new friend. "The winters out here are brutal."

Pete swallows, visibly intimidated by my brother. "I bet."

The conversation keeps going from there. Pete tells us about him, how he was a lawyer in LA and when he found out his wife was cheating on him with his brother, he sold his practice, his house, and all his earthly possessions, and decided to come up to Washington to hike the mountains and do some soul-searching. He seems like a good guy. He's older than us, though it doesn't necessarily seem it. Drake just turned eighteen, and my birthday is next month, whereas Pete is twenty-eight.

But age is just a number. Drake and I have seen enough shit in our lives, been through unparalleled horrors which have given us the kind of wisdom only life experiences can provide. So we're getting on just fine with this older dude.

We agree to let Pete camp on our land, and he sets up his tent about a quarter-mile north from our trailer, closer to the mountain. Drake went inside before we did, so by the time the fire is out and I'm heading in, I expect him to be asleep. But when I get inside the trailer, I find him by the window, staring out in the direction of Pete's tent.

I sigh, audibly, to make sure he knows he's being ridiculous. "Why are you so paranoid?"

He aims his snake eyes at me, and I want to tell him that shit doesn't scare me like it does other people. "I'm not paranoid, Darian. I'm being smart. We don't know this asshole. Outsiders can't be trusted."

"Outsiders?" I grin, crossing my arms over my chest.

"Yea." He glares. "People from society." He lets out a breath and blinks hard, standing up and inching to me, placing his hands on my waist.

Insecurities take over, and my eyes fall to the floor between us. "You didn't want to touch me in front of him…"

His slips his fingers under my chin, lifting my gaze back up to his. "We don't know him, baby. I'm sorry… I didn't mean to hurt you, but I just…" he trails off and shakes his head. Speechless and sincerely confounded. I know the feeling.

It's easy for us to play pretend out here in the woods, when we're all alone. We can act like whatever we're doing is fine. But when strangers come in, it doesn't necessarily feel fine. And the thing is, I can't tell if I would rather give up humans for Drake, or if that's stupid.

People are a resource; humanity is civilization and vice versa.

Drake is happy with me now, but in two more years? Five, ten, thirty? I can't make him stay out here, just him and me, forever. He needs more. He deserves better.

"I get it." I nod, pulling him into me, wrapping my arms around his neck, hugging onto him hard.

His arms slink around my waist and he holds me harder, kissing my hair.

"I love you, Drake," I murmur, and I feel him shudder. "I think we should let Pete stay. I think if we meet more people along the way, like Chet or anyone else… I think we should take them in, too. We can take in strays because we're strong. And it's the right thing to do."

He's still for a while, just breathing while we hold each other, his lips lingering by my neck while he stays in his thoughts.

And I wish, so badly, that I could hear them.

CHAPTER EIGHTEEN

DRAKE

D inner will be served soon, but I can't even think about that right now.

I need a fucking drink.

Making a beeline to the study, I dart across the room toward the bar, pouring myself some whiskey from the decanter. I sip from the glass, my mind reeling from the conversation I just had with Abdiel.

He's internally distraught. That much was clear from hearing his thoughts for all of five seconds. He's hung up on the deaths of his parents, and in all honesty, I get it.

I still think about all the death I've experienced in my life... A lot more than the kid has. I found my own mother dead, killed by my father, which set off a chain of events, molding my existence based on a cosmic plan. Everything that's happened since then was a result of that day.

In the bathroom... Her body lying stiff and cold.

"Mom...?"

A chill runs through me as I gulp back my drink, draining the glass and immediately pouring a new one. I sip it slower, contemplating what Abdiel said... what he wants.

To go up on the mountain. To where they died.

That's not a good idea at all.

But how could I tell the kid that? How could I explain?

And if it's part of his Ecdysis...?

"Two nights in a row." The familiar voice startles me out of my head, and I look up at my brother, entering the room slowly, closing the door behind him. "I must have done something special to deserve this."

I try to huff out a chuckle, but it doesn't really work. So I just take another swallow of burning liquid.

Darian immediately knows something's up, though I'm blocking out the specifics. He narrows his gaze at me, walking over to the bar slowly. When he gets up next to me, he pours himself a glass, brushing against me as he does.

Then he leans up on the wood, taking a slow sip, all the while watching me closely.

The tension in the room is as thick as the waves of frustration coming at me through his head.

He saw me talking to Abdiel.

My eyes lift to his.

"Drake, for the life of me, I can't understand what your angle is here," he finally sighs, the tapping of his brown dress boot on the wood floor distracting me from his investigative tone. "Do you really care about the kid? Or are you just trying once more to hurt me?"

The fuck??

The words, the accusation causes my eyes to spring back to his. My jaw strains as I take in a breath, reminding myself that he's my brother and I love him.

Don't hit him. That would be wrong.

"Excuse me?" I growl, gripping the side of the bar as I face him. "You think *I'm* hurting *you*?"

He appears momentarily stunned before his brows zip together. "What's that supposed to mean?"

Shaking it off, I mutter, "Never mind. The point is that I'm not trying to do anything, and I have no angle. I care about Abdiel as much as I can, but I didn't know he was your *property*, brother." I slant in closer to his face. "You should probably tell him that, because he came to me to talk about his Ecdysis."

I knew saying this would push Darian's buttons, which is confirmed by the stabby look he's giving me. Darian is smitten for the kid. It's obvious. He might even be falling in love with him...

Swallowing suddenly becomes much more difficult.

"He wants to go up the mountain," I say the words he already knows, watching as his gaze lands on the floor and stays there for a while.

Sucking in a long breath, then letting it go, he taps the rim of his glass over and over as he glances at me. "I suppose I understand why... But it's not safe."

"No, it is not."

Quiet hangs in the room again before Darian mutters, "Abdiel thinks I should tell everyone the truth."

With my gaze on the side of his face, a desperation unlike anything I've ever felt crawls up my esophagus, burning worse than the liquor I'm sucking down. I almost cough it out like a cloud of smoke.

I focus my thoughts, so he can't hear my truth. It kills me to cover it up, but I do. I must.

And I mumble, "That's not what the Regnum wants. You know that."

He nods and goes mute for another moment, while I stand still beside him, stinging all over like my entire existence is one big gaping wound.

Darian turns his blue eyes on me. "You know, he also thinks it's bullshit that you won't accept happiness. He wanted you to stay last night..."

My face is tight, a pressure building behind my eyes that I force away with every bit of strength I can muster. "Did he..."

Darian nods slowly, our eyes locked in a battle, one that's been ongoing for more years than I'd care to count. He parts his lips, then snaps them shut. And I both dread what he was going to say and crave it, like a next hit of deadly poison in my veins I can't seem to live without.

A knock on the door breaks through the ripples of unspoken pain as Darian calls out, "Come in."

The door opens a crack, and Gina pokes her head in. "Dinner, sir."

"I'll be right there," he tells her, eyes never once abandoning mine.

She leaves, and he finishes his drink, setting the glass down right next to my hand on the bar. His fingers graze mine, that one movement speaking volumes more than either of us will allow, from our mouths or our minds.

He leaves the room for dinner, and I'm stuck.

Nailed to the floor.

I don't join them for dinner. Instead, I stay in the study the entire time, drinking and smoking. Trying to get my head on straight.

When I'm fuzzy yet somehow seeing clearly, I sneak out and cross the house to the lounge. Darian will likely bring Abdiel in here after dinner, at least to talk, and I'm not sure why but I feel like I should be there. It's completely ludicrous, I know.

If Darian wants to enter a relationship with the kid, I should back the fuck off and not interfere. This is what I've been telling myself is necessary for years. Although subconsciously, I always knew it wouldn't take, him attempting a relationship with females.

The wives have never been a true threat. Abdiel is.

Although, no, he isn't. He's a sweet kid, and I like him a lot. Contrary to what Darian would believe, I *do* care about Abdiel. Maybe too much, hence the problem.

What the fuck was I thinking last night, being with them together? I should just leave them alone to do their thing... Like I was going to with Lars.

Did it kill me a little every time I knew Darian was with him? Sure. But I'm used to pain. It's part of my existence.

And now the pattern is being repeated with his son. Only this time, I've inserted myself where I don't belong.

I'm confused, and a little drunk. I hate this feeling. The confusion, not the drunkenness.

When I hear footsteps, my heart begins to race. Leaning up against the edge of the desk, I watch the door with wide eyes as it swings open.

"You're being unnecessarily overprotective," Abdiel grumbles as he wanders into the room, loosening the collar of his uniform button-down. "I mean, don't get me wrong, it's hot, but I just don't get it."

Darian steps in after him, peering out into the hallway one last time before closing the door and locking it. "We need to talk about this, my prince. I want to understand your feelings. Your motivation."

Abdiel opens his mouth as if to speak, but then their eyes land on me, and I wave.

196

"I um… I thought maybe I could help," I say, even though it's the stupidest possible thing I could utter right now.

Darian looks shocked, as if he truly didn't expect me to stick around, and Abdiel looks pleased. Pleased to see *me*.

I'd deny it if anyone asked, but honestly, it thaws my chest. *A lot.*

He steps up to me and gives me a small smile, propping next to me on the desk, basically mirroring my stance. And now we're both staring at Darian, waiting for him to explain himself. I would feel bad about ganging up on him, but he's the Head Priest. It's his duty.

"You were the one who told me I *must not squander* the Empyrean. Remember that?" Abdiel lifts his brow at my brother, and I have to suppress my smirk.

I can't believe he's already giving Darian the business like this. It should make me jealous, but I actually happen to think the kid is pretty adorable, and I've always enjoyed watching my brother squirm.

"That's true, I did say that," Darian rumbles, approaching us slowly. "But I didn't know your rebirth would include journeying up a dangerous mountain for days by yourself."

"I won't be by myself," Abdiel counters. "I'll have Mother." I can see the grin trying to pull at Darian's lips, and it makes me want to smile, too. We both hide it. "Plus, the Tribe is always around, aren't they?"

Abdiel looks to me, and Darian raises a brow in my direction.

"They don't typically go up farther than the lab, unless they have to." I breathe out a sigh. "Look, little mouse, I won't tell you not to go because I understand why something like this is important. But I will tell you that the mountain *is* dangerous. We're not just saying it to stifle you. Your parents' deaths are a mystery for a reason."

Abdiel looks between Darian and me. "But you can't tell me exactly what's up there, can you?"

"It's… not of this earth," Darian murmurs.

A new, different chill sheets my flesh.

Abdiel blinks over wide, green eyes, as vibrant as the trees outside. The color he possesses is beautiful and bright. I'm not sure what I would do if something were to happen to him.

That said, I live on that mountain. Not all the way up, of course, because I'm not a total psycho. But I've seen things up there. Things no one else on the Expanse has seen and lived to talk about. Not even Darian.

"I have to do it." Abdiel shrugs on a strong exhale, his eyes staying

197

with my brother's. "It's my one request."

Darian stares at him for a long time, so long that it appears he's staring at both of us. It's strange, this little threesome we've entered into. I don't know what to make of it, maybe because it's still so new. Or maybe because I know eventually I'll need to walk away…

At last, Darian hums and rubs his eyes with his fingers. "If you must go, at least wait until after the solstice festival. We'll be requiring your culinary services. Plus, I… I need you here. Please."

Darian is distraught. I hate seeing him this way, and for the first time, it's not my doing. I guess I should be pleased by that fact, but I'm not.

"Wait… what?" Abdiel's head shakes. Darian grins. "You mean… I get to cook? For the festival??"

"As Ryle's sous chef. But yes." Darian steps up to Abdiel, brushing dirty blonde curls with his fingers. "Collectively we all agreed your talent needs to be showcased."

Abdiel smirks. "Really? It was a collective decision?"

"Fully." Darian's lips curve, and Abdiel lets out an elated chuckle.

He kisses Darian, hungrily, yet apparently lovingly tender. It gives my bones an ache.

I look away until I feel something… A hand on my hand.

Abdiel's fingers graze over mine as he kisses my brother, and suddenly, I can't breathe. I'm gasping for air, but there isn't enough in the room.

He wants me to be with them…

Moving my hand away, I stalk toward the door.

If I can't be with Darian, what on earth would lead me to believe I could be with both of them? It can't work, and I'm a fucking idiot for hooking up with Abdiel in the first place. Now I've dug myself into a goddamn pit, and it'll take all of my stored-up self-loathing and misery to get out.

"I should go," I mumble, going for the door. "Glad I could be of assistance."

I hear them both say my name, but it's too late. I can't stay.

I just fucking can't.

Leaving the Den quickly, I storm off into the night, scolding myself all the way. My ATV is where I left it in the garage, and I hop on, starting it up and pulling away. I drive slowly past Domestic housing, then Regnum housing, heading toward my home. The mountain.

Once I get to the farm, I can speed up, and I rip it past the crop fields, then up to the Field of Influence. My guards on patrol nod at me as I zip by, maneuvering the trails I know like the back of my hand, leading through the Field and up to the lab.

But I don't stop there. My place is farther, about a half-mile from the lab, nestled in the forest of White Trumpet Mountain. There's a lookout area, and my cabin is located on it. I'm pretty high up, but not even close to as high as the mountain goes... Where Abdiel wants to go.

I know what's up there, and I don't like to encounter it often. It's a hard one to explain, and even Darian doesn't really grasp what it truly means. All he knows is that we should stay away from it, and keep our family away from it, too. To protect them.

Parking my four-wheeler out front, I hop off and stalk into my house, kicking off my boots at the door. My place isn't even half as big as Darian's, and certainly not as fancy. But then he has five other people living with him. Here it's just me.

Darian's only been to my home twice since I built it. He came up one time to see me, and let's just say it didn't work out well... That night ended in a fight, and I told him not to come back. So now he doesn't.

If he wants to see me, he comes to the lab. Or he waits for me to come to him. And usually I do, but sometimes I don't. Because I'm an asshole, and I have to be one. After everything we've been through, from the time we left home at fifteen to right now, I'm convinced Darian would be so much better off without me, romantically speaking.

I'll still always be his brother, his family. I'll always protect him, lay down my life for him. And apparently, I can't keep my dick away from him, so that will probably keep happening, though it shouldn't. Especially if he has Abdiel now.

Wandering over to my wood stove, I toss a couple of logs in and get the fire started. Then I meander around, going to the fridge for a beer, wallowing in the bullshit I've brought upon myself. I wish there was something I could do, some way I could feel better about this, but it's hopeless.

Abdiel's wrong. I'm not meant for happiness.

It's not his fault. He's young. He's like Darian was at that age; head in the clouds, beautiful sparkling ideas, hearts in his eyes and overflowing with a need to love someone. Darian's still like that deep down, though he's been battered and beaten into something much more cynical over the years, hiding himself and lying and craving...

And most of it is my fault. *I told you, I'm evil.*

Falling down onto my couch, I lie on my back, staring at the ceiling, bottle in my hand hanging off the edge. I don't want to torture myself, but my mind won't stop drifting back down the mountain to a private room in my brother's house... where I know he's fooling around with his new *boyfriend*. If that's what Abdiel is to him, I have no idea.

I'm not meant to be a part of what they're doing, but I can't help closing my eyes and listening, with all my might. Trying desperately to hear that far. To *feel* them.

Darian on his knees, pulling Abdiel's pants down slowly, gazing up at his eyes; ocean blue locked on moss green. His tongue sliding over his lower lip as he wraps his fist around Abdiel's long cock, eager mouth inching closer.

My breaths grow unsteady as my hand drifts into my pants, adjusting my erection, writhing where I lie while I picture it, hearing their gasps and groans in my mind as Darian bows to his prince and Abdiel takes it, loving it. Having a King on his knees.

A small mewl leaves my lips unintentionally while my hand rubs against my cock, hard as stone at the images flooding my mind. They get onto the bed, and Abdiel crawls over Darian, his ass splayed out for my brother like a feast. He sinks his warm, perfect mouth down on Darian's thick cock, already having enough experience now to know what he likes. Darian likes when you tease the head with your tongue, then suck hard but slow. He likes it gradual. He likes his dick to be worshipped by your mouth, and that's what Abdiel will do for him.

That's what I do for him.

A tear sneaks out of my eye, and I turn my face to wipe it on my arm, breathing heavily as I tug my cock, harder and harder, imagining the things I can't have. Being in that bed with them again... touching and kissing and teasing, building lust and need like the spreading of a wildfire.

I see Darian licking and sucking everywhere, holding him so hard he'll bruise Abdiel's milky flesh.

The longing in my chest is palpable, painful. Excruciating, and it gets me off in the end. The aching in my chest, throbbing as hard as my cock while it erupts an orgasm of heartbreak.

SERPENT IN WHITE

Breaths fly in and out of me while I cry silent tears.

They're by the lake, and I'm on the mountain.

I'm alone, and this is how it needs to be. I fooled myself once, and I paid the price for it.

I won't do it again.

CHAPTER NINETEEN

DARIAN

The palette of sunset reflects off the lake. Pinks, oranges, and yellows, swirling together over the surface of the large water body.

The twinkling lights are strung up on the trees, giving us that enchanting feel. The whimsical aura of summer solstice.

It's beautiful.

The festival occurs all over the Expanse, but the real party is happening here, outside the Den. Tables set up for guests to sit and dine, a buffet out back where Ryle and Abdiel are providing food for everyone.

I'm trying to be coy, but I've been watching that area closer than anywhere else.

Abdiel is in his zone tonight. He made some delicious food, roasted corn with vegetables and chicken wings. He also made dessert. Peach cobbler with vanilla ice cream. I'm amazed at his skills, and also not. I volunteered him for a reason.

The party has been ruminating for a few hours, and everyone is having a great time. I suppose I am, too. But I'm anxious.

My awareness is heightened. All evening, despite how busy we've been, I've known Abdiel is leaving. He's going tomorrow, making his journey up the mountain to get his closure. And so it's been difficult for me to enjoy the festivities, knowing my prince is willfully leaving me in a few short hours.

You may think I'm being dramatic. That's okay. It's a fair assessment. To a layman, Abdiel is going on a glorified hike, and it's no cause for concern.

But I know better. *I don't want him to go.*

If there's any potential of harm, I should be protecting him from it. The fact that he's disobeying me makes me itch. I need him safe, and unfortunately, I can't guarantee it when he goes trudging up the mountain by himself.

Not to mention that we basically just started whatever this thing is between us. I'm not ready to lose him for days. Not yet.

Dessert is finally about done being served, and I'm watching Abdiel clean up, pretending to listen as Lauris and Gem commend and complain about various things that either went well or could have gone better tonight. Regardless of their thoughts, I think everything was perfect.

Music is playing, echoing from the booth we have set up on my back deck, easy melodies crooning while people talk and laugh and eat, the merriment palpable.

Yet the only thing I can do is watch my Domestic.

I've been greeting people all night, laughing with them, smiling and playing with the kids. It's quite the political event, if I do say so myself, and now all I want in the world is to see my prince. I want someone here I can curl into, if even metaphorically; someone who will hold me tight and make me feel like less of a *King* and more of a goddamn man.

Drake hasn't shown up yet. I don't know that I expected him to, but I really wish I would've had at least one person to keep me company while Abdiel was working. I need it, and I never realized how much until it was within reach, though just out of my grasp.

"Beautiful night," someone speaks at my side, and I tilt my gaze to find Gina, pouring herself a drink right next to me.

I came over here to get away from all the noise. Thoughts can be overwhelming in a setting like this, especially when eighty percent of them are wondering about my marriages, and when I'll finally decide to give them an heir to The Principality.

My smile is modest. "It is."

Gina finishes pouring and aims her cup toward mine, where we clink in a soft toast, taking our respective sips.

"He did great tonight, didn't he?" She asks, and I notice right away that she's referring to Abdiel, though I'm not sure why she would assume I'd known that without her explaining herself. But following her gaze, I see Abdiel helping Ryle bring pots and pans inside, a smile ever-present on his soft lips.

NYLA K

He's just the most joyous person, and it makes me happy, to know someone like him.

"He did," I answer, purposely keeping the longing out of my voice.

Gina shifts toward me, and I peer in her direction. "His parents would be proud."

Mention of Lars and Jenny seizes up my insides, especially knowing where Abdiel is going tomorrow morning, and why. I give her a sympathetic smile and nod as she takes a long sip of her drink, watching Abdiel all the while, before wandering off, leaving me cold and unsure.

When Abdiel goes back inside, I decide to sneak off, hoping to speak with him. He'll be gone for a few days on his journey, and I'm really yearning to get some quality alone time with him before he leaves.

We spent last night in the lounge again, and it was marvelous. We still didn't have sex, though he's been pleading for it, testing every bit of willpower I have in my body. I still insist that it will be special. Not that I'm not *dying* for it myself, but I want him to lose his virginity when I know he's absolutely ready, and unfortunately, I still haven't felt it in his mind one hundred percent.

So instead, we've just been kissing and touching and sucking like there's no tomorrow. And even then, it's beyond satisfying. My prince is a perfect treasure. I never want to let him go, hence why I'm sort of stalking him tonight.

Lingering in the corridor, I watch Abdiel in the kitchen, instructing his helpers. For as passive a person he typically seems, he's very good at taking charge when he needs to. Tonight really showcased how wonderful he'd be at operating some type of business. I know he loves to serve, but there needs to be more to him than that.

I want to help him soar.

It looks like Abdiel is almost done, and I'm getting ready to tug him away with me so I can kiss him dizzy when I feel cold fingers brush my arm.

Hey.

Turning my face, I'm met with snake eyes, and I get that usual mixture of relief and dread, such a normal part of interactions with Drake at this point, I wouldn't even know what to do if I didn't feel these things so close to one another.

What took you so long? I blink at him, and he looks away for a moment.

"I wasn't going to come at all…" he mumbles. I have to fight not to roll my eyes.

Glancing back to Abdiel, I ask for him with my mind. His face tilts, and he peeks my way, giving me a subtle smile.

I'll be right there, my King.

"Let's go," I rumble to Drake, wandering up the hall.

I know he's not following me at first. I can hear him contemplating his next move, or what he's even doing here. But eventually, he gives in, and his footsteps join mine.

Going into the lounge is the safest bet, to ensure privacy in whatever it is the three of us may do together. But it's such a beautiful night…

And it's the solstice. Mother needs us outside, with Her.

And so I go through the back door, and I can hear Drake's confused thoughts, yet he doesn't argue. He just continues following me, his own inner comforts growing easier once we're outside, in the woods.

This place has been our home for twenty-five years. The forest is a part of us and we're a part of it. Walking in the dark, lighting from the party grows farther as we trace the lake with our footsteps, the nostalgia gracing me. It always does when I'm out here, because it's so pungent; the memories of how we started. Where this all came from… two lost boys finding themselves in the secluded woods.

To think of what it's turned into can be staggering at times. But I sit with the trepidation, the uncertainty and the wondering. I have no choice.

We're here, and this is part of the plan, whether we like it or not.

Drake falls into step beside me, knowing where I'm headed. We walk in silence for a few more minutes, voices growing distant, thoughts rippling across the calm water of the lake. The moon is high, vibrant in its auburn hue, providing us the perfect illumination.

Reaching my destination, I plop down on the old log bench, made by Drake and me, back before The Principality, before anyone joined us or followed us. Before expectations and responsibilities.

It's moss covered now, vines crawling, decorated in scattered clovers and baby's breath. This is a spot I come to get away. It's quiet, serene, and far enough from the Den and housing that I know I won't see anyone else. The festival happening across the water is visible, the twinkly lights reflecting like fireflies suspended in time.

Drake takes a seat next to me, and I let out a breath slowly. Resting my head on his shoulder, I feel him stiffen for a moment. But then he relaxes into me, slinking his arm around my waist.

"Will Abdiel be able to find you out here?" He murmurs, his fingers grazing up and down my arm, giving me chills despite the warmth in the air.

"He'll follow our thoughts," I speak quietly. "He's good like that."

I feel Drake nod subtly. *He is good. He's so damn good, Darian.*

I flinch at the tone in his thoughts. *Is that supposed to be a warning? Because I know, Drake. I know it's dangerous… All of this is.*

Then why aren't you trying harder to stop it?

Lifting my head, I glare at him. "Why is it always my responsibility?"

"Because you're the *King*," he grumbles, and something in his voice catches in my ear. Something like… resentment. It brings on a Deja vu unlike any I've felt in a while.

I'm quiet for weighted seconds, letting the feelings settle over me, like a cloud of dust.

"I can't disrupt fate," I finally mutter.

He lifts a shoulder in a mild shrug, finishing my thought. "Nothing happens by accident."

We sit side by side for more moments of quiet, gazing at the lights on the lake. Drake's fingers creep over mine, and I hate how much it feels like home. I hate how good he feels when he's just going to rip it away for the umpteenth time.

"I used to kiss you out here." His breath brushes my cheek, and I shift. "A *lot*."

His lips graze my jaw, and I whimper, leaning into his touch. "I used to let you."

"You did more than let me." He nips my earlobe. "You kissed me back."

Pivoting my face so that our lips are hovering, I push myself into him. *I would never have been able to resist you. Ever.*

Drake's breaths pick up as pushes me back, one hand on my chest and the other on my waist while he straddles me, making us horizontal. His eyes skate over my face as if he's looking for an excuse to stop. A reason why we can't do this, so he can fight it.

It's always a fight with him.

"I've never wanted anything as much as I want you, *always*, and it's devastating," I tell him the truth, my cock stiffening up like crazy just from being near him like this. Being back where I belong, at his mercy, listening to the war he wages with himself.

"Shut up, Darian," he hisses, his mouth coming down on mine fiercely.

He kisses my lips raw, both of us gasping for air in between the desperate sucking and biting. My fingers tug at his shirt until he grabs my wrists and pins them over my head.

Why do you do this to me? His thoughts are as aggressive as his mouth while he shoves his hips forward, grinding the pole of his erection into my own. *Why do you torture me like this?*

You're just mad because you can't make yourself stop wanting me... My mind hums at him. *Wanting us.*

"Fuck you," he snarls his weak threat breathlessly as he releases one of my wrists to go for the zipper on my pants, pulling it down quick.

He yanks down my pants and boxers rough and fast, undoing his own next to reveal his long cock. I'm salivating from the sight of his pale skin bathed in the moon's glow. He's almost ivory, carved like a wicked sculpture. His dick is sticking out straight toward me, the blushed pink tip swollen, just begging to be licked.

"So do it, then," he rumbles, then wraps his fist around my erection, full and thick, throbbing at the somehow soft roughness of his touch.

With my eyes on his, I part my lips, enough to let him know I would *love* to have his beautiful cock in my mouth right now. The eyes of a serpent sparkle down at me while he tugs his lip between his teeth, sliding his hands up my torso, and taking my shirt with them.

"I want you completely naked," he growls, ripping my pants down my legs the rest of the way. "I want you lying out here at my mercy, like back then."

A moan slips from my lips at the fact that I'm ass naked out here, only a few yards from the festival being celebrated by our family. My nipples harden from the sting of breeze on my burning flesh, already glowing with a sheen of sweat. My cock is stretched, and my balls are heavy, aching with need.

Drake doesn't bother taking off his own clothes. I think that's the point; he wants me exposed, while keeping himself in control. He stands up before straddling my chest where I lie on the log bench, aiming his cock right by my face.

I waste no time licking a line up his erection, swirling my tongue around the tip to lap up a bead of precum. His eyelids droop, and he groans, a sight and sound that has me gripping my own cock behind him. But he swats my hand away and does it himself, stroking me slowly while I take him in my mouth.

I'm sucking his cock hard, hungry as hell for him and that perfect dick, when I make out a distinct sound. Humming.

It's Abdiel.

I can hear him coming to us, growing closer and closer to where we're hidden away at the far side of the lake, me naked and in a very compromising position. And it makes me a thousand times harder knowing he's about to walk up any minute.

Drake fists his hand in my hair, pushing himself deeper into my throat until I grunt, my heartbeat in my ears almost drowning out the sounds of Abdiel humming. But I still hear him, and he's about to stumble upon us, while I'm throating Drake's cock.

"You can't fucking wait for him to see this, can you?" Drake hisses, flicking his hips to fuck my mouth. "You love being used even more than he does."

We love being used by you, my thoughts whisper to him, and he curls his fingers around my balls behind him, squeezing until I whine, choking and gagging on his dick.

"I told you to stop that shit." His jaw ticks visibly at me in his fury. But I know him. I know him well enough to know he likes when I say these things to him.

Nothing can ever come of it, and I know that. I guess maybe talking like this is my way of torturing him like he tortures me. We're both masochistic fucks, apparently.

Abdiel's footsteps approach, and I can tell when he reaches us because his humming comes to an abrupt halt, and his thoughts actually gasp.

"Oh my God..." he whispers.

My eyes fling to him, while Drake is still spearing my throat with his dick and jerking me rough at the same time.

"Hi there, little mouse." Drake's voice calls to Abdiel, who is frozen in place, eyes wider than I've ever seen them before. "Do you like what you see?"

"Fuck yes," he purrs, immediately adjusting himself in his pants while his eyes slide all over me, naked and lying here like a sex toy. A wayward, filthy king.

"You want to come play?" Drake asks, his fingers slinking between my ass cheeks until I quiver.

"*Please*. Dear God."

Abdiel stomps up to us, his fingers visibly twitching from wanting to touch more than he can even comprehend. Drake pulls his dick out of my mouth and moves back down between my thighs.

"Take your cock out," Drake commands Abdiel, and he does. Post haste.

"Look at you, my beautiful prince." I'm breathy and flushed beyond belief as I gaze up at Abdiel, his long, perfectly shaped cock bobbing right above my face.

"Look at *you*, my delicious King." He runs his fingers through my hair.

"I see something delicious I'd like to taste…" I lick my lower lip, and he hums, tracing my jaw and my lips with greedy fingertips.

I'm so busy focusing on how good Abdiel looks with his dick out, I don't even notice what Drake is doing until he runs wet fingers between the crack of my ass. I shiver and pucker at his touch, tightening up like an instinct, though he doesn't stop. He presses his index up to my asshole and shoves it inside, just an inch, until I gasp out loud.

Of course, it burns as usual, but I relax right away and accept the intrusion I love so much. He forces his finger deeper, priming me just enough until he feels I'm ready, which I am. I'm always ready for his cock in me.

"Abdiel." Drake's deep voice vibrates into me, and we both look up at him. "Shall we use our King?"

Abdiel, being the sweet one of the three of us, glances at me first, his eyes asking for verification that this is what I want. Which it is. One hundred percent. So I give him a little nod, pulling my bottom lip between my teeth.

I want it so bad, my prince. I need this before you leave me in a few hours.

Slight guilt flashes over Abdiel's face, but then he looks back to Drake and nods. "Yes. Let's use his body to get off and make him come like the wicked King he is."

Drake shudders visibly. "That sounds like the best use for this forest I've ever heard."

He takes his cock in his hand and rubs some lubrication onto it before pushing my hips forward, bending my knees so that I'm spread open for him. Then he presses the head up to me, swirling it around in the wetness, teasing my rim until I'm practically foaming at the mouth.

Nudging into me, his dick shifts and then breaks through the entrance until I groan in ecstasy at that first feeling of his fat head forcing inside my tight hole.

He stills for a moment, driving me insane with need, waiting until he can feel me wound up and trembling before he surges in farther, *deeper*, his cock ripping me apart in the best possible way.

"Fuuuuck yesss..." My eyes roll back when he brushes my prostate.

I can't believe I'm being fucked out in the middle of the woods, with people so close. We've never done it out in the open before, not since before it all started, when it was just us.

"I think he likes it." Drake slides his hands up my hips. "Your turn, little mouse. Give him your big cock to suck as deep as I fuck him."

"You wanna swallow my dick down, baby?" Abdiel asks, not waiting for an answer before he's pressing the crown of his erection up to my lips.

Moaning around him, I take him into my mouth, struggling to concentrate on sucking, all the while with Drake's dick pushing deeper and deeper into my ass. It's life affirming, being here with the both of them. I'm loving it so hard, I might come any minute.

Drake refuses to touch my erection, but it's bobbing around with his steady thrusts, his hips bucking into me while he ruts into me balls deep. I have tears seeping from my eyes at Abdiel's cock gliding into my throat, his balls on my face while he fucks my mouth, matching Drake's pace, his tempo.

Drake holds my hips, fingers digging in, while Abdiel clasps my jaw, caressing me as he breathes my name on every exhale.

Darian... Darian... God, Darian, you suck me so good, baby.

Drake's hands move up to my chest, pinching my nipples until precum drips from my cock, his powerful hands gripping my pecs while he fucks and fucks and fucks me so good, I'm going cross-eyed.

I groan on Abdiel's cock, telling them with my scrambled brain that I'm about to come. *I can't hold on... I'm gonna fucking explode.*

"Take our dicks, baby," Drake growls, lashing my prostate over and fucking over. "Is this your little secret, your highness? You come out into the woods and get fucked in the ass, tree bark scratching up your back while you suck your servant off? You love all this dick in you, don't you, Darian?"

Yes... yes yes yes...

"Fuck, I'm gonna come down your throat, my King," Abdiel whines, his hands covering Drake's on my chest.

"I'm gonna come deep in his ass," Drake rasps with black hair hanging in his face. I can't stop watching the two of them. How utterly sexy they are...

And I have both of them right now, inside me. Drake is right with his dirty talk. This is my little secret, and it will be my undoing.

I'm fucking coming...

My dick erupts first, the orgasm swirling me up into a tornado of pleasure. Then Abdiel breaks, pulses of warm liquid squirting down my throat as I drink up every drop. Drake busts last, falling over me to bite my neck and collarbone while he stuffs himself so deep inside me, I think his dick is going to meet Abdiel's. He comes hard, filling my ass, while both of them purr and whine and gasp.

Abdiel pulls out of my mouth, leaning down to kiss his cum from my mouth. Then Drake pulls out of my ass, leaning down to lick up the remnants of my cum all over my abs. And they both kiss me, then they kiss each other, all of our breaths echoing the magnitude of our releases, binding us in something deeply profound, sensual and wonderful.

I just wish it were as simple as keeping them forever. But I know it's not.

Because once our dizzying highs wear off, we're reminded of our reality.

Drake helps me up and Abdiel cleans me off. I'm dazed as they take care of me; they tend to me in silence, like a ritual.

My eyes aim toward the peak of the mountain, and I wonder how much of this is just vanity.

Just something to fill my cup until its inevitable end.

CHAPTER TWENTY

ABDIEL

After the adventure in the woods, Drake disappears. Darian and I walk back to the Den separately, just in case someone's watching, which no one seems to be.

The festival was great. One of the best I've ever had, but maybe I'm biased since I got to be such a huge part of it. My meals were a success, as was helping Ryle operate in the kitchen. I loved every minute of it.

Of course, that meant I didn't get to thoroughly enjoy the party like everyone else. And boy, did they enjoy it.

By the time we sneak back to the Den, it's almost three in the morning and people are still drinking by the fire, skinny dipping in the lake, singing songs, dancing and just celebrating. Summer is here and we've felt it all night.

I felt it in my bones while Darian, Drake, and I were doing our thing… The air warm, the moon high, stars bathing our flesh in their sparkle while we performed like animals in the forest.

I'm not as shocked as I was maybe a week ago at the things happening between me and the leaders of The Principality. I'm more concerned about what this all means and where it's headed.

Drake is the most emotionally unavailable person I've ever come across, but I can feel him fighting against himself. Every second we spend together, and more so every second he spends next to Darian, it's like he's in physical pain. I feel him resisting what he wants, *strong*, as if he's trying to repel a magnetic force, and I can't for the life of me decipher what the hell it's all about.

He blocks out his thoughts, that much is clear. I don't know how he does it, but any time he doesn't want us to hear him, his thoughts get this fuzziness to them, like static waves. It's odd, but I'm more worried about *why* he feels he has to do that. Could it really be because of what the Regnum would think about him and Darian being in love?

I don't want to believe that. I don't want to believe that my family would crucify two people for loving each other regardless of their origins in this world. Love is love, and at the end of the day, as long as the people are consenting and old enough to do so, I don't see the problem.

But maybe I'm being naïve. I would hope not, but you never know.

And then there's Darian. My King who is quickly taking shape as the love of my life, and it's so overwhelming sometimes I feel like I could fall down and weep into the dirt.

Is this how it feels to get the person you've been wanting for so long? Is this the kind of gut-twisting satisfaction that comes from finally being granted your one wish, and being so ecstatic to have it you don't even know what to do with yourself?

It's how I feel every time I'm with Darian. The thing is, I know I could be happy with him and only him for the rest of my days. It's not *me* who would be holding up this relationship.

My King has baggage, and a lot of it. It's not my place to urge him into action, and I would never judge. Such is the curse of falling for someone who's in love with someone else, and so detrimentally frightened by what it means.

I just have to sit back and wait for them to figure their shit out. Be supportive, keep my ear and shoulder available to bend or lean on, enjoying the unexpected sinfully hot sex, which is so obviously a crutch for the two of them it's not even funny.

The mild chaos burning between the three of us just adds to my need to break away for a bit. I'm going to get closure on the deaths of my parents. I'll seek answers and information, let Mother guide me to the next, and hopefully final step in my spiritual rebirth.

My *Ecdysis*.

I need to shed the uncertainties of the old Abdiel and reemerge from the woods an enlightened version of myself. Hopefully, this little trip will also give me some clarity on the three-way relationship I've found myself tangled in with two men twice my age. Plus, they might need the alone time to sort out their nonsense.

I just hope I don't return to blood and gore.

Glancing left, I smile at my stubborn king, asleep at my side, peacefully sated and quiet. He's truly beautiful, almost unbelievably gorgeous, and I understand how blessed I am to be in his presence romantically.

He's troubled, sure. Because no one could be that perfect without some inner flaws. I just wish I knew more about what he's holding against himself...

Darian and Drake both seem to feel unworthy of love, but in different ways. Drake won't let anyone get close enough, I think because he refuses to take on the burden of someone else's heart. But Darian...

His heart is yearning for it. Aching to be filled with the love of another. Yet he can't accept it.

Why, my King? My fingers trail his jaw while he breathes softly into the pillow, muscled arm draped over my waist. *What happened to you?*

His eyelids flutter, and I shift to press a soft kiss on his stubbled jaw, before lifting his heavy arm gently off myself. Trying not to wake him, I slink out of the bed as quietly as possible, dressing in the dark, the only light from the partially drawn curtains of the lounge, the moon's glow reflecting off the lake.

I'm glad I didn't go home after what we did in the woods. Darian was almost falling down, he was so tired. I wasn't sure he'd even notice me sleeping next to him, but his mind pleaded with me to stay, though his mouth would never allow him to speak the words.

I know it's killing him to let me go on this journey, and I'm still not sure why. He and Drake say the mountain is dangerous, but it can't be that bad if Drake lives up there. I'm only marginally afraid of what I might find, but I know I need to go, regardless. Even if Darian feels that me leaving could result in the end of us...

I don't know why he feels this way. I couldn't get a straight answer out of his thoughts, but I heard him thinking it, for just a split second, when I told him all I wanted was to make this journey.

He thinks whatever I find up there will make me stop loving him. And I just can't comprehend it.

Giving one last glance to his large form, deep in dreamland, my heart aches as I leave the lounge, creeping out the back door and sneaking around the Den toward my trailer. I have a bag already packed with clothes, my tent and sleeping bag, and enough food to last me four days, just in case. I don't plan on being up there more than a couple, but if I get stuck, I want to make sure I'm prepared. Not that I'm incapable of making my own food in the forest. We learn how to do that at a young age. Still, I've grown accustomed to my bacon, egg, and honey sandwiches.

I've left a note for Gina and Paul. I'm sure they'll be confused at first, but Darian and Drake will intercept them if, for whatever reason, they feel like coming after me. I'm sure they won't, though. I have to assume they want answers about what happened to my parents almost as much as I do.

Lacing up my good hiking boots and grabbing my bag, I leave the trailer determined. There are still people mulling about, but most of them seem a little incapacitated, not exactly paying me any mind. The Regnum knows how to party, and there was no shortage of booze and things to smoke tonight. When I saw Jordan last, a few hours ago, he had just eaten some mushrooms and was waiting for them to kick in. I'm sure he had a great night. Or *is still having* a great night.

Darian offered me his ATV, but I assured him I would rather walk. The four-wheelers are obviously faster, but this journey isn't about speed, it's about following the signs from Mother.

She'll guide me, I know it. I just have to listen.

And so off I set, walking through housing, past the farms, up to the Field. The Tribe is on patrol, but the guys barely even notice me in between their activities, also known as girls in their underwear on their laps, astride their ATVs. I can't help the smirk on my face as I walk right past, shaking my head as the girls' giggles echo over the entrance to the mountain.

I keep going on the walking path at the other side of the Field, the one that leads up the mountain rather than toward the lab. I can still see the lab, though, from afar. It's dark and quiet, naturally, since no one's working right now. Still, just seeing it reminds me of that first day, in Drake's office.

To I'm sure his chagrin, I'm not as afraid of him as I was then, although he still makes me very nervous. But I sort of trust him, which is an odd notion. He seems like the last person anyone should trust, but underneath that intentionally cold facade, the one he gives off to keep people at a distance, he has more heart than most others. He really cares for people. I know he does.

It makes me sad to think of him living up on this mountain all alone. As I walk and walk, already an hour into my journey, I approach a cabin that I just know is Drake's. No question.

Not only is he the only person who lives on the mountain, so this

215

must be his house, but it also screams Drake. Small, not overly fancy, but rigged with any comfort he could need and the most elaborate outdoor garden I've ever seen.

Walking around back, I notice he has a greenhouse too, though not as large as the one outside the Den. Peering inside, I see some very interesting-looking plants. It makes me smile. *He's so damn smart...*

I wish he knew how much of a gift it is to know him.

I shouldn't be snooping around his place, but I can't help it. I don't think many of the Regnum have seen this place, and I feel special even being near it. Coming through the trees past the greenhouse, I almost gasp out loud.

My eyes widen. The cabin is located right at an overlook. I hadn't realized how high I was already...

There's a perfect view of the lake from up here. And the Den.

My heart lurches as I gaze down over the calm waters, and the elaborate home which looks much smaller from this height. Drake built his house so he could always watch over Darian...

He loves him so deeply in secret.

My limbs twitch with the desire to bang their heads together. I wish they could just get it through their thick skulls that they need each other, but I know it's much more complicated than that. Still, I hurt for them. I really hope I'm not coming in between them, or complicating things even more.

Wandering back around toward the path, I hear something in my head. It's like a voice, and it's startling.

It's yelling something at me, so faint yet clear enough that I stop short.

Watch out!

Frozen, I glance around, and when my eyes land on the ground, I curse, my heart leaping into my throat.

There's a bear trap, nestled into the dirt, grass, and leaves, two inches from my foot. One more step and I might've lost it.

"What the fuck..." I breathe, my pulse racing inside me as I back up slowly, eyes scanning the surrounding area to see if I can locate more.

Drake, you fucking lunatic.

I don't see any others yet, but that's not to say there aren't more traps, of different varieties. Slapping my hand over my heart, I breathe out slowly.

Sure, a bear trap is just that. A trap for bears, which are definitely

216

a concern out here. But something about this, and how close it is to Drake's cabin leads me to believe it's not just to maim potential four-legged intruders.

I leave Drake's property slowly, carefully. I find at least one more visible bear-trap, and now I'm on high alert, which I should have been from the start. We're always taught to keep our eyes and ears open at all times in the woods, especially on the mountain, and now I'm kicking myself for being lost in my own relationship drama.

No more. I need to focus.

Back on the path, I keep walking, my mind swirling around that voice. The one that told me to *watch out...*

It wasn't Drake. I know what his thoughts sound like. And as much as I know Mother speaks to me, it's less of a direct voice and more of a feeling when She gives messages.

I can't stop thinking about it as I go, the muscles in my legs burning from the upward hike. Eventually, I decide to take a break, plopping down on a broken tree, pulling out one of my sandwiches and a bottle of water.

I'm content so far with my trek, eating in quiet comfort, eyes flitting through the trees. Aside from Drake's bear traps, I haven't sensed any danger just yet, but we'll see. As long as I keep my awareness up, I should be fine.

A new little chattering voice springs into my ear, and I stop chewing. Glancing around, I see nothing.

Birds are chirping, dawn having broken as an early summer sun graces the forest with fresh light. It's still cool in the mornings, the spring weather hanging on, not ready to hand over the summer heat just yet, which I have to appreciate.

I go back to my sandwich until I hear the tiny voices again. Blinking hard, I wonder if this is some extended side-effect of continued Empyrean use. I got my last dose the day before yesterday, after pleading with Drake to give me more for my journey. So maybe I'm just high, though that explanation doesn't settle me.

My mind's eye is leading me to something, and as I peer around, I notice a small shack, off in the distance. Squinting at it, the chattering comes into clearer focus.

Please. Please please.

"Who's begging?" I whisper, peering at the ground by my feet.

There are three baby ravens in a nest that must have fallen with this tree I'm sitting on. They don't look injured, but I can't help noticing I'm not seeing Mama anywhere around.

Their chirps sound like words. *Hungry. Hungry.*

Blinking again, I think momentarily that I'm losing my mind. But even if that's the case, I can't ignore any animal in need. I'm a servant, after all.

Ripping off a few small pieces of bread from my sandwich, I drop it down to the babies, watching them scamper around, pecking at the food. It nourishes them, and I watch, listening as they praise me.

Thank you! Thank you!

You're welcome, I smile at them.

You will not be forgotten, young Prince. Everything gets a return.

Slowly, I nod. *Everything gets a return.*

One good deed for another.

Wrapping up the rest of my sandwich, I wave to the chicks and pick myself back up, treading carefully in the direction of the shack. As I grow nearer, branches of the trees shift with the wind. I can hear subtle voices, more distinctly human, yet far enough away that they're muffled, and I can't make out what they're saying.

Still, it's something aggrieved I'm hearing. The air feels much colder around here, but I ignore it, stepping up to the door of the shack and pulling the handle. Struggle and pain ripple through the breeze with words I just can't hear, unfocused. My heart lodges in my throat as I peek inside the darkness.

And then I let out a breath of relief. Because it's a hunting shack. There are spare farming tools, some animal furs and hides hanging up. Nothing out of the ordinary.

Shaking off whatever the pensive feeling is in my gut, I close the door, making my way back onto the trail.

The sun is hanging high in the sky as I climb toward it.

I've been hiking the mountain for a few hours, and I'm closer to the peak than I could have anticipated. I'm taking my time with this journey. Inspecting the area, feeling the emotions of this mountain.

It might sound crazy to some, but there's a voice up here. At first, I thought it was Mother, but the more I hear and feel, I'm not so sure.

I stop by the river to splash some cool water on my face. I'm growing closer to where it happened... I can feel it.

My parents' bodies were found in a gully, which sits many yards down from the peak. Their bones were shattered, indicating that they'd fallen... Or jumped.

Or been pushed.

I still remember that day, like it just happened...

I'm cold, freezing, though it's summer and the sun is warm.

My skin is frigid, as if I'm sitting in an icebox.

I wander closer to where everyone is gathered, people standing up on the banks looking down on the rest of us, in the gully, dredging through the water. Hushed whispers surround me, yet I can't hear any of their words.

I'm smaller than the adults, so they don't see me sneaking around them, moving closer.

Finally, I break through, a sharp pain of breath sucking into my lungs like a blade.

Mom and Dad...

They're lying in the shallow water, eyes open.

My father's leg is bent back in a way it certainly shouldn't be, and my mother's arm is folded underneath her. Their faces are right by one another's. And they're holding hands. Actually, their fingers appear tangled together, like it would take great effort to separate them.

Swallowing is a harsh burn, pressure building up in my face so tight I can barely see. My eyes are flooded instantly with tears I don't feel. My face is numb, my whole body is.

My parents... are dead.

I turn and throw up onto the ground. It splatters on my shoes.

"Abdiel, no!" A loud voice booms from my right, but I can't look in its direction.

I can't look away from the bodies of the only parents I'll ever have. The most important people in the world to me.

They're gone.

"Come, now," the voice says as I'm lifted up into powerful arms and hauled away from the bodies.

Away from the pain.

It takes many moments for me to realize it's Head Priest who's carrying me, stomping through the muddy water while I cling to him.

My skinny arms tighten around his neck, and I bury my face in the crook, crying hysterically. He walks for what feels like hours, holding the back of my head, his long fingers gently caressing my curls.

"There there, young one," he whispers in comfort, though his voice sounds choked with emotions. "You're not alone, and you never will be."

I shiver and shake in his grip, but he just holds me tighter. At some point, I think he's sitting down. I can barely register where we are, but I know we're still in the woods. I don't see or hear anyone anymore. Nothing but the consoling murmurs of our Head Priest.

Our King.

"I'm... I'm sc-scared," I whimper.

"Shhh... I know," he says, tone deep in a grief weighting my own chest like a hundred pounds of wet cement. "Feel this, Abdiel. Feel anything you need to. Mourn... but don't fear it."

His words give me some minute comfort, although I don't exactly understand what they mean. I nod into the crook of his neck, and I just cry. And he cries with me.

A loss I've felt in my bones every day since...

Sucking in a sharp gasp of air, I shake myself out of it.

To think Darian was the one who held me that day, when I lost my parents, is a staggering notion. I was just a boy then, and he was a man. Not that it was sexual in any way... Neither of us could have known what the future would bring.

But I remember always watching him, since I was young. When I was little, I didn't understand what my fascination with him was building to. And once I became a teenager, the feelings morphed into more of a yearning I couldn't fathom.

Head Priest paid only enough attention to me, making sure I had everything I would need without my parents. But we didn't talk after that day, no more than a couple of words here and there. And now that things have happened between us, I can't help but wonder if maybe he kept a closer eye on me...

I know it wouldn't be appropriate, but the heart doesn't care about logic or rationality. I've been a Domestic since I was fourteen, and I've been in love with him the whole time, whether I knew it or not. Am I to believe he only just noticed me?

Leaving the river, I walk back toward the path. I stroll for another mile or so until I come to a fork. It's not really a *fork* per se, because there's the way you're clearly supposed to go, the trail which looks like it's been made for quite some time. And then there's a small path going in a different direction, one that appears scarcely used.

And something pulls me that way, those needy feelings of curiosity I possess driving me toward the narrow trail, leading farther into the woods, rather than *up up up* to the top of the peak.

It's much colder up here, which makes sense because of the change in altitude. But then it doesn't really *feel* like that. It's a different kind of cold… The cold of the unknown.

Fear slinks through my chest as I walk slowly, observing my surroundings, listening closely for anything discernible, though it's difficult because I seem to be hearing all kinds of things.

Voices that sound like voices, and those that don't. They sound more like… emotions. Feelings.

Mourn, but don't fear it.

Chills grace my flesh as I walk, twigs and pine needles crunching beneath my boots. I try to step slow and careful, to stay as quiet as possible just in case. I haven't seen any bears or mountain lions yet, knock on wood. I'm hoping to avoid the dangerous, though I keep my knife sharpened and ready, hanging on my pants.

As I walk, my eyes settle on a clearing. It's between enormous trees, and it looks a bit peculiar, as if it shouldn't be.

But it is, and in my mischief, I stagger toward it. The closer I come to it, things begin to echo. The surrounding air is thick, which I attribute to pressure changes and whatnot, though again, it doesn't feel like that.

It's a shift, and it brings my legs to a halt.

Something assaults my chest, a hard pounding, which I think is my heart, though it's much more aggressive. It's like I'm being shot by my own heartbeat.

Struggling to breathe deeper, I suck air into my lungs and hold it while my vision swims and things become blurry. The clearing is twelve feet away, and it almost feels like there's a force field around it.

This makes no sense. It's just an empty clearing in the woods. Nothing more.

Closing my eyes tight, I shake my head to gather my thoughts. And when I reopen them, my stomach clenches like a fist.

There's something there now. Within the clearing.

In the middle of this circle of tall trees, there's a large, flat rock that wasn't there before.

It's black, like obsidian, almost sedimentary in its layers. It looks volcanic, though somehow shiny as well.

It's mesmerizing, and I want to get a closer look, but every internal warning in my mind is telling me to stay far the fuck away from it.

I'm perplexed by this. I don't know why I'm being cautious. It's just a rock.

Yea, a rock that literally wasn't there two seconds ago.

Regardless, I take tentative steps, growing closer. Two more feet. Then another, and another.

The wind whips through my hair, the rock distorting in my vision.

Two more feet, and I'm so close I can feel it. I don't know how or what I feel... but I feel something.

Something dark. Something... evil.

Abdiel... No!

A chirping voice calls to me, breaking through the whispers urging me closer and closer.

No, Abdiel! Don't do it!

Tearing my gaze away from the rock, I gape up into the trees. The baby ravens are there, chirping. Their squeaks and squawks grow frantic, their little bird voices crying out as loud as they can.

Don't go in there!

My heart is thumping so hard inside me, I can barely breathe. Stumbling back in the direction I came, I fumble over my steps until the clearing is farther away and I can breathe better.

I lean up against a tree, clutching its bark while I catch my breath.

What the fuck...

What is that?? What's going on up here??

Pulling in air and holding it, I exhale slowly, propping my head against the tree behind me. I don't know what's happening, but I was in some sort of trance walking toward that rock.

It was *calling* to me... beckoning to my curiosity. And I'm not fully convinced it wanted to harm me, but the raven chicks seem to think it did.

When I glance back up at the tree branches, they're gone.

I'm going fucking insane.

Dropping my backpack onto the ground for a moment, I take out a bottle of water, chugging half of it in two large gulps. My hands are shaking.

My thoughts are stuck on the clearing... that rock. Did it have something to do with my parents? Is that where I'll find answers?

Or is that what Darian and Drake warned me about?

I scoff. *Their warning without a warning.* I wish they could have just been specific about what danger I need to watch out for. Like animals or a fucking mysterious rock that wants to kill me.

Inhaling deep once more, I peer around the trees toward the clearing. My stomach drops into the dirt…

It's gone.

The rock… has vanished.

Motherfucking fuck. What the damn hell is going on up here?

This would be the perfect place to end my life.

I startle at my thoughts as they chill me to the bone. *Why the fuck would I ever think something like that??*

They didn't feel like my own thoughts, though they were in my head. They mirrored my voice, and it's terrifying me. *Why the fuck would I think that?*

No one would even notice, I'm sure…

My heart pumps hard behind my ribs as I look around. The thoughts are inside me, but they don't feel like they're coming *from* me.

There has to be someone else around.

Picking up my bag, I creep through the trees, following the feeling until I see her.

A girl with strawberry blonde hair fluttering around her face in the breeze, sitting on the floor of the forest. And she's crying.

This would be the best place to kill myself.

And no one would ever find me.

CHAPTER
TWENTY ONE

DRAKE

R unning my hands beneath the stream of water, I watch as deep red turns the water pink. I scrub them with soap, *hard*, aggressively attempting to rid all the traces around my nails and on my fingers.

But it's no use. There's a hue I can't get rid of, even after the rest has washed away.

All the blood on my hands…

I've created something special, and for now, it's all mine.

I haven't told Darian yet. I know I will eventually, but he's dabbling in other parts of our new life. He's been rather busy, anyway.

Becoming a leader.

Two years ago, we invited our first new friend to live on our territory. And since then, the plan of the universe has continued to take its shape, everything meant to occur in these woods revolving around my brother.

Darian King, Head Priest of The Principality.

It started as an idea, as anything does. A mildly far-fetched thought about what human existence should look like, why we're here, and what should come of our new lives in the forest. Darian and I decided we mustn't squander the opportunities we've been given to start over.

Because nothing happens by accident.

More people stumbled upon our settlement, and we decided to stake a claim in this land we call the Expanse. It's ours, and we'll defend it or die trying. Darian thinks I'm being dramatic when I say that, but he doesn't know the things I've seen...

The evil I've made to keep him safe.

The funny thing is that each and every person who has wound up here in the last two years, who have wandered onto the Expanse looking for an escape from the outside world and a new community, a fresh start, they've all looked to Darian and me for guidance.

I'm no one's leader. But Darian is.

He's taken to the role almost effortlessly, because of his charisma, his obvious strength, wisdom and patience. He's the perfect person to preach the message of Mother Earth, her gifts, and the transformation of life.

It's really quite simple. We don't call it a religion, because neither of us believe in that. It's just the way of the world. We live by earth and die by earth; our God, Mother. A great spiritual being more than a pronoun, of course, but the way we see it, She's a "she," since She gave birth to us, from dirt and water and air.

In the early days, Darian and I smoked a lot of homegrown weed. We ate mushrooms, and I made an herb to smoke from some flowers I've grown, native to the mountain of their namesake, the white angel trumpets. The plants have entheogenic properties, from the species Brugmansia suaveolens, which I've been studying for quite some time. I've been cultivating them in my greenhouse, synthesizing as best I can until we get a lab built.

I think it could be a tremendous breakthrough in my chemical research, but I need the space. I need help as my operation grows.

Anyway, the first time we smoked it together, we experienced things I could have never dreamed, unlike the relatively basic highs from cannabis or even mushrooms. It was with our minds truly open to the great plan of the universe that we saw it all so much clearer.

This is our purpose. And thus, The Principality was born.

We fucked harder and more intensely than we ever have that first night, in the woods surrounded by colors and whispers and shapes of unknown entities, dancing and singing around us. Even thinking about it now gives me chills... Especially since we don't get to be together all that much anymore.

Darian has sworn to me that he doesn't necessarily want to lead these people. He's younger than most of them, but for some reason, they all look to him for answers. And because of his giant, lovely heart, he feels obligated to give them what they want.

But no one knows about us, and it's been killing me inside a little bit every day. Sometimes I just want to grab him and kiss him in front of everyone, to end the facade that we're brothers and nothing more.

I find myself resenting him, or them, or Mother, for making it this way.

For making me fall in love with him and then giving him to everyone else.

This is what I'm thinking as I sit in my greenhouse, vial in hand. I created something new, and I'm going to try it for the first time. I've made it to be injected rather than smoked, because it's no regular psychedelic. To be honest, I'm not sure exactly what it will do.

But I guess I'm about to find out.

I remove the packaged syringe from my pocket and unwrap it. Sticking the needle into the vial, I suck in the clear liquid, my heart jumping in my chest all the while.

I've never done anything like this before, but I'm very careful as I tie up my arm and inject myself with precision, making sure to see blood fill the syringe before I plunge. As soon as it's empty, I remove the needle from my vein and untie myself, blinking heavily.

It feels like the trumpets at first; warmth and thick, wavy air. Colors and shapes rippling around my head. The Earth speaking to me, telling me how things need to be. How they are.

But then I hear something different... voices. They're faint, whispers unlike those from nature. They sound like people speaking from afar, but I can't tell where they're coming from. I'm in my greenhouse and no one comes up here.

Walking as steadily as I can outside, I wander toward the cliff that overlooks the lake. It's not crazy high, so I can see people mulling about down there. We have plans to build Darian a cabin next year, and a lot of work is being done to make a clearing, chop down trees, create lumber. It's a whole process, but it will be very exciting once it's built.

He deserves to live in a castle, not a trailer.

Watching them scurry to and fro I realize, even much to my own skepticism, that what I think I'm hearing are their thoughts. I mean, it's hard to know for sure, but I'm hearing things that people would think, coming from them. The carpenters are worrying about measurements, the farmers thinking about crops. It's faint, because they aren't close, but still.

I think I can hear them...

Needing to investigate this further, I hop onto my ATV and drive down the path toward the housing trailers. And as soon as I'm closer, the voices hit me like a proverbial ton of bricks.

Slinking off, I'm dizzy as I walk, hearing things; so many things. Everything.

A guy named Jason waves at me, but he's thinking about how I make him uneasy. A woman named Shirley says hi, and she's wondering if I'm seeing anyone. A guy named Justin passes me without a word, but he's also wondering if I'm seeing anyone, the same thing he seems to be wondering about Jason.

Children run past me, and all I hear are thoughts about toys, and the animals they just came from feeding. I can practically see what they're describing in their heads, and it has me spinning.

Blinking over and over, I rub my eyes. It's not fading the way the high from the trumpets does. It's been at least twenty minutes and the voices are as strong as ever, pounding inside my skull.

This is crazy.

I need to get to Darian. This high is so intense, and I have no idea what's going on. Is it possible the psychedelics I've created have given me some sort of telepathic abilities? And if so, how?

My mind aches with the stronger question... Why?

I wander up to the trailer I used to share with Darian. The one I moved out of when people started joining our little community. I still remember the look on his face the day I told him I was leaving...

"Don't go... Please."

I shudder myself out of it as I knock on his door, not waiting for an answer before I push inside.

"Dar... something crazy is going on," I rumble, rubbing my eyes again.

I don't see him, but I can hear him. Actually... I hear two voices.

My heart rate picks up considerably as I step farther into the living room, turning toward the bedroom door, which is only partially closed.

I know I should leave. I shouldn't even look where my eyes are aimed, I know that with every muscle in my body. But I can't stop myself.

Neither can I stop my brain from hearing their thoughts.

"It's been so long since I've been with a man..." says the male voice who isn't Darian. My eyes settle on the bed, the bed we used to share, my breath leaving my lungs in a pained gasp. "It feels so good."

"You're so sexy," says Darian in a hushed, aroused whisper only I've ever heard before. Or so I thought... "Keep touching me."

The man is named Lars. I recognize him right away. He and his wife have been living here for about six months. He's very nice, quiet and polite. And he's gorgeous, a fact that's hard to ignore, though I've tried. More so, I've tried to ignore how my brother notices it.

And now he's on top of my Darian, kissing his lips.

My lips.

My heart is screaming inside my chest. I can hear it, louder than anything else, the sound nearly drowning out their thoughts about how good it feels to do something forbidden, something secret. The sounds are almost as painful as what I'm witnessing; Darian's hands on Lars's abs, slipping beneath his shirt. Lars's hand on Darian's crotch, rubbing him through his pants.

I feel sick, like I might throw up. I need to move; I need to leave, but I can't stop watching. I'm frozen to the floor like a masochistic statue.

"Are you sure your wife doesn't mind?" Darian hums into Lars's mouth.

"Positive. We've done it before, together. She told me to just keep it discreet."

"She's wonderful."

"She is. Are you really single? You seemed... unsure at first."

Darian stills, and I hear him thinking about it. The sound is so strong, my knees buckle, and I almost fall down.

Drake will never be able to love me back... *Darian's voice speaks in his mind.* He's ashamed of wanting me.

"I'm single. I'm just... experimenting," Darian whispers, his words and the tone of his voice striking me down like a thousand knives cutting me all over.

The regret lining them... it's damning; coated in unrequited feelings and uncertainty, two things Darian has never been.

Until me. This is what I've done to him.

"Can I take you in my mouth, Head Priest?" Lars's voice stings my ears once more, and I turn, quickly storming away as quietly as I can, though I'm sure they heard me slamming the door.

I can't be bothered with it. I just need to get the fuck out of here.

The thoughts of everyone around me assault my mind as I jump onto my ATV and peel off, dirt and dust kicking up behind me as I tear up the path. I rush back to my trailer at the bottom of the mountain, the farthest from the rest of housing. But when I get there, I still don't stop. I keep going, up the mountain.

I go up and up and up some more, driving for a long time, farther than we tend to go.

This is uncharted territory.

I come to a fast stop when I almost crash into a tree, jumping off the ATV and immediately falling onto my knees in the dirt. I clutch my chest, because I think I'm having a heart attack, and I can't breathe. I don't know what this feeling is, but it's like a tight, suffocation in my chest, squeezing me from the inside out.

"Fuck... fuck fuck fuck." I cough, covering my eyes, forcing away tears.

This is stupid. Why am I reacting this way?

I left him. I moved out. I told him we couldn't...

This is what I wanted. But why?

Why, when I'm so clearly in fucking love with him...

Climbing to my feet, I stagger around, stomping through my thoughts. I walk for a while, weaving between the trees of the mountain until my feet start to ache and my body feels heavier than my heart.

And when I stumble upon a clearing in the woods, I decide it's the perfect place to sit down.

As I saunter into the clearing, a rock appears before my eyes. It's dark, black and smooth. It just looks like a seat, and my tired, tear-filled eyes land on it right before my ass does.

Plopping down, I bury my face in my hands, and I cry.

I cry vicious tears, agonizing tears. Tears that sting my eyes and my cheeks, and my hands. They're like acid, and when my lids creep open, there's red on my hands.

Deep, thick red, staining my pale skin.

A chill brushes my skin until all the hairs on my arms stand up.

"Why am I bleeding?" I whisper to no one.

My chin lifts as a form steps in front of me. It takes a few blinks over my blurred vision before I recognize the person.

My gaze narrows suspiciously.

"Well, look what the cat dragged in," the all too familiar voice stabs my ears. "Hey, shrimp. Long time no see."

"Dan." Pure hatred etches my tone as I stare up at him in rage and disbelief. "I thought I killed you."

He laughs. "Oh yea, you did alright." He grins, and I notice the bloodstains on his shirt, right at his stomach. "Great job, by the way. I didn't think you had it in you."

"Yea, well... you underestimated me, you fuckin pig." I stand up, ready to attack his perverted ass.

But I pause and look around when I notice that the forest suddenly looks different.

Swallowing hard, I cringe as my jaw sets. I'm in a bathroom... A familiar one.

Shivers rack my body when I look down, my mother's body lying on the floor by my feet.

"Fuck..." I whimper, covering my eyes with my hands, trying to rub this shit away, but it just won't go.

"Don't be a pussy, shrimp." Dan's fucking prick voice slithers into my ear, and I turn to glare at him. "You killed me. You're not a bitch like I used to think you were."

"Yea, you wanna get stabbed again, asshole?" I growl at him, getting up in his face. "Keep talking."

"I was wrong about you," the fucker chuckles. "I admit it. You've got loyalty to that boy."

He's talking about Darian, and I'm seconds from strangling his dead ass with my bare hands.

"You don't talk about him," I hiss in his face. "I killed you once for touching him, I won't hesitate to fuck your ass up for speaking about him."

"Language, baby boy." A female voice rasps, and I jump, glancing down at Mom, who's now awake, speaking to me.

Her face is still blue, eyes circled in black. She looks dead as fuck, yet she's talking...

To me.

"What the fuck is going on...?" I breathe, stumbling away.

"Drake, you needed to see this today," she says. My brow furrows. "You're not afraid of anything, my love..."

"Except one thing." Dan grins, evil.

"Oh yea? And what's that?" I rumble while my head spins.

"Losing him," my mother sighs from the floor. "But what you need to understand, baby, is that he's not yours to lose. He belongs to them now. You can protect him and love him as your brother. But he can never be yours, Drake. Do you understand?"

More pressure builds behind my eyes as I remember the sight of him with someone else...

"I love him..." I cry, to my mom, the woman I only knew for the first portion of my life. She's nothing but a vague concept, a distant memory to me now.

"I know, darling. But you have to stop."

"Go, shrimp," Dan says, and I seethe in his direction. But he simply nods toward the bathroom door.

And as much as I want to ignore him, I open it, and step through.

On the other side, I'm in muddy water, surrounded by ledges of land on each side. I think it's a ravine, or a gully of some kind. It looks familiar as part of the mountain, farther down than where I am, or where I was.

I'm not sure why I'm here... Or how I even got here from all the way up where I was just a moment ago.

Confusion is holding me captive, my movements slow and murky as I look around. It's the pale daylight of early morning, no longer the dimming of sunset. The cool air of spring no longer surrounds me, but the humid heat of late summer.

How has everything changed in the blink of an eye? How did I get here, and where did I come from?

What's happening?

A sudden sound catches my ear. My face pivots all over, searching for whoever is making that noise, though I see no one.

The closer I listen, the more I realize that someone is crying. More specifically, a man...

The sound is familiar...

"Darian?" I call out. "Dar, where are you? Are you alright?"

I know it's Darian crying. I can tell, but I don't see him anywhere. I don't see anyone.

"Dar?!" I scream louder, spinning around and around, searching for him while he weeps.

Darian's hushed cries are accompanied by smaller ones. The sobs of a younger boy echo Darian's. But who?

Who is that? And why is Darian crying with him?

I stumble backward when I see the ground by my feet, covered in stiff limbs and dead torsos. Bile rises in my throat, and I swallow over and over, my hands shaking with fear.

And when I lift them once more, they're still drenched in blood.

All the blood is on my *hands...*

My mind lingers on that clearing in the woods while I continue scrubbing. I remember all the times I've been there since that first instance, and the things I've done, what I've seen. The things it's *allowed* me to see…

I hope Abdiel is okay.

Surely, he's reached it by now. I know he was nearby. I could hear him shortly after I *took care of* the prisoner. I wondered for a moment if he would find me.

But of course, he didn't. He's on a different path, and I just have to hope he'll be strong enough to overcome whatever the forces in that clearing want to show him. Others haven't been so lucky…

Shrugging off my bleak mood, I stomp up the stairs from the dungeon and saunter back out of the shack into the woods. Snatching my walkie from the ATV, I radio Lorn.

"Grab Xander and get up here," I bark, feeling eyes at my back. "I've got a body for you to burn."

"Yes, sir," Lorn replies, but I'm barely listening.

I'm too busy turning to face the familiar gaze watching me with a quiet scolding.

"What brings you up here, your majesty?" I grunt at him. He says nothing but lifts a brow.

He's silently simmering in my direction, and of course, I already know why. But this dance we do is like a second language at this point. Actually, it's the only way we communicate anymore.

We don't do real conversations. We haven't in years. It's strained between us… I know that. I wish it weren't, but there's nothing I can do about it.

My mother's corpse was right all those years ago when it told me I can't have him. It's turned my black heart even blacker, but again, there's nothing to be done. This is how it must be.

The universe showed me something that day, in that clearing. It showed me the location where Lars and Jenny would die, thirteen years before it happened. It showed me and I couldn't stop it. Because it's my curse to hold all the pain.

The blood is always on *my* hands, so it doesn't end up on anyone else's.

Darian looks like he wants to say a million things, but he sighs and settles on, "What did you find out?"

"It's like we thought," I answer, leaning against my ATV and pulling out a rolled joint. "He and some friends were spying. They've got drones. They decided to sneak in and attempt to steal whatever they could."

His jaw tightens visibly. "So… you don't think it has anything to do with the business?"

I shrug. "You know I don't believe in coincidences…"

"Yea, neither do I. But this shit is serious." Darian rubs his eyes. He looks tired, weakened. Abdiel's only been gone a day… Does he really miss him that badly already?

Maybe he's just worrying. Or maybe it's something else that's stressing him out…

"We'll go to war if we have to." I light my joint and take a drag, trying to remain as impassive as possible.

"Not everyone loves killing as much as you," he murmurs, and I flinch.

That hurt. The truth usually does.

"I resent that." I step closer to him. "I get shit done, *Head Priest.*" My fist pounds over my heart. "*I* protect this place." *I protect you from me.*

Darian pushes into my space, the warmth of him immediately crowding me, though I don't show it. "Why do you keep doing this? Why do you keep it going when you know you don't have to? You're damning yourself, Drake. It's like you do it on purpose…"

"I *am* doing it on purpose," I seethe in his face. "I do it because no one else will. It's the balance, Darian, and you know it. You can keep telling yourself that's not the case, but it fucking is. Just accept it so we can all be on the same page."

"I don't want to accept it," he snarls with pain in his eyes. "I can't. The natural order doesn't have to involve you compromising yourself." I scoff over his words, looking away, but he moves his face in front of mine again. "It doesn't. You're hiding… Using the drugs, the mountain… the *evil* as a crutch. A buffer so you don't have to face the truth."

"Oh yea? And what's the truth, Darian? *Hm*??" If flames could come out of a gaze, they'd be doing it now, aimed right at my brother. "You think you know everything… Well, you don't know shit. You have no idea the kinds of things I live with. What I live with!"

I back up before something bad happens, pacing about in my rage, the fury rippling off me in waves. I can feel it up here. The night gets darker, colder, and the leaves tremble the way my fingers are.

Darian looks up, looks around, at how the trees are moving and the sudden shift in the atmosphere. But he doesn't appear scared or concerned. Not for himself…

He looks worried for me, sympathy shimmering in his blue eyes. They're darker now, and I'm sure he'll be craving soon. And I'll shoot him up, like a fucking dealer, because it's the last remaining connection I have to him.

Everything he just said is entirely true. I *am* hiding. I'm hiding so much more than he even knows. But such is my burden. And he's wrong about one thing...

I don't have a choice.

"Thanks for coming up, brother," I mumble, stomping out my joint and hopping onto my four-wheeler.

I don't hesitate to start it up and peel off, leaving him alone in the dark.

Because I have to.

CHAPTER TWENTY TWO

RHIANNON

This is the creepiest forest I've ever been in.

I still can't remember if I came here intending on killing myself, because by the time I got up here, close to the peak of this mountain, I'd convinced myself to do it.

It's better this way.

These woods are already a little shady, what with all the strange noises; the endless quiet sprinkled with forest sounds, so unlike the bustle of Seattle it's not even funny.

But the forest has strange feelings, too. Like it *knows* you the moment you set foot on its ground. It knows what's inside your head and your heart, and it'll play on that. For what reason, I'm not sure. But even if I hadn't been dead set on killing myself when I left home last night, by the time I got settled up here, I was filled with the certainty that I need to die.

It's the only way.

As if all of this isn't creepy enough on its own, a tall boy emerged from the trees, scaring the ever-loving shit out of me. I jumped so hard I might have peed a little. *Okay, that's an exaggeration, but still. It was startling.*

Peeking up at him from where he stands over me, I wipe my nose on the back of my hand. He doesn't look scary at all, which is comforting. He's actually... pretty damn beautiful.

Trying not to focus on that, I pull a scowl, looking away from him while I wipe under my eyes, attempting to rid the mascara smudges I just know are there. I don't like how he's just hovering over me while

I sit on the ground. He's like six feet, and while he doesn't appear menacing, the way he's towering over me is more intimidating than I enjoy.

"Go away," I grumble, aiming my face at his boots, my hair hanging around it like a curtain so he can't see me.

I'm such a child. As if me not seeing him means he can't see me.

"Are you alright?" He asks, ignoring my grouchiness as he takes a seat on the ground, right in front of me.

That gets my face up. Our eyes meet, and I'm once again momentarily captivated by how gorgeous he is. He doesn't even look real. Green eyes, a few shades darker than mine, dirty blonde hair in these lush curls that look softer than silk. A perfectly pointed nose, plump pink lips and a jawline that goes for miles.

I blink myself out of the fascination with this stranger and peer down at my hands, picking chipped nail polish from my fingernails. I didn't come here to make friends, and I don't want this kid sitting here trying to talk to me.

I came here to escape my horrible life, and possibly to kill myself, which I still kind of want to do, even though he's interrupting me.

"I'm Abdiel." His hand juts forward into my vision, and I glance at him again.

He's just staring at me, a pleasant almost-grin on his pillow-lips, hand extended, waiting for me to shake it. *Shake hands with a stranger in the woods who just found me crying on the ground? Well, how can I resist...*

Ignoring my inner sarcastic thoughts, I shake his hand, quick and unenthused. "Okay, I know your name. Now can you leave me alone?"

"No." The almost-grin turns into an almost-frown as his forehead lines in something like unease. "I can't leave you alone."

"Why the hell not?" I gape at him like he's nuts, and a shiver brushes through me at the thought that he might not be as nice as he looks.

But then he says, "Because you're obviously upset. You're crying, and you were thinking about..." His voice trails, and he clears his throat. "You're obviously upset. I wouldn't feel right about leaving you alone."

"Look, stranger—"

"Abdiel," he corrects me, grinning. My eye twitches.

"... *Abdiel*," I huff, and his smile widens. "I'm not your

responsibility."

"Actually, you kind of are," he jumps in. "Because you're on my land."

My jaw drops, and I stutter, "Oh my God. I'm so sorry." My head shakes over and over, conveying my confusion. "I didn't know anyone lived up here. I didn't mean to trespass…"

"Well, I don't live up here," he says. Now I'm confused. "I live down there." He points in the direction that would lead back down the mountain. "Between the mountain and the lake."

"So then how is this your land…?" My brows pull together. "You can't own an entire mountain. You're like twenty-five."

He beams at me. "I'm actually nineteen, but thanks. I was hoping I looked a little older." I can't help but roll my eyes as he chuckles. "Anyway, it's not just me. My family owns this land. It's called the Expanse."

"Okay, I have no idea what the hell you're talking about," I mutter, "But I promise if you just leave me alone for like fifteen minutes you won't have to deal with me on your land anymore. Well, you will, in a sense, but it won't be my problem after that."

Abdiel's smile disappears, and he blinks those large, sparkly, moss-colored eyes at me. I'm trying not to focus on how lovely they are, but it's hard when he looks like a baby deer.

"You can't kill yourself," he whispers.

My heart thuds, and my stomach jumps into my throat as I glare at him. "How did you—"

"I just know, okay? And you can't do it." He sighs and shakes his head. "Look, I obviously don't know you. You haven't even told me your name yet…"

He lifts his eyebrow at me, and much to my own trepidation, I murmur, "It's Rhiannon."

"Rhiannon." He nods, as if he approves of my name. It pleases me deep in a place I want to kick because I don't need this random person to like my name. "Well, Rhiannon, I have to tell you… you have every reason in the world to live."

"Is that right?" I scoff. *If he only knew…*

"Yea, it is." He reaches out, abruptly taking my hands in his. It startles me, and I try to tug them away, but he just holds on tighter. "All life is precious, and all life is necessary. Each one of us is a part of the great transformation. Even you."

I can't help giving him a look like he's certifiably insane, because honestly, he fits the bill. He sounds like a total whackadoodle.

"What the hell does that even mean?" I finally break my hands free from his grip. "You sound nuts, you know that?"

He shrugs, unaffected by my words. "Maybe so, but at least I know the truth."

"The truth about what?" This kid is starting to hurt my brain. "The things I may or may not be planning to do up here are none of your concern. I didn't ask you to come rescue me, *Abdiel*. I came up here to be alone. To escape. I saw that clearing over there and figured nearby would be a perfect place to…" My head gets a little foggy, and I squeeze my eyes shut. "It doesn't matter. Please, just leave me alone."

Quiet surrounds us for what feels like an eternity, and when I finally reopen my eyes, I find Abdiel looking at me with much more concern in his deep green irises. His eyebrows are practically knitted together, and he's gnawing on his lip, like he's overwhelmed by whatever is happening in his head.

"That clearing…" he mumbles, voice low, almost inaudible. "When you looked over there, did you see a rock? A black one…?"

Fear zips up my spine. I can't tell him about what I saw… About what happened over there that led me to where we're sitting right now. My lip trembles as I whisper, "No."

He blinks at me, like he doesn't necessarily believe my answer, but he doesn't call me out. He simply glances up for a moment, then breathes out steadily.

"It's getting dark. I'm going to set up camp for the night, and I think you should stick around. It's dangerous to be out here alone."

"You're out here alone," I murmur petulantly.

"I'll start a fire," he goes on, ignoring me again. "I have some extra food you're welcome to."

He stands up and holds out his hand for me to take. And after staring at it for a solid ten seconds, I do. Holding his hand feels nice, comforting though it gives me tingles all the same, which makes me uneasy. I don't know this kid. I should get away from him…

I didn't come here to hike and camp and roast marshmallows.

I open my mouth to tell him that, but he cuts in before I can. "Why don't you just stay for a bit, and we can talk? No strings attached. And if by tomorrow morning you still want to go off on your own, I won't stand in your way."

I give him a skeptical look, but he just keeps blinking those eyes at me like a cartoon character until I sigh, giving in to his persistence. I suppose there's no harm in talking to him. He seems like a nice enough guy, and if he's not, well... I always have my knife.

"Fine, but if you're hoping to get laid out here in the woods, you can just think again. No fireside makeout sessions, got it?" I fold my arms over my chest, letting him know I mean business.

He shows me an amused smirk. "Yea, I wouldn't worry about that. I'm seeing someone, so..."

"That doesn't mean anything," I counter. "Men are scumbags."

He laughs out loud. "Oh, is that right? All of us??"

I can't help the quirk to my lips. "Yes. Every one of you. All shit."

"I would apologize on behalf of my gender, but I doubt it'd be sincere," he chuckles. "However, speaking on behalf of just me, Abdiel Harmony, I'm with someone. And I love him very much, so there won't any attempted fireside makeouts, I promise." He taps the spot over his heart with his finger.

My face goes blank at his words. *Oh... he's gay. Alright, then... that settles it, I guess.*

I'm not sure why I'm disappointed all of a sudden. I have this weird stinging feeling in my gut, like jealousy, and it's ridiculous. It goes against everything I just said to him... Plus, again, can't stress this enough, I don't know this person.

I shouldn't care that he's in love with someone, or that it's a man, so there's probably no hope of him ever being attracted to me. None of that matters, and neither does this stupid inner monologue I'm having while he stares at me, wearing a content smile on his full lips.

He's not affected by me... clearly. Not one bit.

Shaking my head, I pick my backpack up off the ground and sling it over my shoulder. "Great. I'm super happy for you and your loving relationship. Now, where are we setting up this fire? I actually am pretty hungry..."

Abdiel makes a face, something I can't exactly detect flashing through his eyes, disappearing quickly. "Let's get away from that clearing. I don't want to sleep anywhere near it."

Yea, me neither. I should ask why not, to play it off like I don't have any feelings about the clearing, or that black rock, but instead I just nod along.

Abdiel suggests we backtrack to a spot south of here, where he can set up his tent and start a fire.

And without any further preamble, I leave with the stranger. This could be a really stupid decision on my part, but I'm feeling significantly more positive already, the farther we get from that clearing.

"Do you even have a tent?" Abdiel asks as we walk, his boots clunking into the solid ground, snapping twigs and crushing leaves, while my sneakers make much less noise.

"No."

"What were you going to sleep in?" I peer at him, and realization dawns on his face. "Rhiannon, I won't let you hurt yourself."

"You don't know me at all." My forehead lines "I'm not your problem or your concern."

"You are, because you're a human being," he says with certainty. "All—"

"Life is precious. Yea, I heard you before," I mumble.

He chuckles, and it makes me smile, though I cover it up. "It's interesting meeting an Outsider. You're so different from everyone I know."

"*Outsider*?" My eyes dart to his while we trek, side by side.

"Yea. I'm part of a community," he explains. "That's the family I was telling you about before. We're our own society, and this is our land. The mountain, the lake, this whole part of the forest."

He's throwing a lot at me right now, and it's hard to process it all. My head is spinning through everything he just said.

"So, kind of like a commune?" I ask, confused by this whole notion. I've heard of things like this on TV and in movies, but I never really knew they actually existed.

"I guess." He shrugs. "We're a big family, and we believe in the same things."

I'm not even sure what to say, so I just stay quiet while we walk. Only ten more minutes and Abdiel stops us, dropping his large backpack on the ground.

"This will do. You wanna grab some wood for the fire?"

I nod and do as he asks, gathering up wood, from twigs for kindling to larger pieces to burn, piling them all up in one spot while Abdiel assembles his tent. The sun is setting, and it's getting dark fast. But he manages to get it up just in time.

I have to cover my mouth so I don't look crazy as I giggle at my little internal joke. *I'm such a fool, I swear to God.*

Abdiel then digs a groove into the dirt, arranging the wood for the fire. He lights it in less than a minute, with nothing but a match and his pure skills.

I'm surprised. I have no damn clue how to start a fire, or set up a tent, and this kid did both in a matter of minutes. I suppose it makes sense, if he lives out in the woods. He probably does stuff like this all the time.

He's pulling food out of his backpack while I ask, "Do you live in a tent? Or do you guys have, like, houses in your commune?"

He grins over his shoulder while tossing the rest of his things inside his tent. "I live in a trailer. We all do, except for Darian. He has a house. A massive cabin. Like, mansion-sized."

"Wow." I take a seat on my backpack, beside the growing fire. "Sounds fancy. What makes Darian so special?"

Abdiel steps over and drops to his knees, fiddling with some metal items. "He's our leader."

Leader? Like a cult??

I'm really hoping that's not what he means, but I can't help gawking at him while a million and five questions bounce around inside my brain. "Your *leader*...?"

"Yes."

"As in like... what? What does he do?" I'm so curious I'm practically inching into the fire to get closer to him, as if that will get me answers faster.

"He started The Principality. With his brother, Drake, when they were just kids, younger than us. They've formed this entire community, brought us all together and taught us to praise Mother, and to sacrifice for the great transformation."

I'm certain my eyes are bugging out of my skull.

I'm mesmerized. I've never known anyone who's been in a cult before. I have to admit, it's always been a macabre interest of mine. I've watched dozens of documentaries on everything from The Children of God, to NXIVM, to L. Ron freaking Hubbard.

This is totally fascinating, and I've already forgotten about all my own problems. This kid and his crazy life are a great distraction for me. I guess I should be thankful for that.

"You've said that twice now," I inquire while he sets a thin grate over the fire, then opens a jar and pours something into a small pan. "What is the *great transformation?*"

"It's life. Existence, for the entire universe, not just for us," he answers, like it's the most basic thing in the world. He places the pan on the grate, stirring what's inside it with a wooden spoon. I'm not sure what it is, but it smells delicious already. "Think about it. Transformation is change, right? Well, that's what we all do. That's what the world does. It changes. Head Priest teaches us to think about our lives as a piece of the puzzle. We're all connected, even after we die. It keeps going, here... and in other places."

I blink several times before I can even respond. "I feel like a just smoked a huge joint."

He laughs out loud. "That's good. I think."

"No, it is. I've never... thought of it that way. Life like a transformation." He nods, and I'm quiet again... considering everything he's said. "Who's *Mother*?"

"Mother Earth." He smiles. "God is in the earth, in the elements, in all of us. So we call It Mother."

"Oh, man. I love that," I chuckle, and he grins along. "So God's a woman. Not an old man sitting in the clouds with a long beard. That makes me very happy."

"Well, God doesn't have a gender," he corrects me with amusement lining his tone. "But yea, we've learned about the cultural expectations of God in the outside world, and it's pretty ridiculous. No wonder there are so many nonbelievers out there."

"Wait, so you've *never* been outside these woods?" I ask, flabbergasted again for like the eighth time in ten minutes.

Abdiel shakes his head. "I was born into The Principality. I've lived my entire life on the Expanse."

All these words he keeps using. Jeez, I need a cult dictionary.

"What about your parents?" He flinches visibly at my words. "I mean, were they born into it?"

"No, they joined when they were about my age, and had me shortly after." He pauses for a moment, staring into the food that just started bubbling in the pan. "They um... they died when I was twelve."

My heart actually aches inside me, and it's such an odd sensation, since I only just met this guy. I don't know him well enough to sympathize so hard, but for some reason, I can feel his pain. He glances up at me, cocking his head to the side.

I don't know what that look means, but I mumble, "I'm so sorry for your loss."

"Thanks." He eyes me carefully.

It's making me sort of uncomfortable, the way he's staring at me. Like he's reading me somehow. I feel like I'm back in the shrink's office, and it makes me itch.

"So, this Darian... is he a huge pervert like most cult leaders?"

Abdiel's eyes widen, and for the first time since I met him, he doesn't look happy or sweet. He looks suddenly enraged.

"He's not a cult leader, and he's *not* a pervert," he hisses, eyes reflecting the flames from the fire to mirror the fury in his tone. "He's the kindest, most caring man I've ever known. He couldn't hurt a fly, let alone a human person."

I hold up my hands, stunned at his reaction. "I'm sorry. I was just kidding."

His brows pinch together. "You were?"

Not really, but sure. "Yea." I nod. "I'm really sorry. I meant no harm."

"No, I'm sorry," he breathes, features relaxing a bit. "I'm not used to Outsiders. You clearly have different opinions on what's funny."

I swallow a lump in my throat. "Sure. I guess that's it. Listen, I really didn't mean to offend you. If you say Darian is a stand-up guy, then who am I to judge? I'm no one, anyway."

"Don't say that." He lifts the pan off the grate and begins spooning food into a small bow. "You're important. Remember that."

"Right." I nod, only partially sarcastic. "The *transformation.*"

"Exactly." He finally smiles again, and I'm reminded of how nice it is to see.

As wary as I am of this *Darian* person, I'll steer clear of talking shit about him as long as it keeps this beautiful boy smiling.

He hands me a spoon and the bowl of food with steam billowing. "What is it?"

"Corn chowder." He dips his spoon into the pan to take a bite.

I scrunch my face. "I'm not a fan of chowders."

"Just try it," he says in a commanding tone that makes me unexpectedly tingly.

Lifting the bowl to my nose, I take a whiff. It smells amazing. "Did you make it?" He nods, and so, for him, I dunk my spoon into the creamy soup and take a bite.

As soon as it hits my tongue, the flavors explode. It's by far *the best* soup I've ever had in my life. I'm not even a huge fan of the ingredients separately; corn, potatoes, bacon. But all together like this, it's amazing.

"Oh, my God. Abdiel!" I squeal, and he grins. "This is delicious!" I shovel another bite into my mouth.

"Be careful," he laughs. "It's hot, you weirdo."

"I don't even care." I'm smiling while scarfing it down. "This is awesome. Are you sure you made this??"

"Positive." He beams. "I love to cook."

"That's great. No one in my house cooks. Except the housekeeper." I roll my eyes.

"Housekeeper?" His forehead creases.

"Yea. Betty. She doesn't cook like this, but she makes healthy shit. Salmon and brown rice. Pretty boring. But that's what my mom eats, and she forces me to eat like her."

He tilts his head like a puppy. It's the cutest thing I've ever seen. *This kid is seriously adorable.*

"A *housekeeper* is like... a Domestic?" He asks, and I stare at him for a moment.

"I have no idea what you're talking about," I mutter in between practically licking my bowl clean like an animal. "A housekeeper is like a maid, I guess. Someone who takes care of the house."

"Ohhh." He purses his lips. "Yea, we call it a *Domestic*." I shrug. "That's what I do."

"Really?" He nods again. "For who... Darian?"

He nods once more, something flashing over his face as he stares at the pan, biting his lip while swirling his spoon around in the soup. Squinting at him, I pick up on something. Something... interesting.

"Is Darian your *boyfriend?*" I ask, fully invested in this juicy gossip like it's reality TV.

Abdiel's eyes shoot up to mine, and I realize his cheeks are flushed. I gasp.

This Darian guy is fitting more and more into the cult leader mold with every little detail I learn about him. I wouldn't be surprised to find out he's banging multiple members of this *family* of his... this *Principality*.

"He's not... we haven't..." Abdiel stutters. "We haven't figured out what we are to each other yet. But I... I'm in love with him."

I give him a sympathetic little pout. "Of course you are."

His gaze narrows at me. "Why did you say it like that?"

Sighing, I place my bowl down. "Look, I don't know you, or Darian. But I just hope you aren't letting him take advantage of you because he's in a position of power. You might not know it, never having been in the outside world, but that happens a lot. So much so, in fact, that I'm able to piece it together without even meeting the dude, just based on things you're telling me."

He scoffs and shakes his head, clearly not wanting to hear what I'm saying. "Has it happened to you?" He cocks a brow at me, and I freeze.

My stomach crawls up into my throat, and I glance down at my hands, picking off more nail polish. "No. We're not talking about me. We're talking about you, and your secret relationship."

"It's complicated," he hums. "I wouldn't expect an Outsider to understand."

"Right." I fight not to roll my eyes. "So, what... are you out here to escape the drama or something?"

"No," he grumbles. "I came up here to..." He pauses and brushes hair away from his eyes. "I needed to find answers. I wanted to find myself, or some closure or *something*, but when I saw that clearing, I just sort of freaked out."

Memories of myself in the clearing flutter through my mind, and I cringe. Abdiel's gaze jumps up to my face, and he gives me that look again, like he can hear what I'm thinking. It brings the unease, fast.

"Maybe there was a point to all this," he says quietly. "It led me to you, after all."

"Some luck." I let out a sarcastic puff. "I'm not exactly a prize."

"You are," he whispers with confidence. "And I don't believe in luck."

Something about the way he's looking at me, and speaking to me, feels good. It's comforting and intriguing. There's something about this guy, and I really have to hope I'm not crushing on him or anything. Because not only is he gay and in love with his cult leader, but I just can't fall for anyone.

It's a dead end and it won't happen. It can't.

"Where are you from?" Abdiel asks, changing the subject, which takes a weight off my shoulders.

"Portland," I tell him. "But I've been living in Seattle for almost a year, going to University of Washington."

"That's a school?" He asks, and I have to grin. It's interesting speaking to someone who doesn't really know anything about anything relating to life outside of the woods. *I wonder if they even have the internet or TV.*

"Yea, it's a college. I'd wanted to go to Business School, but now I'm not so sure."

His forehead lines. "It doesn't make you happy?"

Not allowing my mind to go into the specifics, I mumble, "No. Not really. I mean, I would like to have a business someday, but I don't know why I have to go to this stupid school for that. It seems like a trap from corporate America. And my asshole stepdad."

"You don't like him?"

"No. I hate him."

"Why?"

"Alright, that's enough of the third degree," I mutter, and he gives me that confused puppy look again. "I mean stop asking so many questions."

"Oh." He grins. "Well, you came over here with me to talk, right?"

"Yea, but that doesn't mean you need to know everything about me."

"Fine, then ask more about me." He settles, sitting cross-legged, like he's preparing for a fireside chat. "But no more about my relationship with Darian, please."

"But it's so juicy!" I squeal, and he makes a face. I have to giggle. "Okay, okay, fine. No more relationship talk. So you like to cook... what else do you do for fun?"

"I'm a singer." He releases another dynamite smile, the perfect lines of his face illuminated by the glow of the fire.

"Really?"

"Yea. My best friend, Jordan, and I perform once a week at reflection."

"Reflection?" *Another word to add to the dictionary, I'm guessing.*

"It's a fire we have every night, where we all get together and catch up. Either reflect on our day, or decompress, or just talk and hang with the family."

Warmth pools in my gut. "That actually sounds really nice."

"It is. And once in a while, Jordan plays the guitar and I sing."

I can't help the longing on my face as I listen to him talk about this. I've literally never done anything like that with my family or my friends. We've always been wealthy, and my family's ideas of fun include vacationing in London or New York, sipping expensive wine and bragging to friends about achievements. What few friends I have are the exact same way.

I started meeting some different people in Seattle, but then it got all fucked up, just like it always does.

Blinking it away, I ask, "You have a good voice?"

"Hence the name Harmony." He smirks.

My brow lifts. "Wait, so *Harmony* isn't your real name?"

"It is." He looks confused. *The feeling is mutual.*

"Was it your parents' last name?"

His head shakes subtly. "No. We get surnames based on our attributes. Elders call me Abdiel Harmony."

"That's fucking crazy," I laugh, and he looks offended until I correct myself. "I mean, in a good way. This community sounds amazing. Everything you're describing makes it sound like paradise."

"It's not perfect, but it's a great place," he states with conviction.

The thing is, I can't tell if he's brainwashed—cult mentality, cognitive dissonance and all that—or if he really just loves his family and his life. It might be a little of both, but I can't judge since the outside world is total bullshit, hence why I came up here to *escape.*

"You should come back with me," Abdiel says. My eyes widen. "I'm serious. You could come meet everyone. Meet Darian and Drake. Maybe they'd let you stay."

His offer chokes me up for a moment. I can't believe this guy I just met is offering to bring me into his secret community. He doesn't know me. I'm kind of a trainwreck.

Also, I can't believe I'm sort of considering it, because *I* don't know *him.* He could be a freak show. After all, he's head over heels in love with his cult leader.

"Who's Drake?" I ask, then I recall. "The brother?"

Abdiel nods. "He's Darian's foster brother. They escaped to these woods when they were teenagers and started everything."

"Escaped what?"

"I'm not exactly sure." His eyes glimmer with contemplative sadness. "Bad things."

"So Darian is in charge... What does Drake do?"

Something shifts in Abdiel's expression again. It's like an introspective wonder as he gazes into the fire. There's something else going on here, but I said I wouldn't pry into his relationship again, so I choose to leave it alone.

"Drake is called The Alchemist. He has a lab, and he creates things for our community, along with running the business side of things."

"Business?" I'm beyond interested in this. I've never been so riveted in my life.

How is it possible I stumbled upon the most captivating mountain in all of Washington on my first shot, and met the most interesting guy in the Pacific Northwest?

"There's a lot to unpack here." His lips curve as he stands up slowly with the dishes. "But I can't keep spilling all our secrets. If you want to learn more, you'll have to come back with me."

"Rude." I smirk, and he laughs. It's a great sound.

You know what else is great? The sight of him walking away.

Seriously, the guy is insanely attractive, and he clearly has an impressive body hidden beneath his clothes. It's a shame he's into dudes, older ones too, from the sound of it.

Not that I shame people for an interest in older guys. I mean, I'm nineteen too, and I'd never consider dating anyone from school or anything. The last guy I hooked up with was thirty, and I thought that was a good age difference.

Though if others were chill like Abdiel, then I might consider wading into the guys-my-age pool.

I shake my head. None of this matters. Abdiel's unavailable, I'm never dating again, and I shouldn't even be thinking about willingly entering a cult tomorrow.

I'll just get some sleep tonight and take off in the morning. We'll go our separate ways and chalk this up to a pleasant distraction from my bleak existence, and an entertaining way to spend a Saturday night.

Abdiel comes back from cleaning the dishes and packs everything up. "I'm pretty exhausted. I've been on my feet all day, so I'm gonna crash. If you're staying up, can you put out the fire?"

I'm suddenly feeling sort of awkward. It's like having a sleepover with someone I just met.

He chuckles. I must be making a desperate face because he asks, "You want me to put the fire out?"

I nod weakly. "Please."

The smug grin doesn't leave his lips while he does it, and I try not to just stand around, shifting back and forth like an idiot.

I don't even have a sleeping bag. I have a blanket, no pillow, and a couple changes of clothes. I didn't really expect to be hanging around up here for long.

"I think you should sleep inside the tent with me," he says, and then catches himself. "I mean, not *with* me. Just in the tent. In case it rains, or animals come snooping around."

"Animals?" I squeak, to which he laughs.

"You're on a mountain, Rhiannon. This isn't a joke. There are bears and mountain lions up here."

"Holy fuck." I gulp. As much as I should worry about getting into a tent with a strange man, my main concern has just become not reenacting the Leo DiCaprio bear scene in *The Revenant*. "Okay, fine. I'll sleep in your damn tent. But if you even inch next to me, you're losing your nuts."

He throws his head back in a cackle that ripples through my insides. "That's quite the threat from such a tiny little girl."

Why is the way he just said that so motherlovin sexy...? And from a very irresistible mouth...

I swallow my errant thoughts and grab my backpack, diving inside the tent before I have to look at him for one more second, with blushing cheeks like a total loser.

Abdiel climbs in, and I'm already under my little throw blanket, curled into a ball, back to him. I hear him shuffling around, but I don't dare glance his way.

"Goodnight, Rhiannon," he whispers, voice rich and smooth, like caramel and hot fudge drizzling over an ice cream sundae. "I'm glad I met you today."

My stomach flutters. "Me, too. Goodnight, Abdiel."

I try to close my eyes, but some animal makes a strange noise outside and they spring open.

I physically feel every inch of space between me and the hot boy with the pink lips, the sexy voice and curious eyes.

I won't be getting a wink of sleep tonight.

CHAPTER TWENTY THREE

ABDIEL

I fully expected Rhiannon to be gone when I woke up. Even outside of what I heard her thinking about when we first met, she just seems flighty. She's jumpy and a little untrustworthy… *Skeptical* seems like a good word.

Yet she's been trusting of me. And I've been trying not to intrude on her thoughts too much because it's one thing with my family, but with a complete stranger… I don't know, it just seems like a dick move. Certain things, however, I couldn't stop myself from focusing on.

She's broken. Inside, she feels damaged, and she's searching for something to believe in. Something to give her faith in life again.

I think The Principality would be perfect for that. So last night, I decided that if she was still there when I woke up, I'd bring her back home and see what Darian thinks.

We haven't accepted strays into the Regnum in as long as I can remember, but Rhiannon feels different. Whatever was going on with that black rock… in the clearing… I think it was affecting her.

I think maybe it affects others.

Rhiannon doesn't want to kill herself, otherwise, she would have done it. I believe Mother brought me up the mountain for this reason. Rhiannon could be a part of my Ecdysis… She was lost, and now she's been found.

As much as I think that rock might have something to do with what happened to my parents, I believe saving a life is more important that

So much to my own surprise, and relief, I roll over in my sleeping bag to find her blanket still beside me. She's not in it, though.

I consider that she may have left it behind, since her backpack is gone, too. But when I emerge from the tent, I find her plopped on it next to the makeshift fire pit I created last night, trying her damndest to light a fire. I can't help but grin to myself as I tug my hoodie onto my arms and zip it up. She's such an interesting creature, this girl.

She's small, and rather pretty, but with sarcasm practically oozing from her pores. I'm out of my comfort zone with her, being that I've never really interacted with Outsiders… like ever. She seems witty and strong-willed, but also sweet and caring. I heard her thoughts last night when I told her about my parents. Her empathy was palpable, and that's the number one quality a human needs to fit in with our family.

I think she'll love The Principality. My main concern would be introducing her to Darian and Drake…

"Are you just going to stand there staring at me, or are you going to help?" Rhiannon mumbles, while literally rubbing sticks together… as if that could ever start a fire anywhere other than in fiction.

"You could have woken me up," I chuckle, stepping over to help her, minding my feet.

She glances down as I rearrange her kindling. "Are you barefoot? In the woods?"

My eyes dart to hers briefly. "Is that weird?"

"Uh yea," she breathes. "Unless you're a hippy, I guess, which it kind of seems like you are."

"I was born and raised in the woods," I tell her, making the perfect teepee of twigs before grabbing my matches out of my pocket, lighting one and sticking it inside. "The forest is my home. Do you always wear shoes in your home?"

I give her a pointed look, and she rolls her eyes. It makes me smile. I'm already picking up on her snarky attitude, and I think it's sort of adorable. She reminds me of a cross between Gem and Lauris.

"Do you like tea?" I ask, in between blowing on the fire just enough to get it going. She does a little half-shrug and a nod. "I have some chai that's great for breakfast. And I have sandwiches too, if you're hungry."

"I don't usually eat breakfast." She combs her fingers through her long, wispy locks of hair. It's mostly blonde, but with these auburn natural highlights that give it an almost pinkish hue, especially when bathed in the light of early morning.

"Well, we have quite the journey ahead of us, so you'll need sustenance." I get up and go to the tent to grab my bag so I can boil us water for tea.

When I come back, she says, "Look, I stayed because I thought it would be rude to just disappear on you. You've been so kind to me, and I really appreciate it..." I pause with sandwiches in my hand and glance at her. "But I don't think I can come with you. It's not a good idea. You don't know me, and I don't know you."

"Well, exactly," I mumble. "We'd be getting to know each other. That's the point."

Her forehead lines and I can hear her thoughts trying to fight against her obvious desire for a change. I know she wants a new life. Of course she does. It's better than ending your life altogether.

But she's afraid. Most people are, and it's fine. Still, I don't think she should use that as an excuse to bolt.

"No, the point is that I think I'm best on my own for now," she sighs.

"You see, the thing is, Rhiannon, I know you don't believe that," I tell her with certainty. I can hear her thoughts, after all. She doesn't want to be alone. She actually hates it. But she's been building a wall around herself based on something that happened to her... something she doesn't like to think about, so I haven't caught onto it yet.

"And how would you know?" She huffs, again with the attitude. It makes me want to smile, but I keep it under wraps.

"I just do. I know you think you deserve to be alone and unhappy... You're not the only one. There's someone I care a lot about who does the same thing." My mind drifts to Drake, wondering what he's doing right now... Slithering through the lab or the woods, or his cabin by himself because he doesn't believe he's worthy of the love Darian and I want to give him. "But it's a mask, a crutch. It's a Band-Aid, Rhiannon. Eventually you'll have to face what's bothering you and let people in, because—"

"All life is precious?" She cuts in with a smirk, and I laugh.

"Because you deserve to be happy, too," I tell her, handing over a sandwich.

She gapes at it, taking it hesitantly, all the while wondering where I came from, and how it's possible for me to be so sweet and kind. Her thoughts bring warmth to my stomach. I'd like to be her friend,

252

and introduce her to all the amazing members of my big family. I'm still not even exactly sure why, but I feel a kinship with her.

There's something about her that's slinking into me. I found her up here, by such a terrible place rife with bad feelings. She's like the good that came from the bad.

"I guess... I'll think about it while we walk." She unwraps the sandwich and takes a bite.

I release a smile. I just won't mention that if she decides against entering The Principality, she won't be welcome on the Expanse. *I could potentially be fucking shit up here... But we won't think about that right now.*

"Holy crap!" She shrieks, and I flinch. "This sandwich is so good! You made this, too?"

I nod, chuckling. "It's my famous bacon and egg sandwich with a secret ingredient. Honey."

"Okay, that sounds completely disgusting in theory, but it's freaking delicious," she raves.

"Sweet always compliments savory." I give her an unapologetic shrug. "Don't knock any weird combos until you try them."

"You're preaching to the choir, kid. I love Hawaiian pizza."

"Oh, I make the best Hawaiian pizza," I tell her. "Bacon, not ham, of course."

"It's really the only way," she agrees, giggling through her massive bites.

I like this girl a lot. She's super cool, funny in her own aggressive Outsider way. Just very different, and I like that.

I make us some tea, and we drink it by the fire as the sun rises into the sky. I haven't checked the time, but I'm sure it's probably close to seven by the time we're done with breakfast.

"The hike down will take all day," I tell her, packing everything up after disassembling my tent. "But if we stay on track, we could be back by dinner."

Rhiannon looks nervous, and her thoughts reflect the same. She's afraid no one will like her, that she won't like them. She also seems to be harboring some ideas of what The Principality is about... like mind games and manipulation. I can only assume it's from something she's seen on TV or in movies. She has a vivid imagination, that's for sure.

But I want her to know, "The Principality will be different from how you've been living your life, sure. But I mean... you clearly haven't been thrilled with how your life has been going up until this point, right?"

"Wow." She folds her arms. "Someone's been drinking the Kool-Aid."

My brows zip together in confusion. "What *Aid*?"

She bursts out laughing and shakes her head. "Never mind. Keep going with the hard sell, dude. I'm into it."

I grin and roll my eyes. "You'll accept that our way is better, Rhi. I'll even throw in a sweetener for you. Unless you're chicken..."

Her gaze narrows. "Alright, I'll play. But what could *you* offer *me*? I doubt you have money..."

"Money is unnecessary."

"The entire world would disagree with you, but go on."

"I have something much more interesting I could give you." My eyes lock on hers, brow cocked. "*If* you stay with us."

She visibly shivers and bites her lip, her thoughts going to an... unexpected place. *She's turned on...?*

I pause for a moment, my gaze landing on her mouth, her pouty lips. Up until this second, I hadn't really thought about it, but now I'm wondering if she would want to kiss me...

It's entirely insane. I don't know this girl at all, and I'm in love with someone else. Two someones, if we're being technical. And they're both men.

I've never been sexually attracted to a woman before... And this girl kind of feels more like a sister than anything.

And yet, she's thinking about it. So now *I'm* thinking about it.

I blink myself out of the trance and clear my throat. "I can't tell you what it is until we get there. But I promise, it'll blow your mind."

Why does everything I'm saying sound sexual now??

"Okay," she rasps breathlessly. "And what if I don't stay?"

"I don't think that'll be an option." I wink.

Then I go on packing up my things and start putting out the fire. Rhiannon just stands there the whole time, wondering what the hell I'm talking about. But the intrigue is working in my favor.

More than anything, she's anxious to meet Darian, since she seems to have this idea about him in her head, already formed. But I know she'll change her mind the moment she meets him.

He's our King for a reason.

"Hey... last night you said you came out here for some closure or something," she starts, and I pause what I'm doing. "What did you mean by that?"

I contemplate making something up but decide against it. If she's going to become a member of my family, I'll need to trust her fully.

"The circumstances surrounding my parents' deaths were suspicious." I busy my hands by getting my tent secured in its bag. "They were found in a ravine halfway down the mountain, and it looked like they'd fallen, or jumped... or something like that." I swallow hard. "The thing about this mountain is that people don't come up here often, and there's a reason for it. Strange things occur up here. Even our security patrols are warned from coming all the way up. But I've always wondered about what happened to them... I just," I pause and shake my head, breathing out slowly, "I don't think they would have willingly jumped. They wouldn't leave me behind like that, not on purpose.

"I wanted to come up here and try to find answers. I think the not knowing has held me back from a lot of spiritual growth and acceptance. Based on the feelings I got from that clearing, I know there's more to it."

The quiet stretches for miles, and when I finally glance over at Rhiannon, she's staring at her shoes, chewing vigorously on her lower lip. Hearing what she's thinking about the clearing, she lied to me last night when she said she didn't see that black rock. She did, and it showed her something that now has her clamming up.

"We should go back to it," she finally speaks, straightening up as she turns to face me.

"What?" I'm sure my face and tone convey how baffled I am by this statement.

"I can't let you forfeit your search for answers just for me," she insists. "You're right. There's something going on up there in that clearing. We should at least go check it out one last time before we head back. So you'll know for sure."

I give her a studious look. I don't think she's manipulating me into taking her back there in some attempt to resume her suicidal plans. If she were, I'd hear it.

What I do hear is her considering that the clearing was trying to convince her to kill herself last night...

And maybe it did the same to my parents.

I already don't feel right about this.

I agreed with Rhiannon's plan to make a detour on our way down, and we trekked back to that clearing just to see.

See what, I'm not entirely sure, because last time I almost walked up to that rock, baby birds warned me not to do it. I mean, if that isn't a sign from Mother, then I don't know what is.

Yet I still chose to come back, because in the corners of my mind, I know these forces had something to do with my parents' deaths. And even though she won't say it outright, Rhiannon does, too.

As we come up to the clearing—it's about twenty feet off in the distance—my heart rate increases to an almost unhealthy level. Sweat breaks out on my forehead, and my vision blurs.

I stop and close my eyes for a moment, swallowing over and over because I feel sick.

"Are you okay?" Rhiannon squeezes my arm in her small hand, her voice echoed.

"I feel like I'm going to pass out," I breathe, swaying on my feet.

"Here, come rest." She tries pulling me over to a tree, but I shake my head.

"No. I can keep going. I have to."

It's not lost on either of us that there's no black rock in the middle of the clearing right now. But that doesn't stop it from feeling like something is very wrong up here.

"Do you see it?" I ask her hesitantly, in case it's something that only shows itself to one person at a time.

"Not yet," she whispers, her voice shaking.

It's then that I notice she's still holding onto my arm; gripping it tightly, nails digging into me while her hand trembles.

"We've got this." I move it into mine, entwining our fingers.

I feel her nod at my side, though she doesn't respond, and I hear her thoughts swimming...

I can't tell if what she's thinking is based around what I told her about my parents' deaths, or something she saw herself.

She's remembering the gully... But it can't be just from what I mentioned, because it's the exact gully where my parents were found. And I didn't describe it to her in really any detail. So how would she know what it looks like?

Unless she was down there, maybe before she came up here?

But even that explanation doesn't settle my mind. In her thoughts, she's remembering the ravine as it looked the exact day my parents were found, in late summer, almost fall.

While I'm mulling this over in my head, and we're taking the tiniest, most hesitant steps ever, the wind ripples around us, and Rhiannon gasps.

The black rock. It's there now.

It just appeared... popped out of thin air.

What the hell, man? This is weird shit.

"Please tell me you see that..." Rhiannon murmurs, and this time I nod, wordlessly.

When we get up to the edge of the clearing, ready to pass through the first trees and approach the rock, Rhiannon's grip on my hand tightens. I feel her emotions, and I'm taken aback by the hurt radiating through her brain. I can't hear what the source is, and I don't want to ask. I don't want to make her any more uncomfortable than we both currently are.

Still, something painful is ravaging her head. A monster she rarely lets out of its box.

"Don't let go," she whimpers as we move into the clearing, the rock only a few feet from us.

"Wouldn't dream of it," I tell her in the most confident tone I can muster.

We reach the rock. It's just a rock, I guess, in theory, but there are so many things happening around it.

The only way to describe it would be a shift in the atmosphere. A sudden change in the air around us, like when there's radiation nearby or something.

Everything just feels *off* all of a sudden.

Rhiannon is remembering how she touched it last time; she sat on it. She's afraid to do so again... but she wants to. For me.

"You don't have to..." I whisper. She looks up at me, her face radiating confusion, likely at the fact that I just read her mind.

"We're doing it. Together." She tugs me forward, and we both sit, side by side, on the black rock.

As soon as my ass hits it, I realize this is no rock, like what you'd

257

find in nature. This is something else entirely. Something dark; a living, breathing creature.

I can feel a heartbeat in it, linking to my own.

It doesn't even feel like a *rock* beneath me, but rather water and mud. I actually look down at my pants to see if they're soaking through.

I don't see anything.

Rhiannon's thoughts are spiraling. Her breathing has picked up next to me, and she's sucking in air fast, her chest heaving beneath her hoodie.

"Don't let it take you, Rhi," I mumble to her, though I'm not so sure I can keep this thing from sweeping me up.

"What do you see?" Her voice asks, and as soon as the last syllable leaves her lips, I'm in a different place entirely.

I'm in the ravine, on the day my parents were found. I can see myself, my twelve-year-old self, gaping at their dead bodies with anguish in his eyes. He throws up, and then Darian rushes over, scooping him up and carrying him away.

Darian looks younger too, obviously. He would be about twenty-one at the time. *Our young leader.* Yet he still looks the same as he does now, a little less wisdom around the eyes, a little thinner and slightly longer hair.

But he's beautiful, and oh so sad as he carries a young me through the woods, shushing my cries. He brings me to a spot I recognize now as the overlook by Drake's cabin. There's a bench, and he plops us down on it, holding my younger self, comforting him.

But from this angle, I can see us both. And my focus is on Darian.

He looks distraught. I knew he was upset about the deaths of my parents. They were his family, and Darian feels a lot. It was a devastating hit for him; for all of us.

But the way he's crying, quietly, likely so that the new orphan doesn't hear him... He's almost inconsolable.

It hurts my heart to see this. For my parents, yes, and for my young self, who was so very affected by the loss of his parents. But also, for Darian. For what he lost, which seems to be more than just two family members...

I feel tears seeping from my eyes, though I don't even know where I am in this vision. It's like I'm up in the sky, in the trees, looking down on the whole scene. And then movement nearby catches my vision.

Drake.

I catch him lingering a few feet away, watching Darian hold young me. He also looks upset, but in a different sort of way than Darian and me.

He doesn't necessarily look surprised by what's happening. He appears somber as he rakes his long fingers through his hair, keeping himself hidden from us. He slinks around a tree and leans his back against it, closing his eyes tight, his head shaking over and over again.

There's something I can hear... It must be in his mind, because his lips aren't moving.

I'm sorry.

That's it. On repeat, in Drake's voice. His deep tone of typically indifferent emotions.

Guilt-ridden and exhausted. *I'm sorry I'm sorry I'm sorry.*

Confusion racks my mind. There's no way he could be guilty of anything... It's impossible. I refuse to believe Drake had anything to do with my parents plummeting from up here.

Yet he's apologizing. He's so very deeply sorry, I feel it in my bones.

He knows something about why they're dead in this moment, but I just can't get to it. And for some bewildering reason, he thinks it's his fault.

But it's not... It can't be.

Drake straightens and stumbles off, staggering through the forest, up the mountain. He walks for a while, and I can see him the entire time, like I'm right there with him, chasing him. I can't see Darian anymore, but I still hear him crying.

Eventually Drake gets to the clearing. He comes to right where me and Rhiannon are, right now, though we're nowhere to be found.

He falls to his knees in the middle, and the black rock appears, in front of him.

Please stop this... His mind bellows as he removes something from his pocket.

It looks like... *a razor blade??*

"No!" I shout, but he can't hear me.

He angles it to his wrist, pressing into his pale white skin. His fingers tremble, and he gasps. *Make this stop!!*

Blood, deep red, bubbles from the cut he just made. It flows, slowly, dripping from his arm onto the ground.

I try to run to him, desperately pulling through wherever the hell I am to get to him fast, as he lies down on the ground, blood seeping from his arm.

"Drake! Drake, no. Don't do this. Please!" I sputter, fighting and fighting through thickness, like quicksand pulling me and holding me back.

I could have stopped it... He whispers sleepily, his eyes fluttering shut.

"No no no. Come back!" I shout, and suddenly, I feel something tugging on my arm.

Tugging my hand.

I blink hard and try to look around, a cool wind brushing my face.

"Fuck," I growl, covering my eyes with my fingers, rubbing them hard. "Wake up!"

"Abdiel... don't... let... go..."

It's Rhiannon. That was her voice. *Where is she??*

Shaking myself over and over, desperate to awake from whatever this dreamland is that I'm lost in, I finally I pull myself out and look around.

I'm no longer in the clearing. I can't see Drake anywhere.

I'm lying on the ground, and when I turn my heavy head, I see a rock ledge. It's an overlook, like the one Drake lives on... only much, much higher up.

"Where the fuck am I...?" I murmur.

My head weighs a million pounds as I lift my neck. And when I take in my surroundings, my eyes widen, and my body launches upward.

Rhiannon is scooting toward the edge of the cliff. My right hand is still locked in her left one, but she's trying to pull herself toward it.

She's trying to jump.

"Rhiannon!" I shout, rolling onto my knees and yanking her back, as hard as I can.

She's stronger than she looks, still fighting to get closer. I have to be careful here. If I move too hard in one direction, we could both go over.

We're so damn close to the edge.

"Rhiannon, please," I gasp, pulling her as hard as I can while simultaneously trying to roll away from the cliff. "Wake up!"

"Abdiel..." she cries, voice overflowing with fear and unease.

I can't see her face as she attempts to crawl closer to the edge of the cliff I'm trying to get us away from, but I hear her tears. I hear her mind... It's vague, but there's a faint whisper of a voice, calling to me.

She doesn't want to do this.

"You don't want this, Rhiannon. I know you don't," I grunt, tugging her hard as I finally get some traction beneath my boots. "All life is precious, remember?"

"Wha—" she whimpers and then she screams. "Abdiel, don't let go!"

"I wouldn't dream of it, love. Hang onto me tight, okay?"

I see her nod as she finally turns her body toward me, her goddamn feet dangling off the edge. I tug her closer to me by her arm, hauling her weight until I have her wrapped in my arms. And then I roll us farther away, putting distance between us and the edge. I physically have to hold her to my chest while crawling us in the dirt and grass, my knees scraping on rocks as I do.

But eventually, I breathe easier, when I get us enough feet from the cliff that I know we're safe.

"Fuck me..." I exhale, loosening my grip on Rhiannon. But she doesn't let up.

She clings to me for dear life, crying hysterically into the crook of my neck.

What the fuck on Earth was that??

"Shh... it's okay," I whisper, hugging her tight. "I have you. I'm not letting go."

"What the fuck happened...?" She sniffles, finally pulling back to look me in the eye.

I have a strong urge, one I don't understand very well, to wipe away her tears. And so I do, brushing them with my knuckles, combing her hair behind her ear. She still looks worried, but now I can hear her thoughts again, more calmed, her mind eased because I'm here.

She trusts me, and it gives me peace, comfort.

"I don't know," I sigh. "Let's get the hell out of here."

I help Rhiannon up, and we head back toward the clearing, though we walk around it this time.

Of course, the black rock is gone.

"How the hell did we go from sitting on the rock, in the middle of this clearing, to like more than thirty feet away on the cliff?" Rhiannon asks, disbelief lining her tone while we pick up our bags and head back in the direction we came from this morning. Down the damn mountain and back toward home.

I can't wait to get back. This has been a strenuous trip, and even though I sort of expected it to be, I wasn't prepared for the emotional toll all this shit would take on me. I'm exhausted, and the thought of hiking all damn day is daunting.

Plus, according to the watch I keep attached to my bag, we were in that bizarre trance for five hours. The sun will be setting in only a couple more, which means we'll have to camp out tonight before we can make it home.

A bewildered sigh leaves my lips. "I really have no clue, but I'm even more disturbed at how much time passed. That was fucking crazy."

Rhiannon huffs a small chuckle, and I peek at her. "Sorry, it's just funny to hear you curse. You don't do it often."

"Oh, so you know me now, is that it?" I tease, grinning at her.

"I think I'm getting to," she mumbles while we walk. "A little bit." Her chin lifts in my direction. "You're a good guy, Abdiel. You saved me back there..."

"That wasn't you," I say with confidence. "We both know it. It wasn't you when we met yesterday either. You don't want to die, Rhiannon. There's something up here, and I think it plays on your fears... maybe. I don't know." I shake my head, exhaling hard. "It's really messed up."

She's quiet for a moment before she asks, "Is that what you think happened to your parents?"

My pulse pounds for a moment while I consider this.

"I kind of do," I answer, hesitantly. "I don't know... I saw some shit while we were on that rock. Some things that are really strange, and I... I need to talk to someone when we get home."

Drake. I need to ask him about the day my parents died.

I need to know if that was an actual flashback, or some weird dreamlike situation.

"Home," Rhiannon scoffs, pulling me out of my thoughts. "It's *your* home, not mine. I don't have a home."

"You will." My tone is genuine, and I don't care if she doesn't believe me yet. She will when she meets everyone and sees what an amazing community we have.

If all she had before was a house of pain and neglect, then I think it's time for her to experience what a real family is about. And what we can do for her. What we do for each other.

262

We're quiet as we walk down the mountain. We eat on the go, our last sandwich, knowing that the farther we get tonight, the less we'll have to travel in the morning. But we definitely have to spend one more night. That's a given.

The sun will set in less than an hour at this point, so my goal is to find us a comfortable spot to settle in. We've made good time since we left the clearing. We're close to Drake's place, and his cabin isn't that far from the bottom.

I find a spot I like, off the trail a ways, between a few tall trees. I have just enough daylight left to show Rhiannon how to properly start a fire, then get the tent set up, with her help. She's taking to the camping stuff pretty quickly, which is surprising since according to her, she's never spent time in the woods before.

She told me her family always had a yard and room for her and her friends to play outside, but her mother isn't exactly a fan of being outdoors, unless it's on a beach with a drink in her hand.

"If you don't mind me asking, what happened to your father?" I turn my face to Rhi while setting up some food for us over the fire. Vegetable and bean soup.

I don't usually eat soup every damn day, but it's the easiest thing to heat over a fire. Otherwise, it would've been sandwiches for every meal.

"I never knew him," she tells me, fiddling with the remaining chipped polish on her fingernails. She does this a lot, like a nervous habit, so most of it is gone by now. "He left when I was a baby. My mom used to tell me he was a piece of shit... a deadbeat. But I don't believe her. I think she kicked him out. She's an asshole like that."

"That sucks," I reply, empathy fresh in my words. "Still, you don't think he'd try to reach out to you over the years, even if she made him go?"

She shrugs. "He might've. Who knows."

"She would keep it from you?"

"Hell yea. Like I said, she's an asshole. Typical entitled rich bitch from a rich bitch family."

I swallow hard. The way she speaks about her family is so foreign to me.

I'm not a naïve idiot. We study the outside world a lot when we're young, so we're aware of the things that go on. And some of the Regnum who came in as strays tell us about their lives before The Principality. It's rarely good.

Even so, I'll never be able to commiserate with hating my parents or my family. I'm very blessed, and I realize that now more than ever. *I will never take this life for granted.*

"That's sort of fascinating to me." She gives me a look, to which I chuckle. "Not your mom being an asshole. The wealth. And the generations of wealth. I've never even held money before."

"That's insane," she laughs, eyes lighting up with disbelief. "I can imagine that right there eliminates most problems from your society. Money is the root of all evils, as they say."

"I've heard that one before!" I gasp, and she giggles.

We eat our dinner, chatting about this and that. Rhiannon tells me about her favorite things to learn, her favorite music, and she even gives me breakdowns of movies she loves that I've never even heard of. She has an interest in learning to cook, which I tell her I'm more than happy to help with, and she wants to learn more wilderness survival skills, which she'll definitely get with The Principality.

She also wants to hear me sing, but I tell her she'll have to wait until her first reflection for that. To which she does her little scowl, and it's all too cute.

I think Rhiannon is cool. She's the exact kind of girl who would have been my best friend if we'd grown up together. And who knows... Maybe I would have even had my first kiss with her.

Maybe I would have lost my virginity with her, experimenting, to see if I liked it.

I'm not questioning myself, or doubting what I've learned about my sexuality in the last few weeks with Darian and Drake. I know I like guys; love them, in fact. But I'm not *repelled* by the thought of kissing Rhiannon. It doesn't gross me out or anything.

So what the hell does that mean?

We sit by the fire, talking until it practically burns out. And when my eyelids are drooping, Rhiannon suggests carrying my sleepy ass into the tent with a chuckle. She goes off a few feet to use the metaphorical bathroom and brush her teeth while I put out the fire, then do the same. When I come back, she's already inside the tent, all huddled up under her little blanket.

"We can share the sleeping bag," I suggest, taking off my pants and my hoodie. Rhiannon shifts her blanket enough to glare at me, and I laugh. "I don't mean get into it together, zipped up. I mean I'll unzip it, turn it into a big blanket, and we can both sleep underneath. It'll be more comfortable."

"That seems odd, new friend." She blinks her wide green eyes at me. "It seems like you're trying to make a move, and I would insist, for your Head Priest boyfriend's sake, that we stay as far apart as possible." I can't help but snicker again. "I'm serious. You're already stripping down in front of me!"

"I'm wearing boxers and a t-shirt," I grumble, crawling over to my sleeping bag and climbing inside. "I'm not *naked*."

She turns onto her side to face me. "What would *Darian* think?"

Even hearing his name twists my stomach up into a knot. "I miss him."

She lifts her brow. "You've been away from him for two days."

"I know. It's crazy." I pull the sleeping bag up to my chin as my eyes stay locked with my new friend's. "I don't want to keep us a secret anymore. I want... I want to love him out in the open."

"Why can't you?" She asks, curious.

"It's very complicated."

"Since he's the leader?"

"Well, yea... And for other reasons."

She blinks. "Like what?"

I already know she'll be judgmental over what I'm about to say, but I need to talk to someone. I haven't been able to tell any of my friends or family about my relationship with Darian, and it's eating me alive inside. Regardless of what Rhiannon says, she's impartial, and she's a friend.

I need to get this off my chest.

"He's... married," I tell her, and immediately, her face contorts like she's trying not to react.

Unfortunately, I can hear her thoughts, and they're not very supportive.

Married?? Why am I not surprised...? This guy is certainly shoving himself into that typical, chauvinistic, narcissistic cult leader box, isn't he? I really hope Abdiel smartens up and stands up for himself to this Head Priest.

"And let me guess, he thinks it's okay to be with multiple people at once?" She mutters, her skepticism on full force.

"Well... not exactly." I chew on my lip. "I mean... it's—"

"Complicated. Yea, so you've said." She rolls her eyes. "So he's just going to stay married while he fucks you, and his husband, and everyone else he wants to fuck, should the mood strike?"

"No. No, that's not it," I reply, defensively. "He's married to

265

women, but he only did it to please the Regnum." Her eyes glaze over. "Our *family*. He's never been with them romantically. He... can't."

Some sympathy shines in her eyes. "Because he's gay?" I nod, and I see her losing some of the know-it-all frustration as she nods along. "Well, I can understand that."

"It's a tough situation," I go on. "I don't want to push him. It's not my place, but I really want him to be happy. And if it's with me, that would be an added bonus."

"Abdiel, it *is* your place to push, at least within reason." She scoots in closer. "He involved you by sleeping with you. He put you in the middle, and now he has a responsibility to consider your feelings."

"We haven't slept together..." I mumble.

"What was that?" Her lashes flutter as if she didn't hear me.

My cheeks flush, palpably. "We haven't had sex yet. We've done other things, but... I'm still a... uh... a virgin."

Rhiannon's eyes go round, sparkling from the dim light of the flashlight I have on by my head. They're very green, almost teal, like the lake in spring.

"Is he the only person you've been with?" She asks, her voice hushed, intimately wondering, as if she thinks someone might overhear, but she can't not ask.

Images of Drake flit through my head, and I'm momentarily nervous until I remember she can't hear my thoughts. But I can hear hers...

She's turned on again, only this time it's from thinking about me with Darian. She's wondering what he looks like, thinking about if he's rough or soft with me.

I can't even pretend it's not stiffening my dick in my sleeping bag, hearing someone else think about me and my Head Priest... together.

I want to lie, and I'm not sure why. I'm not a liar, and I don't care what anyone thinks. But the addition of Drake into the equation of Darian plus Abdiel equals something none of us understand, not even a little.

Still, I answer, "No. There's one other... person."

"A guy?" Her tongue slides over her lower lip, drawing my attention to how pink it is. I nod slowly. "You've never been with a girl... ever?"

"No," I whisper. And suddenly, I'm very aware that we're closer than when I first laid down. We're still separated by my sleeping bag, but her face is only a foot from mine.

"Have you always known?" She asks, nestling in even closer.

I can smell her, like fresh-cut lilies and wild lavender.

"Known...?" My voice trails, sounding raspier to my own ear than usual.

She tilts her head. "That you're gay."

"I'm not..." I start, then pause, considering my words. "I'm not sure that I am... gay." She blinks. "I mean, I've never... tried. So I wouldn't... know."

Man, that was hard to get out.

Tension is enveloping us like a balloon filled with buzzing energy. I think I must be fucked up in the head, because I can't stop wondering what it would feel like to kiss her... And this is someone I compared to a sister earlier in the day.

I'm clearly a little sick, but my curiosity is winning out as I move in closer.

"Abdiel, don't try to kiss me," she murmurs, even though my face is inching and inching, until our lips are hovering. "I mean it. Do *not*."

"Why...?" My voice is a barely-there whisper.

"Because you're in love with someone else." Her words are telling me no, but she's not moving away. And I hear her thoughts, fighting what's coming from her own mouth. A mouth I'm sincerely interested in right now.

Two someones, but who's counting? "I am."

Her small body has crept so close to me, we're practically melting together. Thank God these blankets are in the way... Acting as a buffer. Because as curious as I am, I know I really can't let this happen.

I'm at war with myself, and it's crazy confusing.

"I don't want to be an experiment, Abdiel," she says with conviction that stops me; freezes me in place.

"I would never want you to feel like that." Our eyes hold one another's gaze, waves of arousal fluctuating in the air between us.

"Then why would I let you kiss me?"

"You shouldn't," I hum, and she bites her lip. "But maybe you'll kiss me..."

She shivers visibly. "And why would I do that?"

"Because you want to." My pulse is rapping hard against my chest. "And I want you to..."

"But you love him," she whimpers, sending a strange jolt to my erection.

"I do," I say again over her plump, trembling lips. "And he loves someone else, too."

"This sounds like a soap opera," she mumbles, her slender fingers reaching out to touch my neck.

"I don't know what that is."

She giggles a breathy sound, hitting me in the junk once more, before muttering *fuck it*, and pressing her soft lips to mine.

It's such a foreign feeling. It's kissing, sure, which I've done multiple times now with Darian and Drake. Darian and I have spent *hours* kissing ourselves stupid, yet when this *girl* kisses me, I've completely forgotten what to do.

But apparently, Rhiannon doesn't mind, and she parts her lips over my lower, sucking it gently, just enough for it to feel really damn good.

And I moan.

I fucking *moan*, from a small, simple kiss.

I don't know where that noise came from, but she obviously likes it because she whines and slides her fingers up into my hair, gripping while she kisses me more.

It's so different from kissing men... so so different. It's almost impossible to explain, but the only thing I can register is how soft she is.

There's no stubble bruising my face as it picks up force. I miss it, but not enough for me to want this to stop. Her lips are plush and eager as they come to devour me, while she keeps it slow and *leisurely*.

I'm brutally aware that she isn't Darian, or Drake, but it still feels good. I like kissing her, although I can't tell if it's because I also like girls, or because I like Rhiannon.

Either way, I slide my tongue into her mouth, just to see, and she purrs, meeting mine with hers. She tastes sweet, and she smells very good, like a flower garden. I'm enjoying this, I can't even pretend I'm not. Plus, my dick is hard. It's definitely trying to fight its way out of my boxers, and my sleeping bag.

But I refuse to let it. Despite how good this feels, and how much Rhiannon is smooshing herself into me, I refuse to remove my hands from where they're trapped by my sides. I can't let this go further than a kiss. It feels far too disloyal to my King... and his brother. *My Serpent*.

Still, Rhiannon's thoughts are driving me insane. She's thinking about things she would let me do to her... and what she would do to me.

She wants me to pet her pussy, and she wants to touch my dick. She wants to know if it's big...

She wants to know how I would react to her sitting on my face.

That thought, and the image it drums up in my brain causes a major throb in my balls and forces me to pull away. We're both crazy breathless, the sounds of us sucking air into our lungs bouncing around the inside of the tent.

"I'm sorry..." she breathes. "I'm so sorry. That was too much."

"No, no. It wasn't." My eyes reopen, and I look over her flushed face and dilated pupils. "Don't apologize, that was..."

"You liked it?" She asks, inquisitively.

"Yes," I mumble, then start chewing on my lip. Because *yes*, I did like it.

So what the hell does that mean??

"Will he be mad?" She asks, and her thoughts are rife with guilt. I hate hearing it.

I don't want to make her feel bad. That wasn't what I was going for at all.

"He would never be mad," I tell her honestly. "But he might be hurt. And he'll definitely be jealous."

She sucks her lower lip between her teeth before muttering, "Then don't tell him."

"That's not exactly an option when it comes to Darian," I sigh.

I contemplate telling her about his ability to hear thoughts, or even about my own. But I can't tell her about Empyrean now. That's not my secret to share. I have to wait and speak to Darian and Drake first.

"I like you, Abdiel." Her voice is timid, unsure.

"I like you, too," I tell her honestly, because it's true.

But...

"But," she sighs, "I won't get in the middle of a relationship. I won't be a wedge between you and the man you love."

"I know." I give her a small grin, swiping my thumb over her lower lip. "Thanks for being my first straight kiss."

She huffs an easy giggle. "Thanks for not deciding you're fully gay mid-kiss and throwing up."

I have to laugh at that. "I doubt that's something that happens, but don't worry. Vomit barely graced my mind."

She shoves me in the chest while I chuckle teasingly. She rolls her eyes and spins around, nestling her back up against my front.

"Goodnight, jerk. And if you rub your boner on me, I'll beat you to death with my shoe."

I swallow hard. "Then you might want to give me a minute…"

"Abdiel!"

"I'm sorry!" I huff, flipping my dick up into the waistband of my boxer briefs. "Okay okay. You're fine."

She exhales, and I reach over to the flashlight, switching it off. We're both quiet for a few minutes, though I can tell she's still awake from her thoughts running wild. Honestly, they're sort of mirroring mine.

I hope Darian won't be upset…

And what do we do about these new feelings?

CHAPTER TWENTY FOUR

DARIAN

I haven't slept in two nights.

The last solid night's sleep I got was with Abdiel in the lounge. When I awoke, he'd left for his journey. And since then, all I've been able to do is stress in one form or another.

Stress about Drake… the distance between us. The things he's been doing to these spies and trespassers.

Stress and worry about Abdiel, up on that mountain alone. Wandering, unknowingly into that spot…

Over the years, I've done a decent job of keeping the Regnum from stumbling across the clearing by the peak of the mountain. It's not somewhere people should go, intentionally or by accident. But on occasion, they come across it.

They rarely live to tell what happens when they do.

Drake and I have been trying to keep the mountain patrolled by the Tribe, but there simply aren't enough of them for so much space. We're still recruiting, so I suppose we'll see how many new members we can get.

Worst-case scenario, we might have to start taking in strays again. I'm not completely opposed to it, but Drake isn't typically a fan of that idea. He doesn't trust anyone. I suppose he wouldn't…

For now, it's all just rampant concern, clouding up my mind until there's so much racing around in there, I have no hope of ever falling asleep. All of this chaos rippling through me… the Regnum wanting an heir, Drake pulling away from me, Abdiel finding out the secrets we try so hard to keep buried… getting a *divorce*?

"Fuck this." I whip my blanket off and stomp over to my closet.

Pulling on some sweats, I grab a towel from my bathroom, heading downstairs. At first, I consider going into my gym to work out. But when I pass the backdoor, my eyes fix on the lake.

I think I see someone out there.

Mischief coiling inside me, I wander to the door and head outside, strolling toward the lake, gaze stuck on a figure I immediately identify.

He's out pretty far, floating with his eyes closed. I worry for a split second that something is wrong with him, but then I hear his thoughts, vaguely. I haven't had Empyrean in a few days, and I could definitely use more.

But regardless, I can hear whispers from his mind, all twisted together. Pain and anguish, joy and elation, desire and lust, needy torment. I can't even fathom what it feels like to be inside his mind sometimes. He doesn't think like a regular person does.

He's a maze, a riddle to decode. I've spent most of my life trying to figure him out, and I'm beginning to think it may never happen...

Watching him float in the lake, basking in the glow of the moon, my head tilts. He's dressed... in white linen clothes. The ensemble he usually wears to weekly sermons or on special occasions. Because white signifies rebirth.

Ecdysis is our personal transformation. I remember the first time he told me that.

The first time we tried Empyrean together.

In that moment, we were one. With each other, with Mother. With the universe.

It's all I can see right now while he swims in the lake, a serpent in white, so lovely and dangerous as the human representation of everything we've done to get right here. He's lodged directly in my heart, wickedly beautiful... quite possibly *evil*, as he says, yet I wouldn't want him any other way.

I can't hate him the way he craves. I can only hate how much I fucking love him, and how much I'll never stop. An infinite truth.

Dropping my towel at the shore of the lake, I step out of my sweatpants and wade into the water. It's cool, but refreshing in the night air, still warm. Solstice has come and gone, and now we're in summer. The most important time of the year.

Swimming out to him, deeper and deeper, I keep my lungs full of oxygen in order to help my cause. I'm not even sure where the bottom of the lake is right now, but it's nowhere near my feet, that's for sure.

As I approach him, he barely moves. His fingers flutter through the water, and I watch them; those hands. All the things they've done...

You need settling, do you, brother?

My feet kick in the water, gracefully while I keep myself afloat by his side. *Yes. I need you.*

His eyes creep open, head turning just enough to lock me in place with those marbled irises. *You don't need me. You* want *me. There's a difference. A big one.*

You see, that's where you're wrong, Serpent, I tell him, my fingers sweeping through the water slowly, toward his. *I do need you. You just don't want to be needed, not in the way I need.*

He blinks at me slowly, in that way he does. Inquisitive. Seeking.

But rather than answering me, rather than fighting me, like he did last night, he simply turns his face back up to the stars.

And he remembers...

"Are you sure you're ready?" Drake's voice shakes, his hands gliding over my flesh. I'm hot everywhere... Burning up and so ready.

"I need this," I tell him, pressing my face into the bed, writhing my ass up against his erection. So long and stiff, like a stone carving. If he puts it all the way inside me, it'll probably reach my stomach. My toes curl at the thought.

"I don't want to hurt you, baby," he whispers in my ear from behind me, fingers pressing into my cheeks, bruising in his eagerness. I know how badly he wants it.

We're teenagers, and we're virgins. Well, sort of. But I know he wants to fuck me, and I'm sick of waiting. I'm sick of fearing this.

I can't let him *keep it forever.*

"Erase the memory, Drake," I plead. "You would never hurt me... I know you wouldn't."

His cock slides into the crack of my ass, and a shiver spreads up my spine. His tongue traces it, moving down, kissing me everywhere.

He's put his lips there before... stuck his tongue inside me. It feels amazing. Even his tongue is long.

"I need lube," he breathes, sounding as dizzy as I am.

"There's some stuff in the drawer." My face burns with the mild embarrassment of what's happening. Thank God it's dark and he can't see.

I hear him shuffling around while I lie, naked on the bed with my

273

ass exposed. It should feel uncomfortable, but I'm so hard and my balls are throbbing.

I don't want to remember what I felt the last time this happened, because as terrible as it was, somehow my body responded. I didn't want it to, and it fucked me up for a long time.

But Drake is the only person I trust. He loves me, and I love him. Whether we're brothers, or best friends... whether we should be doing this or not, I still need it.

I need him. All of him.

He comes back to me, running slick fingers between my cheeks until I'm trembling.

"I'll give you my fingers first," he mumbles, draping himself over me, his warm chest to my back. I whimper when he swirls them around on my rim, one wet digit slipping inside.

"Fuck," I purr as his other hand comes up to my chest, gripping my pectoral.

His lips are on my neck as his finger pushes deeper into my ass, pausing to let me adjust. "You like this?"

"God, yes..." I gasp, rutting into the bed to get some friction on my aching balls. "More."

He removes the finger, and when it pushes back in, there's another one with it. It burns, but I like it. I like the way it hurts. It's one of those things that's wrong but feels so damn right.

His fingers work in and out of me, slowly, building up a deep storm in my loins. Then he adds a third, and I groan, out of mild discomfort that has my cock leaking onto our bed.

"This is only a portion of what my dick will do to you, Darian." He licks my ear.

"I want it." My voice is a hoarse plea.

"You're sure?" He sounds hesitant still, and I know it's because of what happened to me.

I hate it. I hate that he thinks I'm broken. Damaged.

A tear slips from my eye, and I wipe it away before he can see. "Please. Please, Drake. Fuck me."

"I will do literally anything for you, do you know that?" He pulls his fingers away and sits back.

I think it's a rhetorical question, but even if I wanted to respond, he's distracting me by spreading my ass open, dragging the head of his cock up and down over my hole. Straddling my thighs, he holds me down with his weight while my hands linger. I don't know what to do with them, one gripping the blankets, the other coming up to brush my nipple. It feels good; we discovered that a few months back.

Drake was sucking on them, and it made me come in my boxers. The memory has my dick flinching hard into the soft comforter.

"Making you happy is like foreplay." He grips my ass in his hands, holding me open while he nudges the fat tip of his dick up to my entrance. It's nice and lubricated, but still, he has to shove hard to even attempt getting it in. "Relax for me, baby."

I'm nervous, and I don't want to be. It's all in my head, the thoughts keying me up. I let out a slow breath, attempting to mollify my muscles enough for him to break through. Peering over my shoulder, I see Drake staring down at his cock, biting on his lower lip while he presses inside my asshole.

The head finally slides in, and we both groan. It's the craziest feeling ever invented, a tight burn that feels bad and good at the same time. The good definitely outweighs the bad, though.

"You okay?" He asks, voice rough and aroused beyond belief. I love the sound. It drives me to shift upward to him.

"I want more, Drake," I beg.

"God, you're gorgeous." He lurches in farther, sliding a couple more inches until my back arches.

"Fucking holy fuck..." I purr, fisting the blankets on both sides of me.

"And you're so goddamn tight, Darian," he whimpers, like he's falling apart already.

I'm sure he is... it's his first time fucking something other than a fist, or a mouth. I fully expect him to come just as quickly as I'm going to.

"Fuck me deeper," I rasp. "Please."

He wastes no time giving me what I need, sinking into me, farther and farther, until he melts over my back, his pelvis resting on my cheeks. When he moves in one spot, my eyes roll back in my head.

"Oh God oh God oh God..." My toes curl.

"Was that it?" He hums by my ear, fingers twisting up in my hair.

"I think so," I croak, then his hips shift, and he hits it again, sending a bolt of lightning zapping through my loins. "Fuck, yessss. Yes yes yes, that's it. Fuck, baby, more."

He pulls back, drawing himself out almost all the way before thrusting back in, deep, so deep his balls are on mine, and it's a fucking fantastic feeling.

275

His hips work with me, pumping his length into my ass, slow but fierce, a hand sliding up my torso. He squeezes my nipple between his fingers until I shudder. And then he grips my throat.

"You feel like heaven on earth," he rumbles, stroking every inch inside me while I lose my damn mind.

My hips grind into the mattress, my cock bereft of attention, though it stands firm, harder than it's ever been before. I think I could easily come without touching it, a mesmerizing thought.

The sounds of our little bed shifting, mixed with our harsh breaths, greedy grunts and groans bounce off the walls. His movements pick up in pace just a bit, just enough for me to know I'm moments from exploding. And he'll be following me right over the edge.

"Fuck me," I pant, forcing my eyes open, past the love drunk heaviness of my lids, to watch him over my shoulder.

His snake eyes meet mine while he bucks into me, again and again, hovering his mouth above mine. "I love you, Darian. I'm... I fucking love you, baby."

My heart bursts in my chest, warmth sheltering me from the inside out as he presses his lips to mine, kissing me hard and desperate while his dick erupts inside me.

I can feel it. I can feel him coming inside, and for a brief moment, it terrifies me.

A string pulls on my subconscious, and I begin tumbling into darkness. That is, until my own orgasm rips through my loins.

It sneaks up on me, the sensation of Drake's big cock pulsing inside me, pushing me over a climax so intense, I have tears pouring from my eyes.

I think I would be screaming if he weren't kissing me feverishly. My brain is all scrambled up, and I can't even think. I don't remember where I am or what's going on. All I know is that I'm coming...

"I'm fucking coming so hard," I cry into his mouth, and he purrs, sucking at my lips hungrily, biting me, licking, lashing, still thrusting.

His hands are everywhere, all over my body, grasping and caressing. As our heart rates even out, the aggression turns treasuring. His kisses go from ravenous to erotic as all hell. Sensual and sleepy, his hands no longer gripping and squeezing, but massaging.

It's like he's loving me with his kisses, with his touch.

And we stay like this for a while, breathing one another in, and out.

276

SERPENT IN WHITE

It will feel like this forever, I'm sure.

I will never love anyone the way I love the boy with the snake eyes.

Ripping at his wet clothes, I fumble to get his pants down.

His lips capture mine, sucking and biting me, his hands on my face, holding me in place while mine go for his dick, and his balls.

"You make me fucking crazy," I whisper into his mouth, stroking his wet cock in my fist.

Listening to that memory, hearing our first time from his thoughts while we reminisced together was unlike anything I've ever experienced.

I remember that night like it was yesterday, just as I remember everything that's happened between Drake and me. The good things, and the bad.

But hearing how he remembers it… He was in love with me. I can't even tell if he still is, but he was. Before things started pulling him away. But I want it back.

I need it.

"You, brother, have been driving me goddamn crazy since the moment I met you," he growls, kissing my lips once more before pushing my head down.

We managed to swim over to an embankment, hidden enough between some trees, all the while pawing at one another, dicks rubbing together in the cool water of the lake.

And now I'm going to fuck him with my mouth on the muddy ground, and I'll love every minute of it.

I go willingly with his fingers in my hair, my knees in the dirt as I kiss down his pale skin, tracing the wet curves of his stomach with my tongue. The V-shape in his lower abdomen, each side getting a kiss and a bite.

"So I guess we're both insane, then." I gaze up at him while slipping my mouth over the head of his perfect cock.

"Motherfuckin lunatics," he sighs, eyelids drooping while I suck him steady, cherishing him with my mouth.

It only takes five minutes before he's spilling on my tongue and down my throat. And thirty seconds after that, I come in his hand and in the grass.

Something about being out in the woods with him has always turned us into voracious animals. It's just another part of our dynamic, and it feels too good to overthink.

I just wish I could keep him afterward. But he slithers off like the serpent he is.

Never to be captured.

The sexy lake fun with Drake got me a couple hours of rest. I ended up passing out on the chaise on my back patio, in only my sweatpants, using a towel as a blanket. Not that it's cold outside or anything, but when I opened my eyes to Gina staring at me like I'm insane, it occurred to me that I probably should have made the extra ten steps inside the house.

The sun is up over the lake as I get out of the shower and get dressed, going to the kitchen for some tea and maybe a piece of fruit or something. I'm really still on edge. Last night helped, but sex with Drake always ends up feeling like a backslide. We don't get anywhere.

Maybe we're meant to just be fuck buddies. But that doesn't make sense, because I'm in love with him. Plus, he's my brother. Add Abdiel to the mix and I'm back to square one with my confusion.

I hear Gina coming and try to pull a mildly less despondent face, though it's not really working. I kind of feel like everyone knows there's something up with me, but it could just be the insecurities that come with a need for more Empyrean.

Her thoughts are faint as she brings a basket of strawberries up to the counter and begins separating them to wash. She's worried about Abdiel. She wishes she knew when he was coming back.

You and me both, girl.

Bringing the mug of tea to my lips, I sip slowly while I watch her. I wonder what she would think about me being in love with her adopted son. Would she hate me? Would she think I'm a creep for being much older than him?

Would she ever condone our relationship? If I wanted to divorce my wives and marry Abdiel, would she and Paul give us their blessing?

My stomach is in knots. I've completely lost my appetite, and I'm even more worried now than I was yesterday.

"Are you alright, sir?" Gina grumbles, pulling me out of my head.

"Why wouldn't I be?" I blink.

"Because you're just standing there, staring at me." She drops a berry into the basket and turns to face me.

My mouth opens, stunned at the brazen attitude she's giving me. People rarely talk to me like that, except Drake, obviously. Sure, I've known Gina for a long time, but still. I'm taken aback.

Does she know something? Has she picked up on the way Abdiel and I have been looking at each other? Did she see us together?

I straighten and resurge my confidence as Head Priest, folding my arms over my chest. "Is everything alright with *you*, Gina? Why are you being so short with me this morning?"

She glares at me for only a moment longer before her shoulders slump and she sighs, rubbing her eyes with her fingers. "I'm so sorry, Head Priest. I'm just... very worried about Abdiel. It's not like him to go off by himself like this, and well... you know about the mountain. After his parents and everything, I'm just..." Her forehead lines in duress I can feel in my gut. "I want him home."

Me, too.

"He's a very strong boy. *Man*," I correct myself, clearing my throat. "He's smart, and he knows what he's doing. I'm sure he's fine, and I'm sure he'll be back very soon with some stories for us."

I wink at her, and she smiles, chuckling and nodding along. "You're right."

Taking my mug of tea, I pat her shoulder, picking a strawberry out of the basket and popping it into my mouth on my way out of the kitchen. I leave out the front and walk to the far end of the porch, watching as everyone prepares for work, beginning their days.

Some commotion trickles down my way. I see a few people rushing around up the trail, and then I hear a faint thought that sends my heart into my throat.

Abdiel's back!

I heard it, and before I can even process what's happening, I'm diving off the porch, ready to run to where he is. But I stop myself.

Fear of how it would look stops me.

My fingers flutter at my sides while I pace back and forth. *He'll come to me first, right? He has to, he lives over here.*

I'm dying to rush to him, pull him into my arms and kiss all the breath out of his lungs, but I can't and it fucking *sucks*. I hate keeping this a secret. I've hated it with Drake for all these years, though I understand why it's necessary. And Drake doesn't want anything out in the open; he's made that abundantly clear.

But Abdiel is different. He deserves a *real* relationship. He deserves a King, not a sordid affair.

Pacing the porch for what feels like hours, I'm so antsy I could fall down, and I'm so excited to see my prince, I could physically implode.

What I'm not prepared for, however, is the parade of drama he's seemingly brought back with him.

I finally spot Abdiel, strolling down the path toward housing, smiling, as usual. But with a strange girl by his side.

A young girl, likely close to his age, with long, wavy strawberry blonde hair, wearing a University of Washington sweatshirt and a backpack slung over her shoulder.

And because this person is clearly an Outsider, there's a pack of people following behind them, including at least three visible patrolmen from the Tribe on their ATVs. I don't see Drake, yet, but if he gets wind that there's an Outsider on our land, especially being led in by one of our own, he'll be appearing any moment.

Gina comes out of the Den behind me, but I don't wait to see her reaction before I'm stomping down the steps toward Abdiel, his little friend, and the anxious family members practically chomping at the bit.

As I approach Abdiel and the girl, I hold up my hand to the Regnum and the patrol, signaling that I've got this. But really, I don't.

I have no fucking clue what's happening right now.

Abdiel steps up to me, and he's still smiling. So sweet and wholesome, if not a bit naïve, with no real awareness of the kind of shit he's stirring up right now.

"I'm glad you're back, young servant," I address him, politely, a hundred million degrees watered down from what I'd like to be doing. But we have an actual audience right now.

"Me too," he breathes, then bites his lip. My dick stirs, and I shake myself out of it, eyes flitting briefly to the stranger.

I'm kind of hoping that if I just ignore her, she'll go away. But unfortunately, no such luck.

Abdiel turns over his shoulder, like he's going to introduce her, or give me a much-needed explanation, but before he can, Gina stomps past me, grabbing him for a giant hug.

"Thank God you're safe," she whispers, squeezing the air out of him while he chuckles.

Then Paul pushes his way through the crowd, jogging up to envelope the both of them. I smile at the heartwarming scene, until

280

my reluctant gaze flicks to the girl once more, narrowing in suspicion.

Her eyes narrow at me in return, and I hear her thinking... about me.

That must be him. The Head Priest... Abdiel's secret Daddy. He's definitely hot, I'll give him that, but I don't trust him.

My jaw clenches. *Who the hell is this rude little girl on my land??*

"Abdiel, I'll need a word," I tell him as he finally manages to dissect himself from Paul and Gina's welcoming grip.

He glances up at me, his smile fading as worry and guilt line his eyes and he nods. "Yes, sir."

Ignoring the flinching of my cock at those two simple words, I nod at the patrol, telling them without words to keep an eye on the girl until I decide what to do. With my hand on his back, I guide Abdiel inside the Den, bringing him somewhere we can speak privately.

"H-how have you been?" He stutters while we walk toward the lounge. "Is everything okay?"

"Debatable," I grumble, opening the door and pushing him inside, before stepping in and locking it behind us.

When I turn to face him, he looks nervous. I can almost feel him shaking, his thoughts jumbling together. There's so much we need to discuss, but first thing's first...

Stalking up to him, I grab his face, wasting absolutely no time pressing my lips to his. He gasps in my mouth from the unexpected force of the kiss, his hands flinging to my waist, holding on for dear life while I unleash.

My breaths are harsh in between sucking him so hard I might bruise his precious mouth, nipping it for good measure in between our tongues swirling like they missed each other. *They missed each other so bad...*

"I missed you." I push him until he crashes into the desk. "I fucking missed you, my prince, oh my God, so so much."

"Mmmf," is all the comes out of him as our tongues tangle, lips sucking, teeth biting.

I can't help the breathless chuckle that flees as I grind my hips into his, purring at the feel of his erection, already nice and stiff for me. "Did you miss me?"

"Are you kidding?" His firm hands land on my ass, pulling me into him harder, parting his legs so we can really rub our stuff together. "I missed you the second I left. I thought about you constantly."

Humming, I pry myself off of him, knowing we can't do this right now. Not with all those people out there, wondering what to do next. *Speaking of which...*

I give us both a moment to breathe before I straighten up, running my fingers through my hair. "Who is this person you've brought me, young prince? An Outsider?"

Abdiel's eyes are still hooded with his arousal, but his brows are now knitting together in unease. "Yes, sir. She's an Outsider. I met her on the mountain."

I don't want him to fear me. I feel bad that he's worried about what I'll do, so I reach out and brush his silky curls away from his face. Taking a lock between my fingers, I twirl it while my other hand runs up his chest. I just missed touching him, beyond belief. I *love* the feel of him beneath my fingers.

"So she was on our land?" My brow arches.

He swallows visibly. "She was. But she didn't mean to—"

"Abdiel, how could you bring a stranger here without consulting me?" My eyes fall to his puffy lips, needing to be kissed by me, for hours. This isn't how our reunion was supposed to go.

"She was in danger. She needed help," he tells me, sincerity in his tone and thoughts. He's such a kind heart. Sometimes I'm surprised he even eats meat.

Lars used to scold him for naming the animals.

"People from the outside can't be trusted, Abdiel," I sigh.

"Her name is Rhiannon," he jumps in, eyes pleading with me to hear him out. "She's smart and kind, and she ran away from the outside world."

"We don't know her, my love." My tone holds no room for nonsense or negotiation. "We can't trust her."

But Abdiel is one of two people who will argue with me, zero fucks given.

"Aren't those the exact kinds of strays you and Drake used to bring in, though? Who became the Regnum... our *family*?" He gives me a pointed look, pulling away from my touch to make his stand. "The Principality was born on strays, was it not? My parents... Gina, Paul, Lucy, Perry... Pete."

He blinks his wide, mossy eyes at me, making it virtually impossible for me to put my foot down. He has a point...

I was just thinking about bringing in new strays. I can't write this girl off just because I don't know her, and because she doesn't trust me for some reason. The feeling is mutual.

But we don't know each other. *Not yet.*

Letting out a breath, I leave Abdiel, wandering to the door and opening it, peering out into the hall. One of the patrol, Jeremy, is up the corridor, so I bark at him, "Bring me the girl."

Jeremy nods and dashes away as I come back into the room with Abdiel.

"Thank you, my King," he whispers, a small smirk curving his mouth while he runs the tip of his thumb back and forth over his lower lip.

That mouth is hypnotizing.

"You're not off the hook just yet, baby," I say firmly, shifting from the stiffness happening in my pants.

"I love how you're looking at me right now," he breathes, and I rumble a seductive chuckle.

I want to pull him on top on me on the bed right this instant and let him fuck me for hours. But unfortunately, a monkey wrench has been tossed into the plans.

My brow lifts. *Can you hear what I'm thinking, my prince? About what we should be doing right now?*

He laughs. *Yea... But Rhiannon is worth the minor setback. She's great. Trust me?*

I roll my eyes and nod.

A quick knock on the door signals that she's here. I can already hear her before I open the door, and I'm on edge. It's been a while since we've accepted a stray, and there's a reason we stopped actively recruiting Outsiders. *Drake will have a lot to say, I'm sure.*

The small girl gazes up at me as I step aside, motioning for her to come in. I nod at Jeremy, and he takes position across the hall while I close the door.

Blinking at the tiny creature, I assess her for a moment. She's not dressed very girly, which I suppose I can appreciate. She's like Lauris or Emithel that way. Her hair is red, but not like Gem's. This girl's is almost pinkish blonde, and she doesn't have the freckles of Irish heritage that Gem has either.

Her eyes are huge and quite sparkly, an interesting shade of green, with some blue to it. The rest of her features are almost elfin. If we're being honest, she looks like she could be related to Abdiel. Though of course, he's much larger than her. She's almost the same size as Emithel, who's by far my smallest wife.

Listening to her, I hear her thoughts running wild as she looks around the room. The first thing she's wondering is if this is where Abdiel and I sneak around. She seems very protective of him when it comes to our relationship, unnecessarily so, since she doesn't know me, and barely knows him.

Folding my arms over my chest, I cock my head to the side while I wait for her to pay attention to what's happening. Abdiel says she's smart, but so far, she only seems distracted and inherently cynical, like all Outsiders.

She isn't doing much to impress me right off the bat.

Abdiel steps nervously between us, eyes coming to mine first. "Um, Darian, this is Rhiannon." Then he turns to the girl. "Rhi, this is our Head Priest, Darian. Leader of The Principality."

Rhi?? A nickname already, and they just met?? What is this nonsense?

Rhiannon steps up to me, wearing a polite smile, though I can still hear how incredulous she is. But apparently, she's willing to give *me* the benefit of the doubt, for Abdiel.

Aw, how sweet.

"Very lovely to meet you, Head Priest." She extends her hand. "I've heard only wonderful things about you from Abdiel."

I glare at her small hand for a moment before Abdiel clears his throat and I reluctantly shake it.

"And yet you don't believe any of them, do you, Rhiannon?" I call her out based on what she's thinking at this exact moment.

Her eyes widen, and her mouth drops open, her hand slowly tugging out of mine. "Well, I..." she stutters, peeking at Abdiel, who appears equally uneasy. "I've just never encountered any sort of community like this before. You're from the outside, right? I'm sure you can understand."

She has a point. I nod, remaining suspicious as I feel her out. "Where are you from?"

"Portland. I've been going to the University of Washington. Living in Seattle..."

"And why have you decided to leave?"

She freezes for a moment, unpleasantness slinking through her thoughts. There's something she doesn't want to talk about, something she doesn't wish to relive, and so she lies, "I couldn't deal with school anymore. The people were unkind, as most people are out there. I'm really not a fan of how the world is going, so when I met Abdiel and he told me about your community—" I peer at Abdiel while she speaks, giving him a scolding look. His forehead lines with guilt. "—I thought it sounded amazing. I mean, you guys don't use money." She scoffs in disbelief. "Do you know how incredibly bizarre that sounds? But it's awesome."

"It is." I wander to the desk and lean up against it. "I haven't had money in twenty-five years. It's entirely unnecessary."

Rhiannon grins and looks to Abdiel. "That's what he said."

I can't help giving him an appreciative look. "Alright, Rhiannon. I'll be blunt. I don't trust you."

Abdiel mumbles, "Darian…"

But I hold up my hand to stop him. "Don't take it personally. I don't trust anyone from the outside. We've been scorned before. That said, I trust him with my life." I nod in Abdiel's direction. "So if he trusts you, then I'm happy to have you as our guest until we decide what to do with you."

The girl pales. "What to *do with me?*"

"You'll stay in Abdiel's trailer." I ignore her, glancing to him. "You'll stay here." His face flushes, the sight of which might make me rock hard if I'm not careful. "Abdiel will show you around the Expanse, and you can work with Gina on chore duty. Even our guests must contribute."

"What do *you* do, Darian?" She asks in a stubborn, bratty tone that fills my limbs with rage.

My back straightens as I tower over her. "I'm in charge, tiny girl. This is *my* land, my family… *my prince.* It'll do you good to remember that."

Much to my surprise, she doesn't back down, aiming her angry little glare up at me.

"Alright, alright. Enough." Abdiel comes in between us. "Thank you, baby." He places a kiss on my cheek. "I'll get her settled in my trailer and bring my things over. I'm sure Gina will want me to get back to work soon."

I tear my burning eyes off the girl long enough to peek at him. "No work tonight, beautiful. I want to hear all about your journey." He gives me a sweet grin, tugging his lip between his teeth.

The girl's thoughts are distracting me, and I break my gaze on Abdiel to squint down at her. "Run along now."

She's practically seething as Abdiel drags her away, out of the room to go on with their business.

As soon as they're out of hearing range, I grab Jeremy. "Let the

Tribe know we have an Outsider staying with us. Top priority is watching her every move. She doesn't take a breath without us knowing about it, understand?" He nods. "Does my brother know she's here?"

"I don't think so, sir."

"Well, then... I suppose we'd better alert the Serpent."

CHAPTER TWENTY FIVE

DRAKE

I slept in my office last night.
It's been a strenuous few days, and after wandering to the lake, then seeing Darian… Well, needless to say, I couldn't just go back to my cabin alone. I mean, I *could* have, but my brain was too busy, my thoughts too hectic.

It's irritating. Mind-blowing orgasms are supposed to clear your head, not muss it up more.

So instead, I went to the lab and fucked around with my hybrids for a few hours until the sun was coming up. I actually don't remember passing out on the couch, but that's where I woke up just now.

And glancing across the room at my clock, I see that it's after nine. *Jesus.* I haven't slept this late in years.

Getting up slowly, I stretch my arms out and rub my eyes. I use the en suite I have off my office, and when I'm freshened up, I open my office door slowly, peering out into the lab to see what's going on. People are mulling about, working. Understandable, since it's late. Even so, you can pretty much always find at least a few someones in here working, at all hours. We could be considered *workaholics*, though we don't see it that way.

Our work is important. We create fuel, medicine, recreational and therapeutic psychedelics, which are exported in trade. We keep this place as self-sustained as possible and growing stronger every day.

My team is solid. Between the chemists and the Tribe, everyone knows how things work by now. We're like our own little family within a family. I trust them not to spill our secrets or make comments on things they don't need to be concerned with.

Like me coming in late, disheveled and dripping wet with mud all over my dress whites, then sleeping for hours in my office.

Stepping out of said office, I keep my head down as I make a beeline for the exit. I'd like to try to escape without anyone stopping me. Unfortunately, no such luck when I push open the door and almost crash right into Jeremy, one of my top patrolmen.

Disguising my shock and the insecure air I haven't been able to shake since last night with Darian, I clear my throat. "What?"

"Sir, Head Priest sent me," he starts, then pauses, his eyes shifting all over the place, as if he doesn't know how to tell me what he needs to tell me.

It only serves to irritate me further. "*And?* Get on with it. What's the problem?"

"There's an Outsider on the Expanse," he grunts.

"A breach?" My brows shoot up.

"Uh, not exactly..." His blinking becomes rapid, and my head shakes to showcase my confusion.

"What the hell does that mean?"

"She's a... guest," he fumbles. "Brought in by Abdiel Harmony."

My limbs actually freeze. I can feel it, like someone pressed the spectral pause button. "What...? He brought her... from where??"

Jeremy does a little shrug, making it apparent that he only has the information he's just given me, no more, no less. Scoffing, I rake my fingers through my hair, reaching for the walkie on his belt. But then I stop myself and brush past him, toward the exit. I need to get to Darian.

We need to talk about this face to face.

My pulse is increasing steadily with my bemused frustration as I stalk the long corridor, my mind a jumbled mass of queries.

Abdiel's back? Relief floods my chest at that thought alone, though it's stomped out quickly when I remember he brought a stranger onto our land. *Why on Earth would he do such a thing?*

And Darian is allowing her to stay? That's ridiculous. Typical Darian, putting us all in danger because of his giant heart overflowing with human compassion. Bleh.

He and Abdiel are so similar in some ways, it's startling.

Still, there's no way Darian is pleased with Abdiel encountering random strays and bringing them back to us, especially after all the shady things that have been occurring lately with trespassers.

SERPENT IN WHITE

There are no coincidences. This is happening for a reason.

But what is it?

Shoving myself through the large doors, I'm hit with late morning sun which blinds me momentarily. I rub my eyes hard, trying to push away the grogginess and the stress of my overall existence as I stomp to my ATV.

I'm about to jump on when I hear something... A familiar voice.

His thoughts ripple around his actual words, and I glance up to find the tall, slender yet immaculately defined form approaching, his dirty blonde curls shining beneath the sun. Full lips pulled into that permanent grin he wears, dimples resting comfortably at its corners like little signs that say, *There's no possible way I wouldn't be modeling in the outside world.*

I'm taken aback by how relieved I am to see him, back and safe. So much so that I almost completely miss the tiny red-haired thing at his side.

My eyes take her in before they spot me, dancing over her long hair, billowing in the breeze, not quite red, but more blonde-meets-coral or something, that blushed color combination emphasized by her pale complexion, similar to mine and Abdiel's. The shape of her face, her nose and large eyes actually resemble Abdiel's a bit, which has me wondering if maybe they're related. Though I'm sure Darian would have mentioned that in his relayed message...

The girl is wearing jeans and a flowy top, loose enough to hide her figure. She seems mousy from afar, though she's laughing and chatting with Abdiel, so clearly, they get along.

But where the hell did she come from?

I'm just kind of standing around, wondering if I should walk up to them and introduce myself, or wait for them to get to me. Or hop on the ATV and drive away, which is what I probably *should* do, though I must admit, I'm intrigued by the girl; by her presence. I need to know why she's here, what her purpose is, and why Abdiel would bring her onto our land without consulting anyone.

That's something that just does not happen on the Expanse. Ever.

Abdiel's gaze finally breaks away from their conversation, and he notices me, his grin widening significantly as he offers me a small wave. I narrow my gaze at him, rooting my feet to the ground and conveying my immediate feelings so only he can hear.

Welcome back, little mouse. You've got some explaining to do.

His grin fades, teeth sinking into that plush lower lip of his. I hate when he does that. It makes me lose control of my thoughts, forcing me to blur them out to disguise my uncertainty.

They saunter up to where I'm standing and finally stop, the three of us just staring at each other for a solid three seconds before anyone speaks.

"Drake," Abdiel says my name in a sort of sigh that tells me he's glad to see me, which doesn't placate me at all since I don't know what to do with that bit of information. "Good morning."

My brow cocks. *Pleasantries, little mouse? Really?*

His cheeks flush, and he breaks our eye contact, glancing at his shoes. "This is Rhiannon. Rhiannon, this is Drake. The Alchemist."

When I remove my glare from the kid and slink it on over to the girl, I find her already staring at me. And I mean *gawking*. I know why, of course, so I make a point to give her a slow-blink, really showing off the eyes.

A word splashes from her thoughts in my direction, *Wow...* followed by, *He is beautiful.*

An itch travels up my spine from the way she's thinking about me, so boldly. It causes me to shift in place, breaking my gaze with her glistening eyes, the color of deep waters. I'm already feeling off today, and having this stranger in here, assessing me, is just making me even more itchy.

"Great to meet you, Dra—"

"Where did she come from, and why is she here?" I address Abdiel, ignoring the girl, who doesn't even seem put off by my interruption. She just goes back to staring at me.

Like I'm a goddamn sideshow act.

Abdiel stammers, "I met her on the mountain. She's from Seattle." His words pause and go quieter. "She needed to be here."

The craziest thing is that I already know what he's talking about, before he even elaborates. *The mountain... They must have been to the clearing.*

Abdiel hears my thoughts and does a brief nod, subtle enough, though when I glance at the girl, she's watching our interaction with some curiosity in her eyes and lining her forehead.

"I need to speak with you," I mumble to Abdiel, watching the girl with reticence. "Privately."

"Sure." He nods. "But first we're supposed to give Rhiannon a tour of the lab."

I scoff, "No. Absolutely not." My head shakes firmly. "I don't bring strangers into my operation, and I don't make a habit of giving out the secrets of The Principality to every little spy who comes stumbling onto my land."

I glare at the girl, and she shivers. I can see it, *feel* it from her thoughts. She's fascinated by me; nervous yet so intrigued it's radiating from her mind. I simply blink at her.

"But Darian said..." Abdiel's voice trails, tugging me back to him.

"Darian said to have me show her the *lab*?" It isn't hard to miss the disbelief in my tone.

He rubs the back of his neck with his hand. "Well, no... But he said to show her around, and she's really interested in the business."

"Of course she is," I huff.

"I go to Business School," the girl chirps.

I roll my eyes. "Of course you do. Look, I don't have time for this. I need to speak to my brother."

I turn away from them but feel a hand on my arm. I already recognize the firm yet tender grip.

"Drake," Abdiel says my name in that voice again, and I don't know what the hell is wrong with me that it creates a tiny flutter in my gut. He just has the sexiest damn voice... "Please? Just a quick tour. Nothing too involved. Even just your terrarium in your office would suffice." His pouty lips pull into a tempting grin. "For me?"

Honestly, what is it about this kid that makes me want to push him onto his knees right here?

Taking a deep breath, I watch him carefully, his thoughts telling me about how he missed me, and how much he loved what we did in the woods before he left. It's twisting me up, which is beyond frustrating, since I'm already twisted up. *How much more can a person twist??*

"Fine," I growl.

Abdiel smiles before his tongue trails his lip, the sight of which is hardening me up good in my pants.

The girl's thoughts are simmering beside me, distracting me with all her mischievous wonderings, about me, what I do, where I'm from... About me *and* Abdiel together.

There's tension between us. I was hoping it wasn't obvious, but if this stranger is picking up on it, maybe someone else could, too?

It's not good, and now I'm even more irritable as I bark, "Five minutes inside the lab. That's it. Stay by my side. If you wander off, I can't promise my men won't shoot you."

Abdiel grins, likely believing that I'm kidding as I stomp in the direction I came, back up the steps to the lab. The girl's head is ridden with angst at wondering if I'm serious.

Hopefully she doesn't find out the hard way.

We go inside and walk the corridor, toward the lab. With the girl by my side, I hear her scattered thoughts while her face bounces back and forth, taking everything in.

"When did you get back?" I ask Abdiel.

"Earlier this morning. We've spent the last hour or so getting her settled in my trailer and taking a tour of the lake, housing, the farm…"

"She's staying with you?" My shock is apparent. *Darian would never…*

"She'll be using my trailer," Abdiel corrects me. "I'm staying in the Den."

My chest tightens. "Are you now…" My jaw does, too.

Abdiel gives me a side-eye. *You can come stay with us… You know that, right?*

My gaze narrows, chest tightening at the thought, for just a moment before I shake it off.

Pushing open the large double doors, I bring them inside the lab. There's a platform with handrails where you stand to overlook everything happening below, in the actual lab, stairs leading down to where my chemists are bustling about. The three of us stand up on the platform, observing them hard at work, mixing, stirring, and boiling in beakers and flasks, using machines to create and measure.

"Wow," the girl sighs. "This is incredible. This place is so different from everywhere else I've seen."

"How so?" I ask, knowing what she means, but wanting to watch her as she explains her thoughts. I like that.

"Well, this entire place… the *Expanse*… there's so much going on here. Little sections, almost like boroughs within your commune. And this place, this lab, is the only spot with technology, it seems." She pauses to collect her thoughts. "I could be wrong. Obviously, I haven't seen everything in only a couple of hours. But… I like it in here."

I nod, accepting her compliment. And it is one, for me, since this lab is mine. I designed it, set it up. I run it.

It's my haven within our haven.

The business side of it is something I have to do because I don't trust anyone else with it. Darian helps, sure, but he focuses more on dealing with the political side. I have to run the exporting and trade, even though it's not my favorite thing.

I just want to be with my plants. I want to be in the lab, creating things. Dealing in science. Business is just a means to an end for me.

I decide to take them down to see one part of what we're doing. My chemists are cultivating spores that will be turned into penicillin for new antibiotics. Very important.

"I can't believe you guys make your own medicine here," Rhiannon says, observing everything closely. And I'm stuck observing her. Making sure she's not some kind of spy, gathering intel for a bunch of assholes who will try to rob me.

I'm not paranoid. That dickhead I wasted the other night was trying to do exactly that. I've worked too hard to allow worthless scum from the outside to trickle in and steal from my family what I've been building for two decades.

She doesn't seem like she's one of them, but I can't know that from interacting with her for five minutes. And you can never be too careful.

"What about long-term illness?" She asks, turning wide, teal eyes on me.

I shake my head. "Rare. But we have the means to treat lupus, multiple sclerosis, fibromyalgia, things of that nature."

"I only saw the med trailer from outside," she murmurs.

"There are four." I nod for them to follow me as we ascend the stairs. "Three surgeons, two in training. Two obstetricians, a neurologist, optometrist, dentist, orthodontist, psychotherapist. You name it, we have it. Pretty much."

Once up on the platform, I take them back through the double doors. When we're outside again, Abdiel steps away to speak with a few of the guys on patrol.

"How have you done all of this?" Rhiannon's voice is full of awe. Honestly, it feels good. I suppose having an Outsider around can be useful for ego stroking. "It's just... it's amazing. You've created an entire community, a society, apart from everything else. It's baffling to me that you're completely self-sustained."

"Well, not *completely*." I lean up against my ATV, folding my arms. "We trade for a reason. There are some things we can't manufacture for ourselves just yet, like the four-wheelers, other vehicles, certain medical and farming equipment... Though we do have some pretty excellent blacksmiths, mechanics, and a training program."

Her face is one of pure shock, eyes wide, mouth hanging open. I have to laugh a little.

"Rhiannon, where do you think things come from? Human beings make them, with supplies provided from the earth and created by other human beings. A person can learn to do just about anything. So that's what we've done. We have talented individuals here, who were cast aside in the outside world. Outside, most of them were nothing, barely working to their full potential. Living paycheck to paycheck, scraping the bottom of unattainable success, or even just struggling to find their self-worth. In here, they're leaders. Masters. They've taught others, and from there, we grew.

"The problem with the outside world, with America in particular, is that it rarely rewards the hard-working. It focuses a lot on the teaching, but not on the application and allocation of knowledge. Here, that's exactly what we do. If you have a skill, it's put to the test and celebrated."

I pause for a moment, letting it sink in. Allowing her to grasp what I'm saying. "Nothing is perfect, shy of our Mother Earth. The Principality understands that. We cherish it, the imperfections of the world. The natural balance."

She blinks a few times, her gaze going to Abdiel, as does mine, watching him as he laughs. The sound is infectious, and it almost makes me smile. I glance back at Rhiannon to find her giving him the same sort of look. Her eyes dart to mine, and we squint at each other.

"You're in love with him." I give her a smug smirk.

"How could I be in love with him?" She scoffs. "I barely know him. We just met two days ago."

"Irrelevant. Love isn't as definitive as you Outsiders like to make it seem. Love can fade, it can expand. Over long periods of time, or short ones."

She grins, a snide little thing. "You sound like you're speaking from experience." I freeze, my spine stiffening, though I make a point not to react to her comment, ignoring it. And then she says, "Tell me about your brother."

I turn a warning glare on her. "I'm not in the business of discussing my family with strangers."

"Well, I'm a guest." She twirls a lock of hair around her finger as she peers up at me. She's so small, it feels like she's half my height. "You could indulge me."

"Anything you'd like to know about him you can find out for

yourself," I grumble. "He's a pretty transparent person."

"Yea, except for the secret affair, right?"

Her words grip my gut, my heart thumping quick behind my ribcage. *Abdiel told her so much. Is he insane??*

"Does it bother you?" I decide to twist her know-it-all attitude back on her. "Knowing you won't have him? Because he's in love with my brother…"

A wounded look flashes through her eyes, revealing that I was right. She definitely has feelings for Abdiel. *I mean, who doesn't at this point?*

But then I hear something… a flicker of a thought I grab onto.

She's remembering a kiss. A searing, scorching, forbidden kiss between her and Abdiel. I can practically see it from her memory…

The two of them in his tent, her fingers in his hair, his soft lips giving in to her desire.

Holy shit.

I'm taken aback. I didn't expect that. I hadn't even considered that Abdiel might have feelings for this girl in return, and now that I'm thinking about it, I'm not sure why. She's beautiful… and they seem to have some friendly chemistry, which I suppose could turn into lustful wanting.

But Abdiel is head over heels in love with Darian. That much I know for a fact. He wears his love for my brother on his sleeve, out in the open for anyone with half a mind to see if they wanted to.

I gulp over my suddenly dry throat. What does any of this mean?

Darian won't be pleased. I can understand the feelings, but jealousy is a form of pain, and pain usually turns me on. Watching Abdiel and Darian together hurts sometimes, sure. Okay, most of the time. But I also know that they want me, and that applies a small bandage to the gaping wound I let fester by standing on the sidelines of their budding relationship.

It's all so fucked up. I'm not angry with Abdiel for kissing the girl. He's young, and as I told Darian, he'll need to explore all avenues of his sexual awakening before he decides what he likes. My brother is jealous, he always has been. And he doesn't let it fuel him, like I do. Rather, he despises it.

Something jolts me out of my thoughts. It's a fear I recognize, coming from the mind of the tiny girl next to me. She's remembering something else now…

Something they saw up on the mountain. Something that almost took them...

"Excuse me," I grunt, stumbling over to Abdiel, who's still joking with Lorn and Jasper.

Taking him by the arm, I pull him away, and he gives me a peculiar look.

"What's wrong?" He mumbles, glancing over to where Rhiannon is crouching down, looking at some flowers.

"What happened? On the mountain." My tone is more frantic than I typically allow it to be in front of others.

Abdiel's face goes ashen. His eyes dart around us, then he blinks slowly, remembering it. He remembers so I can see, from his thoughts.

The clearing. The black rock, like a piece of obsidian out of place, yet its existence is subjectively necessary in this one spot. It belongs there, when it's there. But that doesn't mean it's good.

It's not. It's very very not good.

I see Abdiel and Rhiannon, sitting on it. And Abdiel is crying.

Tears flow from his eyes while he grips Rhiannon's hand.

And then I see myself. I see myself as he saw me, a vision of that day... That terrible, awful day that changed so many things.

It had to happen; it was part of the plan.

But it still hurt.

Gasping, my eyes widen at Abdiel as he stares at me, and we speak without words.

Did that really happen? He asks me. *Did you really cut yourself the day my parents died?*

I blur my thoughts fast. I'm afraid if I think too much about this, he'll hear something that will upset him. The kid isn't stupid at all, because he catches on, stepping in closer to my face.

"Stop hiding it from me, Drake," he rumbles, close enough that I feel it on my chest. "You can't hide forever. You went to the clearing that day. Why? What do you know about my parents' deaths?"

"Little mouse..." I breathe, shaking my head. *There is so much you don't know. If I were you, I'd keep it that way.*

He seethes in my direction. I feel his frustration, coming off him in waves. "I'm not satisfied with that. Something happened to us up there. That spot... there's some spooky, other-worldly shit living in it, and I think you know that. I think you're..." He pauses and gulps visibly. "I think you're feeding it."

My jaw locks, and this time I inch closer to him, my face hovering over his. "Listen to me, kid, and listen close. I've been on that mountain for half my life, for years before you were even born. I appreciate that you went up there to learn. I think it was necessary for your Ecdysis. And whatever happened with you and the girl, it led you right here, right now. Don't push it. Just because something exists, doesn't mean it's for you to know about."

Abdiel looks like he wants to keep arguing, but it's not in his nature. Eventually he sighs and runs his long fingers through the waves of his golden hair.

"You should come to dinner tonight." His eyes settle on mine, and he's not shy about unleashing his thoughts on me.

He wants to see me tonight. He wants more of me, him, and Darian together. I appreciate how bold the kid is. For a virgin, he's pretty forward with what he wants.

I let out a small chuckle. "As much as I'd love to be present for the shitshow that will undoubtedly be tonight's dinner, I think I'll sit this one out, little mouse. I have work to do."

He leans in to whisper by my ear, "All work and no play." I shiver.

When he pulls back, he smirks, and I can't stop staring at his mouth. *Temptation, baby.*

He blinks, *Come over tonight, then.*

I think you need some private time with my brother, I tell him, fully serious. And the jealousy I feel at knowing they'll do all manners of dirty stuff together without me is a jab to my chest, one I use to drive me.

It makes me feel good to hurt.

Abdiel keeps up the direct gaze, though there's a blush on his cheeks that I crave to watch spread all over his flesh. If I went with him tonight, I could probably get my wish...

But he doesn't know what's been going on with Darian and me. It's strained, and it's my fault. I need the pain of knowing they're together without me. I need that dull ache in my chest, the unease in my stomach. It's my burden.

"See you around then, Serpent," he whispers, spinning to walk back to Rhiannon.

I watch after them as he takes her by the arm, asking her if she'd like to go meet his best friend, Jordan. She grins and nods, beaming for the kid. I can see it, plain as day. And again, I don't blame her.

Abdiel is a light, for Darian, and myself, though I'm reluctant. Darian used to be my light, but I've tarnished his brightness over the years. And now I'm left with only animosity, resentment, and regret.

297

Deciding that I'm not in the right headspace for work, I think I'll go up the mountain instead. I'll go home, tend to my greenhouse, maybe relax. Get rid of some of this inner anguish I'm carrying around like a sack of bricks.

When I get there, I end up wandering around the woods for a while. These are my woods. There's a reason I live up here, alone. And it's not because I don't crave human connection. I do. I'm not as much of a loner as I make myself out to be.

But I need to be up here. I need it to settle me.

Like the first time I used Empyrean, when I saw so many things I never expected to see. Ever since then, I've used it on occasion, to reach into the depths of my mind. But the trumpets do that, too.

I named my drug *Empyrean* because that's the highest part of heaven. Where human will and the will of God become one. This is exactly what my Empyrean gives us.

It's a power, and it's sacred, which is why I don't allow just anyone to use it. The trumpets are synthesized into psychedelics used by the Regnum, for rebirth. But the effects of Empyrean, the telekinesis... That's just for us.

That's what Darian doesn't understand, though. Once the window of the mind is opened, empathy allows you to hear your fellow man. Maybe you could even hear other things...

And it doesn't wear off. He doesn't need a weekly injection. Neither does Abdiel.

That's my fault, too. I keep them thinking that's how it works, because I crave the connection, with Darian especially, and I just know it would fade if he knew the truth. My manipulation of my brother dives deep, like the depths of the lake we swim in. I never meant for it to come to this...

And now he's growing to hate me.

It started when Lars died. They weren't an official item, nothing like that. Lars was happily married to Jenny, and they were loving parents to Abdiel. But Lars was bisexual and purely smitten with my brother. He and Jenny had an understanding.

And Darian was craving things he couldn't admit to himself out loud; things we were certain the family wouldn't understand or approve of. Though I know that's not entirely true either...

I left him when he needed me. *I* convinced him we could never be, and so he sought out someone else. It wasn't either of their faults. It was entirely my problem.

But then Lars and Jenny died. They fell from the overlook, near the peak of the mountain. They fell from thousands of feet and landed in a ravine.

No one ever knew what really happened. But I do. I know in my heart…

The mountain made them jump, and I could have stopped it.

But I didn't.

And so it goes, blood for blood.

CHAPTER TWENTY SIX

ABDIEL

Dinner tonight is awkward, for a myriad of different reasons. First off, Rhiannon and I are dining *with* Darian and the wives. I'm not serving the dinner, I'm eating it, and that on its own is beyond bizarre.

Also, having Rhiannon here seems to be setting Darian on edge. He doesn't trust her. I get that. Apparently, the feeling is mutual, because Rhiannon is like a dog with a bone. She's convinced Darian is up to no good.

When she found out he has *five* wives? Forget about it.

"Abdiel, he's using you," she said while we were getting ready for dinner. "He's in a position of power. He convinced all these women to marry him for his own selfish reasons, and now he's doing the same thing to you."

"You sound jealous." I'd given her a pointed look.

We're friends, but still. She's a *new* friend. I've known Darian all my life, and I've been in love with him for a while, even if we did just start hooking up. He's a part of my world, ingrained in who I am. She's wrong about him, and I just wish she could see that.

But she's triggered, and it's very uncomfortable for all of us.

We sat down for dinner pretty much knowing it would be tense. And it certainly has been, worsened by the fact that I can hear everyone's thoughts.

Gina is onto us. Not *exactly*, but she knows something is up. She's wondering why I'm eating dinner at the table I've served for years as she and the other Domestics serve our meals and replenish the drinks.

The wives are wondering the same thing. Kiara and Alissa are jealous of Rhiannon. They don't even think twice about me, whereas Emithel and Lauris seem keen to Darian's homosexual tendencies. I can barely even eat, or look in his direction, for fear they'll see the eyes I give him and call us both out.

Rhiannon is quiet the entire time, seething about our little disagreement from earlier. She also happened to pick up on some of the tension between Drake and me when we visited him at the lab, and now she's convinced there's shady shit going on in The Principality.

What she doesn't know is that it has nothing to do with our family or our community. It's the three of us who are tying each other up into knots, lying and hiding things, from each other and the rest of the Regnum.

And then there's Darian. I feel awful for bringing all this stress into his home and laying it all on his table. He just missed me so badly, as much as I missed him, and all he wanted was to celebrate my return with lots of kissing and touching.

But instead, we're dealing with the Rhiannon stuff. He's tense as hell, wondering what to do about her, listening to her half-cocked theories about him while sitting there trying to keep a polite face.

So by the time dinner is over and everyone retreats, I feel immensely guilty. Darian goes up to his bedroom and slams the door. I flinch as he does, my heart aching to run up there and be with him. The fact that I can't is making me nuts.

We meander around for a bit afterward, talking with the Domestics. Rhiannon seems to be getting along with Gem and Emithel, and they take her around the Den, giving her a tour while I talk to Gina. I'm working a day shift tomorrow, which will be good. Believe it or not, I'm excited to get back to work after all the craziness we experienced up on that mountain.

I need some stability.

As the house goes quiet, and the Domestics all retreat to their trailers for the night, I take Rhiannon outside to talk.

"Look, Rhi, I'm so happy you're here, you know that," I start while we walk down to the lake, "But you have to lay off Darian." She looks like she wants to protest, but I cut her off before she can. "It's hard enough for him knowing he's disappointing his family by not being able to give them an heir. But to be made to feel like he's doing something wrong by being with me... It kills him. He already carries so much guilt."

She gives me a wide-eyed stare, considering what I've said. "I'm sorry, Abdiel, but I just… I've seen it enough times to know. If he wants to do right by you and his family, he needs to tell the truth."

"Okay, well that's something he'll do on his own time," I sigh. "You're not making it any easier."

"He doesn't need it to be easy," she says. "Tough love time for the Head Priest. And I'm not talking about him coming out. I mean getting rid of the wives."

"Yea, well, I think most of them know his situation, anyway." I rake my fingers through my hair.

"You seem really stressed." She squeezes my arm. "Oh, Abdiel, I'm so sorry. I don't want to upset you. You're the only friend I have at this point. I know I'm skeptical of a lot, but you weren't wrong about this place. It's amazing…"

She says this, though I can hear her thinking about how we all seem brainwashed. She's just so damn suspicious of it all, and I'm not sure what would help her see that we're not full of shit.

"I'm gonna crash." I give her a quick hug. "You remember how to get back to my trailer?"

She nods. "Yea. I'm fine. Go, get some rest. I'll see you in the morning."

We go our separate ways, and I head inside, to the lounge. I change into sweatpants and a t-shirt, getting settled in the giant bed. It's strange to be sleeping in here, in the open. For people to know I'm here is odd, and I think it's part of what has Gina on high alert. I mean, I could have just slept in their trailer, or at Jordan's.

Darian so quickly insisted I sleep here—in the lounge too, not even in the guest bedroom—and my heart wants to believe it's because he's done hiding.

Maybe he really wants to figure out how to tell people about us.

I don't know… My thoughts are scattered, making it virtually impossible to get any rest. I've been lying here for hours, staring at the window. Partially drawn curtains hang around the view out to the lake, and I remember the night I peeked in here like a total weirdo. I remember it like it was yesterday, though it has only been a few weeks.

Still, it's hard to believe how much has changed since that night. The night I found out the truth and inserted myself into something I would now die before giving up. It's so complicated between the three of us, but I can't find it in myself to regret anything.

SERPENT IN WHITE

I love Darian, and I think I love Drake, too. I wish they could admit they love each other.

When I'm sure I've been lying awake for three hours, no sign of slumber in sight, I decide I can't take it anymore. Sliding out of bed, I creep to the door, opening it slowly and peering around the hallway for signs of anyone.

The entire house is quiet.

Leaving the room, I tiptoe up the hall, toward the stairs. I know there are guards by the front door on patrol, but they wouldn't hear me from over here, so long as I'm very quiet. I sneak up the steps, taking two at a time to ensure I don't make any noise. Then I hold my breath as I pass the other bedrooms, reaching Darian's last. The largest bedroom in the house, the master, all the way at the end of the hall.

Twisting the doorknob, I pray it's not locked. It isn't.

Slinking inside, I close the door softly, locking it behind me. Finally, I can breathe again, letting out a long one I'd been keeping in while I look over the room.

It's massive. Probably as big as the sitting room downstairs, and equally fancy. All the furniture is large; dark tones, a regal elegance to every detail.

It fits Darian perfectly. Of course, I've been in here before, cleaning. But never in that bed...

The bed where he's lying beneath his comforter, a giant lump in the middle of the mattress. I see him stir. He must have heard me come in.

Wandering up to the bed, I waste no time lifting the covers and sliding in next to him where he lies, wearing only boxers, his smooth skin available to me.

His scent hits me immediately, enveloping me in his warmth; the masculine smell of his flesh and the soap he uses. Sweet and fiery, like hemp, amber, and lush leather.

His back is to me, so I slip my arms around his waist, pulling myself as close as humanly possible, until my chest melts into his muscular back.

He eases himself into me, awakening more from his slumber to recognize it's not a dream, a long hum leaving him while I press my lips to the nape of his neck.

"My Prince Abdiel," he whispers, then spins in my arms. "What took you so long?"

"I wasn't sure..." My voice is gruff, hesitant. "If you were upset with me…"

"I could never be so upset I wouldn't want to see you." He cups my jaw with his large hand. "That I wouldn't crave your body against mine."

"I missed you so badly, my King." Impatiently, I press my lips to his.

No more waiting. No more hiding. I just need him, now. *Right fucking now.*

Darian kisses me brutally, holding my head still as his lips devour mine, sucking in between nipping me with his teeth until a chill runs all over my body. His tongue glides in to meet mine, and we both hum, licking and lapping at one another, reuniting the way we should have earlier if it hadn't been for my unnecessary drama.

Guilt weighs on my chest like a sack of potatoes. The fact that I kissed someone who isn't him only yesterday has me trembling, and not with arousal.

"Abdiel," he whimpers into my mouth. "Please come back to me. Stay with me, baby."

"I'm so sorry, Darian." I pry my lips away from his. "I need to tell you something…"

I witness his jaw flex, eyes dark in this light, almost black. It's a bit frightening, if I'm being honest.

"I know," he mumbles, breaking our stare for a moment. "I know you kissed the girl…"

My lashes flutter at him. "You already know?"

"I can hear both of your thoughts, Abdiel… Remember?" A small, reluctant smirk crosses his lips as he scoffs.

"Oh…" I mutter, feeling immensely foolish. "Right."

"Do you… love her?" He asks, his tone cracking my heart in half.

He doesn't sound like my King in this moment… He sounds like a child. Insecure and afraid, and I hate that I've made him sound that way. *I* did this to him…

I'm a piece of shit.

"I don't think so." I take his hand in mine, locking our fingers. "Not like I love you…"

He shudders, forehead dropping forward to rest on my shoulder, nuzzling his lips in the crook of my neck. "I can't lose you, my prince. I can't lose both of you…"

Wrapping my arms around his shoulders, I hold him close to me, kissing his head, his cheeks, his jaw, then finally, he gives me his lips once more. Our kisses are slow, sensual and intense, confessing of feelings we don't need to speak out loud. They're here, rushing between us like a waterfall.

I need you, baby, I tell him, sucking his mouth raw.

I need you more. He tugs at my shirt, yanking it over my head and tossing it, coming back to my mouth instantly, like a magnetic force is pulling him to me. I feel the same way.

He places his hand on my chest, gripping my pectoral muscle while my heart bangs beneath his palm. Our lips glide and tumble, tongues tasting, teeth biting in urgent need.

Running my hands down his back to his ass, I grasp and squeeze, full and round in my hands while I bring him closer. He grinds against me, his erection stiff as it writhes on my own, sending an eager throb to my balls I haven't felt since that last night in the woods.

"You're so precious to me, baby," he says with his other hand in my hair, tugging, keeping me still to kiss me steady. "I'm jealous, of course I am. I want you all to myself."

"What about Drake?" I breathe over his lips, slipping my hands into his boxers, feeling the smooth skin that covers the rock-hard muscles of his ass.

"That's different." He pushes my sweatpants down. When he discovers I have nothing on beneath them, his dark eyes gleam.

An aroused grin covers my lips, a flush traveling up my neck, palpably. "One less piece of clothing in our way."

He growls, easing himself on top of me, straddling my waist. "Be my feast tonight, baby. Please... I'm *starved* for you."

A mewl escapes me while I push his boxers down, large, erect cock flopping out onto my abs. Making a fist around it, I stroke slowly, holding our eye contact the entire time, until his eyelids droop and his head falls back.

"Fuck, I missed your touch." He takes my other hand in his, running it up his chest to hold his pec. I circle my thumb around his nipple until it hardens, and my mouth is watering.

"I need to taste you, my King," I plead, chest heaving from beneath him.

His eyes open, and he glances down at me, sucking his lower lip between his teeth, the sight pulsing my balls. He moves his hips until he's sitting astride my chest, massive dick right in my face, waiting to be sucked dry.

Parting my lips, our eyes remain locked while I open wide, ready to receive his delicious cock. He shifts once more, pushing the head up to my mouth. The fat tip shoves inside first, and I immediately suck hard, tasting some of him already. I whimper, and he bucks his hips, giving me another inch.

Darian reaches forward to hold his headboard, guiding himself deeper into my mouth, slowly, so that I can adjust to him. Still, when he hits the back of my throat, I gag, and he groans. He sits up on his knees, angling himself deeper into my throat, pulling out and pushing back in while I hollow my cheeks.

He's fucking my mouth, like I did to him the other night in the woods, while Drake was railing him in the ass.

And in this moment, I miss Drake. I would love to see him behind Darian right now, fucking him... Fucking *me*, who knows. My cock flinches at the thought, and Darian reaches one hand behind him, fisting me tight. He jerks me slow while he fucks my throat, pushing deeper and deeper until his balls are on my chin.

"God, baby..." he groans, sliding in and out of my mouth, saliva dribbling from the corners, my eyes watering. "Does my Prince like to take his King's cock deep in his throat?"

I nod, and he hums, hips flicking steadily, my jaw going numb already from his girth. His hand travels down to my nuts where he plays with them, fondling and rubbing and toying with me until precum is leaking from my cock.

Abruptly he pulls his dick out of my mouth, a trail of my spit going with it. Then he runs the head over my lips, down my chin. He drags his cock all over my mouth, and I fucking love it. I *love* this, feeling like his pet, his toy, to do with as he pleases. To suck him and make him feel good, to treasure his dick like royalty, because that's exactly what it is.

"Do you love my dick?" He rumbles down at me, dark eyes glimmering wickedly.

"Yes, sir," I answer immediately, witnessing his cock flinch.

He moves up farther, dragging his balls over my chin, up to my lips. "What about my balls, baby? Do you love them, too?"

I groan and nod, parting my lips to suck on his nuts, licking them all over, using my whole mouth to cherish them; *him*. I'll gladly fucking worship every part of him.

He moves again, spreading his legs wide while I lick a line up his taint, moving back. Using my hands to spread him open, I slide my tongue over his hot hole.

"*Fuck…*" he whimpers. I wish I could see him, but my face is quite literally buried in his ass.

He's practically sitting on my face, holding himself up so he doesn't smother me, but still. My mouth is in between his cheeks as I grip them hard, fluttering my tongue over and over.

I have no real notion of how to do this, but I think I get the general idea. Licking him like he's a delicious treat, I kiss and suck everywhere my mouth can reach while he groans and strokes my cock roughly in his fist.

"That's right, my prince," he croons, riding my face. "Eat my ass. Eat me so good, baby. *God…*"

His voice, that rumbling deep voice like thunder, mixed with his filthy words… They have me soaring.

Anything for you, my King. I will do fucking anything to make you feel good.

"Is that right?" He answers me with his mouth while mine is preoccupied.

I mumble into him, shoving my tongue into his asshole.

He groans. "You are *mine*, Abdiel." Then he tugs himself away from my lips.

I whine at the loss, wanting more. I want to spend all night eating him like a snack I could never get my fill of.

But he moves down, writhing along the length of my body with his. His rests his cock over my own and takes my face in his palm, gazing deep into my eyes. "I want everything with you."

His lips lower to mine before he kisses me deep, sucking his own flavor off my mouth. It's dirty, and luscious, and I can't get enough. I'm desperate for something more, and he knows. Because he's my King, and my lover.

He yanks my sweats off the rest of the way, then crawls to his nightstand, opening a drawer and taking out a small bottle. A frisson of nerves run through me, because I think this is happening.

We're finally going to fuck. I think I'm going to lose my virginity to the man of my dreams.

I'm fucking *high*.

"We'll have to be quiet," he whispers, opening the bottle and squeezing lubrication out onto his hand. Then he reaches behind himself. "The drawbacks to not doing this downstairs."

"You can cover my mouth if you want," I rasp, and he grins.

"Mmm…" He kisses me softly while gliding lube between his

307

cheeks.

"Can I?" I ask, and he nods, handing me the bottle.

My hands are shaking as I squeeze out more, stroking it onto my erection. Then I move my wet fingers between his cheeks, tracing a slick finger up and down over his rim. I feel him clench beneath my touch, and I think it means he's excited. That he likes what I'm doing.

"I can't wait to feel your giant cock inside me, Abdiel," he purrs as my fingers swirl. "I've been dreaming about this."

"Me too," I hum. "Good God, I've wanted to fuck you for so long."

"We shall wait no longer." He positions himself so that his legs are spread wide where he sits on my hips, his ass open for me. "Get inside me, my prince, before I die of starvation."

Shivering, trembling head to toe, I take my lubed erection in my hand, aiming it up to his hole. Our eyes remain locked where we stand, in this moment, frozen in time together.

This is unlike anything I've experienced up to this point, because I've been waiting for *him*. Waiting to give myself to him in every way humanly possible.

I nudge my head up to Darian, while at the same time he presses down on me, sitting himself on my cock. The tip struggles for a moment before it slides in, and I groan out loud.

"Quiet," Darian growls, though his voice is breathier than I've ever heard it, his eyes barely able to stay open.

Squeezing my lips together, I grip his ass with one hand, the other still holding my dick to push into him. It's the most intense feeling of my life. His body is clutching me, so hot and tight, like a fist made of fire. He sits down on me farther while I give a little thrust, my erection disappearing into his ass, fitting snugly into his body like this is where it belongs.

We're one.

"*God*... fuck, Abdiel... your cock is huge," he groans, taking more, deeper.

"You're so... tight." My chest shudders, a sheen of sweat covering my body already. "I can't believe I'm inside you right now."

He breathes an erotic chuckle, gripping my chest hard with his fingers as he hovers over my lips. "You're not a virgin anymore, sweet prince."

My next groan is cut off with a kiss.

Finally releasing my erection, my hands slide up his hips, holding him where he sits on top of me. He just stays there, seated on my cock, not making a move to go anywhere while he kisses me with gradual passion, building a slow burn.

My entire body is wound up like a rubber band. The desire to stroke in him is overwhelming, the need to move driving me wild until I growl into his mouth.

He grins deviously on my lips. "You want me to move, baby?"

"Yesss," I whimper. "Yes yes yes please. *Please*."

"I love hearing you beg." He shifts on his knees, just enough to pull his ass up my cock, only an inch or so, but it feels divine.

A moan leaves my lips, and I slap my hand over my mouth. He presses back down, then lifts again, swelling up an easy rhythm, riding my cock like he was made to do it. Seriously, the way he works his hips is so graceful, rippling his movements; swiveling, welcoming me as deep as possible, then pulling up on my shaft, taking me over so good I'm crying beneath my hand.

"Fuck yes, my prince," he grunts, panting with his hands all over me, pinching my nipples between his greedy fingers. "You feel so good, baby. Is this a good first fuck for you?"

"God... God, *yes*... I can't... fuck me, Darian..." I have no idea what I'm even saying, this is the most amazing thing I've ever felt.

His body squeezes me tight, clamping and clenching in pure heat while he strokes my cock in his tight ass. My hands travel up his body, feeling his skin, treasuring his lines of strength. Tracing his muscles with desperate fingertips, my thumbs flick his nipples until he hums. My eyes move from the salacious need on his face to his erection, hard as fuck and bobbing up and down between us.

I curl it in my fist and jerk, pumping up and down to match the tempo of his hips riding me.

"Baby..." he whines, bringing his face down to mine, kissing my lips, my jaw, my neck. "Baby baby *baby*..."

"Does it feel good, my King?" My voice is hoarse with arousal as the orgasm builds up in my loins so strong, so fervent I'm about to burst.

I need to hold out, to make him come first, but it's my first time fucking, and I'm dizzy. I'm going out of my mind.

I need to come.

"You fuck so good, Prince Gorgeous." He licks a line down my throat, lapping up my sweat, biting me to cover up his groans.

"I want to make your big dick come," I tell him, and he whimpers.

My fist slides faster, his movements mirroring my speed while he

309

fucks my cock, his ass holding me tight. The only reason it's even able to move is the slippery lube we're wearing.

"Fuck me, Abdiel." He trembles on top of me, drunk with lust. "Fuck me like I'm yours."

"You *are* mine," I growl.

His lips dance on my flesh. "Worship me, boy, for *I am your King*."

Possession fills my heart as I flip him abruptly onto his back, our connection never severing while I settle between his legs. The look on his face is priceless. He clearly didn't expect that at all. His pupils dilate, a quiver on his lips at me taking control of him.

Spreading his legs wide, I pick up the movements where he left off, thrusting into him so deep my balls press at the entrance of his body.

His eyes roll back in his head. "Abdiel... Go harder."

"Your wish is my command, your majesty," I pant, pounding my cock into him as rough as I can.

This time he groans out loud and I grin, covering his mouth with my hand as I push and pull, pumping my cock between his legs while he squirms. I'm not even touching his dick and it's flinching, stretched long, engorged. Watching it closely, I swirl my hips. Every time it moves, I can tell I'm hitting a spot, that spot he loves, deep in his body. The one that gives him blazing euphoria.

Removing my hand from his mouth, I grasp his chest with both hands, kissing his lips, then biting him, hard. He's whining and panting unlike anything I've heard before, and it's quixotic music to my ears. I think I've gotten the hang of fucking, rippling my hips into him while his cock twinges out sticky liquid between us.

"You feel so good stroking me," I tell him, breathlessly. "Your tight ass fits me perfect." The bed is moving all around with my rapid thrusts, the sounds of our animalistic sex bouncing off every wall in the room. "Open your eyes, love," I demand, slinking my fingers into his hair. "I want to watch you fall from grace."

He forces his eyes open, gazing up at me as he moans a song of only one lyric. *Abdiel... My prince.*

"I'm going to..." he mumbles, his words dissolving into a gasp.

"Close, beautiful?" I purr, straight up crumbling myself, using every piece of willpower I have while I move in him. "God, Darian, please tell me you're gonna come... I can't hold on..."

"I'm... I'm..." His lips are trembling, eyes threatening to close. "I'm... *coming*."

He whines out loud, and I cover his mouth with mine, his rigid length erupting between us, throbbing cum all over our joined bodies while he cries between my lips. And that's all I need to let go myself.

"I'm coming too," I rasp as my dick explodes, pulsing long streams of cum, jetting, filling him all the way up. "I'm coming in you, baby. Coming in your ass... fuck fuck *fuck*."

"God, baby, come in me..."

Our mouths stay together, licking, sucking and biting while we inhale each breath, exhaling to fill one another's lungs.

The world around us swirls for an eternity, the words of our thoughts ricocheting everywhere while our hearts regulate. Darian's hands treasure me, rushing all over my body, down to my ass, up my back, down my shoulders and arms, massaging me like I did good for him.

Like he's endlessly appreciative of how good I fucked him into oblivion.

"You're everything to me," he whispers up to me with wonder in his beautiful eyes.

Pushing back his hair with my fingers, we're nose to nose, staring; gazing.

In this moment, I don't believe I'll ever love anyone this hard, for the rest of my existence. I never even comprehended that I could fall so deeply into a love like this.

Taking his hand in mine, I thread our fingers. Then I bring our joined hands up to my mouth and kiss his knuckles.

"I'm in love with you, Darian," I murmur, not giving one single fuck if I'm supposed to play it cool, or be aloof. There are no games to play with a love so vibrant. It's serious. "I want to be with you and do this all the time. I want you, no matter what that means."

He blinks up at me, his eyes glistening for me. But his thoughts turn suddenly troubled, a somber tone which tightens my chest.

He says nothing, but shifts beneath me. Breaking the spell of his hypnotic gaze, I pull my hips back, tugging my softening cock out of his ass as it clenches on me while I go. Glancing down, I watch my cum dripping from his body.

"Was I not supposed to come inside you?" I ask, feeling like a foolish former virgin for just doing it without asking.

Drake does it... that's the only reason I did it. But that could be their thing.

"Abdiel, my beautiful young prince, I *loved* you coming inside

311

me," he rumbles, still holding onto my hand tight, as if he won't let me go. He refuses. "That was your first time ever doing that. I'm honored to share it with you. For you to be... mine."

My chest warms, and I go to him, nuzzling my body on his, though I still feel his unease. It's making me uncomfortable.

"Did I do something wrong, my King?" I hate the insecurity in my voice, but I can't help it.

"You did *nothing* wrong, baby," he says, though he's reticent. I can feel it, in his twitchy fingers as they brush my jaw. "I just... before we enter into anything, there's something you must know."

I gulp. "What is it? Are you alright?"

"Yes, yes. I'm fine. But this is something that... it will come as quite the shock." He pauses to breathe, and I'm shaking. My heart is in my throat. "I should have told you sooner..."

"What, Darian? You're scaring me..."

"I'm sorry, baby." His brows zip together, worry lining his eyes. "I'm so sorry."

"For what?" My tone is more frantic now, impatient and terrified.

He goes quiet for minutes, shifting beneath me so that he can stare at my face. His silence is suffocating me, choking the air out of the room while I await his words. Some truth I don't think I want to hear.

Finally, he says, "You know your parents meant a great deal to me, yes?" He pauses, and I nod, hesitantly. "They were my closest friends. It was hard when we first began The Principality. It was just Drake and me for so long, and when people began joining, they all looked up to me. They followed me, as their leader. In the beginning, I didn't know what to do with that. I was young, and still figuring myself out. I needed a friend to confide in, and then your parents arrived."

My eyes are so wide they're starting to ache. I don't think I've blinked in a while.

"Before you were born... before you were even conceived, your father and I... became close." He stops and swallows visibly, the slope of his Adam's apple dipping slowly while he stares up at me from where I'm resting against his chest.

I move back.

"We were friends. And then we also... were together." His eyes fall away from mine as he clears his throat. "Romantically."

I have no thoughts. No reaction. My mind is a blank space.

Since I'm barely even breathing, unable to form words in my mind, let alone from my mouth, Darian keeps speaking. "Your mother knew,

and she was fine with it. It was something... they used to do together."
He shakes his head. "You don't really need to know that. They're your
parents... I'm sorry. I just... I needed you to know that no one was
unfaithful to anyone."

"But you fucked my dad," my voice scrapes from inside my throat,
the words simply ejecting themselves on their own.

Darian's eyes widen, and his mouth hangs agape. He looks more
uncomfortable, more insecure than I've ever seen him. I wish I could
say it dampens his attractiveness, but he's even gorgeous when he's
fumbling about.

"I... I..." he stutters before stopping to take a breath. "I did."

"For how long?" I ask, and he appears startled by my question. My
brow arches. "You said *before I was born*... Does that mean it stopped
after?"

He clears his throat a thousand more times. Then he answers me
with his mind, too uneasy to say the words out loud anymore. *No...
We saw each other on occasion.* His eyes lift to mine. "Very rare
occasion at that point." He scoots up, coming after me while I back
away. Still, he manages to grasp my face. "Abdiel, it wasn't anything
serious. We weren't *together*. He was married to your mother, and
they were madly in love. It was just something that happened on
occasion. Something... physical."

My stomach turns violently.

I just fucked my dad's lover.

God...

"Abdiel, please don't be upset," he begs, eyes rounded with guilty
sorrow. I hate seeing him this way, but I feel very strange about this.
"As I said, I was figuring myself out. Drake and I... we weren't
together in any real way at the time. He'd made it clear that he
couldn't, and I was feeling so very hopeless. Your father was my
closest friend, and he was a wonderful man." He stops short, as if
preventing himself from saying something, unsure if I can handle it. I
blink at him. "You remind me very much of him."

Pain and joy meld together in my chest, twisting up like a length
of rope. I love hearing that I remind anyone of my parents, because I
loved them and they were, indeed, wonderful.

But they're not here, and it does hurt to think about them,
especially now. Especially from the lips of a man we've now shared.

Swallowing hard, I back up slowly while my chin wobbles. Darian
sits up, wincing as he does, bringing my attention back to what we

313

just finished doing.

"We should wash up," I rumble, robotic. There's so much pinging all over the inside of my skull now, I'm finding it very difficult to decide how I should feel.

I love Darian. I can't just turn that off. I'm not even necessarily angry with him, or hurt. I'm just... confused.

"Baby?" Darian's voice calls to me, and I think he's been trying to talk to me for a few seconds, but I didn't even hear him. "My prince... are you alright? I think we should... talk this through."

I shake my head again. "No, let's just get cleaned up and go to sleep. I'm tired."

Darian appears distraught. He looks like there's so much he wants to say, but he doesn't want to push me, which I appreciate. He just dumped a lifetime supply of nonsense on me.

All I want is to take a shower and curl up in bed.

He stands slowly, legs visibly like jelly. I look him over for just a moment, admiring how beautiful he is. And then I remember that my father probably looked at him the same way.

Was it destined that I would fall for him? That he would captivate me the way he did my father? And what was my mother doing while all this was happening? Just sitting around? Or was she hooking up with someone herself?

I can't fault them. Free love is a thing here. As long as everyone is old enough and consenting, as long as it's mutually agreed upon by both partners in the relationship, there are a lot of couples who do similar things.

But it's a different notion when it's your own parents. Especially when it also involves your lover.

My King... Or my *father's*...

Stalking away, into the en suite, I immediately turn on the shower. I feel for the water to get warm and then hop in, not waiting for Darian. I know he's there, though. I'm not facing the doorway to his bedroom, but I can tell he's standing there staring at me. I *feel* him.

Closing my eyes, I let the water run over my tired mind, my aching muscles. I just lost my virginity. I should be in bed with him, loving him. Instead, I'm in the shower, all torn up.

I hear Darian approach, then I feel him step into the large shower stall behind me, circling my waist with his big arms. He does so slowly, hesitantly, as if he's not sure I'll want him. As if he's afraid I'll push him away.

It breaks my heart in half.

I spin in his arms and hug onto his waist, so hard that his back bumps against the wall of the shower. Burying my face in his neck, I let his warm, wet flesh comfort me. It takes him a second, but he accepts my embrace, fingers running up and down my back. He clutches my head in his hand, stroking my wet hair.

Tears slip from my eyes, masked by the running water, soaking into his skin while he holds me, and our hearts beat in truth, together.

CHAPTER TWENTY SEVEN

RHIANNON

Mornings in the forest are especially beautiful.
I've never really been a morning person. I have a tendency to resemble an ogre who lives underneath a bridge, and it takes me a solid hour to maneuver myself back into a functioning human being.

Out here, however, I wake up early. Well, *everyone* wakes up early here. You can hear people up and mulling about as early as four-thirty. Which makes sense, since a lot of them are farmers, fishermen— fisher *people* actually, a few women—carpenters, and such. They have to be up early.

And I've seemingly caught the bug. I enjoy being up to watch the sun rise over the lake. Sipping a nice cup of coffee and feeling the breeze brush my skin, before it gets too hot. The weather has been exceptional lately, but the temperature at sunrise in the summer is now my favorite.

It's seven-fifteen, and I just finished my coffee. I haven't seen Abdiel yet. I was hoping to catch him, to apologize for our disagreement last night. I'm guessing he spent the night with the *Head Priest…*

It's not that I'm salty, or jealous or anything, though it probably seems the opposite. I'm genuinely just concerned for Abdiel. In the short time I've known him, I've come to realize how sweet he is. It's basically unheard of, for someone to be that damn kind. He's a generous, accepting soul, with loyalty in his marrow. People like that are hard to come by in regular society, let alone guys my age.

There's no other way to say it. Abdiel Harmony is a unicorn.

And the last thing I would want to see, now that I feel so personally attached to him, is someone abusing his never-ending trust. Especially someone he's madly in love with.

Darian. I want to like the guy as much as everyone else does, but it's hard. He checks off so many narcissistic asshole boxes.

Older. Beautiful, almost unbelievably so. Strong, capable. A leader, a manipulator. Someone who looks at you like he can hear every thought happening in your head.

That part isn't specific to him. Abdiel does that too, and so does Darian's creepy brother, Drake.

Drake is another interesting piece of the puzzle of this cult I would love to figure out. That's why I have a plan for this morning...

I'm going back to that lab. I want to see him again. I need to.

The first time I set eyes on him, he was painstakingly familiar to me for some reason. It didn't take me long to remember why...

I saw a vision of him, when Abdiel and I were in that clearing. Before I almost tried to off myself, completely unintentionally.

Now, I'm not sure what that means. Why out of all the people in the world, I would have seen his face, his bizarre snake eyes, in my mind at such a poignant moment. Especially since I'd never met him before.

My brain was showing me his face... Or whatever forces that live on the mountain were. *But why?*

When I saw him, he was just standing there, exactly where we were in the clearing. He was looking, staring, right at us. Right at *me*. And he was crying red tears.

It's strange, but when I was talking with him yesterday, I got the sense that he was trying to figure me out as much as I was trying with him. Only he was doing a much better job of it. He has this way about him, this air as if he can see into your soul. Like he can read what's happening in your mind, and he'll have no qualms about using it to his advantage. It spooked me. I fear he'll be able to see what I saw when I was up on that mountain... and that it'll upset him.

But even so, I have to go back to him, back to his lab. I need more answers.

It's not that I'm *against* this place. In fact, the opposite is true. I think it's every bit the heaven on Earth Abdiel had described when we met. But the thing is, I've never fit into any societal molds outside of this cult, and the same seems to be happening in here.

People don't trust me. It's apparent when I speak to them. Darian doesn't, and I think they're all so brainwashed by him that his skepticism of me is trickling down to his people. Of course, I have Abdiel, when I'm not pissing him off by talking shit about his man. And his adoptive parents, Gina and Paul are just as sweet, if not still wary of me, since no one knows me well at all. But they haven't tried.

The only people I've gotten along with even a little are two of Darian's wives, Emithel and Gem. They're the youngest of his five beards, though they're all at least ten years younger than him. Another red flag in my humble opinion, but what the hell do I know?

They're sweet girls. Actually, speaking of them, I see Emithel coming outside now, her jet-black bob of hair shifting just above her shoulders as she walks over, rocking worn Chucks and a hoodie with some logo on it for a band I've never heard of. She's definitely the quietest of all Darian's wives. She rarely speaks, a natural observer if I've ever seen one. I recognize it because I'm the same way.

Lauris watches people too, but I haven't spoken to her much, since she's obviously Darian's right-hand girl. She speaks to him more than the others, and he speaks back, though their interactions aren't affectionate. He doesn't act like a husband to any of the five, and not for their lack of trying. Kiara and Alissa, *the hot ones* as I call them, are constantly vying for his attention, which they don't get.

Honestly, I have no clue how anyone hasn't picked up on how gay he is. I'm not talking stereotypical gay. He doesn't sing show tunes and paint his nails or anything, but he's just solidly not interested in females.

Most of the guys I've met here have checked me out at least once. Not all, but many. And I'm not saying this to brag on myself. It's just something women are used to. It happens. Sometimes it's flattering, sometimes it's annoying, but it's a part of life outside *The Principality*, and apparently, people here aren't shy with their sexual interests either.

Except Darian.

I know he doesn't like me, but still. Not once has he ever looked at me in any sort of studious way revolving around my looks. He's flat out not interested, and it reminds me of the time I went to a gay club with a friend of mine from school. I was the only vagina in a sea of penises, and I'd never felt more invisible.

That's how Darian reacts around me, only worse, because he's jealous. I think he sees Abdiel as his property, a possession of his I'm flying a little too close to. And he ain't having it.

My thoughts are shifted aside when I give Emithel a polite smile and a wave. I'd like to make at least one friend here, besides Abdiel. Em's probably my best bet.

"Good morning." She smiles.

"Same to you." I gaze out over the lake. "This view is spectacular."

"Isn't it?" She sighs. "I come out here every morning, just to enjoy the beauty."

We stand in quiet comfort for a moment before I ask, "Were you born into The Principality? Like Abdiel?"

She nods. "Yes. My parents have been here since almost the start."

"What do they do?"

"My father is a carpenter, and my mother is the registrar for classes. She's like the head teacher."

"That's amazing. What sorts of classes have you taken?"

"Well, I finished the high school equivalency and after that it was all about art." She grins.

I saw some of her paintings inside Darian's house last night. She's incredibly talented, and it's obvious she has a great passion for art.

"Have you ever thought about selling your paintings?" I ask without thinking, and she turns her face to give me a peculiar look. "I mean, at least online…? You don't have to go to a gallery or anything."

Her eyes narrow a bit in confusion. "We have no use for money…"

"It's not about the money," I tell her. "It could be about recognition. Or bringing your art to people who might enjoy it."

"I have all the attention I could ever need right here." Her tone is quietly peaceful.

It reminds me of one of the Manson girls.

Okay, maybe that's an extreme example of brainwashing, but it's just so strange to be around people who have no desire to travel, to see new places, explore new things. They have no earthly want to leave this forest, and it's bizarre to me.

"So Darian… he's just *it* for you, huh?" I peer at her. She starts chewing on her lower lip. "I mean, till death do you part, right?"

"No marriage is without its challenges," she mumbles, awkwardly twirling a strand of dark hair around her fingertip. "Sacrifice is a huge part of the transformation."

"Even if you're sacrificing your own happiness?" I tilt my face toward her. "You're so young, Emithel. Don't you want to experience true love for yourself?"

Her face springs in my direction, eyes widening as if what I'm saying is illegal, and we could be shot for even talking about this. "I *do* love him..." Her voice is mousy, timid. Unsure.

"I'm sure you do..." I mutter, rolling my eyes. "I'll see you in a bit." This debate is pointless, and I have things to do.

I squeeze her shoulder before spinning away and walking toward the path. I can't deal with the robotic conversations right now. I want to go speak to the only person who seems to tell it like it is around here...

The Serpent.

While I make my way, strolling the trail that brings me through their housing, rows and rows of trailers, I contemplate this whole thing. This *place* I find myself in...

I can't deny that running away from reality feels good. I would never say I don't understand these people's desire to leave society behind. I mean, the terribleness I've experienced alone makes me want to hide from life, all the damn time.

I've only ever lived in the States, but it's not exactly as fabulous as us Americans try to make it seem, or some other countries think it is. They glorify the USA as the best damn place on Earth, but beneath the surface of our shiny, apple pie-scented *land of the free* is a dark, seedy underbelly; a prism of evils unlike anything God probably ever imagined when He, or She, created the earth.

Mankind in general has turned this planet into something disgusting, but America really takes the cake as far as cruelty, dissonance, and a blatant disregard for the conscience we so actively try to convince others we have in spades. Maybe it's just because this is where I live, but I've had many friends from other countries, and for everything I love about America there seems to be three things I can't even believe I actually live amongst.

But all of that said, even though I totally get the idea behind wanting to flee the bullshit and take up refuge here in a place that's sustained as well—almost miraculously so—as the Expanse, I can't help but see through their rose-colored glasses.

Call me a negative Nancy, but I'm actually just a realist. I don't think Utopia's exist, and I feel like if I lived here, I would always be waiting for the other shoe to drop.

It's about a half-hour walk from the lake to the mountain. Once you get past housing and all the scattered locations for things like school and manufacture, you reach the crop fields. Rather than going left in their direction, I stick to the trail on the right, leading me closer to the mountain.

At its base is a different field, which is heavily guarded by their patrolmen. Abdiel told me they're called the *Tribe*, which is good to know, since they're the dudes who have been following me and watching my every move since the moment I emerged from the mountain with him. I guess their job is to protect this place, which begs the question... *from what?*

If it's really as harmonious a commune as they all make it seem, then what's the need for all the secrecy? The masked dudes on ATVs with machine guns strapped to their backs. *A bit excessive for a place that doesn't even use money, no?*

My bet would be on the field before me. Abdiel told me it's called the *Field of Influence*, and that different things are grown there. From the smell, I know they must be growing cannabis, but that can't be it. With that level of security, it's like they're sprouting nuclear weapons from the soil.

I want some answers. Not because I plan on leaving and going to the press or some dumb shit. I don't care about anything like that. I just want to know for my own peace of mind. I want to know why these people are so hardcore dedicated to Darian. Why they treat him like a literal King, and what his brother's role is in all this.

I'm... *curious.*

And yes, I know curiosity killed the cat, but maybe that bitch was a simple house cat. I'd like to think of myself as more of a ferocious feline. A jungle cat, disguised as someone mousey and small.

Shaking it away, I cringe at the thought. I *wish* I had that sort of confidence. That's the person I was supposed to be until that scumbag ripped it all away.

Swallowing my unease, I wander over to the entrance of the field, a trail that will take me to the lab, based on how Abdiel and I came up here yesterday. Only I don't get very far.

"Where you think you're going, stray?" One of the guards mumbles from behind his bandana. All I can see are dark eyes, narrowed at me as if I'm the enemy.

It's pretty alarming. But I force myself to straighten.

"I wanted to see Drake," I insist.

Both of the guys are quiet for a moment before they burst into two equally loud, booming bouts of laughter.

"Look at this girl," one of them sighs. "Thinking she can just waltz in here and demand to see The Alchemist. Who the fuck do you think you are, little one?"

"Yea, who do you think you are?" His friend repeats, and now they're both glaring at me, sliding their guns forward from where they're hanging, strapped to their shoulders.

Gulp. "I think I'm a guest on your beautiful land." I step forward, shaking like a leaf and trying my hardest to hide it. "Says the Head Priest."

"He doesn't want you here," one of them growls.

"No one does," adds the other.

My fingers are trembling, the quivers of my nerves trailing all throughout my extremities. I want to keep arguing, but I'm afraid if I speak again, my voice will tremor.

I'm just about to turn around and bolt, when a deep voice calls from somewhere behind them. "Let her in."

The two guards straighten, obviously recognizing the voice without having to turn around and see who said it. I recognize it too, though I'm facing him.

There he is, with his charcoal black hair, longer on top, hanging down almost into his eyes. Equally dark brows resting above two orbs of swirling light and dark… the eyes of a serpent.

The guards back up and say nothing, simply nodding to the trail. Inhaling deep, I stumble around them, toward the tall figure. He's standing with his hands in his pockets, glaring down at me as I approach. He's got a good foot on me, so he really has to angle his chin downward to make eye contact. And I have to pivot my face upward to look at him.

He certainly has a menacing look to him, and he's quiet, inquisitive, which is probably scarier than someone loud and in your face.

All of his angles and lines, his jaw, long neck, broad shoulders, they run in rigid continuation down his body. A body that is slim yet defined, as much is clear from his form-fitting clothes. Right now, he's dressed in skinny black jeans, and a black V-neck t-shirt. Simple as hell, yet on him, it's like making a statement.

I try not to blatantly *stare*, but he's doing it to me, so he's getting what he gives.

"How can I help you, stray girl?" He blinks, slowly, looking exactly like a snake would if it were a person.

SERPENT IN WHITE

Everyone keeps calling me a stray... Maybe I am just the docile house cat they all assume me to be.

"I wanted to learn more about the business." I get right to the point. He seems like the type of man who detests meaningless chitchat. "If I'm going to be staying here—"

"*If...*" he repeats my word, not like a question, more like a scoffing statement. I stare at him with my mouth open. "What would make you think you've been invited to stay?"

"I... I'm not..." I stutter, unable to form words while he glares down at me like that, the darkness of his irises swallowing up the swirls of light. It reminds me of that vision I had of him... in the clearing. "I just thought that, since I was in Business School, maybe it would be cool to see what your setup is like. What else you guys export..."

His jaw clenches. "I told you before, I don't give out information to strangers."

"Yea, but it's not a secret if you're trading with outsiders, right?" I mumble, feeling pretty stupid for arguing with him.

He stays quiet for a moment, giving me a pretty intense look I can't read at all. The silence drags between us. Seconds, minutes, hours... who even knows how many have passed at this point. Time is infinite in his presence.

And then suddenly, he twirls and stomps up the path, saying nothing more. He's walking in the direction of the lab, so I decide to follow him, since he didn't tell me to go away, not outright, anyway.

His long strides are hard to keep up with, and I'm practically jogging behind him. When we reach the lab, he moves up the steps and pushes the doors open, the guards standing off to the side to allow him in. Reluctantly, I follow, peeking up at the guards while they glare at me. None of them appear excited to have me back in this building, but whatever.

I'm not here for them. I'm here for the guy who's stalking away from me right now.

Inside the lab, he goes to a door which is marked as his office, opening it with a key, then moving aside, motioning for me to come in. Those inner alarms I have, the ones that warn against danger, they're pinging all over the place. Entering a confined space with a strange man twice my age, who looks the way he does and is observing me the way he is... Yea, it's probably something our self-defense instructor would advise against.

Yet here's me, prancing right inside and turning to watch as he steps in and closes the door behind him. Locking it.

Gulp again. "This is your office?" My voice quavers as he saunters toward me, slowly, exactly how a snake would move toward a mouse it knows for a fact ain't going anywhere. "It's nice."

His head cocks to the side, studiously. Dangerously. "Why are you really here, stray? Tell me the truth. I can't seem to get a good read on your intentions, and it's... quite frustrating."

What the hell does that even mean?

"It means I want you to tell me *exactly* what you want," he keeps speaking, somehow answering my inner thought, though my lips remain firmly shut. "You have one minute. Make it good."

He stops when he's standing right in front of me, towering. I try to back up, but my ass hits his desk and I startle. My pulse is jumping, rattling my veins while I gawk up at him, a total deer in headlights.

"I..." My voice cuts out with my nerves, his eyes burning me alive where I stand. "I want..."

"Speak up," he growls, barely audible, though I feel it, his voice, rumbling into me.

He smells like flowers, musky ones. Like gardenia and rose oil. And fire...

"I want control back." My words come out before I can even process them. "I want my life back."

His eyes narrow into slits as he stares down at me, heavily, smothering me with that look. My mind is rushing through all the times I was afraid. All the times I begged and pleaded for *him* to stop, and he didn't...

Drake's Adam's apple slides in his throat, a movement that catches my attention and holds it.

I said the words because they're true. That's why I went into the woods that day. That's why I'm here, trying to figure this place out.

Because I don't trust anyone, and I need to. Because I need to get the fuck away from it all and find myself.

I'm not sure if I can do it here... Or if these people will even let me. If the forces up on that mountain will allow me to stay...

Drake leans in closer, gripping his desk on each side of my hips. He's hovering over me, and I slant back. Not that much, not enough for him to be directly on top of me, but enough for me to *feel* him as if he were.

This is usually the part when I'd be able to feel the warmth of the body near mine, but with Drake it's only ice. He radiates cold, and for reasons unknown, it's comforting.

Heat is stifling, but cool is calm. Easy.

"You need to learn…" he murmurs, breath brushing my lips, like a burst of fresh air. Minty. It reminds me of those peppermint candies my grandma used to have in dishes all over her house.

My eyelids flutter, blood rushing in my ears while I await whatever he's about to say. *I need to learn…?*

But before I can hear his words, I hear a knock instead. Three, actually. *Rap rap rap* on the door to his office, causing me to jump and my eyes to fling open. By that time, Drake is already across the room, opening the door a crack. He whispers to someone through it, and I can't hear what they're saying, but his posture is rigid.

He runs long pale fingers through his black hair, then turns back to me. "Stay here. Don't touch anything."

And then he leaves through the door, closing it behind him.

My head is spinning. *What the heck was that??* How did he get me to confess something like that to him? Just by standing close to me, looking all dangerous and smelling fantastic?

That's entirely ridiculous. And what the hell was he about to say? *You need to learn.*

Learn what?? I know there's probably a lot I need to learn. I won't pretend I know everything, not even close. But what would me learning have to do with what I told him? About wanting to reclaim control, of my life, my body, my thoughts…

I rub my eyes with my fingers and get off the desk, pacing around in circles. He's a very strange, intense person, which of course, is incredibly intriguing to me. I've always been drawn to the quiet ones, the scary ones. As much as I thought I was developing a crush on Abdiel, especially after that steamy makeout session from the other night, the Serpent, as they call him, is really winding me up, and it's not good.

He's the last person I should be looking at.

Rumor has it he's an eternal bachelor. He hooks up in secret, interested only in sex. Basically, the exact type of guy I'm usually attracted to. *Great.*

On top of that, he just left and told me not to *touch anything*. That's the sort of thing you say to almost guarantee everything will be touched.

And in that spirit, I sneak to the other side of his desk, poking around while keeping my eyes fixed on the door. I'm not sure what he'd do if he caught me snooping through his stuff, and I'm also not sure why the possibilities excite me so much. *I have issues... Daddy issues too, clearly.*

He has plants everywhere, which strikes a chord in me. For someone so robotic, so cold, it's fascinating that he cares for living things as if they're his children. Or maybe his pets...

But still, he's obviously *The Alchemist* for a reason. He grows plants and turns them into things. Medicine, fuel... but what else?

That Field... What else does he grow there?

Rifling through the papers on his desk, looking for answers, I tug open drawers. I don't find much in the top ones, more papers, pamphlets, packets of seeds, note cards with all sorts of chemical equations on them.

But then in the bottom drawer, I stumble upon something that stops me short. *Needles.*

More specifically, syringes. Packed in plastic, like the ones you'd buy from the pharmacy to inject insulin. I reach inside and pick one up, examining it closely. *Why would he have needles? Is he diabetic?*

Ducking down, I dig farther into the drawer, pulling out one of those large rubber tubes. Swallowing hard, my fingers brush over it. I know what this is for... usually to tie your arm when you're shooting up.

I'm no stranger to drugs myself. Fortunately, I haven't fallen down the addiction hole like some of my friends, but I've tried enough things to know what happens and how it all works. The escape from reality...

Is that what this is? Is Drake a drug addict?

Continuing my search, I reach the very back of the drawer, locating a small vial. Peering back up at the door before I pick it up, I don't see or hear anyone just yet. So I take it out.

It's full of clear liquid, and there's a label on the side that says *Empyrean.*

Empyrean... The highest part of Heaven.

I'm trembling all over as I squeeze the vial in my hand. Maybe that's what this place is about... Drugs. They're making more than just fuel and medicine in this lab.

Are they all on drugs? Even Abdiel... Darian??

For reasons I'm not sure I'll ever understand, my mind urges me to tear open the packet with the syringe and stick the needle into the vial. I'm shaking so hard I almost drop it, terrified that Drake will walk in at any moment. But I barely even care.

I'm trying this shit. *Empyrean.*

And if I overdose and die, well then... it was meant to be.

Grabbing the tube, I use it to tie up my left arm, struggling to do it one-handed. I squeeze some of the liquid out of the needle then tap the most prominent of my veins. I've done this once before, but by no means am I a professional. I had to stab myself four times before I could get my vein, and this time is no different.

I keep stabbing at myself, my hand shaking too bad. Taking a deep breath, I try once more and finally, I see blood flow into the syringe. Pushing down, I empty the contents into my vein, and once it's done, I remove the rubber tie, managing to stuff it back inside the drawer as colors and shapes start popping in my vision.

Sitting back on the floor, I look around the room.

Everything is moving. Everything is *alive.*

"*Fuck...*" My voice travels from between my lips, the word visible, floating up into the air, banging against the ceiling.

Lifting my hands, I observe them. The air is rippling like waves in the lake, my fingers stretching out long, like claws.

Fear clutches my insides while I crawl onto the floor, words attacking me from every direction. *Where are all these voices coming from??*

Stumbling to my feet, I rush to the door, the air in the room trying to keep me there, though I'm fighting against it. I can't stay in here. It's too small. I can't breathe.

When I whip open the door, the voices become louder. They're all different tones, no conversations, more like inner monologues. I can't identify anything they're saying because there are too many of them. The sounds are attacking my brain.

I realize I still have the empty vial and needle in my hand, so I stuff them into my pocket and rush out of the lab, brushing past the patrol on my way out.

What's her problem? A deep male voice comes from one of them, and I look up, my forehead lining in confusion. *Why the hell did Head Priest let her stay here, anyway? I mean, she's hot, but still. She seems like a headcase.*

His lips aren't moving, but I hear him saying these things about me.

My eyelids flutter with rapid blinking as I dart through the hall, away from the guy who's talking like a ventriloquist. I race through the corridor, ignoring all the colors and shapes following me, the voices assaulting my mind. I leave the lab, not stopping for anyone.

I just run. I run into the woods.

I run up the mountain.

It's calling to me. And I have to listen.

CHAPTER TWENTY EIGHT

DRAKE

God, what a disaster.

A local cop came onto the Expanse. It hasn't happened in a while. We have a sort of unspoken agreement with these hicks. They acknowledged years ago that what's best for them is to steer clear. Leave us to do our own thing out here, and now and then we'll make it worth their while.

Money talks in the outside world. I'm no stranger to it, and neither is Darian. Just because we don't let money rule our lives anymore, doesn't mean we won't watch Outsiders fumble for it. If we must.

The growth of the trumpets, the synthesizing of our psychedelics— not including Empyrean of course—is like a DMT of sorts. We trade with a syndicate outside of Boulder, usually for vehicles or supplies, and on the rare occasion, for a delivery of cash to our local PD. Again, we don't touch the money here, but it's something that happens every now and again to shut them up.

If they get greedy, they come up here. And we handle it.

That's what just happened. That's what called me away from my office while I was in the middle of… whatever that was, with the girl.

The guy is in the cell right now. Xander captured him. The rule is always to take hostages, shoot to wound and all that.

Leave the trespassers for me to deal with.

That's the part Darian hates. But I can't worry about that right now. He has Abdiel back, so maybe…

I shake my head. I don't even know what I'm thinking. My heart has been aching more than usual lately. I wish I couldn't feel it, but can. That's the part I don't understand.

If I'm made to be the evil to Darian's good, then why does it hurt so much?

If I couldn't feel it, I'd be fine, but I do, and it's a pain unlike anything else. Sometimes, it reminds me I'm alive. Other times, it makes me want to die.

I should let Darian know what happened, but I have to tend to the girl first.

I come back to my office, opening the door slowly. But when I peer inside, she's gone.

Squinting, I look around. Nothing is out of place, so I shrug it off. She probably got bored and left, to go find Abdiel or something.

The girl is a new piece of the puzzle. After what she said to me earlier, what I heard in her mind... There was an anguish there, one very familiar.

Sighing, I decide to go handle my business. I need to deal with the prisoner.

Leaving the lab, I get on my ATV and drive up the mountain toward the shack. It's not a long drive, but my brain is scattered the whole time. When I get there, I push on the door and wander inside slowly. I lean up against the wall, exhausted mentally. And just knowing I have to go up there... To endure it.

It takes so much out of me. I wish it didn't, but it does.

I carry the burden of who I am on my shoulders, like the weight of a thousand secrets and lies. They're as heavy as boulders.

Thinking about the girl, my eyes close. She was afraid, vulnerable. Damaged inside, and the way she was thinking about it... this is something I recognize all too well.

Her need to reclaim control... To take her life back... It reminds me of someone.

My eyes fling open, sweat trickling down my temple.

Peeking at the clock on my bedside table, I see that it's two in the morning. And when my gaze darts across the room, I find an empty bed.

Swallowing becomes impossible. I have so much saliva, yet I can't gulp it down. My throat is thick and dry, closing up until I almost can't breathe.

I rub my eyes and jump out of bed, walking as slowly as I can when all I want to do is run. But I need to keep quiet. Kara's not home, working the overnight shift. But he's *here...*

Passing his bedroom, I hold my ear up to the door. I hear snoring. But then I hear a different sound, in the room next door. The shower is running in the bathroom.

My hand trembles as I reach for the knob, not bothering to knock. I twist it and open the door, peeking through the crack.

"Dar?" I mutter. "You in here?"

He doesn't respond, but I hear muffled cries.

Fuck… No.

Pushing my way into the bathroom, I dart up to the shower. Darian's in there… on the floor. The water is rushing over him where he sits, propped against the wall. His shoulders are slumped forward, shaking with his ragged sobs.

My eyes have never been so wide at the sight of my brother, my best friend… my only friend… broken. There are bruises all over his torso, the shapes of fingertips and hands. And there's a pinkish hue to some of the water circling the drain.

The pain in my chest is full and thick, an ache unlike anything I've ever felt. And it quickly warps, twists and rolls into an unbridled rage. A monstrous fury so vibrant I can barely see straight.

My vision blurs for a moment while every muscle in my body constricts in pure wrath.

I'm going to kill him.

The decision is made in that moment. No debating, no contemplating. It's been written by the universe.

But first thing's first, I need to help my brother.

"Darian." I stumble to him, falling onto my knees by the edge of the tub, reaching in, not giving a fuck that I'm getting soaked by the spray of the shower.

I grab his chin and tug him to look over his face. There's blood trickling from his nose, too. My jaw sets, my teeth damn near grinding to dust.

Darian is crying hysterically, though still keeping quiet as he does. Of course, we have to be quiet… so as not to anger the evil.

But it doesn't matter. No more tiptoeing or pretending it'll get better. I should've fucking stopped this weeks ago, the first time I saw the bruises. The first time I heard him come in after everyone was asleep. Every time Kara works her overnight shifts…

I cringe as my heart shatters in my chest. I could've stopped it. I should have…

I know in this moment I'll carry this guilt for the rest of my life.

But it stops tonight.

This ends now.

"I'm gonna get you out of here, okay?" I mumble, and he doesn't respond. Sitting like a broken doll on the floor of the shower, my brother crumbles before my eyes.

My six-foot, one-hundred-and-eighty-pound wide receiver foster brother, reduced to a blubbering mess. He's so strong, but in this moment, he's gone.

No. No, I won't let this happen to him. I can't.

He's all I have. I won't let that asshole take him.

Seething inside, I manage to forgo my rage long enough to focus on getting Darian out of the shower. Turning off the water, I grab a towel, wrapping it around him and helping him stand. His legs shake as he moves in slow motion, out of the shower, teeth chattering in between his sniffles.

He's still crying, though no sounds are coming out. He's just sort of shivering, and it's the most heartbreaking thing I've ever witnessed. My face is tight and burning, pressure building up behind my eyes as I dry him off carefully.

"Where does it hurt?" I ask, minding his bruises. I check his nose, and it doesn't feel broken.

"Everywhere…" he mumbles.

My stomach twists in misery, but I don't show it to him. I stay strong for him, keeping the worry off my face while I wipe the blood from his nose and lips.

"Can you walk, Dar?" I keep the towel wrapped around him, noticing that he doesn't have any clothes in the bathroom.

Meaning he didn't have any when he came in here.

My jaw is numb from straining so hard, fist clenching over and over to stop myself from running in there right now. I have to take care of my brother first. He needs me.

"It… hurts, but yea," he croaks.

Draping his arm around my shoulder, I slink my arm around his waist to help him walk better while we leave the bathroom quietly, Darian wincing as he goes. When we pass the asshole's bedroom, he starts to quake. His pace picks up, and now he's *dragging* me *up the hall, yanking me into our bedroom fast.*

He's out of breath once we're inside, and I close the door wishing like hell it had a lock. Now I understand why we aren't allowed one, even though we're fucking fifteen.

"You're okay." I'm fighting like hell to hold on to my strength. For him. "I have you."

He shudders and covers his face with his hands, the towel trying to fall off his naked body. Rushing to his dresser, I grab some boxers and bring them back to him. He pulls them on, steeling his arms around himself.

"You want some sweats?" I ask. Darian usually sleeps in only his boxers, but maybe right now he wants more clothes.

He shakes his head slowly, the cries picking back up again. "What... why... I don't get it..."

Biting the inside of my cheek to keep my own tears at bay, I lunge and hug onto him tight. He latches himself to me and just sobs into my neck.

"It's not your fault, Darian," I tell him. "I'm going to take care of this, okay? I'll fix it."

"You can't," he whimpers. "I'm fucking stuck here... with him. And it is my fault."

My head shakes over and over, but I can't find any words. This hurt of his, I feel it like it's my own.

How is it possible to feel someone else's pain? Is empathy really that strong? Can it be?

Or is it because we're connected, Darian and me?

"Come on." I tug him over to my bed. "You need to rest."

He walks with me, pausing for a moment. "I can sleep in your bed?"

I nod. "Of course."

"You won't leave me, right?" He shivers as he crawls in, nestling up beneath my comforter.

"Never." I climb in next to him, trying to keep some distance, though he snuggles up to me immediately, resting his damp hair on my torso. "Remember what I promised?"

His head moves with his nod, a sleepy sigh creeping from his lips before he murmurs, "You'll never leave me. And you'll always be mine..."

My head tilts as I look down at him where he's curled up on me, already falling, sleep muffling his cries.

I know he meant to say I'll always be his brother, which is what I promised him a few months ago. Well, I promised it out loud, to him. But I'd promised myself that same thing years earlier, when he first came into my life. When he first became my brother.

333

You'll always be mine.

Something stirs inside me, in my stomach, spreading warmth up to my chest. It's tight and hot, and it feels strange. Strange but good.

You'll always be mine.

I watch Darian sleep for a while, almost an hour spent with him twitching and trembling, eyelids fluttering as he dreams. I hope they're not too bad, the things he's seeing in his head.

I can only imagine.

It boils my blood once more. And as much as I can't have him waking up without me, there's something I need to do. And it needs to be done right now.

Carefully wriggling myself free from Darian's hold, I slide out of the bed as quietly as possible. Reaching beneath my mattress on the right side, I pull out my knife. A hunting knife I make sure to sharpen often, although I've never been hunting...

Until now.

Leaving the room, I saunter up the hall, a peculiar calm settling over me. My adrenaline is jacked, sure, and my pulse is thumping in my neck, but it feels right.

This is what I'm meant to do.

Sneaking into the dark room, silent, my eyes adjust to the lack of light as I observe the lump of shit sleeping soundly in his bed. I look around the room, squinting at what appear to be cut zip ties on the floor next to Darian's clothes.

Swallowing a painful lump down my throat, I step up to the bed. My head cocks while I watch him, blissfully unaware in his slumber. Just another rat-faced prick with a vicious monster living inside him, like so many others on this miserable planet.

Moving amongst the rest of us like they belong. But they don't.

They don't get to live.

I crawl onto the bed carefully, pulling the covers down enough to reveal his body. He's on his back, eyes still closed, though his features shift as I straddle his hips. My index finger traces an invisible line from his potbelly up to his chest.

"You come back for more, kid..." he mumbles, eyes still closed. "I told you you'd like it."

My eye twitches as I shift down harder on him, putting pressure as I snap the blade out from my knife, angling it off to the side.

"I knew you'd see my way..." His voice trails when his eyes open and sees it's me. His brows zip together, but before he can protest, I *stick my knife right up to his throat.*

"You were saying?" I hiss.

"What are you doing, shrimp? Don't do anything stupid," Dan grunts, hands out at his sides while he lies still, knowing his slightest move could help me nick his carotid artery.

"I could ask you the same." I lean over him. "You wanna die quick... Or slow?"

"Whatever you think you know, it's all bullshit," he croaks, shifting, which only prompts me to press farther into his skin, drawing blood. "Fuck! You little prick!"

"You're a sick piece of shit, Lannister," I mumble. "I'm gonna take your last breath. Give it to my brother as a gift."

"He liked it." He releases a sickening grin that settles in the pit of my stomach like food poisoning. "He consented."

"Right." I drag the blade of my knife down his throat and onto his chest, just hard enough to scrape him without actually cutting.

I feel him trembling in fear, his eyes widening as he loses his confidence. The look in them gives me the slightest piece of solace. I would like to give this look to Darian someday. For his revenge... Restitution.

But I'm not sure it could work like that.

"I just want you to know, Dan, that it gives me great pleasure to take your life," I mutter, poking my blade into his stomach gradually until he groans out loud. I quickly reach onto the floor and grab a sock, stuffing it into his mouth.

His hands fly up in an attempt to remove it, but I pin one of them down in my wrist. He struggles against me, his other arm flying up. I put my knee on it, holding him down while my blade stuffs deeper into his gut, puncturing his flesh.

His eyes widen as blood pours instantly from the wound.

"To wipe you off this earth," I growl, dragging the blade up, up his stomach, cutting him deep, leisurely and long.

He gurgles, eyes bulging, sweat seeping from his pores while blood gushes out of him, all over me, and the bed.

It's everywhere, the smell of it thick in the air.

But I'm not done.

"For hurting my brother... My Darian... Tonight you die, Dan." *I jerk the blade even harder, farther up until his breastplate stops me, his muffled wails fading into the background to my pulse.*

It's hard with this knife, since it's not that long. But it's sharp as hell, slicing through his skin, tissue, muscle and entrails.

"You die, and he lives."

I'm out of breath, panting while I gut the motherfucker, slow and precise, to ensure he feels every single second of pain, every inch that will never be enough.

Blood soaks into my clothes, coating my arms and legs. The whole room reeks of copper, the metal in the air so thick you can taste it.

My hand keeps grinding, digging the blade into him as rough as I can.

Dan sputters for only another minute before he gives up and stops breathing.

And I let out a long exhale, peering down at the mess I've made. I can see into his body, his ruptured organs visible beneath the vibrant red of blood everywhere.

I close my eyes and wipe my forehead with the back of my hand, trying to brush the hair out of my eyes, feeling a smear of blood on my forehead, sticky.

It makes me chuckle.

"Bye, Dan," I breathe, slithering off him and staggering away from the bed. "Thanks for dying so well."

Staring down at the scene before me for a moment, I wonder if I should even bother cleaning it. But I shake my head, and step out of my sweats and boxers, both of which are red and completely soaked through.

I go to the bathroom naked and jump in the shower, quickly washing the blood from my body. I wash my knife too, admiring it; the small item in my hand. I used it to kill my foster father.

I took a man's life. And I don't really feel bad about it.

If that makes me a sociopath, fine. I'll live with it. But honestly, it needed to happen.

Dan had to die for what he did to Darian. My brother will never be the same. He'll carry this for the rest of his life.

Something that permanently damaging... it's unforgivable.

I get out of the shower and go to our bedroom. But when I see the time on the clock, I become a bit frantic.

We have to go. We have to go now.

I think leaving this place could only be a good thing. There's been too much pain here. Too much hurt and misery.

We can go somewhere far away and keep breathing. We can live, because that's why we're here.

Our purpose.

A sound brings me out of my memory, and I look around.

I gaze out into the forest, the sunlight barricaded out by the trees and all their many branches of full leaves. I see nothing, so I shrug it off and prepare myself for what I need to do.

It does weigh on me, everything I hide from Darian. Over the years, convincing him we could never be together; that the Regnum wouldn't approve, and that they couldn't understand.

Darian is smart as hell, but he's also been weakened by what happened to him. It doesn't matter if it was a hundred years ago, or ten minutes ago. It still affects him, and the unfortunate fact is that I played on that.

I used his insecurities to convince him we could never be together. *It had to be done.*

Unlocking and lifting the trapdoor, I head down the steep steps. I saunter slowly to the cell, occupied by one Officer Hoyt.

He's pretty young, probably in his late twenties. Built, but not too much. Not as big as Darian.

I toss that thought away and glare at the man where he sits on the floor, holding his tied hands to his head in the spot where Xander hit him. It's still bleeding. He probably has a concussion. Not that it will matter for much longer.

"You'll burn for this." His raspy voice quavers up at me, through the metal bars.

My head pivots right. "Of that I am almost entirely certain, Officer." I open the cell with my key. "Now, stand up, please. We've got some walking to do."

"No. Where are you taking me?" He stutters, eyes red-rimmed and glistening with a fear he's so clearly trying to cover up.

"I'm going to set you free." I give him a pointed look, folding my arms over my chest.

He doesn't believe me at all, that much is clear from his thoughts and even just the look on his face, but I don't care. "You are?"

I nod. "Yup. Come now. Let's go."

He still doesn't move, and I'm losing all my patience. Stalking up to him, I grab him by the arm until he's forced to his feet, yanking him out of the cell. I'm dragging him along while he does the bare minimum of walking, just enough to keep himself from falling. We get to the steps, and I point.

"Go."

"No."

"Do it, Officer. My patience is wearing thin."

He hesitates for another moment before climbing up the steps into the shack, with me right behind him. I catch him looking around, assessing items he could grab as weapons. Contemplating running. I hear him thinking it all, running through his potential for survival.

"You won't get far," I tell him. He turns to me, gaze narrowing. I blink.

Brushing past him, I grab his arm again, pulling him along with me.

"Where are we going?" He asks while we walk, following the narrow trail which leads up the mountain. The path that directs to the overlook.

The cliff.

I don't answer him, but it doesn't stop him from continuing with his pointless words. "My partner will come looking for me. My Captain. You won't get away with this."

"Captain Bellman? I know him." I smirk, peering at him from the side to witness his face drop.

He doesn't say anything else after that.

Many more minutes of walking, I finally spot it in the distance. The cliff, settled just beyond the clearing in the trees.

The black rock isn't there.

Gulping, my fingers begin to tremble. It's not a relief to me, not seeing it. I know it'll come, and I know what it wants.

Taking a deep breath, I yank my prisoner into the clearing and shove him to the ground. He rests on his knees, gaping around frantically. His thoughts are wavering, the forces pulling him. And I hear all of it...

I hear it as he goes through every bad thing he's ever done. My mouth dries while I watch him crumbling, curling into the fetal position as he cries.

"Accept your sins, Officer Hoyt." I step closer. "This is what it wants."

He turns until he's lying on his back, sweat lining his forehead, mixing with the blood in his hair as he gawks up at me. He's afraid. I see it and hear it. But it's not me he should fear...

"You're evil," he gasps. "And God sent the serpent to destroy Adam. To destroy man."

I nod. "Yea. Probably." I pull my knife from my pocket, opening

338

the blade.

"Why are you doing this?" He wails, wetting himself.

"You know why." I lunge at him, grabbing him by the collar. Kneeling over him, I bring us nose to nose. "Evil atones, too. Human sacrifice, Hoyt. Your greed will cost you your life." I bring my knife to his throat. "Any last words?"

"I'm… sorry…" he whines, snot dripping down his face.

"Noted."

And I slice his throat. Blood spurts from the wound, coating my hand.

He tries to breathe, gasping and gurgling, blood spraying from his mouth onto my face.

I close my eyes and wipe them with my hand, shoving his twitching body down into the dirt. "Great. Now I have to go shower."

Standing up slowly, I swallow as I watch his body, giving up its last breath. Movement catches my peripheral, and my head tilts toward it.

The rock appears, right beside me.

That black rock, shiny and layered, rippling in my vision. I blink heavily at it.

"Are you satisfied?" I hiss as the trees move around me, wind whipping through the branches.

The smell of blood is strong, like that night, all those years ago.

I paid the price that night, for Darian. And I'm still doing it now. For him, for Abdiel, for all those people down there.

I'll be the evil, for their good.

After all, it's the balance.

The natural order.

Evil atones.

CHAPTER
TWENTY NINE

DARIAN

My stomach is in knots.

It feels awful, all that twisting and tying. I'm tormented with a guilt so strong it burns my insides like bile.

Abdiel was gone when I woke up. I was relieved when he came to bed with me, after I told him the truth. After I confessed my secret… about my intimate relationship with his father. He was hurt and confused, I could see it, hear it even worse.

But he still stayed with me. He slept in my arms, breathing soft breaths on my flesh, brushing me with his sweetness, his acceptance; his loving forgiveness.

Yet reluctantly, I dozed off. And when I awoke, he was gone.

My fingers rake through my hair, and I pull hard, until it stings.

I took his virginity last night. It was an awakening for my soul, having him inside me. His body in mine and his breath in my lungs, filling me with every beautiful bit of his perfect.

I never knew how much I needed something until Abdiel Harmony stumbled into my bed.

But I ruined it. I blundered our time with the truth, and while he needed to hear it, I just wish I could've hung onto that bliss for a little while longer. Just a few more minutes of blind love, before I decimated it all.

I'm a disaster.

It's just after dinner. Abdiel was nowhere to be found tonight, bringing my inner turmoil to the surface. Everyone's been watching

They can tell something is off with me, and I'm too exhausted, too strained to hide.

Abdiel worked a morning shift, then he took off before I could attempt speaking with him. I haven't seen him since he fell asleep by my side with the pale light of dawn streaming in through my bedroom windows.

I *need* to talk to him. I just need him to understand that I don't want to hurt him.

I need him to know that I love him, too.

And I know where he'll be so I can try...

It's time for reflection. Night is upon us, and I decide to walk, with the wives, to the fire pit. Abdiel is set to sing tonight. Everyone's been looking forward to it.

Usually, he sings once a week or so, but he hasn't done it in a few weeks. I can't bear to think it's because I've been distracting him from the things he loves, but I also can't deny my own insecurities. I'm fucking the kid up, and that's the last thing I want.

I want him to prosper. I want him to soar...

We get to the fire, and it's a packed house. Hundreds of my family are gathered around, talking, conversing, laughing together. It's the first time in a while that all five of my wives are here, too. It's a big night.

I just can't wait to see him... To hear his exquisite voice.

I pray he'll give me another chance. That this isn't over before it even began.

The noise of the crowd dies down, and my eyes shift all around, searching for Abdiel. When I spot him, my heart tries to jump right out of my chest. He looks gorgeous, if not slightly tired. His grin is warier than usual, and I hear him thinking about me. His thoughts are on me before his eyes are. It gives me some peace, to know he's thinking of me, even in our times of trouble.

He sits on a bench, by Jordan's side. Jordan tunes his acoustic guitar while Abdiel gazes around, smiling and waving at his family. There are so many people here, it's difficult to see over the crowd. But the wives and I are in our usual seats, off to the side.

And then his eyes find mine.

He blinks, and I hear him. *Hi...*

Hi, baby, I bite my lip.

A flush rises to his cheeks, but he looks away, forehead lined in apprehension. I physically *loathe* myself for doing this to him. I never meant for any of it to happen this way.

It's not like I sought him out knowing he was my former lover's son. It just happened, and I don't regret it.

Because I'm in love with him.

I know Abdiel hears my thoughts, but he's forcing himself not to look at me. Jordan strums the beginning chords of their song, and immediately, everyone cheers.

It's a song I know well. A song Drake and I used to listen to when we first ran away...

Nutshell by Alice in Chains.

A sad song, still sung so beautifully by the blonde boy with the evergreen eyes. He's breathtaking to look at, and even more so to listen to. I'm mesmerized as I watch him, his harmonies floating through the air, draping over us all like a protective sheet of serenity.

Out the corner of my eye, I see movement and my head turns to find Drake, off in the woods, a few feet from where we're all gathered. He's wearing his white linens, leaning up on a tree, staring directly my way. My eyes plead with him to come to me, but of course, he doesn't.

He never allows himself to.

Abdiel finishes his solemn song, but despite the lyrics holding a serious nature, everyone jumps up in applause, shouting and whooping. I clap my hands together as hard as I can, my wives squealing at my sides. And Drake bites his lip, watching Abdiel smile from afar.

Something feels so *wrong* with Drake right now. There's something happening inside him that doesn't work. And naturally, he's blocking it all out, covering up his thoughts as he does, not allowing me, or Abdiel, close enough to help.

To tell him we love him. That he's not the evil he thinks he is.

Instead, he stays keeping us at a distance, keeping me away from him, just as Abdiel is.

I've never felt so alone.

"Encore!" The crowd is shouting, and Abdiel laughs with Jordan. The sight of him smiling always gets to me. It eases the pain in my chest.

They whisper to each other, likely deciding on a second song. Jordan strums a chord.

But it's interrupted by a loud cry. "Stop!"

Everyone looks around, all of our faces mirroring the same

confusion. *Who said that?*

The female voice continues, and as it does, it becomes very clear to me who is disrupting Abdiel's performance, and our nightly reflection. My jaw clenches.

"Stop the show!" The girl shouts, that inconsiderate little thing jumping up onto the bench where Abdiel and Jordan are seated.

The Regnum's eyes are set on her, silence in the crowd deafening. I witness my patrolmen rushing over. Drake steps forward, too. But when they look to me, I simply hold up my hand, signaling them to hang back.

Well, let's hear what she has to say.

This ought to be good.

"Rhiannon, what are you doing?" Abdiel stands, his eyes pleading with her to stop whatever this is.

"I'm sorry to interrupt, Abdiel," she whispers to him, but then stands taller, addressing the crowd, "But the people need to hear this."

RHIANNON

Everyone is staring at me. Gaping, *gawking.*

I'm not a public speaker by any means, so to have this many eyes on me at the moment is very nerve-racking.

That said, it's not exactly quiet.

I can hear *everyone's* thoughts, so loud it's like they're all talking at once. I don't know how they do this…

Empyrean. The drugs I took… I know Darian uses them. And Drake, and even Abdiel. That's how they always answer my unspoken thoughts; that's how they know what I'm thinking.

These drugs… they're miraculous. Unlike anything I could ever anticipate experiencing. I always thought telekinesis was a myth, exaggerated by phonies just looking to take your money. But if this stuff was created in a lab, by Drake, then I can only imagine what else is possible.

My mind has been opened to so many things in the last couple of hours.

But then, of course, there's the fact that this cult, which seems to revolve around these drugs, using them to brainwash people into thinking these brothers are somehow special, or godlike, is also covering up murder.

I witnessed Drake kill that man, in the clearing by the peak. I watched him drag the dude up the mountain, shove him to his knees and slit his throat.

It was terrifying in the moment, but even more so were his thoughts.

I heard him... remembering things. About his and Darian's foster father. About their past.

Drake killed that man, too. When he was only a teenager.

And now, the people deserve to know who they're worshipping.

"I know this won't be easy to hear," I speak over all the hushed murmurs of thoughts. "And many of you won't believe me, or you won't want to... But you need to know the truth. You need to know... that you're living in a cult."

I expect a stream of outraged voices, or at the very least a few gasps. But I'm met with nothing but silence. Even the thoughts are zipped up tight in this moment.

"It's not a commune, this place," I keep going, looking over all the suspicious faces. "It's a cult, and your leader..." I aim my gaze at Darian. "He isn't what he seems."

A few faces turn to Darian, eyes wide, some of them wondering why he's even letting me speak right now.

But Darian just stays quiet with his deep gaze locked on mine, arms crossed over his chest, eyebrow raised in a thoroughly unamused manner. He looks bored, and quite frankly, it's irritating the shit out of me.

"I've been in this place for two days, and already I can see what you people can't." I command my voice to come out loud enough, fighting against the quiver. "What you're incapable of seeing because he's brainwashed you! Him and his brother."

My eyes dart to Drake, standing off to the side of the group, propped against a tree, wearing all white linens. He looks like a ghost, or a demon or something. Actually, right now, *he* looks like the cult leader.

He smirks at me, head slanting to the side. *Pesky little rodent*, his thoughts mumble. A chill zips up my spine.

I can't forget the image of him slicing that man's throat in the clearing. The blood everywhere, all over his arms and face. Or the memory I heard of him gutting his foster father...

I only caught the end of it, so I'm not sure what happened to incite the murder. I know there must have been a reason... There had to have been. Otherwise, he's just a lunatic serial killer, and that can't be it. *Can it?*

"The secrets they're hiding from you all are staggering," I speak to the people. "Haven't you ever wondered why such high security is needed for a place that doesn't even use money? Haven't you wondered what they're really growing in that field at the base of the mountain, what they're really cooking up in that lab?? Haven't you wondered why you never see or hear of any intruders on your land? Because they're there alright! If I was able to make it onto the mountain, you bet your asses others are, too. Which begs the question... what is happening to them?"

A few people finally start to share glances with one another. Their thoughts are considering my words, wondering, at long last, why all of this is necessary. They consider the Field of Influence, the lab, the trading that occurs, all of which is headed up by *The Alchemist*.

Darian's face remains impassive, but Drake is seething. I feel it on my skin, his thoughts like a blazing wrath of fire singeing me. His jaw is visibly clenched, inner voice hissing at me, *You stole from me, stray. You'll pay dearly for that.*

Gulping over my sandpaper throat, I decide to keep going. I have them hooked, now it's time to reel them in.

"And then, of course, your leader. Your *Head Priest*." My eyes land on Darian once more. "Five wives yet still no children? Doesn't make much sense, does it?"

The wives appear worried, peering at one another, then Darian. But to his credit, he doesn't flinch. He stays planted, fixed in his spot, glaring. Even his thoughts are silent.

"Rhiannon, stop," Abdiel whisper-shouts at me. I glance down at him, regretting this move a little just by the look on his face.

He's hurt. I didn't mean to upset him, but he's brainwashed, too. *Why can't he see it?*

"Abdiel... you're in denial, too." I shake my head. "Don't you see how much he lies to you? Manipulates you...?"

Abdiel's brows zip together, his teeth sinking into his lower lip as he breaks our gaze. His thoughts are on something that happened last night, or early this morning... Something Darian confessed to him.

My eyes widen. *He was involved with your father??!*

Abdiel's gaze snaps up at me, his face freezing in shock. *You can hear me?*

I nod subtly. *Don't you see it now, Abdiel? Don't you see how much he's using you?*

Abdiel appears shattered, but he doesn't deny what I'm saying, or thinking, to him. And this time when I peer over at Darian, he falters. Just enough.

His forehead lines; the face of someone wounded. He's hurt that Abdiel is questioning him.

This is all so fucked. "I'm not saying this place isn't wonderful, because it is," I go on, addressing the crowd, who are now shifting uncomfortably. "It's a heaven on Earth. But you need to know who you're following. You need to question their motives, and the things they keep from you. Don't you deserve to be made aware, when it affects all of you, too?? If not more!"

I gaze about the sea of faces. "Dictatorship is everyone's least favorite form of government for a reason. This is America, land of the free. Democracy is the right way, for everyone to have a say in what we do. As a community, as a people, you own this land just as much as they do!"

I point a finger toward Darian and Drake. "Make a change. Vote out the King!"

My voice is so loud it echoes through the trees. I watch the intrigued faces, all eyes glued up on me, and for one very brief moment, I actually expect them to cheer.

But they don't.

The first thing that happens, letting me know I fucked up, is Lauris. She inches up to Darian's side, her eyes hard and unforgiving, aimed right in my direction.

Then Gem and Emithel do the same, standing by him, folding their arms the way his are, glaring up at me in doubt and betrayal. Kiara and Alissa are already there with them—they never liked me to begin with—and more movements happen.

People shift from where they were standing, crowded around the bench I'm standing on, over to Darian's side. One by one, they move up to him, forming a wall at his left and right. A wall of support that is clearly unbreakable, regardless of what I tell them.

It didn't matter.

Either they're so beyond brainwashed there's no getting through to them, or they simply don't care, about any of it.

Loyalty is the key I hadn't anticipated.

Drake moves in between everyone to stand by his brother's side, eyeing me with so much fury my knees begin to wobble. When I look down at Abdiel, his eyes are alit with pity. He feels sorry for me as he stands up and joins Darian's side.

They all do, each and every one of them, their thoughts quickly turning from murmurs of loyalty to their chosen leader, to angry chants about exiling the traitor.

Kick her out.

Get rid of her.

I don't care if she disappears, just get her out.

Down with the traitorous bitch!

Go back to the outside, stray!

Off with her head!

Okay, maybe the *off with her head* was an overreaction, but I can hear a lynch mob forming in their minds, and it's scaring the shit out of me.

I acknowledge that I made a huge mistake here. I may have just gotten myself killed.

My entire body is shaking violently as I watch all the angry eyes aimed in my direction. The patrolmen stalk up to the bench where I'm standing.

I hold up my hands. "No, please. Wait..."

Drake and Darian share a quick look. Abdiel aims a pleading gaze up at his Head Priest.

Darian blinks down at Abdiel, then holds up a hand. "Stop. Leave her be."

Everyone is silent again, even their thoughts. Everyone except Drake.

The girl is mine, brother. Leave her to me.

I'm quaking so hard I might wet myself.

Darian's eyes stay on mine, shimmering with a regal confidence. In this moment, he truly does look like a King.

And that was my biggest mistake... underestimating him.

"You," he barks, finger pointed my way. "Come with me." He turns to his patrolmen, giving them a quick head nod I can't read. Then he looks to Abdiel and Drake. "You two as well. We have much to *discuss.*"

I hear a quiet fuming in his tone, a fizzling rage that surrounds him as he turns and saunters back toward his Den. Abdiel peeks at me, blinking over wide eyes before following Darian like a puppy. Drake stands in place, glowering at me for a few beats until he too turns and storms up the path after his brother and Abdiel.

And me, well, I just look around at the angry mob I've created, and the patrolmen standing guard, waiting to see if I do any more stupid things.

I can't. There are no more options for me. The only leverage I have is in my head. But the question is… is it enough?

CHAPTER THIRTY

DARIAN

The moment I set foot in the lounge, I'm pacing. Back and forth and back and forth. Abdiel comes in after me and doesn't say a word. He stands off in the corner, shifting his weight from foot to foot. Peering over my shoulder at him, I find my emotions torn.

On the one hand, I love him so much, and I'm so very sorry for what happened last night. But on the other, this is all his fault.

This girl he decided to bring here. This girl he has feelings for…

Even if they're different from his feelings for Drake and me, they're still there. And I just don't understand them. The girl is a nuisance, and she needs to be dealt with.

Drake comes stomping into the room and goes straight for the decanter of scotch on the desk. He pours himself a glass, then pours another, handing it to me fast. I take it, and he clanks his against mine aggressively before tossing it back.

Watching him carefully, I know something is up. There are so many things he isn't telling me, and somehow this girl seems to know about them.

Lastly, the girl steps into the room. I hear her fright immediately, and it only serves to annoy me further. She sure wasn't lacking in confidence five minutes ago when she was trying to rally my people against me.

She leaves the door open as she stands there like a small, trembling statue. I catch Jeremy out in the hall and nod for him to close the door, which he does, posting up just outside as I've directed him.

I take a small sip of my scotch, all the while observing the girl over the rim of the glass. Her eyes dart briefly to Abdiel, who won't look away from his shoes, and then to Drake, who is radiating an anger unlike any I've felt from him in quite some time.

Sucking in a breath, I'm unable to hide my vexation. "So, what seems to be the problem here?" My question is directed at everyone in the room, though I'm looking primarily to the girl right now. Clearly, she has grievances.

Time to air them.

"I know about everything," she speaks, keeping her wide eyes on me. And for as much as she is driving me insane, I have to give it to her. She's a ballsy little thing. "You two, the drugs, the trespassers, your affair with Abdiel's father... All of it."

I glare at her. "It wasn't an *affair*." My gaze flings to Abdiel, and he rubs his eyes.

Huffing out a rough exhale, my fingers sift through my hair as I address Abdiel and Drake. *How does she know all of these things??*

I can hear you, Rhiannon's thought breaks through, and I turn my eyes back on her. She's smirking. My blood fucking boils.

But my brother gets there first, stepping forward with his fists clenched. "Lock her up."

I ignore him, looking to Rhiannon. "How did you get it?"

She doesn't speak, but I hear her recalling stealing the Empyrean from Drake's office. My eyes dart to his, and honestly, I've rarely seen him this enraged.

"Sticky fingers, tiny stray." He moves in closer, towering over her, intimidating her with his height. "I should cut them off."

Abdiel finally speaks. "Don't threaten her."

Drake squints at him briefly before falling back. "Lock them both up. As far as I'm concerned, they can both rot."

Hurt flashes over Abdiel's face, while fear covers Rhiannon's. She knows he's not kidding.

"No one's locking Abdiel up," I intervene with a hand held up to my brother.

"What about me?" Rhiannon squeaks.

I shrug. "I don't care about you."

"Darian!" Abdiel scolds.

"He's killed someone!" Rhiannon points an accusatory finger at Drake. "I saw it! Witnessed it with my own eyes!"

"Ease up there, toots. I've killed lots of people." Drake folds his arms over his chest, and I rub my eyes.

Mother, these kids are testing me.

"I mean, someone you know," Rhiannon says quietly, aiming a defiant scowl at Drake, though she's speaking to me. "Someone from your past… And he's been manipulating you for years. Making you think you can't—"

"Shut her up before I do it myself!" Drake roars, crowding the girl quickly, combatively.

I don't think he would lay hands on her, but I'd rather not stand around and find out.

Abdiel comes between them, protecting Rhiannon while holding Drake back with a hand on his chest. "Alright, that's enough," he growls. "No good can come from attacking each other like this." He angles his chin to the girl. "You have to stop. Even I can't protect you from this mess you've made."

Dismay frames Rhiannon's face. I hear her regretting everything she's done, but mostly for hurting Abdiel. She cares greatly for him.

"Secrets, secrets everywhere," I sigh, waltzing up to the three of them. I place my hand on Abdiel's shoulder until he steps back a bit. Then I move in close to the girl, cornering her while she backs up into the wall. "You come onto *my* land, steal from my brother, then try to blackmail us into… what? Giving up control? Silly girl, you should know by now that *nothing* is greater than control."

She swallows visibly, her pink little lips quivering. "I just thought… I was just… trying…"

"You were trying to rally my people against me," I growl inches from her face. "You were trying to take what's mine. People on this land have died for less."

I know, she thinks, even her thoughts trembling in fear. *I saw it.*

Every ounce of my fury burns at her through my eyes. "You. Know. *Nothing.*"

Backing up, I straighten and pull open the door, addressing Jeremy. "Lock her up."

At those three words, my patrolmen rush into the room and grab the girl, tying her hands behind her back and hauling her away.

She shouts in protest as they drag her out of the house, but I ignore it, eyes stuck on my two men. My lovers, my friends, my family.

All the secrets, the betrayals. It ends now.

We need to get to the bottom of this.

"Darian, is that really necessary?" Abdiel pleads with his despondent gaze, forehead lined in concern for his friend. "Locking

351

her up? Where are they even bringing her?"

"We have cells," I breathe, exhausted from all this already. "On the mountain, there's a hunting shack with a trapdoor leading down to a jail of sorts."

He looks stunned but for only a moment before nodding, accepting the secret I'm sharing with him. "Do you use them often?"

"Depends on your definition of *often*," I mumble. He flinches but says nothing. "Sweetheart, I know we still really need to talk." I grasp his face in my palm, and my heart soars when he lets me, leaning into my touch. "There is much for us to discuss, but first, I must speak with my brother. Alone." My eyes flit to Drake, and for the first time in a long time, I catch him wavering.

Abdiel nods. "Yes, sir."

Resting his hands on my chest, he angles his face in close, so that our lips are hovering. There are so many things he wants to say, so many thoughts, questions, worries in his pretty head. But instead of voicing them, he simply presses a velvety soft kiss on my lips, enough to melt me into a puddle on the floor.

"Wait for me upstairs... in my bedroom," I command, quietly, my tone wrapped in the fuzz of my lust and love for this beautiful boy.

"What if someone should see?" He asks, curious fingers tracing the lines of my torso through my shirt's fabric.

I place another quick kiss at the corner of his mouth. "That's the least of my worries right now."

He nods once more and breathes slowly, backing up and leaving the room, his mind swirling as he does.

And now I'm left with my brother.

My lover, my partner, my Serpent... Holder of all the secrets.

We stare at one another for a while. Eyes locked, thoughts scattered, lips sealed. I'm really not even sure where to start. So I decide to go for a simple request...

"Tell me the truth," I demand, though the moment the words leave my mouth, I fall to my knees. I kneel before him and rest my head on his legs, trembling at the impending revelation.

Rhiannon said he killed someone we knew... Someone from our past.

There's only one person it could be.

"Tell me what you did..." My voice quivers with emotion. With the need for this... This *truth*.

Drake's fingers comb through my hair, leisurely, treasuring. He strokes me, petting me like a cat while he whispers from above, "I did it for you."

My face springs upward, chin tipping so I can look at him.

"I killed him because he hurt you," he confesses, and with his spoken words, I hear the memory of what happened that night.

I can almost visualize it, based on what he's thinking. That night, before he frantically woke me in the dark, where I was sleeping in his bed, bruised and battered.

He avenged me.

He killed our foster father.

"I bathed in his blood, brother," Drake growls. "That was the night I took on the evil. I did it for you, and I've been doing it ever since."

"I didn't ask you to do that," I mumble, stupidly, because I can't think of any other way to respond. But it's the truth.

"You didn't have to." He drops to his knees in front of me. "Don't you see, Darian? That's why I'm here... It's the balance. The natural order. I'm the dark to your light."

My head shakes, not liking this one bit. "No. I don't accept that. You're here because..." I stop and gulp. "You're here because *I need you.*"

He takes my hand in his, holding it up to his chest. "I've killed them all for you, Darian. To protect you."

My eyes are wide as I stare at him, gaping in shock and awe. I can see into his mind. I see him covered in blood, in that clearing on the mountain. Beside the black rock...

I see him bleeding. I see him making others bleed.

Feeding the evil. For *me*.

In this moment I know, deep down in my conscience, I should object. I should say no to this, because he's *mine* and he's ruining himself... When he doesn't need to.

But my heart feels too much. I love him too damn much. He's already fed me until I'm full.

Grabbing his face, I pull his lips to mine.

I kiss my serpent hard, ferociously ravaging, our teeth clashing before our tongues do the same. I suck wildly at his mouth, tasting him, biting him. And he groans into me, fingers wasting no time running down past my waist, stroking me over my pants.

My erection throbs in his palm as it grows, stiffening by the second while we maul one another, panting and gasping, sucking and licking.

Pushing him onto the floor, I straddle his hips and grind into him while we kiss deeper, rougher. I pin his hands above his head, and he whimpers into my mouth, a sound I devour like the most delicious of treats.

His vulnerability, which I get so rarely, is like the first drops of water after a drought. I love it far too much.

"You killed him for me," I purr, visualizing him vibrating in sexy anger, a rage so strong it caused him to seek revenge. *For me.*

"I *gutted* him," he breathes ragged, lifting his hips to mine. "I took his life as tribute for you, baby."

I groan onto his mouth, kissing his lips raw. "I accept your offering, my Serpent."

He grins, lazy with lust as he writhes beneath me. "You should take something else... Take more."

Gazing down at him, my chest flutters while his eyes sparkle. He wants me to fuck him. I can hear him, practically begging for it in his mind.

"We've never done that before." My lips trail his jaw, my cock so hard it's about to snap.

"We haven't..." he whispers. "But I've imagined it."

"Have you?" My heart thumps from my chest into his while I suck his pulse.

He nods. "Sometimes... when I'm all alone..."

Returning my face to his, I suck hard on his lower lip while he tells me in his mind, *I stuff my fingers inside myself and wish it was you. My brother...*

I whine out loud, hoarse and trembling. This is what he does, and he does it so well. He gets to me. Everything about him...

"You are meant to be mine, brother or no brother." I thrust my erect cock into his. "We could share blood and I would still want you desperately. I can't help it. I've always been..."

"Lost to you," he finishes my thought. "I'm sorry, baby."

"Why do you torture me so much?" I breathe at his throat, sucking and biting to leave him purple. Marking him so everyone knows he's mine, even though he can't be. "Why do you tempt me, knowing I can't have you the way I want?"

Our panting breaths echo off the walls. Drake strains his muscles, lifting himself so he can squirm into me.

"You *can*, though," he murmurs. "You could. The girl was right... It's been my fault."

My movements slow. "What?"

"I've been convincing you we could never be more than secret lust," he admits softly. "For years, I've pulled away, making you think we can't be together. But it was because *I* was afraid. Because... you're too good for me, Darian."

I back up, a strange foreboding crawling through my insides as I gawk down at him. His cheeks are pink, like his lips, puffy from our kisses, his broad chest moving with unsteady breaths. He's the most beautiful beast I've ever seen...

"You... You've been manipulating me." My forehead lines. Drake blinks. "The girl *was* right... It's been you all along. You're the reason I've felt so insecure. You're the reason I married those girls. To escape my feelings for you."

Hurt and anger weave together in my heart as I stumble off of him. But he scrambles on top of me, this time pinning me down.

"Darian, please," he insists, holding me while I struggle against him. "Listen to me. You have to understand where I was coming from..."

"No. I don't give a fuck," I hiss. "All I've ever wanted was you, and you've done nothing but run from me!" My voice raises as I shout up at him, the tension from the last twenty-five years finally erupting like a long dormant volcano. "Pushing me into Lars's arms, then convincing me I needed to marry, to give the Regnum an heir. It's been you all along, hasn't it?? Whispering in their ears!"

I keep fighting against his hold, but he's using all his weight to keep me beneath him.

For the first time, I'm seeing the truth. His thoughts are on display. No more hiding, no more blurring it out to *protect* me. To subdue me.

Drake's brows zip with his guilt, his shame, as he moves his lips up to my ear. "I'm so sorry, baby. I never wanted to hurt you... To make you feel like loving me was wrong."

"But that's exactly what you did," I snarl. "Now, get off me."

"No." He stays planted over me while I try to wriggle free.

"Get off me, Drake! Now."

"No, please. I need you to forgive me." He kisses my jaw, my neck, my throat.

The feeling sends chills rushing across my body, but I'm so angry with him, I don't want it. "Drake, stop."

"You love me, I know you do," he whispers.

And it triggers something in my mind.

A flashback I've tried so desperately to bury.

Him *on top of me, my hands zip-tied to the headboard.*

His *lips drag over my throat while he spreads my legs. "You love it, I know you do…"*

Fear clutches me, burns my limbs, smothering me from the inside until I can't breathe.

"Drake, stop." I gasp for air. "Please stop. Get off…"

He moves back, likely hearing the shakes in my voice. His eyes widen, and he releases me immediately.

I sit up, clutching my chest while sucking air into my lungs, sputtering to hold on to it before letting it go. My vision swims, and I close my eyes, squeezing them shut hard while I focus on catching my breath.

When I finally reopen them, I see Drake leaning up against the bed, gaze wide with dread and shining regret. He won't even speak to me, but I hear him thinking…

Hear his guilt.

I reminded you of him… I scared you like him.

I shake my head slowly. "I know you'd never hurt me."

"But I did," he grunts, standing up fast.

I turn and watch as he stalks to the door. "Drake, don't go."

He stops, shoulders slumping while his head falls forward. He says nothing, but I hear him as he leaves the room…

This is why, baby.

You're too damn good for me.

CHAPTER THIRTY ONE

RHIANNON

It's cold down here. Dank and dark.

I don't know what time it is, but I'm trying to keep track. I think I've been in this cell for at least four hours.

For as much regret as I have over my petty attempt at speaking the truth, and how terribly I mistook the situation, I'm still pissed. I can't believe they locked me up in a cell.

Well, actually, I sort of *can* believe it. If they kill people, what would stop them from taking prisoners? I'd rather be locked in this dungeon than dead, although now I'm beginning to worry about what the endgame is here.

What are their plans for me?

I'm kicking myself. I let my pride and my misguided attempts at informing people drive me to make this stupid mistake, and now there's no telling what kind of hot water I'm in. And mostly, I'm mad at myself for betraying Abdiel.

He trusted me. Brought me to his home and introduced me to his people, after saving my life. He sensed my loneliness immediately, and without a second thought, he offered his hand. He offered his help.

And what do I do? I come in here, investigating his friends and family, snooping and stealing, then call his man out in front of everyone.

I feel like such an asshole.

Covering my face with my hands, I exhale a rough breath.

Who am I?

My anger's bubbling inside, a thick rage chugging through my veins like molasses. *The scumbag* took my identity. *He* stole it from me, and now I have no idea who I am… Who I'm meant to be.

My soul is broken. I'm damaged, scraped up and dented. One moment contemplating suicide, the next reaching out for someone, *anyone* to trust; someone to love me, to give me a chance. But then the immediate distrust swallows it all.

That perpetual suspicion. The *doubt.*

I hate feeling like this. I despise the wariness inside me. Why can't I break it?

Why does it have to be like this?

A faint voice ripples from somewhere off in the darkness. Sitting up straight, I scoot away from the bars, zipping my back to the farthest wall. I'm scared down here. I can't really see anything, and I don't like being underground. I feel claustrophobic.

It only takes a moment for me to recognize the voice, or rather the thoughts, as they grow nearer.

Drake.

Swallowing becomes more difficult as my limbs tremble.

Here kitty kitty…

I clamp my jaw to stop my teeth from chattering.

Herrree… kitty… kitty…

Snake eyes appear in the black, between the bars of my cell. My blood is rushing so fast, practically drowning out any sound. But his thoughts are visible to me, as if they're in my mind already.

Hi, tiny stray girl. He blinks.

"W-what do you want?" I stutter, feeling around the floor next to me for a rock or something sharp I could use as a weapon.

He rests his forehead on the bar. "You're a problem, you know that?" His hand slips into his pocket. "I'd been wondering what to do about you before… And then you stole from me."

Keys jingle in his fingers as he holds them up to the door, inserting one into the lock. Then turning it.

Fear lances my spine, and I can't move. I'm frozen, just watching him. Staring at his pale skin, contrasting the darkness surrounding him. His black hair is all disheveled, mussed up as if he's been yanking at it for hours. He has circles under his serpent eyes.

The lock clicks as the door opens, and he pushes it, stepping inside. "You turned my brother against me." His head cocks as he stares down at me.

There's something very threatening about how quiet he is. Even his thoughts are soft murmurs. He doesn't seem anywhere near as angry as he was in that room earlier.

I'm not comforted by it.

But in this moment, looking up at him, the light in the dark, all I can feel is… strength. Protection.

It's odd. Beyond odd… It's fucking crazy.

Before I'd even met this man, I saw him in a vision, crying tears of blood. Right before I tried to kill myself, *unintentionally*, I think.

And apparently, he's been killing people since he was a kid. There would be no earthly reason I should ever feel safe around him.

And yet…

He steps forward. I stare. He steps again. I keep staring.

He reaches me, then drops to his knees. "We never finished our conversation yesterday. Before you stole from me and freaked out like a little psycho."

I scoff out loud. "*I'm* the psycho? Uh hey, pot, this is kettle. By the way, you're black."

A small grin tugs at his lips, but he pushes it away before I can focus on how abnormally beautiful it makes him look.

"You said you wanted control back… of your life," he speaks in a soft, growly sort of tone that does things to me inside, things I can't exactly fathom right now. "Is that why you did what you did today?" He tilts his head again and blinks slowly.

I'd love to lie, to hide my truth, but I know it's no use. He can hear me as much as I can hear him, and surprisingly, it's a comfort. One I've obviously never experienced, but I have to admit it brings me a sense of peace.

So I nod, swallowing a dry gulp before admitting. "I think so—"

"Well, you went about it the wrong way," he jumps in before I even have all the words out.

My gaze drops to my fingers as they twist in my lap. "Yea, I picked up on that. Is that why you came down here? To gloat over how misguided I was before you kill me?"

His brow arches, a dark curve that brings on more tingles to my belly. "Why would I kill you?"

"First of all, you told me you were going to…"

"No, I didn't."

"Not in so many words." I shrug. "And second of all, isn't that your thing?" This time both brows move. "Murder…?"

He lets out a deep, rumbling laugh, more subtle than anything, but it's somehow one of the greatest sounds I've ever heard come out of a person. "You have interesting ideas about me, kitty cat."

Suddenly, he's on his hands and knees, crawling, inching closer to me slowly. I'm already up against the wall, so I have no place to go as he cages me in.

"I saw you..." I murmur. He grabs my ankle and tugs me until I slide down onto my back. "I heard your memory. You told me... you kill people."

"I kill people who need to die," he mutters, hovering over me while breaths fly in and out of my lungs. His snake eyes are shimmering down at me, and as freaked out as I am, I can't deny the clenching happening between my legs. *This is so fucked.* "There's a difference. But you, little stray kitten... you certainly don't *need* to die."

My lips shiver through the words, "H-how do you know that?"

"I can feel it," he says softly, leaning in, that scent of him intoxicating me until I feel drunk. "You were up on that clearing and you *lived*."

"Because of Abdiel," I croak, my head spinning.

He shakes his. "No. Because of you. This is your Ecdysis, Rhiannon. Here, on our land, is where you'll get your life back. But you must want it. *And* you must deserve it."

For every ounce of confusion bubbling inside me, there's twice as much realization. Understanding.

Somehow, I get what he's trying to tell me. I'm not sure how, but it's not lost on me that of all the wilderness in the state of Washington, I found my way onto the Expanse. I met Abdiel in that clearing. He saved my life.

Taking those drugs was like a religious experience. Maybe I was meant to witness that murder...

Maybe it has something to do with the vision of him I had...

"I fucked up," I whisper up to him while my heart gallops in my chest. He nods in agreement. "These people... your family... they follow you and Darian for a reason. I think I see that now."

"They follow *him* for a reason," he mumbles, something serious flashing in his twisted eyes.

"No." I shake my head. "Both of you."

Making a snap decision, which for the life of me I can't even understand, I reach forward, my fingers grazing his jaw. He actually flinches, which brings a rampant heat to my gut.

"Take back your control, stray," he rasps, only an inch from my face. "It's why you're here."

My heartbeat is booming inside me, my stomach twisting up. I can think of many things I'd like to do to regain control of my life, after what I've been through.

Or I can stop thinking. Stop rationalizing.

Stop making excuses.

And fucking *take* it.

My lashes flutter, and just as I'm about to pull the Serpent's lips down to mine, he hops off me, rises to his feet and stalks out of the cell.

I'm still lying on the cold floor, breathing like I've been underwater for ten minutes while the door locks and he disappears.

ABDIEL

I think I've walked about fifty circles around Darian's bedroom by the time he comes upstairs.

He slides into the room, stealth even with his stature, like a panther. And when he closes the door behind him, he leans up against it as his eyes droop, breathing long and slow. I *feel* his angst.

I wish I could take it from him. Hold it, bear his burden. I would do that for him, and I realize it's a symptom of love I have felt before, though never truly this heavy.

In this moment, I would do any and every possible thing to keep my King happy.

I just want to know if he would do the same for me…

His eyes reopen, and he gazes at me, irises a tumultuous blue ocean of varying emotions.

I wouldn't be able to stop myself if I wanted to.

Stalking up to him, I grab his face, holding his chiseled jaw in my hands while I kiss him, gently greedy, until he hums satisfaction into my mouth like a scrumptious delicacy. When we pull apart, we're both breathless, even though it was only a couple of seconds.

But that's what he does to me… He renders me without air.

"I'm so sorry I did this, Darian." I kiss him once more, quickly. "I'm sorry I brought this drama back with me." Another peck to his soft lips. "I never anticipated that she would… I don't know," I sigh, dropping my forehead to his. "Maybe I am naïve. I wanted to believe the best in her… In people. But you guys were right about Outsiders. They can't be trusted."

A small grin tugs at Darian's mouth. I feel it on mine as his large hands slide up my chest. "Shh. Hush now, my sweet prince. No apologies from you. You've done nothing wrong. Your trust is one of the things I love most about you. And in all honesty, the girl wasn't *wrong*."

I pull back enough to gawk at him like he's lost his mind.

He chuckles. "I'm not saying I endorse her wayward actions. And she will suffer repercussions for that little scene. But the thing about being a leader is knowing when to speak up, and when to listen."

Watching him, in this moment, I'm not sure I could ever respect anyone more than this man. He *is* a King, regardless of how strange that might sound to an Outsider. I don't give a single fuck what anyone thinks.

Darian is a Royal. Born for it.

This time when my lips grace his, they're as cherishing as they are desperate; hungry. I'm giving him all my love through my mouth and gradual flicks of my tongue while we taste each other, sucking with punishing force. And to my delight, I think he's giving me the same thing back.

"Abdiel," he murmurs on my mouth, pushing against me until I'm backing up. "I'm the one who's sorry, baby. I wish I had told you about me and your father sooner. I was just… *God*, I was so worried it would mean the end of us, and we just started, baby. We just fucking started."

"Maybe this makes me naïve too, but I don't give a damn." I pull him on top of me on his bed. "I don't think anything could end us."

"Nothing?" He grins in between our ferocious kisses, hands running all over.

"Not one single thing."

He whimpers and sucks harder on my lips, giving me his tongue, brushing it over mine as he lifts my shirt. I help him get it off, and then I remove his, pulling him down so we can press our heated flesh together.

Next stop, we're ripping at each other's pants, fumbling to get closer to where we both want to be. Naked in his bed, loving with our bodies until there's nothing left but luxe sensation.

Darian yanks away from my merciless kisses when we're in our boxers, my hands inside his, exploring. "There is something I'll need from you, my love."

"Mmm… and I'll give it to you," I growl through a wicked grin, trailing my lips down his throat. "Deep and *hard*."

He shudders. "No, not that." He chuckles out a breathy rumble that's so sexy I want to flip him over and penetrate him right this second. "After everything that's happened in the last few days… Your leaving, whatever… *feelings* you have for the girl…"

He pauses after that part, his Adam's apple dipping in this throat before my eyes. Glancing up, I witness the shining vulnerability in his gaze, hearing it in his mind all the same. It makes me feel like a giant piece of shit.

"Baby, I don't know how I feel exactly, but I know it's not even remotely the same as what I feel for you…" I start, but he stops me with a kiss.

"I know," he breathes when he pulls away. "I know. I'm just saying, after all of it, I need to know that I have you, Abdiel. I need to know you're not going anywhere. Because I don't think I could handle it… Losing you."

He gulps again, and I feel him pleading with me; a trembling need, yearning in his heart for me in a way that sends mine leaping with joy, yet still bogs it down.

"I would love to give that to you, my King," I confess. "There's nothing I want more, but you need to understand things from my point of view…"

"Prince Abdiel." He settles over me, fingers rushing to hold my waist. "You know I want you. Do you want me?"

"I *love you*, Darian," I tell him with absolute certainty. He smiles, biting to contain it. "But—"

"No," he whispers, brushing his lips over mine. "No *but*."

I chuckle. "Yes but. You're still married." He flinches, opening his mouth to argue. "And you're in love with him, too."

That gets him. This time he's quiet for many long, strenuous seconds, blinking down at me while his thoughts rush all around Drake.

I see so much happening in his mind. Their history, what they've been through together, the hardships they've endured and what they've built. It would be so easy to fear competing with that. And I suppose a lesser man would feel crazy jealous, or intimidated.

But I'm not. And I don't think it makes me awesome or anything. It's not about that…

It's about my own feelings for Drake.

"He's… complicated," Darian finally speaks, then takes in a breath and rests his head on my chest. "It's complicated with us, and it never won't be. He's my brother…"

My heart thumps into his cheek. "Not technically."

"He is, though. I've always thought of him as a brother, even after I fell in love with him. He's done things for me, Abdiel… Things other people would never understand."

Rhiannon's words from earlier spring into my mind, verified by what Darian's thinking.

"He's killed for you," I mutter.

Darian freezes, but then he softens a bit and nods on my pectoral. "He has."

My mind rushes over many thoughts, eventually settling on a pertinent question. "Did it need to happen?" His face pivots to peer up at me. "Did they need to die?"

The oceans in his eyes crash like waves of the tide as he says, "Yes. They did."

My fingers roam up into his silky hair, brushing the strands while I nod. "He's an exceptional being, isn't he?"

Darian melts into my body, holding me close. "That he is."

We're quiet for another few moments, just listening to each other breathe and think. Darian knows I have feelings for Drake, too. He doesn't need to ask. He's seen all the things we've done together in our thoughts, read our story from our minds. It's nothing like what they've experienced together… I'm not sure anything is. But it's the kind of bond I hope to one day have. With Darian.

And maybe with Drake, too.

"If you can prove your loyalty to me, sweet prince, it would be my greatest pleasure to return the favor." He rests his chin on my chest so we can make eye contact.

I don't need him to elaborate either. I know what he means.

If I can assure him I'll be his always, he'll divorce his five and tell the truth.

364

DRAKE

What am I doing?

I think I've gone off the deep end. The things I've been doing...
The ways I've been acting...

This isn't like me. My hardened exterior seems to be crumbling,
shedding from my body, leaving me exposed, pink, and vulnerable.
And I can't identify how or why it's happening.

I'm the evil one. That we've established. I've taken that burden,
worn it like a medal of honor. I haven't wrestled with the things I've
done in years, so why now?

What is this sudden *need* I have burning inside me to settle the
turmoil? I must have some immense messiah complex, because this
shit is simply unreasonable.

Protecting Abdiel from the truth, confessing to Darian, even
though it opened his eyes to the monster he's been in love with since
we were kids, offering myself up to the girl, even though she's
technically the enemy...

What in the name of our sacred Mother is wrong with me??

Even now, I've been sitting outside the hunting shack for hours.
After just barely escaping the abruptly salacious thoughts of the stray,
I ran up here and dismissed the patrol Darian had assigned to guard
the place. I parked my ass in the dirt, where I've been since, smoking
joints and contemplating what exactly it is I think I'm doing.

And how it all became so diluted.

I know there are answers my Mother wishes to give, but I'm in
denial. I'm being intentionally dense about this, because I don't want
to accept it.

This is my purpose...

We're all connected. Darian and me... Abdiel to us... Then the
girl. She fits into the puzzle, I know she does. I'm reluctant, because
after the shit she pulled, it feels like a betrayal to Darian.

That said, I know she's remorseful. I could feel it, the moment I
stepped into the cell last night. Even before, in the lounge. She regrets
what she did.

She was just confused. She didn't understand her reason for being
here. The others might not understand it, but Darian and I do. We
remember what it's like for Outsiders when they first arrive. We dealt
with it for years.

Skepticism, suspicion. Doubt.

Still, it's not my place to give her a pass. Darian has to do that himself. They need to work out whatever bad blood is between them. For me, it's a bit more complicated.

She reminds me of him.

When we were younger, back in Michigan. Before the night we left…

And that's what she's been carrying this whole time. I feel it. It sits heavy on my chest.

I don't know the girl at all, but I want to help her as if I do. Like it's my purpose.

A blood-curdling scream jolts me out of my contemplations and without thinking, I jump, stumbling to my feet to an almost dust-scattering degree, darting back inside. Opening the trapdoor, I climb down the steps to another deafening wail of pain and devastation.

My heart is thumping hard as I race to the cell at the end, finding the girl on her side, arms covering her head while she thrashes about. Eyes wide, I fumble the keys out of my pocket, unlocking the cell door and whipping it open. I burst inside and fall to the ground by her side, looking over her small, fragile frame, where she wriggles on the ground, tears staining her flushed cheeks, eyes squeezing shut in her state of anguish.

I'm not sure what to do. I'm powerless, impotent and confused. Reaching out, I try to brush hair away from her face, but an arm surges out, whacking me in the gut.

"Sonofa—" I grunt, gripping my stomach, my jaw clenching in irritation. But then my muscles ease, because it was clearly an accident.

"No… no no no, please…" she whimpers and whines, digging her fingers into the cement floor. "Please stop!"

Blinking, I remember something…

Darian used to have nightmares. Not often, but every once in a while, when we first moved out here, he'd wake me up in our tent or our trailer, squirming all around, shouting in tears.

And then it stopped… But not because it actually stopped. Because I stopped sharing a bed with him.

For all I know, he could still have them.

A sickening feeling slithers through my chest, my hands fisting at my sides. I'm the worst. *Worse* than that…

I'm an abomination. A plague. How he even still loves me is

beyond all reasoning.

Making an impromptu decision I know I'll probably regret later, I grab the girl in my arms, lifting her onto my lap. She's still wiggling around like a worm on a hook, but I simply clutch her tighter, stroking her hair with my fingers. It's as soft as pure cotton...

My fingertips brush it away from her forehead and temples, where it's matted with sweat from her fear and strenuous movements. Sitting back, I prop against the nearest wall, and just hold her. I fasten her to my chest while she whimpers, her sobs eventually turning to easy mewls. She really is like a stray kitten...

The thought makes me grin. And then it falls away, when I remember where I am. In a cell, where she's our prisoner, because I don't know her at all, and she doesn't know us.

Yet, maybe I *do* know her... It certainly feels like I do. Because right now, here in this moment, I'm holding my brother. Comforting him, easing his pain as best I can.

Maybe the evil can be good sometimes...

Something tickling my throat wakes me up.

My eyes flutter open, then dart around, confusion holding me, but only for a moment until I remember what happened. *Fuck...*

I came in to comfort the girl during her nightmare, and I must have passed out. *When has that ever happened??*

She's still in my arms, and when I drop my chin to look at her, I find her gazing up at me. Her eyes are traced with sleep, but still so bright; a gleaming teal unlike almost anything I've seen in nature. It's sort of mesmerizing, but I quickly push the thought away when I remember she can hear me.

My throat dips with a swallow, and her eyes fall to it. I shift, my lips parting as if to say something, *anything*, but before I can, she leans forward and presses her mouth to my clavicle. A soft kiss that could be mistaken it's so small, but her warm breath gives it away as her lips drag up, kissing a line on my flesh, which feels clammy. That never happens to me.

It's the girl. She's burning me up, and I suddenly realize that I'm

367

sitting with her in my arms, her breasts pressing into me, ass resting on my erection.

I really shouldn't be hard. Call it morning wood, I guess, but it's still inconvenient all the same, because it could give the girl the green light to keep kissing me, or scare the shit out of her. Either way, it's bad.

I attempt to say her name, tell her to stop, produce really any words that could help, but all that comes out is a rumble, like a hum. And then she purrs.

She fucking *purrs*, like a kitten.

My balls are suddenly aching, and I recognize how bad this is. I do... But that doesn't make it feel any less good.

She writhes into me while kissing and sucking all over my neck, moving up to my ear.

Oh no... No no no. Not that spot.

"You have to stop." My voice comes out exactly like the groan of someone whose words mean jack shit. "We can't..." And then it trails off when I feel nipples... on my chest. Through two separate outfits...

I'm dying.

I haven't been with a woman in so long. For as much as Darian thinks I sleep around, it's been maybe a quarter of that. Most of my sexual exploits are with him, and lately, Abdiel, too. The last woman I was with was almost a year ago...

And I can't think about that right now.

"We *can*, though," Rhiannon murmurs, her voice all breathy with arousal. It sounds like the wetness I just *know* is seeping into her panties, and I'm going out of my mind. My fingers twist into the fabric of her shirt. "You said it yourself, I have to take back control. This is how I do it..."

"Not with me." I force myself to pry away, though it just gives her the opportunity to shove me onto my back, straddling my waist. "This can't happen..."

"Because of Darian?" She asks over my lips, and I feel her falter.

Something in her mind stands out... A memory of her and Abdiel, alone in a tent. Doing basically the exact same thing.

"Because of Darian," I whisper, though she already knows.

"What is this connection I have with you two? You and him..." Wonder lines her tone. "Something is holding us all together, and it makes no sense."

"Nothing makes sense," I rumble, inching up closer to her face, my hand sliding until it's resting on the nape of her neck. "And the thing that's holding us all together... is him."

She gives me a look of reticence, biting her lip for a moment in thought. *But he hates me.*

My finger twirls a strand of her long, strawberry blonde hair. *Don't be so sure, kitten. My brother doesn't have a hateful bone in his body.*

She still looks skeptical, but this time she forces it away and nods, accepting my words. It makes me smile. She wants to be one of us, I can feel it.

I don't know where this girl came from, how or why she would ever fit into our plan, but something about her settles me inside. I'd love to know what it is... To pluck it out and put it in a jar, study it in the lab.

Her mind races with questions, all sorts of wonderings, about me and Darian, me and Abdiel, the things we've done together. Me, up in that clearing.

My chest caves.

Before either of us can speak again, footsteps turn our heads. And we're met with green eyes, wide like that of a cartoon character.

We're shuffling apart, but it's too late. Abdiel already saw us, as evident from the way he's gaping, stunned like he just caught cousins fooling around.

He blinks a few times while I brush my hair back with my fingers, wanting to stand but knowing my hard-on will be totally visible right now.

"Uh..." he croaks, then clears his throat. "I'm um..."

"Yea, the feeling's mutual," I mutter, the awkwardness of it all working to kill my erection enough for me to rise to me feet. I brush off my pants, my body stiff from sleeping for hours sitting on a cement floor, with the girl on top of me.

Glancing at Rhiannon, I find her flushed on all visible skin, chewing her lip like it's the food she's been denied all day. *Oh, that's why he's here.*

"I brought you a... uh... sandwich." Abdiel steps hesitantly inside the cell and places it on the ground by her feet, immediately backing up slowly as if he'll be struck down by association for even being near us.

"Thanks," Rhiannon mumbles with her face beneath her palms.

"I should go." I shake my head at my own stupidity while stomping to the entrance of the cell. But Abdiel blocks me.

"Drake." He grasps my shoulders, the softness in his touch bringing on more need to my chest like embers I just can't douse for the life of me.

What is my problem? Am I turned on by everyone now??

"Back off, little mouse," I growl, inching closer to his face. "This isn't your fight."

"It doesn't have to be any of our fights," he insists in that tone of his. He's so damn good, it's almost unbearable at times. "Go talk to your brother. *Our* King."

My jaw clenches while I stare into his eyes, a green so deep it's like an overhead view of the forest we call home. The thing is, deep down, I know he's right. I know something needs to be done about all this yearning between the four of us.

About the secrets…

But I close my eyes and shake it off, pulling away from him. Because adding the girl just adds another person for me to protect… For me to kill for.

As if there wasn't enough blood on my hands…

CHAPTER THIRTY TWO

DARIAN

Last night with Abdiel was everything I needed.

I know it had only been a day since he fucked me for the first time, but said day was full of turmoil so strong it was like having teeth pulled.

After telling Abdiel the truth about me and Lars, the drama with Rhiannon, finding out about Drake's betrayal and all the anguish that always beats me over the head when it comes to him, I wanted nothing more than to hold on to my headboard with white knuckles and get fucked within an inch of my life.

And as sweet as he is, my prince certainly has no shortage of filthy desires and wanton dominance hiding within his strapping young body. He was all too eager to oblige his King.

Honestly, I had trouble walking when I first woke up this morning.

Yet for all that satiating, I'm still brewing uncertainty inside.

I asked Abdiel for a devotion last night. But the truth is that I don't only need it from him.

Things are tense as the day moves on. I'm getting odd looks from just about everyone in the Regnum, shy of the Tribe, because they know better. But Gina and Paul in particular…

I overheard them wondering why Abdiel has been spending so much time with me lately… Why he came into the lounge last night while we were talking with Rhiannon and then disappeared until early this morning.

I feel really bad. I don't like lying as it is, but to my family, especially the guardians of my Domestic, whom I've fallen head over heels in love with, it's hard. My mind is just as much of a clusterfuck as my heart. It was so bad I actually told Gina I'd be skipping dinner tonight.

I've spent most of the day wandering around the lake, just thinking. I'm purposely avoiding Abdiel. I don't want to make this decision any harder on him. *What if he chooses not to dedicate himself to me? What if he decides it's too much, loving someone who is also madly in love with his evil brother?*

And then Drake... *What is there to do about him?*

I haven't seen him since he stalked off yesterday, and I assume he's up on the mountain somewhere. Doing things he thinks he needs to do to protect me. And of course, I feel responsible. Not that I ever asked him to kill for me, but Drake's that kind of person.

I made him promise never to leave me. He thinks this is the way to do it...

Maybe he's right.

And who could forget the most confounding of my immediate problems... The prisoner.

I can't hold her in there forever. It's been a full day, and I'm already going out of my mind with guilt. This isn't the same as the other trespassers and thieves we've held. For as much of a pain in the ass that she is, Rhiannon is Abdiel's friend. He believed in her enough to bring her here.

I have a responsibility to her, too.

Last night, or early this morning, actually, when Abdiel was lying on my chest, regaling me with all the details of his journey we didn't get to discuss the other night, he told me about how they met.

In the clearing... The girl tried to kill herself.

I know better than to assume she would have tried it anywhere else in the world. That clearing is something I've purposefully kept guarded, even within myself, for decades.

But I'm not sure that's the right approach anymore.

I didn't want to admit it before, or think about it in any real way, since she's been carrying herself like a blatant foe of mine since the moment she set foot in front of me, but I've sensed an off-handed kinship with Rhiannon. A force of something holding us together that I can't rationalize or truly understand.

And I don't think that can be avoided any more either.

Coming back from my walk, when I'm sure dinner is over, I saunter toward the Den right as Lauris is stepping outside. I give her an easy smile, because Lauris has always been the one of my wives I know I can trust. She's dedicated, loyal, smart, and everything I look for in a partner, which is why I married her first. Well, that and because her thoughts always gave away her utter lack of interest in my dick.

Lauris and I suffer from the same sorts of insecurities surrounding our sexual preferences. Though hers were more about being unsure of what she wanted until we tried to have sex one night, drunk and fumbling around like two gay morons. Needless to say, it didn't work, and she's been in love with Gem since basically the day I married the tiny redhead.

That's the biggest pinpoint here. Not only do I owe it to myself and my family to be honest about who I am, but I really owe it to my wives. They deserve to have relationships, real ones, if they want. They don't deserve the sneaking around and secret affairs they're forced to engage in to protect my reputation.

After all, my *reputation* doesn't mean shit without the love of my family.

Lauris stops walking when she's in front of me, folding her arms over her chest. Naturally, I know what she's about to ask before the words leave her lips.

"Are you alright?" The concern on her face gives me the warm and fuzzies. And then it makes me feel like an asshole. Because of all the lying.

I nod first. It's a habit to act like everything is good, one I really need to break.

So I shake my head instead, rubbing my eyes with my fingers. "I'm tired, Lauris. I'm so fucking tired of wearing this mask."

Gazing over the foot of space between us, I watch her forehead line as she reaches out and brushes my hair with her fingers. "Then take it the fuck off."

"I'm terrified that if I do, everything around me will crumble." My confession. The first time I've ever said this out loud.

"Your highness..." she breathes, squeezing my shoulder. "You can always rebuild from rubble. Don't forget that."

Something comes over me, and I grab her, pulling her in for a hug, damn near squeezing the air out of her. But it just makes her chuckle while she wraps her arms around my waist, holding me back.

"Do you love him?" She mumbles into my neck.

My first instinct is to freeze, because even if we know things about each other, we've never discussed it out loud.

How much time have I spent hiding? Covering up my truths because I'm afraid?

How much of that was Drake's fault...?

"Which one?" I mutter, unable to keep the grin off my lips as she gasps, pulling back to give me an outraged smile, jaw hanging agape. I can't help but laugh.

"You're not as regal as they think you are, are you?" She teases.

I wink at her. "None of us are. That's the point."

I made a decision.

I'm still unsure if it's a good one, but good or not, it's definitely necessary.

Wandering in the dark, I ignore the eyes on me. The way the trees curve with the winds, as if they too are gawking, wondering what the hell I'm doing.

I wish I knew, guys.

At the door, I stop to take in a long breath, preparing myself. Then I open it, stepping inside the small shack, bending to pull on the trapdoor. I trot down the steps into the icy darkness. It's almost seventy degrees outside at midnight, yet down here it feels like winter.

Mother, please forgive me. Guide me on this path.

The sound of my boots clomping on the cement travels, erasing the silence from a moment ago. And once I get to the last cell, I peer in between the bars.

I'm not sure what I expected to see. The girl digging into the ground, attempting to burrow her way out. Or her lying on the floor, miserable and on the verge of death. Maybe sobbing, openly weeping for freedom.

What I don't expect, however, is what's happening, which is her doing a headstand.

I'm not even exaggerating. She's on her head.

Propped against the wall, for assisted balance I'm guessing. But I find myself tilting my own head to observe her face. Her eyes are closed, and when she opens them, she simply blinks at me.

Head Priest... She thinks.

I'm momentarily floored at her calling me that. Her thoughts don't even sound sarcastic.

"What are you doing?" I ask, unable to hide the amusement in my tone.

She gracefully pushes herself off the wall, flipping onto her hands and knees. Then she scoots over to the bars, sitting on the floor while she gazes up at me.

"I was doing yoga, and then it somehow turned into... that." She shakes her head subtly. "What are you doing here?"

Letting out a long sigh, I take a seat on the ground by her side, with only the steel bars separating us. "I came to speak with you. Because you're my guest, and I know next to nothing about you."

"Yea, well... you never tried," she mumbles, not sounding as accusatory as I'm sure she was going for.

"Neither did you." I fold my hands in my lap.

Point well made, she thinks.

"Rhiannon." I turn to face her better. She does the same. "I'm sure you've picked up on this by now, but Empyrean is more than just a high that opens your mind's eye to all sorts of things you may have never considered. Its power lies in the breaking down of walls. The light it sheds on our fellow humans."

She blinks over wide eyes, glistening in the low light of only a couple lanterns. "Because of the telekinesis?"

"Yes, but it's more than just that, too," I explain. "Being completely exposed is something many of us find... difficult. I know I'm one of them. For a long time, the only person I've ever been vulnerable to, by choice, was my brother. And then Abdiel... And now you."

I watch her swallow, her nerves making themselves visible.

"How did you feel when you found out we were listening to your thoughts? It was unnerving, wasn't it?" I lift my brow in question.

She nods. "Yea. To say the least."

"But once you get past that part, it's freeing. For example, right now, all my secrets are bared to you. It's a power unlike anything else. It's *godlike*, Rhiannon. What you have in your mind right now..."

"*Is* empyrean," she finishes my thought, and a small smirk graces my lips as I nod.

"Exactly."

We sit in silence for a moment, listening to one another, thinking about the power exchange, the control we both possess together.

Her eyes lift to mine, riddled with unease. "You were vulnerable to someone before... and not by choice. Weren't you?"

My gut crawls up into my chest, and I have to clench my jaw to stop the desire to curl into a ball and hide. But I do, stop it.

I force myself to sit up taller, and confess, "I was raped by my foster father when I was fifteen."

Rhiannon's eyes go round. The empathy in her mind seems to wrap around me, like arms.

"That's why Drake killed him..." she whispers. I can do nothing more than nod.

And then smile, a chuckle leaving my lips as I look down, shaking my head. "Honestly, I should've known. Maybe I didn't want to think about it... As soon as he told me we had to leave, my main priority became surviving with him. I didn't care about a single other thing. Loving him consumed me for a long, *long* time."

She nods along, praising what Drake did in her thoughts. It's familiar... It reminds me of how I felt yesterday when I found out what he'd done to Dan.

Being avenged. *She loves the idea. She wants it herself...*

I try not to think about it too long, because I don't want her to feel cornered, since she's in a cell and all, but I'm picking up on all the familiarities now. Many things are clicking into place.

And so, I keep talking to her. Because I think she needs it. "He used to pay me extra attention... my foster father. And truthfully, I liked it. I never had a father... So this father figure, I thought it was what I'd been missing. No matter how wrong it felt at times, how wrong I *knew* it was... the alone time, the lingering touches... I held onto it. I was in denial. I didn't want to give up my *father*, no matter what. I mean, I wasn't that young, and I'm not stupid. I knew he wasn't supposed to touch me like that. But I just... couldn't stop wanting it. Even when I hated it, I just couldn't stop feeling like it was... the only way."

Scoffing to myself, I press my back against the wall, dropping my head to it. I'm surprised when I hear Rhiannon relating to what I'm saying. Her thoughts are practically nodding along, commiserating.

"Anyway, that night, the night Drake and I left, that was the first time he got, like... *aggressive*. Really aggressive. He waited until Drake was asleep, then told me to come into his room, which had happened before. Said he wanted to talk about football, wanted some company." I roll my eyes at the black ceiling, recalling these details I choose never to think about, though they're always in my skull. "He got my guard down and tied me to his headboard with a fucking zip tie, then stuffed something into my mouth, some cloth. I'm not even sure what it was... A sock or a tie." My gaze goes far away for a moment. "It tasted like fabric softener."

I blink and gust out a rough breath. "He fucked me. He fucked me until I was bleeding, then he cut me loose and dragged me into the bathroom naked, shoved me into the shower and told me to get cleaned up. And that was it..."

I trace the dirt on the floor with my fingers. "That was the last night of his life... And I guess the first night of mine. My life... *living* with that. Because it's been twenty-five years, Rhiannon, and I still live with it. I never won't."

The silence stretches for miles. Not an uncomfortable one, though. It's a weighted silence, heavy with all my words. My truths.

Darian... Her voice speaks to me in the open air of her thoughts. My neck curls until I'm looking at her, giant orbs of teal shining at me.

She wets her lips. "I... I..." Then her voice dissolves while she shivers in place. She wants to tell me her own truth.

I turn my body toward hers, sitting cross-legged on the hard floor. "You have to know this one thing: *nothing happens by accident.* For a long time, I wondered why something like that would be a part of my existence... Part of the plan for my life. I questioned why any God would let such vile things happen. And that's when Drake and I realized, it's the balance. Good for evil, Rhiannon. God did that to me because She knew I could handle it." I pause and grin. "Well, with Drake by my side, at least."

She chuckles, a tear sliding down her cheek, gaze locked on mine. She doesn't move to wipe it or hide it. There's no point. We're open with each other right now, and honestly, it feels fantastic.

"You're a King, Darian," she whispers. "Born in blood."

"Coming from you," I lean in closer to the bars, "That's the ultimate compliment."

She giggles again, and we stare at one another while she builds up to it. I give her time, as much as she needs.

It doesn't feel like long, but it could be hours for all I know until she mumbles, "My stepfather... he..." Her voice goes out again, and I don't make any moves, I give no encouragement. I just sit and wait. "He raped me."

Her head falls forward, and she rubs her temples. My heart tries to jump out of me and go to her, to soothe her because I know exactly how much gut-churning discomfort is eating at her right now.

"I've never told anyone that before," she breathes, face aiming back up to mine. I nod, watching as she reaches forward, gripping the bars in her fists. I do the same, covering her hands with mine. "Six months before graduation, he... came into my room when my mom was out. I never liked him, and I knew there was a reason. I never fucking trusted him, and I was right."

Nodding again, I keep quiet. I give her empathy in my thoughts. I give her my strength in our joined hands. At this point, we're so close the bars may as well not even be here.

"My mom never cared that I hated him," she huffs. "All she cares about is money, success. Showing off to her silicone-stuffed friends. She never stopped to consider why I was suddenly depressed and desperate to live on campus at school. And of course, he paid for my apartment in Seattle. He has a fucking key."

My eye twitches with rage. "He has a fucking *key* to your place?"

She nods, solemnly. She looks so small in this moment. It's apparent how petite she is, like a baby bird I just want to hold in my palms, petting gently until she's ready to fly.

"I tried to change the locks once." She glances at the floor. "That didn't go over well..."

"So you ran away?" I ask, head cocked right while I watch her closely, reading her thoughts in between her story. A story we share, yet hers is her own.

All of ours are.

"I was supposed to go home for the weekend to spend time with him and my mom," she tells me, her hands settling beneath mine. "He'd already been texting me, and I was sick to my stomach at the thought of seeing him. So instead of driving home, I took a different drive. It took me a while to get to the mountain. I've never been a big hiker, but I swear I walked for five hours until I found that clearing."

At mention of the clearing, both of our thoughts immediately go to Drake. I watch her face as it flushes, and she tries not to think about something. She's trying to hide it from me... her attraction to him.

"Rhiannon," I murmur, inching in closer, "Don't feel bad about being drawn to him. Don't feel guilty for wanting him. Everyone does... It's just part of what makes him the Serpent. Temptation is his thing."

She blinks hard, her head spinning, visibly to me. "Darian, I'm *so* sorry." Her chin wobbles. "I have to apologize... I caused a huge mess for you guys."

"Water under the bridge," I assuage. "I mean, sure, you weren't easy, but what kind of leader would I be if I couldn't handle a little insurgence from a total stranger?"

She grins. "You're a true leader. I see that now."

Letting go of her hands, I stand as her forehead creases. She misses my touch. I have to chuckle at it.

She's cute, this kid. I don't know what that means, or where that leaves us, but it feels good to have another ally.

Pulling a key from my pocket, I unlock the cell, opening the door for her. She doesn't dive through it like I thought she might. She gives me a wary look, questioning my forgiveness.

So skeptical, stray princess, I purse my lips to cover my grin.

She lets out a small laugh, then does something I really wasn't expecting. She lunges at me, hugging onto my shoulders with all her tiny might. I'm much taller, and wider than she is, but she still almost knocks me over with her force.

She's a fierce one.

"Now what?" She asks, lips brushing my neck as she does.

"Well, you're here, Rhiannon," I rumble into her. "So I'm going to request something of you... something I've asked of everyone in my Regnum. Your loyalty. I need a guarantee that you're here to stay."

"Here to stay..." she whispers, her tone draped in awe.

"This isn't something you can just drop out of in six months if you don't like it, like Business School." I pet her long, silky hair. "You don't get to leave me."

"No one leaves?" Now she sounds shocked.

"No. No one leaves," I reply, firmly. "I'm a possessive King. My Mother made me that way."

She nods as she pulls back, the saucers of her eyes locked on me. For the first time since I met her, she's on Team Darian. I hear her thoughts, practically pledging my allegiance.

This talk we've just had, opening up to one another, and finding out how much we have in common... It gave me a new piece to my puzzle.

I have to appreciate it, even if it's something I never expected.

The thought brings on an idea. My next questionable one...

379

Something needs to be done.

"I'm calling a meeting." I take her hand in mine and pull her out of the cell, toward the steps.

"A meeting?" She's nervous.

She should be.

"A meeting in the woods."

CHAPTER THIRTY THREE

RHIANNON

Well, this is an unexpected turn of events.

Darian sent me to go collect Abdiel. When we parted ways at the hunting shack that secretly houses the jail cells, he told me he was going up to the clearing to find Drake. We both knew he was there.

I'm not sure how I knew… Darian, sure. They've been connected since they were kids. Connected through blood and pain and emotions so deep they're permanently carved onto their souls.

But me? I just got here.

I don't even really know what I'm doing. All I know is that I'm infinitely grateful to Darian for his forgiveness, and now I truly see what Abdiel was clamoring about in the woods a few days ago…

He's a King. The leader of The Principality… And potentially my leader? *My* Head Priest?

I'll need to decide. Either I'm staying, or I'm facing whatever consequences come with choosing to leave, which is a terrifying thought now that I've seen what normally happens to trespassers on this land.

The thing is, though, it doesn't really feel like a decision.

It feels like it's already been decided.

Either way, Darian had one of the patrolmen drive me back. He told me to go get something to eat, get cleaned up and grab Abdiel, then bring him to the clearing.

We have work to do, he said in his mind.

He sounded determined. I'm nervous as much as I am anxious.

I just got done showering and dressing in something acceptable for frolicking in the forest... a light, flowy sweater dress and some boots I borrowed from Gem. It's the middle of the night by the time I'm going to find Abdiel. I have a backpack ready, filled with items I found in his trailer. Flashlights, batteries, granola bars and water, a blanket, matches.

I hope I got everything... Darian didn't exactly tell me what we'll be doing up there, but I know it will be fucked up, because... ya know. That clearing gives me the creeps.

Yet with the three of them, I feel safe. It's a crazy notion, one that has me greatly questioning my sanity. Feeling safe with three strangers, at least one of whom is a murderous sociopath, and another, his brother/lover, who locked me in a jail cell not twenty-four hours ago.

But after everything I've endured over the past two years, I want this crazy. I'm welcoming it. Maybe that's what facing real evil does to you... It gives you the ability to seek out the light, even when it's buried within the shades of your comfort.

Drake isn't evil. I know he's not. The things he's doing, he thinks he has to. For Darian, and Abdiel and their family. But it doesn't need to be that way.

He's not a monster. We've known real monsters, and he couldn't be more different from them.

Walking up to the Den, I see the patrolmen, recognizing two of them as the guys who put a bag over my head and drove me up to the jail. I gulp down my nerves, expecting them to stop me from going inside.

But to my surprise, they don't. They simply stare me down, all eyes, the rest of their faces covered by bandanas. They don't look like they'd want to engage in friendly chitchat with me anytime soon, but at least they're not stopping me. *Darian must have radioed to them...*

It's wild, being in a place without cell phones. They use walkie talkies to communicate with each other, but outside of that, you're stuck searching for people. Like right now.

If we were Outside, I would just text Abdiel and tell him to get his ass down here. But I can't do that. I'm left wandering through Darian's house in search of him. First, I try the room we converged in those two times. But it's empty.

Walking through these dimly lit halls at night, there's a log cabin ambiance I really like. Sure, it's summer, so there's no fire burning or snow outside the windows, but I can only imagine how beautiful it is in winter.

I'd like to stick around to see it...

Creeping up the stairs, I pass a few bedrooms, all doors closed. I have no clue which one is Darian's, but I have to assume it's the one on the end. When I reach it, I decide against knocking, since I don't want to wake anyone else. It would be difficult explaining to the wives what I'm doing...

I turn the doorknob, and it's unlocked. Opening the door a crack, I peek inside to find Abdiel, sitting in a large, beautifully upholstered chair by the window. He's dressed only in sweatpants, his features highlighted by the glow of the moon as it reaches inside to adorn him. His worry is prominent, around his eyes, the creases in his forehead.

I step into the room, and he turns fast, clearly anticipating Darian's return. There's no disappointment on his face when he realizes it's me. Just surprise.

"We have to go," I tell him softly. His brows zip together. "Darian called a meeting... On the mountain."

His eyelashes flutter when he's shocked and confused. It's adorable. "What...? What kind of meeting? And how are you out?"

"He let me out," I answer with a calm smile as I walk to him. He stands. "You were right. He's a great man. Pretty much the best."

His confusion morphs quickly into elation, eyes brightening with the grin on his full lips. "*Pretty much?*"

"You guys are all equally awesome." I take his hands in mine. "Which I think is what the meeting is about. Drake is up at the clearing. Darian wants us all to go. We can take an ATV to get there faster."

His brow arches. "You know how to drive one?"

I can't help the scoff that bursts from my lips. "Yea, right. That's funny."

He laughs and shakes his head. I go to turn so we can leave, but before I make it, he grasps my face. His lips are on mine quick, a shock so thorough it turns all my limbs into jelly. I whimper into his mouth as he kisses me, just as soft and eager as I remember.

Abdiel has this elegant way of kissing that's unlike anything I've felt before. Our lips dance a tango, sensual and seductive in its steps.

He pulls away, releasing a tender breath as he pulls me into his chest, hand on the back of my head, cradling me to him. "I'm so glad you're alright. And that you're *here*, Rhiannon."

I nod, locking my arms around his waist and taking in his perfect smell. The smell of someone so inherently selfless, and beautiful down to the core of his person.

Abdiel Harmony is one-of-a-kind perfect.

"I'm here," I whisper, warmth overcoming me.

Right now, I'm standing in the bedroom of someone I considered an enemy only days ago, who is now something of a guardian. It happened so fast, which is how I know it's the real deal.

Darian is my leader. And I want to stay.

Regardless of what this all means, my attraction to Abdiel, my odd obsession with Drake, the chemistry between them all, and then me… I really have no idea how it will shake out.

But either way… *I'm here.*

"Let's go," Abdiel says.

He pulls on a shirt and his standard black boots, grabs the backpack for me, and we're off. Fingers remaining threaded, we leave the Den, passing the patrol on the way out. I can't help but smirk.

I don't know what's about to happen, and theoretically, I could be treading into certain danger.

But sometimes it's fun to take a walk on the wild side.

DARIAN

The woods guide me. They always have.

This forest is a part of Drake and me, and we're a part of it. We breathe together, sing together, laugh and cry together. When we rage, the ground rumbles, and when we ache, the rains soothe us.

Being in this clearing brings a different sort of awareness. It still reminds me of when I came here seven years ago. The day after Lars and Jenny were found dead in the ravine beneath it.

I remember that night, after grieving for hours with tear-stained cheeks and red-rimmed eyes, confusion and anger clouding my mind.

I came up here to seek answers.

And I found them. But the thing about searching for the truth is that you always end up finding something you wish you hadn't.

The *forces* didn't show Abdiel the full scope of what happened that night... the night his parents fell from the cliff.

Tonight, they might.

"My jealousy did it," the familiar voice rumbles at me from the ground as I walk up to the clearing, lantern in hand. "It was my fault."

Stepping between the trees, I glance down at him where he's lying, arms out wide at his sides. He's wearing white linen pants only, his pale skin scattered in occasional black symbols, and scars.

And his eyes are closed while he speaks. "Evil atones."

Placing the lantern down, I stand over him. "You've made many messes over the years, brother."

His forehead creases in his clear anguish. I don't enjoy seeing it. For as much as I crave his vulnerable side, I don't want him to hurt. But with Drake, the hurt is inevitable. *Eternal.*

"I went to see the girl," I tell him, pacing around in the clearing.

His eyes spring open, and he turns his head to watch me. "You did?"

"I did." I nod. "Because after I got to thinking, about her misguided attempts at what she thought was saving people, I realized she reminded me of someone..."

My eyes find his once more, and I see him swallow.

"You've done so much for us, Drake," I continue. "For *me*. My debt to you is endless..."

"You owe me nothing—"

"It wouldn't matter anyway," I growl, coming back to him. "Because I never wanted this. I wanted a *partner* in you, Drake. Not a henchman." There is sorrow shining in his eyes, while mine smolder with frustration. "But you couldn't give that to me, could you?"

He crawls onto his hands and knees, gazing up at me. "I *wanted* to... But I was afraid."

"Afraid?" I crouch down to make us eye-level. "Of what?"

He pulls his bottom lip between his teeth. It stirs my dick. "Of losing you. Of hurting you..."

"You wouldn't—"

"Not on purpose, but it would happen. It's bound to." He scoots closer. "I'm not good, Darian. I never have been, but since that night, something has lived inside me. Something I can't control..."

I take his face in my hands. "What I hear you saying, brother, is that I was never enough for you."

385

"You always were," he whispers.

"Then what is it really, Drake?" My tone fizzles in anger, volume rising. "What's the fucking problem? Because I would have given up *everything* for you! But you couldn't bring yourself to do the same!"

The earth beneath us vibrates in a matching fury. Drake's chest is heaving back and forth as he grabs at the collar of my shirt. "I'm a monster, Darian! Don't you get that??"

"We're all monsters!" I roar in his face, pushing him back onto the ground.

I straddle him and hold his throat with my fingers, not tight enough to harm him, but enough that his pupils dilate as he gapes up at me, the winds whipping around us in turmoil.

"You don't want me." My voice snaps enough to prove the hurt behind my words. "You left me. That was why I went to Lars. Because you *left!*"

"I know..." he croaks.

"You packed up and moved out. Like I wasn't yours. Like we weren't meant for each other, when you know damn well we always have been. Don't you?" He's quiet until I bark again, "Don't you?!"

"Yes," he rasps, his fingers digging into the dirt by his sides. "We're meant for each other."

"You promised you'd always be mine." I lean in closer, my face hovering over his. My hands are no longer holding his throat but caressing it. I feel him swallow on my fingertips. "Not just my brother... *Mine.*"

"Don't you get it, Darian?" His hands move up onto my thighs. "We're *all* yours. I couldn't let you give it up for me... All of this, everything we've made. *We* built this, Dar. Us, together. And I've always been yours, baby. You're *my King.*"

A breath leaves me at his words, a warm brush of air sweeping over our flesh.

He's not being sarcastic or snarky, he's not hiding me from his true thoughts, or covering up his feelings to keep me from seeing them.

He's mine. I'm his King.

Always my King, beautiful. His snake eyes call to me, craving me as I hold his jaw and kiss him slowly. We both groan together, hands rushing all over, lips melded, tongues mingling while the trees rock above us. Our movements are instantly frenzied, his fingers ripping my shirt over my head, and mine dragging down his pants.

"I'm in love with you," I whisper into his mouth while he unzips me, hand slinking inside to feel how hard I am for him. "I never won't be."

"I've been in love with you since I watched you sleep from across our bedroom," he confesses, his truths like sugar on my tongue.

"Mmm... creepy." I grin, and he chuckles, shoving my pants down below my ass, until my cock flops out onto his abs.

"I'm being serious," he rumbles, though he's squirming beneath me, arching his back to rub himself on my body. "It didn't matter that you were my brother, or my best friend. I would have killed for you no matter what, baby. It was written."

"Always." I suck on his lip, fisting his inky black hair.

"Infinitely always." Drake's hands travel over my skin, a cool contrast to its heat for him.

We're fire and ice.

Nothing has ever been this clear, and I feel momentarily stupid for never having seen it. The answer was here all along...

Pushing his back into the grass and dirt, I yank his pants off the rest of the way, then rid myself of mine until we're both naked, shadowed by the darkness of the night, moonlight etching us while we kiss, rich with passion, writhing together in lust and even more love. The need I've always had for this man can't be sated.

But I shall try.

"Fuck me," he pleads, leaning back to present me his throat.

Trailing my lips down it, I scrape him with my teeth before sucking and biting, giving him marks from his King.

"I have literally nothing to use for lubrication." I make my way to his chest, licking the lines, sucking his pink nipples between my lips until he cries a soft noise, his long cock flinching between us.

"There's a bottle in my pocket," he breathes.

Reaching to his pants, I pull out a small bottle of what looks like oil. Opening it, I'm immediately hit with a floral scent. It's intoxicating.

"What is this?" I ask, my senses opening up as I continue to sniff.

"It's an oil I made..." he mumbles, curling a fist around my erection, "From the trumpets."

My eyes snap to his. "You mean... this..."

He nods, gaze flickering with voracious desire. "It has psychedelic properties, yes."

"Holy fuck." My eyes widen, a chuckle of disbelief leaving my mouth. "That's incredible. I'm totally using this to fuck you."

He laughs. "Okay, just be careful. That's all I have. Don't waste it basting your dick like a Thanksgiving turkey."

I can't help but cackle, pouring out a few drops onto my cock while he strokes me. "How fucked up will this make us?"

"I'm really not sure." He grins, jerking me to spread the oil all over my erection.

I take his chin in my fingers and bring his mouth back to mine, kissing him, lapping and sucking at his mouth in leisurely movements. The surrounding air is calmly erotic, though there's a buzzing chemistry popping like lightning.

Drake spreads his legs, and I take just a dab more of the oil before putting it away, sliding my slick fingers between the crack of his ass.

I'm already shaking. I've never done anything like this with Drake before. I mean, we've done *a lot*, but to my knowledge, nothing has ever gone into his ass. My love for being on the bottom always defined our sex, so I'd never considered that maybe he wanted me to...

"Put your cock in me," he whines, circling my nipples with his thumbs while we grind our hardened dicks together. "I've been fantasizing about this for years."

"Are you fucking serious?" I ask breathlessly. "Why have you never said anything?"

"I wanted you to figure it out on your own," he mutters quietly. I pull back enough to give him a look.

"You're the ultimate stubborn brat, you know that?" I bite his lip hard until he mewls. "Honestly."

"I love you," he whispers, looking every bit like the temptation his serpent personifies. Wickedly sinful in every sense.

And my chest is on fire.

"I love you so much," I mumble, taking my cock in my fist, dragging it down to his ass.

Swirling the crown around on his hole gives me his shivers. "Don't hold back... Please."

My balls are aching. "You'll be the death of me, Serpent."

With his hands on my ass, trying to pull me into him harder, I have to take a moment, let him sweat it out. For all those times he controlled me with Empyrean, for manipulating me when he didn't have to...

Wait... Something clicks in my mind.

I blink at him.

"What?" He asks in a desperate whisper, his mind echoing his need.

388

SERPENT IN WHITE

I can hear his thoughts, plain as day. *Stop fucking around and fuck me, Darian. Please... I need it.*

Drake, I think. *I can hear you.*

Yea, no shit, his impatient and irritable thoughts respond.

You haven't given me Empyrean in like... a long time. It's been... I literally can't even remember the last time I had it. *Solstice? Earlier??*

Drake's face is still while he shimmers up at me. The corner of his mouth curves.

I shake my head down at him. *What else have you been hiding?*

This isn't a secret, baby. I've tried telling you, but you wouldn't listen. He grabs my face in his hands. *Your mind's eye is open, Darian, and it has been for many years. Your Ecdysis happened long ago. You don't need Empyrean to hear anymore. You don't need the drugs to see... You're awake.*

My heart jumps inside me. My fingers are trembling as I touch them to his lips. I'm blown away by what I'm hearing. All of his thoughts, everything in his head.

I never needed solitude; I never needed a weekly injection of Empyrean...

My gifts live inside me.

"Well, I would argue that you still needed your solitude," Drake says. "You definitely needed your weekly dose of me."

I narrow my gaze at him. "I'm going to eat you alive, snake eyes. You better be careful."

"Do lions eat snakes?" His grin goes wide.

"I guess we'll find out."

My mouth takes his in a kiss that doesn't stop, not while I hold his waist, aiming my cock into him. I suck his lips as I push, fighting the resistance of his body. He shivers in the grass while I force myself inside him, and finally it breaks.

"Fuck..." he hisses as I nudge my cock into his ass, trying like hell to be gentle, but *holy fuck this is amazing.*

So tight... so so tight. "You're strangling my cock," I growl, thrusting deeper while he whimpers.

"You've never fucked before, have you, my King?" He gasps when I hit that spot, the one that makes me soar. I shift to do it again and he cries, digging his fingers into my skin.

"My dick technically went inside Lauris once." I huff a breathless chuckle, holding his throat while my hips push into him, slowly, pulling back and then pressing deeper.

"That's a disturbing thought," he rumbles. Then his eyes roll back in his head. "Good God, fuck me. Your cock is too fucking thick..."

My lips lower to his jaw. "You love it."

"I do," he groans as I pump between his legs.

He wraps them around me, our hands all over one another, touching and squeezing and holding while I bottom out, dick so deep in him, his balls are on my pelvis, and it's the most exquisite thing I've ever felt. *Shy of him doing it to me, of course.*

The sounds of him being fucked into the dirt, his deep voice rasping out *more more more*... I can't tell if they're his thoughts or his actual words, but it doesn't matter. This is everything I need right now, to soothe my soul.

It's a balm for the hurt we've unintentionally caused each other over the years.

It's healing. Cathartic.

We're one, in this moment. The King and his Serpent.

I hold his hands down, threading our fingers in the damp earth while I push and pull, stroking my cock in and out of the tight depths of his body. Our foreheads together, breaths mingling, praises singing like the songs of doves.

I love you, my King.

I love you so much, my Serpent.

It doesn't take long before Drake's hoarse, choked words are tumbling from his lips, "You're making me... *come*."

And his long cock pulses out streams of slickness, all over our chests while we rub together, muscles straining and skin sticky from sweat and his orgasm.

I break next, sucking vigorously on his neck as I explode into a mind-numbing climax. Colors zip all around behind my vision. I'm not sure if it's from the trumpets in this oil on my cock, or if the orgasm is just that spectacular. Probably both.

But either way, I'm free falling into an abyss, surrounded by rippling light and shapes. My loins are racked apart, crumbling like old stones as I cry into my brother's throat.

When we catch our breaths, clutching one another for dear life, we both turn to the side, our hearts collectively thumping into each other.

It's here.

The black rock.

SERPENT IN WHITE

CHAPTER THIRTY FOUR

ABDIEL

Rhiannon and I see light up in the distance.

We ditched the ATV at the entrance to the trail, and now we're on foot. Approaching the clearing, I can already spot Darian and Drake. One lantern provides a dulled glow, the breeze sifting through our hair as we walk, hand in hand, closer to a place that scares me down to my bones.

Because it knows things I don't. Because it has control unlike any human beings could fathom.

I'm wary about returning to the clearing, and as we step through the trees, my unease is verified.

The black rock is there. *It's already here.*

All the hairs on my arms and the back of my neck stand up, chills rushing all over my body.

My eyes find Darian first, my King, sitting in the grass. He's naked, with leaves and twigs in his hair, which is all mussed up. Dirt sprinkles his golden skin, dusting his muscles. He looks... gorgeous. As usual, but seeing a King like this, naked in the soil... Believe it or not, it does nothing to diminish his commanding confidence.

Especially because he's sitting, calmly, staring at the black rock. Drake is by his side, also naked and much dirtier than Darian, though it's more visible on his skin because of how much paler he is. Still, his hair is tousled about, blades of grass and forest debris scattered along the wall of his muscular back. And he too is staring at the rock.

I peek at Rhiannon. She's observing them, appearing worried, bu seeing as they stare at the rock. Their clothes are scattered next to them, the sight of which gives my dick a stir in my pants.

I know what they were doing. I only wish we could have arrived in time to catch the show.

"Sacrifice," Darian's voice rumbles deeply through the quiet surrounding us. His tone isn't loud by any means, but it still catches mine and Rhiannon's attention. We stand up straighter. "I called this meeting because it's necessary for us all to be on the same page."

He looks up at Rhiannon and me, motioning us over.

I pull Rhi with me as we wander up to them and take a seat on the slightly damp earth, keeping the rock in my peripheral all the while.

I'm nervous about it. I don't know if you have to touch it for it to fuck with you, or if just being near it could ripple us into another dimension. Who knows at this point.

Rhiannon seems to be having similar thoughts, though she's simultaneously distracted by the two very hot, very naked older guys we're now sitting in front of. I want to grin, but I press my lips together to cover it up.

We sit in the grass, the four of us in a little circle. Drake still hasn't spoken a word, or even looked at us. He seems to be in some sort of trance, staring at the rock, his gaze far off, as if he's not really with us at all. It's worrying, but Darian doesn't seem nervous, so I try to remain calm.

"We are bound by our places in the transformation," Darian says to us.

Peeking at Rhi, I find her eyes locked on Darian while she listens intently to his words. I can't believe this is the girl who was ever so suspicious of him for days, because now it's as if she's the one who's been *sipping the juice*, or whatever the expression was she used the other day.

"Tonight, we will render our Ecdysis complete." Darian takes Drake's hand in his. "And we're not leaving until it's done."

Reaching forward, his eyes connect with mine. *Your hand, my prince.*

I nod and take his hand, our fingers weaving together. The comfort I feel in simply holding his hand is unlike anything I could describe. Rhiannon and I are already holding hands, and she takes Drake's other hand in her right. He makes no move whatsoever to react.

Her thoughts echo her concern, but Darian assures her he's fine.

My eyes close while I remember to breathe, since it's becoming difficult. My chest is heavy, as if something is weighing on it.

Let the truth in, my prince, I hear Darian. *It will hurt, but it's necessary.*

Mourn, but don't fear this.

The fright, though, is gripping me; that familiar thickness in the air flooding me with trembles. In my mind, behind my eyes, I can see the black rock. I know it's there, and I know it has more to tell me.

I knew finding Rhiannon last time I was up here wasn't the sole purpose of my journey. I've still craved learning the truth of my parents' deaths…

But even though I want it, I'm terrified of knowing.

My memories float back to the vision I had the last time Rhiannon and I came here. Of Drake, on the day my parents were found. Him cutting his wrists, bleeding into the earth.

A flash comes into my mind… A memory that isn't my own.

It's Rhiannon's. She's remembering a vision of Drake, when we were here. Right before she came to, trying to pull us both over the edge of the cliff.

She saw Drake, crying tears of blood.

My heart rate speeds up, pulse ringing in my ears as wind whooshes through the trees. My body goes numb, everything around me falling away as I'm lifted and delivered into the eye of the storm; a vision in my subconscious I don't know how I've accessed.

I see Drake, visibly younger. Not by much, but it's clear this is from the past. He's wandering through the woods. He doesn't look happy, and I can hear his thoughts.

He's upset with himself. He regrets pushing Darian away…

Pushing him into the arms of my father.

He comes up to the clearing and stops in the middle, rubbing his eyes with his hand. The trees move with his unrest, the winds brush, birds' chirps go silent.

It's palpable, the change in atmosphere.

His eyes spring open at a noise. Footsteps. *He's not alone.*

Stepping in the direction of the sounds, he peers through the trees and his eyes widen to find my parents. They're by the overlook.

They're holding hands. And they're stepping up to the edge.

Drake blinks in disbelief, and then looks to his right. The rock is there.

"No…" he whispers, his thoughts clicking into place as his head turns back to my parents. "No no no. Stop!"

He calls out, rushing toward them.

But it's too late.

Everything happens in a matter of seconds. My mother goes over. My father's head turns at the sound of Drake's voice.

His eyes widen as he awakens from the trance. Fear graces his features.

But it's still *too* late.

"No!" Drake screams, diving toward the cliff. He reaches out.

But... it's... too... late.

Drake peers over the edge. He cries. His tears turn red.

"I didn't want that!"

Yes, you did, the rock says.

"No, I didn't! Fuck you. Fuck you fuck you fuck you. Take me!"

Evil atones, Serpent.

And nothing happens by accident.

Drake curls up into a ball as he weeps. "It's my fault."

His words echo in my brain. I look to him, now, naked and dirty, crying as he whimpers it, over and over again. *It's my fault it's my fault it's my fault it's my fault.*

I can do nothing more than stare, for so long my eyes are dry enough that they could fall out of my head. My heart pumps in pain, as if I've been stabbed. *My parents killed themselves...?*

They jumped, because whatever forces that are here told them to.

"The good and evil..." I whisper, finally realizing.

Finally understanding.

"It wasn't your fault," I murmur, crawling to Drake.

"It was." He nods.

I grab his face. "No. Don't you see? You're making yourself a martyr, but you don't have to be. There's good and evil in all of us. It's meant to be this way."

"It showed me the ravine," Drake croaks, his snake eyes locked on mine. "Years before they died. I knew about it, and I could do nothing to stop it. Your parents are dead, Abdiel! How can that be *right??*"

"It's not." I shrug. "But that's part of it. Fucked up shit happening, to make us stronger. *That's* the balance. It's not some burden you have to carry on your own. I know you want to protect us, but it can't all be on your shoulders."

"Let us help you carry that burden." Rhiannon's voice breaks through, and we both turn to her. She's kneeling right next to us.

"We've all experienced the pain of life," Darian says, squeezing

Drake's hand. "And we're still here. We're still standing. Because we're meant to."

"To overcome," Rhiannon adds. She and Darian share a look, reflecting a bonded experience.

Something detrimental they both overcame. I can hear it in their thoughts, see it in their memories.

It hurts to think about it... It pains my heart to know the things they've been through. And that's exactly what we're coming into... Sharing our pain, overcoming our pasts.

Becoming one in this transformation.

"I can't..." Drake's head shakes a bit. "I don't want you to have to..."

"But we will," Darian insists, with authority.

Like a King.

And Drake immediately nods. He accepts his King's ruling.

My heart jumps.

"Sacrifice, for the greater good." Darian brings Drake's hand to his lips and kisses his knuckles. Then he does the same to mine. "We all must sacrifice to come together in this. I'm going to give up some control... I must, in order for this to work." He blinks, vulnerability shining in his blue eyes.

"I'll sacrifice my life on the Outside," Rhiannon says, mostly to Darian, though she looks to me and Drake as well in the process. "I'll sacrifice my pride to you... my King."

A subtle grin tugs at his lips. Then his eyes jump to mine.

My pulse rocks, knowing what I must do. "I sacrifice my independence and pledge you my loyalty. I sacrifice my subservience to everyone but you, my King. I'm yours. Forever."

He sweeps in a breath, his joy audible as it shouts in his mind. I can't help but lunge forward and kiss his lips, delicately fierce.

For us, it was inevitable.

I never possessed a single shred of doubt that I would be his for all my days, and in whatever afterlife we find ourselves in.

"My Prince Abdiel," he sighs on my mouth as we pull apart.

Breaths shallow as we all look to Drake. The Serpent, and final piece to our puzzle.

He stares at Darian, dark brows pulling together while his thoughts sort through all these things they've been through together. All measures of pain and pleasure, love and loss, aching serenity. So many years, longer than Rhiannon or I have been alive.

The marble-like colors of his irises darken as his chest expands with a powerful breath. "You know what you're asking of me, right?"

Darian nods. "And I know what I'm promising you in return."

Drake's head drops forward for a moment, before he brings his gaze back to our King. "I sacrifice the wicked for you. I'll give up my holding of the evil for purposes of the order, and in turn, I give you myself... I give you my honor, forever. My King."

This time Darian smiles, and it's radiant. Luminescent, lighting up the darkness around us as he pulls our Serpent to him, to his lips. Never have I witnessed a more devoted kiss.

I adore watching them together, the love they share, seeing it freed from the chains of fear and secrecy. It's miraculous.

Looking to Rhiannon, she still wears the wide eyes of someone who's new to all this, and I tug her into my side. She smiles up at me, and I down at her. Then I press a kiss in her hair. She smells like flowers and hope.

New beginnings.

When Drake and Darian pull apart, they're practically slobbering on each other, which Rhiannon and I think is funny. And hot.

Darian gives Drake a look. "You've been feeding the forces of this mountain with blood..." Drake's eyes sparkle. "But what if we give it something else?"

The Serpent smirks. It's a salacious one, holding all the temptation possible. I shudder.

Drake and Darian turn to Rhiannon and me. They look us over, slowly, and now I'm really squirming.

Too many clothes, they both think at the same time.

I look to Rhi. She's nervous, but also there's a heat she hasn't felt in quite some time simmering in her belly. I feel it through her.

Drake moves in closer to Rhiannon, brushing her hair away from her shoulder until she shivers. "Do you want to play, kitten?"

RHIANNON

My eyes go to Darian first.

It's amazing that I'm looking to him as a lifeline now, since we just made up. But when it feels right, you don't deny it. You don't question it.

I've had enough bad in my life. It's time for the good.

Are you comfortable, princess? He asks in his mind. *It's fine for you to say no, just know that.*

I swallow, considering what could happen.

The four of us, out here in the forest, alone in a clearing where things aren't as they seem. A breach of earthly possibility and physics.

We've all just pledged ourselves to our King. This needs to happen now.

We need to sacrifice ourselves to him.

"I want to play." I grin at him. He smiles back. It's a gorgeous one. He's truly beautiful. Beyond all rationale.

He nods to Abdiel. "You first."

Abdiel wastes no time slipping his fingers into my hair, pulling my mouth to his. He kisses me gently, though his hunger is just beneath the surface. I can taste its notes coming through as his tongue plays with mine. And he lays me down.

Drake pulls Abdiel's shirt over his head, his mouth coming immediately back to mine, teasing my lips, biting and nipping softly until my toes curl in my shoes. My eyes catch sight of Drake, naked as he moves to Abdiel's boots, removing them for him, with his socks.

A fire catches and spreads inside me. They're such beautiful men, between Darian and Drake being older, yet clearly in their prime. Their bodies are so different, defined and hard all over. Large cocks that tighten my inner walls, my panties already soaking through. And then of course, Abdiel, his strength youthful, muscles taut and perfect.

Next thing I know, Drake is tugging my boots off, moving behind Abdiel until I can see his snake eyes. His head tilts, curiously, while his lips trail the nape of Abdiel's neck. Abdiel quivers, and I feel it while he peppers his kisses from my mouth down my throat.

I'm stiflingly hot already, as if there truly is a burning inside me.

"Can I undress you?" Abdiel's rough voice catches my attention, and I look to where his moss eyes are aimed up at me, with Drake's hands reaching inside his sweatpants. He lets out a small purr, head falling forward onto my chest.

I peek up at Drake again, and he winks.

"Yes." I nod eagerly. "Yes, please."

Abdiel grasps at the material of my dress, pulling it up over my body and tossing it away. I have no bra on, so my breasts are immediately exposed, and a flush crawls up my neck and face, timidity taking me over.

But when I hear the thoughts of Abdiel and Drake with their eyes stuck on my breasts, my inhibitions seem to dissolve. I comb my fingers through Abdiel's silky curls as his lips find my nipple, sucking it into his warm mouth. My back arches off the ground, going to him as a moan escapes my lips.

"Fuck..." A grunt comes from Drake as he kneels behind Abdiel, shoving his sweats all the way down and yanking them off his feet.

He takes Abdiel's cock in his hand and tugs it slowly while Abdiel's mouth worships my tits.

I'm simply flabbergasted at the sheer size of all three dicks around me. It's nothing shy of a miracle from the heavens.

Abdiel's lips make a slow descent down my body, kissing and nipping all over my shivering flesh, and I'm so distracted by how good it feels that by the time my eyes are searching for Drake again, I find him with his mouth wrapped around Darian's cock.

Darian is lying right next to me, biting his lip with his hands tangled in his brother's hair as Drake slurps him back.

My core clenches hard while I watch. I've never seen something like this in front of my own two eyes, and it's probably one of the most arousing things I've ever witnessed.

I can't get enough. That is, until I feel Abdiel's tongue circle my clit.

A loud whimper escapes me, and I actually slap my hand over my mouth. Darian and Drake both peer at me. Then they chuckle.

"Sorry." Abdiel grins from between my legs. "I've never done this before."

"Scoot over, kid." Drake inches off Darian, moving up next to Abdiel. "I haven't done this is a while, but I'll show you my moves."

"How long has it been?" Darian teases, heavy lids lazy in his arousal as he presses his head back into the grass.

"Mmm... like a year." Drake's breaths tickle my soaking wet flesh until I'm trembling.

His thoughts are on a memory... of him going down on a very familiar blonde.

Abdiel's and my eyes fling to Darian.

"You went down on my wife?" Darian gasps an outraged chuckle.

"Guilty," Drake sings, casually, his strong hands rubbing my thighs, massaging them.

"I should cock-slap you for that," Darian laughs.

"You probably should." Drake winks at our King.

"You *definitely* should," Abdiel and I say at the same time.

"Okay, enough chitter chatter." Darian shoves Drake.

Drake grabs Abdiel's jaw and kisses him. The way their mouths move together is nothing shy of hypnotic. I could watch them make out for hours.

But then both of their faces are between my thighs, right next to each other, and they're both kissing all over, my inner thighs, then my pussy. My legs are spread wide enough to fit them both, that balmy flush still burning up my face as I watch Drake's long tongue slink out to graze my clit. Then Abdiel's does the same.

I whine, fingers on each hand in both of their hair while they French kiss each other over my clit, tongues lapping and circling. Drake goes in for some suction that crosses my eyes. Then Abdiel does it. Drake sticks his tongue inside me. Then Abdiel.

It's like they're playing a game of Horse on my vagina.

Meanwhile, they're writhing together, rubbing their erections into one another, muscles touching, large, masculine hands fondling everywhere. It's amazingly hot, watching these two men together while they're eating me, savoring me like a delicious delicacy.

Drake pulls away and leaves Abdiel to feast on me while he goes back to Darian. My eyes can't decide where they'd rather be, on the beautiful boy eating me out for the first time ever, or on the sexy as fuck dude deep-throating the other sexy as fuck dude until he's practically choking.

Abdiel leaves me at the brink of orgasm, and I whine, watching as he comes up, wiping his mouth with the back of his hand.

"Kiss me," he growls, not giving me a moment before he's sucking at my lips. "Taste how delicious you are, baby."

I'm melting everywhere as his long, thick erection settles over me, slipping and sliding in my arousal.

"Fuck me," I plead into his mouth, and we both purr.

"You sure?" His hand glides up to cup my breast, thumb brushing my pert nipple.

"Positive." I grab at his firm ass, trying to get him inside me faster.

Darian's panting distracts me for a moment, and I peek over to see Drake's fingers between his legs while he sucks and sucks, all the while watching Abdiel and me like a live show.

There's so much going on, I don't know how I'm even functioning.

Abdiel presses the tip of his cock up to me, sinking into my body, slow, careful, and treasuring. His eyelids flutter as he drops his forehead onto my shoulder.

"Motherfuck, that feels good..." he rumbles, shoving inches into me until I'm breathless.

The sensation of having him inside is unlike anything I've felt before. It feels... right. More *right* than anything ever has. Like we're Legos, snapping together in just the perfect shape.

Abdiel pushes into me, deeper and deeper, my moans and whimpers saturating the air as his big, perfectly rigid cock fills me, all the way up.

The smooth feel of his skin inside reminds me that we're bare, unprotected. But then that doesn't matter, because they're all safe here.

We're not on the Outside, with death, disease, and consequence.

We're The Principality. And everything is perfect.

"Fuck... yes..." I sigh as he bottoms out, clawing at his shoulder blades.

His mouth moves onto my breasts while he thrusts, in and out, stroking himself in me, over and over, building up a rhythm in friction that has me soaring. I'm moving up to the edge of a climax already when I see movement.

Drake has pulled himself away from Darian, who's looking all sorts of restless and flushed, moving over to Abdiel. He drops kisses all over Abdiel's back and shoulders as Darian hands him a small bottle. He opens it and pours out some liquid, rubbing it onto his erection. Then he swipes his fingers between the cheeks of Abdiel's ass.

"Good God..." Abdiel whimpers, pushing his hips up on a backstroke, giving Drake more access.

Drake grins, humming as he does something that swells Abdiel's cock like crazy inside me. I think I have a guess as to what it is...

"That feel good, little mouse?" The sound of Drake's voice alone is enough to have me shuddering, but Abdiel's dick is basically living on my G-spot at the moment.

"Yes yes yes..." Abdiel cries. "*More.*"

I'm desperate to see what's happening, peering around Abdiel's torso to watch Drake's movements. I hear someone's thoughts, about fingers, and Abdiel is shivering.

Drake works his fingers in Abdiel's ass while Abdiel rocks between my thighs, spread-eagle and fucking loving this, until he removes them. Abdiel whines at the loss, until Drake scoots up behind him.

"Jesus, I'm gonna come soon…" I mewl, watching with wide eyes as Drake kisses, licks and bites Abdiel's neck and shoulders, taking his cock in his hand and pressing it in.

I can tell the moment he slips inside Abdiel's ass, because Abdiel melts over me like a slab of butter on a stack of pancakes.

His arms are resting on either side of me in the dirt, and he's rutting into me, his cock so deep inside me, I'm sure it's touching things, while Drake holds his hips and pushes deeper.

Abdiel releases a desperately hoarse noise into my neck, his lips kissing, teeth biting at my flesh as Drake gives him more, and more. When he turns his face, I see him looking at Darian, biting his lip, eyes locked on our King while he's sandwiched between Drake and me.

Darian scoots over and grabs his face, kissing him in such a deeply sensual way, swallowing up all his moans, pants and purrs.

"Abdiel," I whisper, hoarse myself from all this lust and hedonistic activity happening between us.

"Mmm," he responds with a hum, sucking on Darian's lips while he thrusts into me at Drake's pump into him.

"Give the King his praise," I tell him, and he and Darian pull apart, looking up at me with mischievous sparkles in their eyes.

Darian gets up onto his knees by my side, and Abdiel lifts himself just enough to wrap his lips around the swollen head of Darian's massive cock. Immediately, Darian's eyes roll back in his head, and he groans.

As the rest of us do.

I can't believe what's happening right now. I'm on the brink, ready to tumble at any moment. But honestly, I think the King might break first.

He grasps Abdiel's jaw, thrusting into his mouth, steadily, gazing with the hungriest of eyes while Abdiel's cheeks hollow, and he sucks and sucks.

"That's it, my beautiful prince," Darian's deep voice rumbles, eyes flicking to Drake, watching while he strokes his cock into his prince from behind. "You love being right in the middle of all this, don't you?"

Abdiel moans on his dick, cheeks flushed, eyes drunk with lust as he gazes up at Darian.

"Drink me, baby," Darian whispers, his thumb tracing the stretch of Abdiel's mouth while his cock spears his throat. He goes so deep, Abdiel's head rests on his pelvis, Darian's fingers gripping those blonde curls as he snaps. "Fuck yes... You're making me come, sweet prince."

Abdiel's barely even thrusting into me anymore, but it doesn't matter. It feels divine as I watch Darian's abs contracting, his seed spilling in Abdiel's mouth. And I watch Abdiel's throat adjust, swallowing every drop.

That's it for me.

"Fuck fuck *fuck!*" I gasp, my inner walls clenching on Abdiel's cock while my orgasm crests and breaks, a tidal wave of pleasure splashing me in cool sensation.

Abdiel sucks up Darian's cock and lets out a hoarse groan, grabbing Darian's hand in his. Drake spreads him open, fucking deep, hips rippling.

Abdiel shifts his hips at the last second, pulling himself out of me while I'm still pulsing, his cock bursting all over my thighs and my navel while he cries, "God... oh God oh God... *yes...*"

We're suddenly a big pile of sweaty limbs as everyone sort of falls apart. Drake pushes Abdiel forward into the cum covering both of us. His dick, which is still hard, brushes over my clit, sending a wave of aftershocks through my body, like a million little bolts of electric pleasure.

"I'm gonna come in you, little mouse," Drake hisses, grabbing Abdiel by the throat, holding him firm.

Abdiel's face is dazed and drunk, but he breathes, "Give it to me deep, Serpent."

Drake whimpers, a sound so foreign on him, it's unbelievably sexy, his forehead dropping forward onto Abdiel's shoulder while he hums that he's *coming.*

He sings it on repeat while the rest of us moan and mumble, clutching one another, the pleasure remaining full and thick all the while. I watch Drake closely as he pours inside Abdiel, and I can't fathom this level of sexual gratification. Feeling it while watching it...

I've never had group sex before, but it's one of those things that will surely ruin you. *This* is an addiction.

I want this eternal.

"Me too," Darian sighs next to me, nestling up to my side. I rest my head on his shoulder.

"Me three," Abdiel whispers, curling up on both of us as Drake pulls out of him.

The three of us look up at Drake while he catches his breath, black hair falling in his snake eyes.

"Well?" Darian growls.

Drake smirks. "Me four."

The two of them chuckle as he crashes down on Darian, knocking the wind out of him until he goes *oof.*

I can't help but giggle and bite my lip as I watch them.

They're here, together. They're finally *here.*

Maybe *I* made that happen...

DRAKE

The trilling song of morning birds rustles me from my slumber. And I'm instantly hit with the feminine scent of flowers, and sex, and the earth.

Lifting my head a bit, I notice that we're still in the clearing, surrounded by the pale glow of early dusk. My first thought is to check for the black rock.

Peering over, I don't see it. It's not there.

I'm not sure what that means...

It's not like it ever truly leaves. It comes and goes as it needs to. But maybe Darian was right... Instead of feeding it blood and death, we fed it sex and love. Lust and pleasure and good things. Could it make a difference? *Maybe.*

Either way, regardless of the sacrifice I made, the sacrifices we all made, this spot will always be filled with the unknown.

And the thing about the unknown is that it's inherently balanced. Good and bad are always possible. Darkness and light... it doesn't matter.

But what *does* matter is that these people made a sacrifice for me last night. They agreed that I no longer need to be the martyr. Abdiel saw the truth of what happened, when I watched his parents jump to their deaths. And he doesn't blame me.

Maybe I still blame myself... I'm not sure that will ever go. But he loves me anyway. And I love him...

I love Darian.

I think I could even love Rhiannon someday. She's a new addition to our world, only present for a few days. It will take us all time to get used to her, but she fits. And if Darian approves, well... who are we to argue with the King?

Speaking of the girl, her tits are smooshing into my stomach, which makes me chuckle to myself. Glancing down, I see her unruly head of pinkish blonde hair resting on my chest. There's a blanket tangled around us—she and Abdiel brought it, thank God, because otherwise, we'd be out here, covered by nothing but our good intentions.

Her face lifts, wide eyes twinkling up at me. I can't do much more than blink.

A deep groan pulls my attention from the wonder shimmering in those teal irises, and I peer left. A chill of arousal zips through my stomach.

Not more than five feet from where we're lying, Darian is on his knees in the dirt, Abdiel behind him, buried deep.

Abdiel is holding Darian's throat with one hand, gripping him by the pectoral with the other. His chest to Darian's back while he whispers things in my brother's ear, plowing him slowly, ferociously consecrated in his thrusts.

I can barely fathom that the kid was a virgin a few weeks ago, because now he's a beast. A forest god, built for fucking and cuddling. The thought widens my smile.

I love my little mouse.

"Love you, too," he pants, voice hoarse in between the slaps of his pelvis on Darian's ass.

"Oh, *God*..." Darian's forehead hits the grass. "Fucking turn me out, baby."

My cock is like steel.

"The sex drive on you guys, I swear to God..." Rhiannon whispers, tone awestruck. I glance back down at her, studying her profile while she watches the King being fucked into the ground by our beautiful servant Prince.

"Does it intimidate you?" I rumble, and her eyes find mine.

Her head shakes in an adorably innocent display that reminds me of Abdiel, that first day, when he came into my office. As curious as a kitten, ready and waiting for his Ecdysis.

Rhiannon was the same way, except she's much less subservient than Abdiel.

She's a spitfire. Something tells me we'll be witnessing it in action more in the near future.

"I like hearing how you think about me." She reaches up to touch my lips with her fingers. Then she shifts on top of me. "And I really like this feeling while it's happening."

The slit of her pussy drags on my erection, causing it to throb and fill rapidly. We didn't have much more than a few cloths and some water to clean up with, so she's still soaking wet, even more so with the show our boys are putting on.

Making a decision, I flip Rhiannon onto her back, and she gasps, chomping on her lower lip as she gazes up at me. "Can you hear what I'm thinking right now?" I hover and swipe her lips with my tongue. Her nipples perk on my chest.

"Oh yea... I can," she purrs, bringing her hands up my sides, scratching me with her claws. It gives me chills in the best way. "I want you to feel me inside, too."

A growl rises in my chest while I writhe into her, the juices from her sweet little cunt lubing me up. My lips brush over hers and she mewls, gripping my arms as I reach between us, pressing the head of my dick into her tight, warm entrance.

"God, yes..." I breathe. "So warm and wet for my cock."

"Drake," she whines, nails grazing all over the muscles in my shoulders, arms and chest.

"Yes, kitten?" I press a soft kiss on her lower lip, pushing my dick into her, only one inch. She moans.

"That day... in your office," she stutters between uneven breaths. "You were going to tell me something, but you never finished. You said, *you need to learn...* and then you left."

I hum, my hand coming up to her perky young tits, cupping and squeezing them tenderly, loving the sound of her purring while I tend to her nipples, my cock sliding into her, just one more inch.

"You need to learn," I drop my mouth to her neck, kissing her pulse in between words, "That to gain control means to give it up."

Granting her a good thrust, I fill her with every inch of my swollen cock, and she gasps out loud, marking my chest with her nails. I lick a line up her throat while I pull back and surge in, holding her hip as she wraps her legs around my waist.

"The most perfect bliss of control comes when you let go."

Pressing my lips to hers, I kiss her hungrily while my hips move, building, rippling as I work my cock in her. I can't keep my eyes off how gorgeous she is, how delicate and beautiful, lying beneath me, submitting to my animalistic need to fuck her good and deep.

"Yea, kitten girl," I pant. "Just like that."

"That's... fucking... *hot*..." Darian's voice comments, unsteady with Abdiel's thrusts. I peek over to find him watching us, but only for a moment before his eyes roll back and he gasps, "Holy fuck, I'm coming, baby."

His cock is thick and full, heavy as it erupts, cum jetting all over the ground while Abdiel holds him close, grunting and growling that he's coming, too.

"I'm filling you up, my King..." Abdiel whines, biting Darian's shoulder.

"Fill me deep, gorgeous."

"So fuckin deep."

Just watching them alone is enough to have me at the edge already. Their hair wet with sweat, dirt-covered skin glistening, highlighting all the muscles. Their bodies are so different, both incredibly masculine in their own ways. Darian, older and all bulk strength. Abdiel, younger and cut up, sinews and lines, like a statue made of marble.

I watch them for another few moments while they hold each other and breathe, my eyes locking on Abdiel's cock as he pulls it out of Darian's ass.

It makes me tremble. He fucked me earlier, my brother, my King... For the first time. *It was like a dream.*

My attention returns to Rhiannon, who was watching the boys as well. Grasping her face, I kiss her again, starved, panting into her mouth while I lift and angle her to get as deep as possible. There's something so primitive about fucking on the ground, surrounded by dirt and grass, leaves and stones. It's not elegant or romantic.

It brings us back to our roots, animals that we are.

Rhiannon's moans and cries are like a sweet melody to my ears. I love the contrast of being with a woman, versus two men. Forgetting gender altogether, we're all so different. There's so much we can do together...

"Yes, *Drake*," she squeals. "Fuck me... I'm so close."

Grabbing a handful of her ass, I plunge into her, feeling her pussy dripping with wetness. It's beyond intense... I'm growing closer myself.

Darian and Abdiel are watching us intently, wide eyes and thoughts echoing the same fascination I was thinking a second ago. Darian is on his back with Abdiel curled up on him like a pet, his hand on Darian's dick, caressing it.

"Fuck." My head falls forward as I wrap Rhiannon's long locks around my fist, pulling her mouth up to mine. "I want you to come on my cock."

She lets out a whimper, practically losing her voice from all the screaming she's done tonight. Her insides begin to quaver on my shaft, and I keep thrusting, keep stroking myself between her tight, plush walls as they grip me and don't let go.

"I'm gonna come." Her back arches.

"Come for me, kitten."

"Come on his big dick, Rhi," Abdiel murmurs while licking and sucking at Darian's neck.

"Come for my sexy Serpent," Darian growls. He reaches out and runs his fingers along my side, casually close to my ass.

It gets me, just like he always does. My balls draw up, tightening as Rhiannon squeals that she's coming all over my cock. Her walls clench over and over on my erection, and it's everything I can do to keep riding her through it.

And then I yank my cock out of her just in time to erupt, fucking my fist while my orgasm shoots from my dick all over her stomach, spraying up to her tits. I milk it all out, then I push back into her. Her lips quiver while she comes again, thighs tightening on my waist, holding me close to her.

My head is spinning, all the heavy breaths singing through the trees. The leaves sway and dance around us, the forest taking a long, collective sigh as the ground beneath us pumps like my heartbeat while it steadies.

Rolling onto my back, I bring Rhiannon on top of me to get her off the ground. Her face is flushed beyond belief as she looks down at me, her thoughts a giant mass of fuzz, which has me smirking.

Then she smirks. I let a chuckle slip, and she does the same. Holding her face, I kiss her lips softly, glancing over as we pull apart to find Abdiel and Darian making out.

I exhale a steady stream of air. "This is wild."

"It really is," Rhiannon murmurs, pushing my hair away from my forehead. "I feel like I just won the lottery."

I can't help but laugh out loud at that. And I catch Darian and Abdiel chuckling through their kisses. They break and turn to face us, scooting closer. Rhiannon grabs the blanket and uses it to cover us all.

"Is it bad that I really want a shower and a bed?" She whines. And the three of us laugh even harder.

"You'll get used to the woods, princess," Darian sighs, brushing her hair with his fingers.

"She really is a princess," Abdiel grins. "From a castle and everything."

Rhiannon sticks her tongue out at Abdiel. "Screw that castle. I'll take fucking in the grass any day."

"That's what I'm talking about," Darian laughs.

"Oh my God, wait until you fuck in the lake," I rumble, adjusting her on top of me.

Her eyes land on mine as she gapes at me. And Abdiel does, too.

"You guys fuck in the lake?" Abdiel gasps.

"It's gonna be a great summer, Prince Gorgeous." Darian pulls Abdiel's lips to his.

"Why are they so cute?" Rhiannon scrunches her nose. It's adorable, like a little bunny.

I tug her chin. "They're the sweet ones."

"And you?" She asks, mouth hovering over mine.

"I'm a little more wicked."

CHAPTER
THIRTY FIVE

RHIANNON

t's time.

It tells me that. The voice is deep, penetrative.

It calls, like an inner beckoning.

It *is* time.

Rolling out from under the blanket and Drake's heavy arm, I shift to my feet.

It tells me to put my dress on, so I do. But not my shoes. *They're Gem's.*

My mind is clear in the pale morning fog. The breeze brushes calm across my skin as I walk.

It's alright, It tells me. *You're loved. You're beautiful. This is necessary.*

In a voice that sounds almost like Drake's, only darker, more cavernous, it repeats his words; *The most perfect bliss of control comes when you let go.*

Let... Go...

Exiting the clearing, I glance back once more at the guys; those three gorgeous souls.

They love you, It whispers.

I think I love them, too.

I feel certain that in a different place, I'm going to live with them forever. We'll work and love and exist together... Start a family.

Finding this land, the Expanse, and all the spectacular things they've made here... It changed everything for me. Last night was the ultimate awakening. And after my realizations with Darian, then the

They're whole, as well. Together.

The three of them are *finally* together, and I think I helped that happen. I did good for It.

In return, my entire life will be different, starting right now.

Just not right *here*.

The black rock isn't visibly there, where they sleep. But it *is*.

Turning, I walk slowly, stepping softly to mind my bare feet. It reminds me of Abdiel, that morning after we first met.

He's such a perfect human.

The closure, the acceptance he found last night in the deaths of his parents…

His Ecdysis is complete.

And so will be mine.

Wandering over to the edge of the cliff, I close my eyes. I take a deep breath. The wind brushes through my hair.

And I smile.

DRAKE

I awaken at the feel of a shift beneath my skin.

Blinking groggily over my tired eyes, I try to remember where I am.

Right. I'm still on the mountain. In the clearing.

We had fully planned to go back down after fooling around some more, but then we passed out. And I get it. I'm exhausted from all the *activities*.

Rolling onto my side, I face Darian and Abdiel, both sleeping soundly, wearing each other like a second skin. My mouth twists at its corners.

I love them.

The things we accepted last night… The truths we found together and the sacrifices we made together…

This is how it's supposed to be.

This is the balance. *Our* order. It makes sense. It feels *right*.

My King, and my Prince… and…

411

My head whips around.

I don't see Rhiannon anywhere.

Sitting up slowly, my eyes scan all over the general vicinity, wondering if maybe she had to pee or something.

But I don't see her.

Rising on shaky legs, muscles strained all over my body, I twirl and twirl around the clearing.

The black rock isn't visible... And neither is Rhiannon.

My pulse is picking up fast, thumping in my neck as my chest tightens.

Tightens as if someone's holding me.

I glance down at Darian. His eyelids are fluttering in his sleep.

He's mumbling out nonsense.

At the snap of a twig, my head shifts. Thirty feet off in the distance, at the overlook, strawberry blonde hair floats in the breeze.

My eyes widen. My stomach plummets.

She smiles.

She steps...

Over the edge.

My hand reaches out.

No!

My heart screams.

I dive forward, reaching... But I'm too far.

And she's already gone.

No no no! I cry.

Droplets of red fall onto the forest floor.

ABDIEL

My eyes snap open at the sounds of aggrieved screaming.

The ground beneath my stiff body is moving, rumbling. The wails I hear echo in my mind.

Forcing myself to wake faster, I rub my eyes and look up to find Drake weeping tears of blood.

My awareness kicks in and I jump, crawling over to him.

"Drake! What's wrong?" I gasp, checking him all over.

He's shivering, still naked and covered in dirt. Shaking through violent sobs.

My face turns left, then right.

Something is *wrong*.

"Where's Rhiannon?"

Drake wipes at the red from his face, streaking over his pale skin. And he slides his snake eyes up to mine.

He says nothing. But I gulp, my heart crumbling inside me.

I already know.

Why...?

My lower lip quivers as my head wobbles, over and over and over. My eyes sweep to the cliff.

My mind fumbles with images of her trying to go over last time.

I swallow, my throat dry.

The wind blows.

No... she wouldn't.

Why??

Standing, I stalk over to my clothes, dressing fast. Drake stands up slowly and saunters over to me, sniffling. "What are you doing?"

"I'm going down there. Maybe she's..." My voice cuts into a desperate whimper I try to cover up with my hands on my face.

Darian is still asleep... But when I glance down at him, I find him shifting all around. His fingers are digging into the dirt.

My eyes linger on him for a moment, as I speak to Drake, "Where is *It*?"

They lift to his, and he somberly shakes his head.

Darian thrashes onto his back, arching as his eyes roll into his skull. A sudden blast of frigid air bursts through the trees, and the scent of musky flowers fills the air.

My forehead is lined in my confusion. *What the hell is going on here??*

Dropping to my knees, I shake Darian. "Wake up! Darian, baby, wake up, please! Something terrible has happened..."

Darian's eyes snap open fast. His irises are black, like charcoal. Obsidian.

He sits up gradually and closes them again, rubbing with his fingers.

And when he reopens his eyes, they're crystalline blue once more.

I peer at Drake for a moment, and he at me.

413

"Darian... my King..." I whisper, reaching out to brush his neck. "Are you alright?"

He shakes his head slowly, peering up at me. "She's gone... Isn't she?"

My stomach ripples in despair as I stand up, not wanting to believe it.

I *refuse*.

"Let's go. Now," I bark. "We have to get to the ravine."

Neither of them say a word, their minds equally quiet as we all redress fast, then stomp back down the trail. We descend the mountain in the direction of the gully.

Where my parents were found.

My pulse is jumping inside my body, fear and devastation bubbling beneath the surface. I don't want to think that this could happen...

I don't want this to be *real*.

When we finally reach the ravine, we walk down into it, only a bit of mud lingering within the gully. We trudge through it, growing closer and closer...

And as we approach, the *exact same spot*, I'm twelve years old again.

Gazing down at the body of my friend, anguish reaches inside me and rips away all the comforts from just an hour ago.

Everything I thought we were building to. The *good*, not the evil.

I turn and throw up on the ground next to my shoes.

"Baby," Darian rushes, grabbing me in his arms. He hugs onto me hard, holding my head in his hand while I cry. "Shh, my sweet Prince. I have you."

For many long, sorrowful minutes, we stand, just holding each other and crying.

Next to the body of our fourth.

Our wails tie together, Darian's and mine, aching in loss.

She could have been so much to us...

She was.

When I finally lift my face from the crook of Darian's neck, I see Drake, lying in the mud by Rhiannon's body.

He brings a razorblade to his chest, just above his heart, and slices.

The red seeps from his pale skin, rushing over into the dirt. He stares up at the sky.

Imbalanced.

414

DARIAN

I'm asking Mother *why*…

We've been sitting in the ravine for over an hour. My face is tight, eyes burning from all the crying. Tears long since having dried up.

Mother… I know nothing happens by accident. I know that. But why…?

Why, after what we just realized *together*, would Rhiannon be taken?

Why, when we discovered we're meant to be in transformation together?

Rhiannon was just like me in many ways… We bonded; linked ourselves together.

Was this to punish me, Mother? Was this to teach me a lesson?

A raven squawks above my head.

Evil does atone, Your Highness.

My jaw clenches, fingers still brushing through Abdiel's soft curls. He's devastated, understandably. I think Drake is, too.

He hasn't said a word so far.

And I'm… well, I'm confused. Confounded.

I feel… guilty.

"Don't," Abdiel whispers, his voice hoarse. "Don't blame yourself. Either of you."

He glances at up Drake, who's propped up against the edge of the gully, dried blood smeared on his chest.

"Mourn, but don't fear this," Abdiel mumbles.

I blink down at him, sliding my thumb along his puffy lower lip. His tone is lined with despondence, but he's still trying to be strong. I hear him doing so, and I just can't believe how blessed I've been to have him.

You're such a gift, Prince Abdiel.

He leans his head into my touch, exhausted and grieving. My neck rolls toward my Serpent.

Baby… come to me. Please.

415

I witness him taking in a deep breath before he stands up and wanders over to where Abdiel and I are seated. He plops down at my side, immediately melting himself into me.

"There was… A different version of the future with her in it," he sighs. "I think we would have liked it."

I nod. "Me, too."

And we sit with this, this *new* present, a different future, until dark. Until it's time to move on… In infinite purpose.

That imperfect order.

EPILOGUE

The entire Regnum is gathered by Lake Willow, all in black.

We will mourn, but we won't fear it. It's just what we do. We move on, we persist...

We *live.*

Members of the Tribe push the wooden pyre into the lake. Once it's a few feet out, Lorn tosses a bottle with a flaming rag onto it. The bottle smashes on the pyre, and the flames begin to spread.

A tear falls from my eye as Darian curls his arm around my waist. I rest my head on his shoulder.

We don't have the energy to pretend anymore. We don't have the energy to *hide* anymore.

As we watch the body of our friend burn, I begin to sing.

Hallelujah.

My harmonies travel through the air, swirling up with the smoke. I give this to my friend Rhiannon...

I sing for her.

When my song is done, Darian, slips his fingers into mine. My face turns up to his, and we share a thought.

It's what she would have wanted...

Darian nods to me, then to Drake at my right. *She wanted me to tell the truth... I'm going to do it. For her.* He blinks. *And for both of you. My gifts, my treasures... My everythings.*

I can do nothing more that gawk at him as he turns to face the crowd in black.

"My Regnum," Darian's voice booms as he looks out over all the faces of his people, gathered under solemn circumstances. What little chatter there was immediately silences. "My family. In the spirit of transparency... What with losing our new friend, I must tell you something... I've been living a lie."

A few puzzled murmurs come from the crowd, all their thoughts reflecting concern and confusion.

"Rhiannon and I had a heart-to-heart, just the other day, before her untimely passing," Darian goes on, his tone reflective. "She wanted to be one of us, and she would have been. But unfortunately, she was taken, for reasons we aren't meant to know. Not yet, anyway. Still, she is one of us, present or not, she's *here*. And so, in her honor, I'm going to tell you some things I had promised her, and Drake and Abdiel, that I would bring forth."

He takes a deep breath, and I *feel* Drake shivering at my side.

"Twenty-five years ago, when Drake and I left our home and came here to these woods we would inevitably claim, I was struggling with

418

many inner demons. We left because we had to... Because I'd been sexually assaulted by our foster father."

The crowd gasps, a collective breath of outrage.

"I've made my peace with it," he continues. "It's been many years of healing, most of which was done by you all. And the ultimate knowledge that I was avenged." Darian's face turns to Drake, whose snake eyes are stuck right on our King.

The love I hear in their thoughts warms my chest immensely. Since the moment I saw them together months ago, when I spied on them in the lounge, I knew they were completely *mad* for one another. It just took a little puzzle of our own to get them to snap into place. We're like a Rubik's cube, the four... now I guess *three* of us.

It's as bewildering as it is brilliant.

"Drake took the life of that evil man," Darian says these words with nothing but gratefulness and admiration. "He did it to protect me, as he's been doing ever since. He's dedicated his life to protecting us from the evils of the world. It's our turn to repay the favor."

Darian looks over the crowd, possibly to assess their feelings on what he's just said. And I'm not surprised to find everyone sufficiently on board, regardless of what it means.

They're here. We all are.

"I want you all to know that starting today, starting right now, I'm going to give you full transparency. Because I can't expect you to be truthful to me in all things if I can't do the same for you. So here it goes..."

Darian peers over my head at his brother once more. Drake's lips curl; subtly, of course. But still, it's quite the sight to see.

"Drake is my lover," Darian sighs. "He has been since long before any of you came here. Since long before The Principality was even an idea. He is my foster brother, yes. But I'm in love with him, and I always have been."

The crowd is much quieter than I expected, but from the thoughts, I'm not getting as much pure shock as I expected. There's some of it, sure, but there are also some people are thinking it's about time he came out with it, which makes me chuckle.

"It was wrong of me to marry, knowing I could never love any of my wives the way I love him, and for that, I'm eternally sorry. My wives and I will begin a divorce process. And I'm sure they'll be quite relieved about it."

He lets a little chuckle slip as he glances at the wives. None of them are upset, or scorned. They all get it. They've long since picked up on Darian's secret need for dick in a relationship, so there's no shock from that side.

Lauris grins at Darian, before pulling Gem into her side.

The crowd is full of smiles, and nods. *Acceptance*, which is a beautiful thing to witness. But we're not done yet...

"So... that said, here's where it gets a little stickier." Darian rubs the back of his neck. "In the interest of no more secrets... I have more than just the one partner. Drake and I have been seeing Abdiel Harmony for a few weeks now. Another thing we're very happy about."

I squeeze my King's hand in mine, and he peeks down at me. I show him a loving smile before my eyes begin to shift at the startled thoughts from some of my family.

This is the revelation getting murmurs of shock. I guess we were pretty good at sneaking around because not one person seems to have predicted this one, except maybe the wives.

"You're the scandal, little mouse," Drake whispers into my ear until I shiver. I shove him, and he snickers.

"The point of all this is that I can't hide anymore. And we shouldn't have to hide anything," Darian's voice thunders. "Secrets were never meant to be a part of this family, this life we've built here on *our* land. Things got muddied up for a while... It was my fault. For not being honest. For not seeing the truths I'd been blinded to."

He looks to Drake, and I hear them sharing a wordless conversation. Drake still insists that he's as much at fault as Darian, if not more. *Our Serpent... He just loves to hold that burden.*

We'll keep trying to break him of the habit, especially since we've agreed to carry it with him.

He's *ours*. Not just evil, or just good. He's the serpent in white. Our holy protector.

"No more hiding. No more shying from it," Darian says, firm and demanding. It's a call to action. "I am your leader, yes. But I want you by my side in everything. We're all part of this transformation together. The strength we hold... it cannot be rivaled. We are... The Principality."

The echo of his final word is barely done breaking as the crowd cheers. People clap and hoot and whistle. The noise is unlike anything I've heard before.

Their applause carries through the air, over the lake.

Darian grins, peeking at Drake, then me. And then the three of us look out whimsically over the water, at the fire that's almost burnt out.

Rhiannon will remain with us in spirit, I know she will. She's a part of this land forever. A part of our hearts... Of our transformation.

And the *four* of us are ready. Ready for whatever comes next... To defend our land, to face any truth we have to. To live, and learn, and love.

This family right here, these partners... They're all we need.

Because today is here... and it's so damn special.

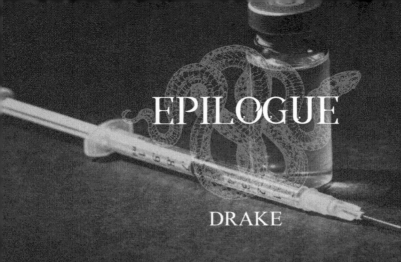

EPILOGUE

DRAKE

Harvest is upon us.

My feelings for this time of year are a double-edged sword. I love it because our hard work pays off. It's a sense of success that gives me extreme joy.

But then of course, the real work begins with making sure distribution is handled properly. It's not my *favorite* thing.

This year, however, I have help.

About a week after Rhiannon's death, I was called up to the clearing. The forces brought me up there; *Mother* did. To tell me something.

I had untapped potential before my eyes.

Lauris is our new *CEO*, if we believed in corporate titles, which we do not. But still, I have her now, and it's been a huge help.

It was Rhiannon who came to me in my mind and told me to believe in someone else, the way I was going to believe in her. Lauris has so much knowledge, so much experience from her time as an Outsider. As it turns out, she's been eager to take on more work around here. She's loyal, trustworthy, and smart as all hell. The perfect person to take over business operations and the trade exporting. It's wonderful.

And it means I can focus on production and creation. The shit I *love*.

The harvest festival is happening in only a week, and the entire Expanse is buzzing with excitement. The rest of Darian's exes are still handling the planning and execution of the whole thing, Gem and Alissa, mainly. Emithel has been commissioned to start painting as a job, which she's more than excited for. And Kiara is dating Perry. From what I understand, they're smitten.

The divorce went through a few weeks back, and honestly, it's been smooth sailing. They're good girls. And really, bless them for taking some burden off of our shoulders, in their own ways.

My stress is understandable, what with overseeing the Tribe and the lab during our busiest season. But Darian's stress comes from a place of protection for his family, so you can't fault the guy. We had a blissful summer, and he's convinced the forces at work up on the mountain will require further sacrifice for the harvest. He's had a few dreams about it... And he's been reading a lot.

Either way, it's nothing we can't figure out, as a collective. The three of us, along with the rest of the Regnum, are pretty amazingly equipped to run this place together. It just seems to work, and I love it.

When Rhiannon died, she took the future I thought I wanted with her, leaving me with the future I *have*. Even if I weren't positive this is how Mother wants things, I would still feel it; crave it in my bones.

Abdiel, Darian, and myself together... We fit. It just works. I sort of always knew it would, but I was afraid before. It took the arrival of a sweet little stray to show me what I have.

That was the purpose, the whole time. To *show* us...

I will die to protect them, *no matter what*. And knowing I won't be the only one sacrificing gives me more peace than I could have imagined.

We're a threesome. *My King and my little mouse.*

I never thought monogamy was necessarily for me, so having two partners is perfect. When I need to get away, to be alone with my thoughts, Darian has Abdiel. And when I need my alone time with either of them, they support that. We make it work as well as we can, knowing it'll never be perfect.

But the imperfections make me want it that much more. For the first time in twenty-five years, I'm done running.

Speaking of being settled, tonight is a big night. It's the opening of the Expanse's first ever restaurant.

Yes, you heard that right. We have an honest to Mother *business* opening here.

Of course, it's only for us. But we made it, so it's awesome. And it's Abdiel's, which makes it even more special.

He named it *The White Snake*; a little cafe-style place. Our construction team spent all summer building it, while Abdiel was working scrupulously on creating dishes and a killer menu, along with hiring a crew. It took a lot of his time and work, a lot of effort in trade to get him everything he needed, but it's finally done, and the grand opening is tonight.

We're all very excited.

It'll be nice to have a chill evening, celebrating Abdiel. We've all been working so hard lately. I can't wait to relax with a drink and some good food, prepared by our little chef.

Speaking of which, I hear him coming. My dick is already hard, remembering how we woke up this morning, with his cock in Darian and mine in him. I swear, there are no shortage of available scenarios in this setup. The opportunities are endless.

And very entertaining.

Abdiel saunters into my bedroom, smirking at me like the sexy little mouse he is. And then Darian swoops in behind him. They both stalk past me, falling onto my bed.

I moved out of my cabin weeks ago. I repurposed it and took up residence here in the Den with my men. We each have our own bedrooms for when we need space, but we typically use Darian's as our master. *Makes sense.*

I give the two of them a curious look. "What's going on here?"

Abdiel grins, lying back, peering at me upside down. "We have an idea."

Darian wraps an arm around Abdiel's waist. "For old time's sake."

"Listening," I hum.

"Empyrean."

Ah.

We haven't used Empyrean in a while, since it was revealed that the telekinesis it brings doesn't actually wear off.

I always knew that whole notion was a mental thing. Because I've had telekinetic abilities since the first time I used Empyrean, twenty years ago. But back then, it was just another way for me to keep Darian close. He convinced himself it wore off, and I didn't argue. Because he needed me, and I liked that.

Little did I realize at the time, he always needed me, drugs or no drugs. He still does, and it's a great feeling.

That said, the high from Empyrean is a whirlwind. It's more intense, more powerful than any other we've experienced from anything I've synthesized with the trumpets, any DMT-like things

424

I've created.

Empyrean is in a category all its own.

And they want some...

"I'm down." I shrug. "But it's in the lab. I'd have to go get it."

"Way ahead of you." Darian smirks, pulling a couple vials out of his pocket.

"You stole from me, my King?" I gasp teasingly. "How purely wicked of you."

"You gonna punish me?" His tongue swipes his bottom lip, and my dick stirs again.

How I could possibly still be getting erections at this point is beyond me. Lately, it seems like I spend a majority of my days twisted up in some sexual position.

Not complaining. Not even a little.

Darian gives me the needles and vials and we do our thing, shooting up together and lying in the bed, giggling at all the crazy things we're seeing.

"How's this for solitude, your highness?" I mumble to Darian, taking his hand in mine and bringing it to my lips.

"More than I could ever ask for," he whispers.

Something in his brain catches my attention. And I crawl on top of him.

"Okay, listen to this memory, little mouse," I tell Abdiel.

And my mind flashes back...

It's getting dark. The sun has set over the trees, and now the moon hangs above, giving us just enough glisten, especially reflected on the surface of the lake.

It's a nice night. Summer warmth lingers in the breeze, though the harvest moon is coming.

My favorite time of year.

Wandering the shore of the lake, I see him off in the distance. It's crazy how quickly my heart rate picks up.

Darian is sitting on the old log bench we'd made, over by the willow trees. I make sure to step slowly, though any time I'm moving toward him I want to run. But I force myself to play it cool, unaffected.

It's all an act. I wonder if he can tell...

Taking a seat by his side, my eyes train toward his. He's looking at his home. Or rather, what will be his home, in only a few short weeks. I'm amazed at how quickly the thing went up, considering its size and how elaborate it is.

I swear, we have some of the best carpenters in the world, right here. On our Expanse.

"I'm going to call it the Den," he finally speaks, voice deep and dripping in contemplation.

He's coming into his own with this leader thing. I'm not sure how it makes me feel...

My chin bobs. "Like for lions...?"

"Or for snakes." His face curls toward mine, and he gives me a look. It's one I'm quite familiar with at this point, and it sets a longing in my chest unlike any other harsh sensation.

He misses me.

I see his feelings in his eyes, that deep, beckoning cerulean, like the ocean I haven't seen in more years than I can count. And my own emotions are radiating from me, like a pheromone.

It gives me a thought. Or an idea... Maybe not a great one, but I suppose we'll find out.

"I made something," I tell him. His brows quirk as he waits for me to continue. "Something... important."

His blue irises sparkle. "Like what?"

Stuffing my hand into my pocket, I pull out a vial. I've been carrying it around with me lately, syringe included, waiting for another opportunity to use it. Or to give it to someone who needs it more...

"Its effects are similar to the trumpets... on the surface." I take out a syringe and unpack it, sticking the needle into the vial and sucking up clear liquid. "But at its core is something much more potent, powerful. Lucid."

Darian's gaze is wide. "What are the effects?"

"Knowledge," I whisper, lifting the syringe and squirting some out. "Capability... Truth."

He worries his bottom lip for a moment, eyes bouncing between mine and the needle in my hand. Then he straightens and scoots closer. "Let me try it."

Amusement dances on my face as I take his arm. I'm struggling to contain my excitement. Because deep within myself I know the entire reason I created Empyrean was for Darian... For us to get closer.

For him to know what I'm thinking, so I don't have to fucking say it.

When my fingers wrap around his lower left bicep, just above the elbow, warmth seeps into me through his skin. I can't help the heavy swallow I try to disguise as I hold the syringe's plastic between my teeth and tap his veins with my fingers.

We haven't been together in months...

And I fucking miss him, so badly it's hard to even be near him right now.

Finding a vein I like, I take the syringe from my mouth and prepare. My eyes hold his, and his mine, the anticipation in his thoughts racing so loud, I can barely think. Blinking at him, I press the needle into his smooth flesh.

Seconds tick slower as I await the blood. And when it swirls, I plunge down and give him Empyrean. Every last drop.

Removing my tight grip from his arm, I drop the empty syringe on the forest floor and watch Darian's eyes. In a single instant, they've gone from dark blue to a crystalline topaz.

Breath leaves my lungs in a gasp as his lashes flutter. That was insane...

"Wow..." *he breathes, face tilting skyward.* "This is amazing."

He's getting the initial effects, the psychedelics.

Now, let's show him what we've got.

It is, isn't it? I think to him with my mind.

"Yea," *he mumbles, completely ignoring me while his eyes dart all around, likely catching sight of things I can't see.* "It's like I can see my thoughts."

I bite my lip to contain my grin. Can you now?

He finally looks at me. And his mind says, Are serpents supposed to be beautiful like that?

I blink slowly. Serpent.

He's never called me that before, but honestly... I really like it.

You're beautiful too, *I tell him, my lips unmoving.*

Darian gapes at me. His eyes, the color of the sky, go round, and his mouth falls open.

But his next words come from his mind... Drake?

Darian, *my thoughts mumble, mouth curved into a subtle smirk.*

I can hear... "I can hear your thoughts..."

You don't have to speak, brother. I can hear you just fine.

Oh my God, how is this happening? *Now his eyes are bugging out. I have to chuckle, because it's thoroughly amusing when he's all flustered.*

Adorable.

He shoves my chest with his hands, a smile taking over his lips.

How is this possible?

It's called Empyrean, *I tell him, reaching forward to grasp his jaw. I hear everything bounding through his head, so loudly it threatens to make me cringe. But I love it.*

Since the first time I used Empyrean, I've loved being inside Darian's head. Sure, it's not always pleasant, hearing what people think about you. Especially when a lot of it, coming from him, is pained. Damaged.

But it's a closeness unlike anything I could have ever comprehended before Empyrean. I've come to crave it. Even the pain sounds good in Darian's mind.

He inches closer to me, leaning into my touch and hovering his lips over my own. My pulse skyrockets in an instant.

I miss you.

His hand flies to the nape of my neck, fingers raking up into my hair. I fucking miss you so much.

Our mouths crash, hard, greedy lust exploding like sparks of color behind my eyes as he kisses me. Sucking my lower lip into his mouth, his thoughts are purring, desperate to get me as close as humanly possible.

What have you done, my sweet brother?

Gripping his face harder, my mouth advances on his, our tongues tangling while we drink each other in, bathing in the unleashed thoughts.

This is Empyrean, *my mind whispers to him in between the frantic breaths, escaping us as we devour one another whole.* The ultimate transformation.

"You're a genius," he murmurs real words on my lips. I'm amazed by the things you do…

Pushing him backward, I straddle his hips, grinding myself into him, shakily ripping at his clothes which stand in the way. I have zero chill right now, but I can't find it in myself to care.

It occurs to me that I may have fucked up here. Having myself unleashed and unfettered at Darian's mercy seemed like a great idea before, but now I'm growing nervous.

There are so many truths I keep from him…

So many of my own I can't bear to let him hear.

And so I push them away and tell him I want him. With our minds, we come together, as with our bodies, humming wordless need until we're naked, flushed and panting.

SERPENT IN WHITE

When I enter him, it's the most spectacular sound, like music that plays inside my brain.

No matter what else happens, for the rest of my days, I just want this from him.

I need to always know that I'm his Serpent.

That no one sheds the layers of the King like I do.

EPILOGUE

DARIAN

"**O**h my dear Mother, that's good." My eyes practically roll back in my head.

Abdiel chuckles. "You like that, my King?"

A groan leaves my lips, muffled by the obstruction. "Fucking delicious." I'm salivating. I can't chew fast enough.

"Alright, don't choke," Abdiel laughs harder. My eyes narrow in his direction while I lap flavor from my lips. "I only want to do that to you in our bedroom."

My gaze darts left and right. The cafe is pretty empty at the moment, so I won't scold him for talking dirty to me in public.

"I'm serious, my Prince." I place the half-devoured pastry down on my plate. "This is amazing. You're immensely skilled."

His head tilts, and he gives me that adorable look of his. Like a curious puppy. He's seriously the sweetest thing in existence. Even more so than this delicious blueberry custard-filled croissant thing he's feeding me.

"Your praise is too kind, baby," he whispers, teeth sinking into his plump lower lip as his forest irises twinkle.

Enough with the sex eyes, my gorgeous Prince, I squint at him. *We've already christened the kitchen. I don't think doing it on the tables is appropriate.*

His head falls back in a cackle that warms my chest like the oven in the back.

"Sorry." He grins, though he doesn't sound in any way apologetic. "You're right. I've got the waitstaff to think about."

He nods just as Kinsey is scampering up to us with a large glass of what appears to be cider.

"Head Priest, I brought you some of the chilled honeycrisp cider."

the Head Chef and owner of this fine establishment. "This one's better cold."

I accept the glass with a kind smile. "Mmm, yes. The one we had at the Harvest Festival was fantastic."

She beams. "That was Abdiel's special batch. Caramel apple hot cider. I'm surprised you even got a taste, it went so fast."

"That it did." I grin, taking Abdiel's hand on the table. "Just like everything else you made that night, my talented Prince."

His eyes gleam at me, and he bites his lip once more. His thoughts are bordering on perverse. It has me shifting in my seat.

Glancing up at Kinsey, I witness her cheeks flush as she turns and scurries back to the kitchen, apron billowing as she rushes away.

That one still crushes on you, baby, I tell him as my mouth quirks.

Abdiel rolls his eyes, though his smile is ever present. *Mmm... Too bad I've been crushing on the man I'm not supposed to have for far too long.*

"You have me now, sweet thing." I absentmindedly trace his ring finger with my index. "Whether you're supposed to or not."

We sit for almost another hour while I finish the breakfast he's made for me, making googly eyes at each other from across the table at his restaurant.

The White Snake was a turning point for The Principality, in many ways. It gave Abdiel his purpose, which was the most important thing to us.

Drake and I have had ours for many years. As does the rest of the Regnum. Even my ex-wives found their new places, rather quickly.

But my Prince needed something to fulfill him, outside of our love. He is a natural-born servant, and it's something he lives for. To make others happy. Now he gets to do it with his cooking, honing his leadership skills more and more each day that he works in this lovely cafe.

I won't lie, I miss having him as a Domestic. I miss seeing him every day, mulling around the house, sneaking glances and tiptoeing around his true feelings. But now when I see him at dinner, he's by my side. As is Drake, every night, not just on rare occasion. And we adjourn to the bedroom we share at night, the three of us together, in the most unexpected turn of events... A polyamorous thruple. Two brothers and their servant...

A lion, a snake, and a mouse.

It makes me chuckle.

They each have their own bedrooms in the Den, because we all acknowledge our individual needs for solitude, though it's very different from what I used to consider a *need* back in the lounge. But they, Abdiel mostly, tend to stay primarily in our bedroom. Worshipping me with their love, which is so vibrant, it turns any previously dulled sensations into a spectrum of color.

And we still use the lounge... though solitude cannot possibly be had in a room where three men physically latch onto each other in ways so illustrious it makes me hard just thinking about it.

When I finally leave Abdiel to his work, I head out on my rounds, sauntering about the Expanse. I check in on a few lessons happening with the kids, who are learning various things, from math to reading and spelling. And in the higher classes, they're bisecting frogs for biology.

It's moments like these when I sit in fascination for a moment, marveling at all that Drake and I have made here.

There's nothing quite like building something from the ground up. Nourishing it over time and developing it into a vast creation.

After that, I go to the fields and observe the farmers. Harvest was over a month ago, but that doesn't mean the work simply stops. They're still working diligently on processing our yields, preserving what needs to be stored for winter. Which brings me next to the base of the mountain.

The Field of Influence.

Weaving in between the rows of harvested plants, I watch the Tribe. They're training a few yards up, taking lessons of their own. Defense is the name of their game. It gives me a tingle of excitement, seeing all the newly recruited faces.

We're more heavily protected than ever. *Good.*

As I wander up past the lab, I find my mind drifting to Rhiannon. It happens, actually quite often. I think of her a lot...

What we would have become, if it had been in the cards. But I suppose it wasn't.

I like to think that in some other realm she's still with us. That we've become a sort of *quartuple*, if that's even a word. *We could make it one.*

She would head up business with Lauris, helping Drake so that he doesn't need to take on the world by himself anymore. It's something we've all given into, after that brilliant, yet tragic, night we experienced up in the clearing.

I imagine that Rhiannon would have been someone I could talk to, relate to in our shared painful pasts. But in her memory, I've started weekly therapy sessions for fellow survivors, of any kinds of abuse. Many of the Regnum have joined me. We talk about anything and everything, really. Our feelings, our pasts, whatever is on our minds. It's been massively helpful, and I have the *Princess* to thank for that.

Continuing the journey up the mountain, my thoughts walk by my side. And as soon as I'm far enough away from everyone else, I allow myself to think about my plan… The one that sends my heart jumping wildly behind my ribs.

I'm going to ask Abdiel and Drake to marry me.

It's an exciting notion, one I'm having for the first time, despite already having done this before.

But when I married my five ex-wives, I wasn't excited. It was just something I did because I felt backed into a corner. It was nothing like the swarm of butterflies flitting through my esophagus I get when thinking about getting down on bended knee for the two most important people in my life.

We've been talking about the future a lot lately. Planning has always been a part of The Principality, and while divorcing the wives and going public with my new relationship lessened the question of an *heir* for a few weeks, no one has simply forgotten about the topic.

Honestly, neither have I. It's something I think about often.

What could it mean…?

Rhiannon would have birthed an heir to The Principality. I know she would have. Of course, it wouldn't have been *my* child, genetically, but Drake's or Abdiel's.

I believe Mother sent us Rhiannon for that purpose. But then She took her away… *What could that mean?*

Does it mean we're not meant to birth a natural heir? Or will there be some other girl who will help it happen?

For the time being, Abdiel will take over The Principality when Drake or I pass, since he's much younger, and will hopefully be around for a long time.

I shiver. I don't even want to think about what life would look like without my Prince.

Alas, after that, I suppose we'll let Mother decide. She will lead us in the right direction for the great plan of this reality.

Proposing to my men is my main concern now, though I haven't decided exactly when to do it. I was thinking maybe after the first snowfall, which could be in as early as a few weeks. I can't wait to see the looks on their faces…

Thoughts slice into my own, and I immediately thwart my excitement, silencing my ideas as I approach the cabin. I can hear Drake as I move closer, which means he can definitely hear me, and I don't want him to know what I'm scheming.

It's hugely difficult to surprise your partners when they can both read your mind.

But even with Empyrean… even with the ultimate openness we share, there are things I've managed to keep to myself.

Outside the former cabin, I take a look around. The greenhouse has been expanded, and peering in through the glass, I see all the colors of Drake's handiwork. Greens of varying shades, flora and fauna, life sprouting from each direction. It's miraculous, and my sudden need to see the inside overcomes me.

Heading to the cabin door, I knock and let myself in, instantly hit with the intoxicating aroma of plants. Drake turned his old home into a protected terrarium of sorts, the entire inside filled with all his most prized possessions. His hybrids, all over the place, surrounded by warming lamps, each tank, pot, and case labeled meticulously with names, kingdoms, and species, chemical equations everywhere.

He still has his shelves set up with hundreds of books, and several whiteboards he uses for math I wouldn't even begin to comprehend.

My brother, my lover, my Serpent… The stone-cold genius.

"I wasn't expecting you," his deep voice murmurs at me, and I spin to find him transplanting something, his fingers digging into the dirt as he massages a new life into it.

"Figured I'd come check you out." I saunter up to him. "Making my rounds and all."

Wrapping my arms around his waist, I press my chest into his back, peering over his shoulder while he works. The sense of calm at being next to him is immediate, though our pulses both pick up, thoughts whirling through all the love we share.

"You've never been able to keep from checking me out," he rumbles, and I chuckle into him, teasing the nape of his neck with my lips. He hums, "Distractions, my King."

"I love distracting you," I whisper, my erection hardening in an instant from just being close like this. From listening to him and smelling him… *Feeling* him, in every single sense possible.

He stops what he's doing, brushing the dirt off his hands before twirling in my arms, zipping our fronts together as his hands go for my throat.

"Maybe it's time for a break." He smirks, eyelids drooping as he leans in and presses an unbearably soft kiss on my mouth.

"That sounds... *so good*," I growl between his lips, and drop to my knees, peering up at him from the floor.

"There is no sight quite like having a King on his knees," Drake hisses as I open his pants, his fingers sifting through my hair.

I lick my lips. This is something I can only ever do with Drake... *Remember.*

I can recall a time when I wasn't a King. When I wasn't the Head Priest of The Principality.

When I was just a man named Darian. A lost boy in the woods, fumbling through pain and pleasure with the other piece of his soul.

And for all the infinite love I possess for what we've built, and our relationship with Abdiel that finally feels like home for the first time in ever, Drake and I hold each other's worlds in our hands.

Hours later, we're curled up on the floor by the fireplace. It's not lit, yet there's enough heat coming from our recently sated bodies that we can lie here naked and not even feel the nip of fall from just outside these walls.

Drake reaches for his pants, pulling a joint from his pocket. He lights it while my head rests over his heart, listening to the steady beat, which has calmed significantly from the loud banging it was doing while he was losing himself deep in my body.

"You should've kept a bed in this place," I grunt at the stiffness in my hip from lying on the wood floor. Still, I would never want to move. I'm at peace.

"I have one," he says on an exhale of pungent smoke. "We just didn't make it that far."

I chuckle, and he does the same, flipping the lid of his lighter over and over.

The sound is familiar, and when I glance at it, I recognize it well as the Zippo he always carries around, with the worn American flag on it.

It was Dan's. And it never occurred to me until after I'd found out the truth about what he did to our former foster father why he had it. I'd always just assumed he'd stolen it from Dan, like he used to steal money, cigarettes, and booze from him.

But it was more like a parting gift. A trophy; a talisman. A symbol of Drake's victory over that monstrous piece of shit, and the vengeance he gave me like restitution.

Taking the lighter from Drake, I hold it in my hand, thumb brushing over the worn face. There's pain inside me from the memories it holds; that will never go away. But the acceptance I feel, the renewed truth in every step that led me to right where I am, is the ultimate rebirth.

Ecdysis.

"I love you, snake eyes," I whisper to him, shifting to watch his gaze with my mouth hovering over his.

"I love you, King Darian." He presses his lips to mine, and we both hum.

"Always?"

"Infinitely always."

When I eventually detach from the lustful hold of my Serpent, I head back out into the forest. The sun has since set and darkness surrounds me as I climb the mountain.

It's calling to me.

And I must listen.

The walk from Drake's cabin isn't that long. Not when your feet glide you in the direction you're needed, as if magnetized to a track just beneath the forest floor.

I barely even remember walking, the daze in me strong as it pulls me closer and closer. Between the trees I march, quiet and calm, the smell of my lover lingering on my skin, keeping me high as I reach the clearing.

And when I see it, it grips me; the empty space settled within a circle of tall trees.

My steps bring me into it, the crunch of leaves and pine needles beneath my boots the only inclination that someone is here.

My breathing goes shallow as I fall to my knees. Right in the center. Memories flood my mind, from the night months ago.

The sacrifice.

Rolling onto my back, I lie, with my arms at my sides, gaze on the starry night's sky where it peeks through the trees, which become barren in the change of seasons.

With each thump of my heart, I'm pushed deeper and deeper into the ground.

My fingers sink into the dirt, feeling the pulse of the earth on their tips. Sucking in a long pull of oxygen, my eyes droop shut.

And I'm swallowed into the abyss.

Behind my eyes, I can see myself. Like a mirrored reflection. I'm watching myself where the forces hold me. On a bridge between two places.

A pop of color appears, out of place at this time of year. Green, vibrant and new, crawls up my arm.

Vines grow over my flesh, taking over my arms. Flowers bloom on my skin. The musky floral scent surrounding me, emanating.

My breathing is one with Mother, the space, the infinite call of the clearing oozing from my pores, where it's housed deep inside me.

Inside of my soul.

And when my eyes fling open, the irises are black.

Stark, bottomless obsidian. Shiny and out of place, layered sediment of sheer evil and pure good.

We are balanced...

For the rock is *me*.

I am the rock.

WE ARE THE END.

A NOTE FROM THE AUTHOR

If you're reading this, that means you've made it through your own personal Ecdysis.

How do you feel?

I hope you're settled, in a sense. I hope this book, this unique and strange story entertained you in some way. Because for all the reality I think weighed heavily on this story, at the end of the day, it's still fiction. And very odd, at that.

There are things I'd like to mention; things I find very important to the story, and thus important to all of you. And yes, I'm long-winded as usual, but trust me, this is necessary.

As you probably know by now, this story was based on a short German fairy tale, called *The White Snake*. It was written by the Brothers Grimm, and if you don't know of them, or haven't read their tales, I highly recommend you change that now.

A lot of times when we think of *fairy tales*, our brains default to Disney characters; Snow White, Cinderella, and such.

Don't get me wrong, those are fairy tales, but many of the versions we know from popular culture are actually based on much darker, and often strange origins, written by people like the Brothers Grimm.

The White Snake is one of the lesser known tales. But it's also one of my favorites. I'm not going to regale you with the whole thing now, but I'll add a resource at the end for you to find it. Take a read. It's… quite bizarre.

Serpent In White is a far stretch from the original. But still, if you look real hard, you'll find the links, the largest of which is my keeping of the *Kingdom* premise.

The White Snake begins with a King and his servant. And while my story takes place in a present-day cult rather than in a seventeenth-century kingdom somewhere, I decided to repurpose a lot of the royal jargon to fit The Principality. I will be including a glossary right after this, so you can see what all the terms mean in relation to the story.

There's a lot of it. Like when Rhiannon said she could use a *cult dictionary*… She wasn't kidding.

The most significant connections, however, are with our main protagonists. The boys.

All of their names are nods to the original story.

The name *Darian* is an Old English name which means *King*. The same goes for Drake. *Drake* relates to *Snake* in Old English names.

And then we have Abdiel. The name *Abdiel* means *servant of God* in Hebrew. Thus, we have our servant; the most important character in the original story.

It's interesting to me that *The White Snake* starts out like, *there once was a King who*... and so on, as fairy tales often do. But the King himself is barely in the story. He's there simply to serve the purpose of presenting us with the white snake. After that, it's all about the servant and his journey. But I digress.

Next, we have the *white snake* itself. In case you didn't pick up on it, Drake is the white snake. The *serpent in white*. He's the one who controls Empyrean, who brings the power and abilities to our King and our Servant.

So where in the original story the white snake is quite literally a *white snake*, which the King eats in order to hear and communicate with animals, my white snake is a troubled and twisted, yet empirically beautiful man who, with his talents for alchemy, created something that helped bring Darian to where he is today, in his position of power, which ends up changing the course of their lives forever.

The great transformation.

There are also many nods to *transformation* in my story. Not only just life as they know it in The Principality, but the word *Ecdysis*, which as Darian described, means molting. It's a rebirth of sorts. Snakes are symbols of death and rebirth. Evil, wickedness and temptation. Sound familiar?

That's Drake for you.

And so where in the original story we have the servant peeking beneath the cover of the tray he serves to the King to find a white snake, of which he takes a bite... Here, that turns into Darian's solitude with Drake, and Abdiel watching in through the window.

Eating the white snake allows them to communicate with animals... and injections of a psychedelic drug allows them to hear thoughts. It's the telekinetic abilities that link the two stories.

Abdiel's curiosity also very much mirrors an unspoken trait in the servant from the original story. I mean, it's a short fairy tale, so it doesn't go into any detail whatsoever on the feelings of the characters. But I think you would need to be super curious to see your King eating from a mysterious tray every night and find yourself unable to keep from sneaking a peek, then a taste. Who wouldn't, right?

After the servant tries a bite of the white snake, the abilities are instant, and very confusing to him, as it goes for Abdiel after the first time he tries Empyrean. In the original, it ends up getting the servant out of some hot water with the King, and in return, the King grants the servant one wish.

The servant's wish is to go off on a journey of sorts. Hence, Abdiel's journey up the mountain.

Here's a cute nod to the original which happens during Abdiel's journey: the baby ravens. If you read *The White Snake*, you'll immediately know what I'm talking about. When Abdiel feeds the raven chicks and they speak to him, telling him, *one good deed for another... Everything gets a return.* That's more or less a direct quote from the original.

Which leads us to Rhiannon.

Rhiannon's place in my story is like a black-mirroring of *The White Snake* storyline. In it, the servant meets a princess on his journey, and then begins vying for her attention, using his abilities to win her over.

Not exactly how it goes down in my version, but there are similarities. Like Abdiel befriending the lonely girl contemplating suicide on the mountain, hearing her thoughts and knowing with certainty that he's meant to help her.

To take her in as his *princess*.

Rhiannon's other main purpose in the story is to bring in the skepticism of an Outsider. If we didn't have her, we'd go through the whole book living and breathing The Principality. Rhiannon comes in like I'm sure any of us would, doubting everything these people are doing in the woods, and it layers the experience.

The fact that she ends up falling in with the rest of them is an interesting piece of the puzzle... Falling for the cult, so to speak.

Rhiannon fulfills what she's made to do, in the story and in her own transformation. Her death may have come as a shock to some... It certainly did to me. That wasn't the ending I had originally planned. But it came to me in an epiphany of sorts, and I think it works perfectly.

I didn't want her to have to die. I never set out to kill characters for fun when I'm writing. The stories very much create themselves. I'm just as much along for the ride as you guys are.

There are little hints here and there, leading up to what's to come. I always recommend re-reading afterward. You'll see things differently.

And so the poly relationship is not quite what we might have expected, but that's how I like it. Imbalanced, complex, raw, and sometimes uncomfortable.

I suppose there's no time like the present to talk about the relationships in this story.

For those of you who have read my work before, you know that I rarely view sex, love, and relationships in the typical ways that romance novels have been doing for pretty much always. The way I see it, polyamory doesn't get enough attention in romance, and overall, it's a vastly misunderstood and misinterpreted topic.

This is probably the hill I'll end up taking my last breath on, but fuck it. I'm here to make sure everyone knows that polyamorous relationships are special; unique, complex and perfect that way.

Sorry not sorry, but I have to be blunt here. Polyamorous relationships are never going to look the way you expect them to. They won't be a perfectly proportionate equal measure between the parties. You need to accept it for what it is.

Okay, now I'm done. (Doubtful.)

Anyway, the reason why Rhiannon comes into the story so late is a direct correlation with *The White Snake*. The servant doesn't meet the princess until his journey. And so of course, due to the history, the intense love and sexual chemistry between Darian, Drake, and Abdiel—we have a thruple between the three of them, a *quartuple* experimented, bordered on, but ultimately abandoned due to fate.

There's a significant relationship between Abdiel and Darian, the King and his Servant-turned-Prince. Like the relationship between Darian and Drake, it has its own footing, as does the pairing of Drake and Rhiannon, Rhiannon and Abdiel before her passing.

You see what I'm saying now? It's never going to be even, all love divided equally between the three, or four, of them. That doesn't make sense.

I won't keep going on about this, but I'm sure if you follow me on social media, you'll see me ranting about it as some point. I'm telling you... My tombstone will read: *Here lies Nyla K. Polyamorous relationships are valid the way they are.*

Sorry. Let's move on.

The part of psychedelic drugs played in this story is an important one of course. Not just because of the telekinetic properties Empyrean provides, but also the effects of psychedelics on personal transformation in general.

The notion of *Empyrean* is built out of some truth. I'm not sure that there is or ever could be a drug that truly gives you telekinetic properties. But the idea is that with the mind's eye open, true empathy, soul to soul, could allow you to hear the thoughts of your fellow beast. In theory.

I know, I know. It's a stretch. But not completely out of the realm of possibility. And that's what we like to explore here in Nyla K Land.

I don't necessarily subscribe to the idea that everyone needs to try drugs at some point in their lives. Drugs can be permanently damaging, we know this. But I also happen to think there are differing effects of drugs for different people, and I think it can be helpful for some in finding their true selves.

That said, I'm not glorifying drug use in any way. This is fiction for a reason. But the White Angel Trumpets are in fact a plant with entheogenic properties. They're a real thing.

My PSA, though, must be; should you choose to try any of these drugs, please do so responsibly. And simply put, **don't** shoot up.

Don't use drugs intravenously. Injections are used for the purposes of this story, but in no way do I condone trying it in real life. There are many easier and safer ways to experiment with psychedelics and things found in nature.

Speaking of nature, how do we feel about the religious aspects of the book? To be honest with you, the stuff they're preaching here isn't far off-base from how I feel, spiritually.

I truly believe that a main reason why many people feel so disconnected from organized religion and even faith in God, is because the constructs that have been set up are downright primitive. I mean, like Rhiannon said, God as an old white man with a beard, looking judgingly down on all of us from the clouds? It's ridiculous.

It doesn't make sense, because it's stupid. The idea of *God* has been so warped through all the texts and misinterpretations over centuries.

And so, to view God as the Earth itself, I think, makes a whole lot of sense. We came from dirt, and we return to dirt. But not in a depressing way.

Honestly, I think a lot of people get bogged down by thinking about an afterlife. But I don't really believe it's any of our places to know what happens when we die. That's a secret for us to learn later, at the end of our transformation.

I might be going off on another tangent here... I also know having a Head Priest spouting sermons feels pretty preachy, although that's done to remind us that The Principality is, in fact, a religious cult.

But that doesn't mean we can't hear and possibly agree with the message.

Okay, last thing, and probably the biggest...

That reveal at the very end. Yea.

The concept of the black rock in the clearing on the mountain is one that speaks to me very much. And for any of my fellow *Twin Peaks* fans out there, I've definitely given some special nods to the black lodge that make me very excited. Yes... I'm a nerd.

If you follow me, you know I believe in and feel strongly about things of this nature. Multiple realities, shifts, doors and gateways. (I mean, I dedicated the book to Agent Cooper... Come on.)

I won't go into the *Darian as the black rock* thing much, simply because I want you to sit with it. I want you to have questions, because questions are good. Questions make you think of answers.

Not that I like torturing people with the unknown... But actually that's exactly what it is. Muahahaha!

No but seriously, is it that Darian only just became the rock? Has he always been the rock? Is the rock Darian, or is he it? And how many joints did I smoke before writing this??

Just kidding. This is my mind totally sober.

All I can say is that if you go back and read into some of the little bits and pieces of things Darian says, and especially the conversation that Drake has with the rock, in Abdiel's vision at the end, when he finds out the truth about his parent's deaths, Rhiannon's suicide... it may allude to some deeper meaning. A connection that Darian possesses to the Expanse. Whether he wants it or not... Whether he's even truly cognizant of it or not.

As we've learned, good and evil are two sides of the same coin. Light and dark. The balance.

Evil atones.

Think about that statement.

To atone is to make amends. Give reparations, which you would only do if you felt *bad* about something; if you possessed guilt or empathy. For evil to atone, it must mean that evil has a conscience.

Okay, I'm sorry. I'm hurting your brains. I'm gonna stop.

Just know that there is still always a balance, in everything. And with true *Ecdysis*, which is really just self-awareness, comes an acceptance, which is what they all found in the end.

Abdiel accepted the deaths of his parents and Rhiannon as tragic, and something that might not have *needed* to happen. But it did, and it can't be changed. Dwelling on the past helps no one. But learning from it... that's important.

Drake accepted that he is worthy of love. Rhiannon did the same, and she helped Darian in discovering acceptance of their painful pasts. Their stories of sexual abuse were definitely heartbreaking, but in coming together and becoming aware, they learned that it doesn't define them.

And then there's Darian. He accepted his truth, his part in the transformation... as the rock. The gateway, the open window. The holder of secrets and stories and truths.

A *King*.

And so that's where we'll wrap up, I guess. A modern-day Kingdom, royalty in the form of a religious cult, who utilizes psychedelic drugs as a form of awakening. There's so much going on with this book, no wonder my author's note alone is pages and pages long, and still I barely scratched the surface.

But I hope you enjoyed it. I hope you were able to make some of these connections yourself, but if not, I'm happy to have given some clarity. But like with many of my stories, I like to leave things open to your own interpretation, while still giving you a glimpse into my head and my process.

And I'm sorry. Because my head is a chaotic place to be. I've put myself on the platter and invited you to take a bite.

Either way, I'm glad you've joined us. Stay a while.

IMPORTANT TERMS

Den
Definition: (n) a wild animal's lair or habitation.

The *Den* is what they call Darian's home; his cabin on the lake.

Domestic
Definition: (n) a person who is paid to help with menial tasks such as cleaning.

This is exactly as it sounds. A *Domestic* on the Expanse is like a house-hand, or a servant.

DMT
Definition: *dimethyltryptamine*, a hallucinogenic tryptamine drug used as a recreational psychedelic drug, and prepared by various cultures for ritual purposes as an entheogen.

Ecdysis
Definition: (n) the process of shedding the old skin (in reptiles).

Similar to molting. After molting happens, an arthropod is described as "fresh", pale and soft-bodied. During this short phase, the animal expands in growth, due to its lack of constraint by the rigid exoskeleton. The new skin could take days or weeks to form, which can make it difficult to identify an individual that has recently undergone ecdysis.

This is all a fancy way of saying *Ecdysis* is a personal growth transformation, though in The Principality, it's a spiritual process rather than a physical one.

Empyrean
Definition: (n) heaven, in particular the highest part of heaven.
Ex. "the unapproachable splendor of the empyrean"

In ancient cosmologies, the *Empyrean Heaven*, or simply the *Empyrean*, was the place in the highest heaven, which was supposed to be occupied by the element of fire. The word derives from the Medieval Latin *empyreus*, an adaptation of the Ancient Greek *empyros*, meaning "in or on the fire".

Drake goes into why he calls his drug *Empyrean*, and I definitely think it's aptly named. Think about it this way, *Heaven on fire* sort of sounds like a mixture of Heaven and Hell. Good and evil.
The balance.

Expanse
Definition: (n) an area of something, typically land or sea, presenting a wide continuous surface.
Ex. "the green expanse of the forest"

This one speaks for itself. The territory was named *the Expanse*, because that is exactly what it is. From Lake Willow to White Trumpet Mountain is the Expanse.

*While the Expanse is a part of Washington state in the story, all of these landmarks/locations have been created in fiction.

The Field of Influence

On this one, we know what a *field* is, and what know what *influence* is. The Field of Influence is the area where things other than crops are grown on the Expanse. Specifically, cannabis and the White Angel Trumpets (the plants with entheogenic properties I discussed before).

Outsider
Definition: (n) a person who does not belong to a particular group.

Outsiders to The Principality are simply that. Anyone who lives outside the Expanse.

Principality
Definition: (n) a state ruled by a prince.

A *principality* can either be a monarchial feudatory or a sovereign state ruled by someone with a title considered to fall under the generic meaning of the term *prince*.

In layman's terms, a principality is a lesser-known royal house, which is why Darian and Drake chose this name instead of something more regal, like *The Kingdom*, or *The Empire*. Because while Darian is often compared to a King, he certainly never intended to be one.

Regnum

<u>Definition</u>: (n) a reign or rule.

Regnum is Latin for Kingdom or dominion. This is one of those nods I was telling you about, to the royal language of the original story. *Regnum* in my version, of course, meaning *family*, and with a deeper dive, the reign of a family over the Expanse.

Stray

<u>Definition</u>: (n) a stray person or thing; (v) to move away aimlessly from a group.

A *stray* is someone from the outside who comes into The Principality.

The White Snake
By the Brothers Grimm

Read Free: https://www.cs.cmu.edu/~spok/grimmtmp/014.txt

Purchase here: https://www.amazon.com/Original-Fairy-Tales-Brothers-Grimm/dp/0691173222

ACKNOWLEDGEMENTS

Let's give some thanks and shout-outs to some special peeps.

First, I need to thank my mother. Thanks, Mom, for reading us the weirdest possible fairy tales when we were kids, otherwise I never would have known about the magical wonders of the strange Brothers Grimm and their mind-bending *white snake*.

Thanks to my family for listening to me talk about this book for months. And thanks for being supportive, even though I'm fairly certain I sounded like a stark-raving lunatic the entire time.

My PA, the beautiful Amber Salazar… Girl, I'm so happy to have you in my world. Thank you for reading this book and loving it SO HARD. She's claimed the Serpent for herself, guys. So the rest of you are shit outta luck.

To Mackenize of Nice Girl Naughty Edits for proofreading this complex book. And as always for creating beautiful graphics and sharing my excitement. And… for helping me with that ending. I think I honestly need you. Don't leave me. Please. Lol, no but seriously. You're a true gem, my love.

AJ Wolf!! Thank you so much for the beautiful interior formatting, but more importantly, thank you for putting together this incredible collection! Honestly, I signed up for Twisted Tales drunk off my ass, and I really thought for a second I'd made a huge mistake. But this book has become one of the best things I've ever written. This story encompasses me as a writer, and I wouldn't have been forced to discover it if it weren't for you setting this whole thing up. Thanks thanks thanks, to you and all the other authors in this collection. Darian, Drake, Abdiel and Rhiannon are in brilliant company.

To Dez from Pretty In Ink Creations for creating this amazing cover. Thank you so much for taking my weird vision and turning it into something dark, ominous and breathtaking.

Wildfire Marketing Solutions. Thank you for working with us on this one! You ladies rock, and you do such an awesome job for indie authors. We love you!

To Brit's Bazaar, who drew the map of the Expanse… Honestly, I'm blown away. Your talent is mind-boggling. Just… thank you. Thank you so damn much for bringing such a vibrant life to the setting I created in my mind.

To the Street Hoes… You guys are *my* Regnum! I can never thank you all enough for the work you do, for pimping me and rocking me with me. My ultimate tribe. And I know it's weird for me to release things this close together, but I just hope I've been doing good for you in return ;)

And as always, the readers. To anyone who makes gorgeous edits for my books, videos, Tiktoks, writes reviews, tags me... Really anything. For anyone who reads and loves my books, and tells your friends, you guys are the reason I'm here. I can never thank you enough, but then I'll never stop trying. I love you all.

BOOKS BY NYLA K

The Midnight City Series:

Andrew & Tessa's Trilogy
(Forbidden/Age Gap, celebrity romance, suspense. Read in order)
Midnight City (TMCS #1)
Never Let Me Go (TMCS #2)
Always Yours (TMCS #3)

Alex & Noah
Seek Me (TMCS #4 – Standalone, Friends to lovers/Angst)

Unexpected Forbidden Romance:

PUSH (Standalone, Taboo/MMF)
To Burn In Brutal Rapture (Standalone, Taboo/Age Gap)

Alabaster Penitentiary:

Distorted, Volume 1 (MM)
Joyless, Volume 2 (MMF)
Brainwashed, Volume 3 (MM) – Coming in 2022!
Fragments, Volume 4 (MM)
Ivory, Volume 5 (mystery, *wink wink*)

Twisted Tales Collection:

Serpent In White (A polyamorous, cult retelling of *The White Snake*)

Twisted Christmas: A Taboo Christmas Anthology

Unwrap Him by Nyla K (An Age Gap, Taboo MM) Coming December 1st 2021!

FLIPPING *hot* FICTION

Hi, guys! I'm Nyla K, otherwise known as Nylah Kourieh; an awkward sailor-mouthed lover of all things romance, existing in the Dirty Lew, up in Maine, with my fiancé, who you can call PB, or Patty Banga if you're nasty. When I'm not writing and reading sexy books, I'm rocking out to Machine Gun Kelly and YUNGBLUD, cooking yummy food and fussing over my kitten (and no, that's not a euphemism). Did I mention I have a dirtier mind than probably everyone you know?

I like to admire hot guys (don't we all?) and book boyfriends, cake and ice cream are my kryptonite. I can recite every word that was ever uttered on *Friends*, *Family Guy*, and *How I Met Your Mother*, red Gatorade is my lifeblood, and I love to sing, although I've been told I do it in a Cher voice for some reason. I'm very passionate about the things that matter to me, and art is probably the biggest one. If you tell me you like my books, I'll give you whatever you want. I consider my readers are my friends, and I welcome anyone to find me on social media any time you want to talk books or sexy dudes!

GET AT ME

AuthorNylaK@gmail.com, or my PA
amberbookobsession@gmail.com

Sign up for the Flipping Hot Newsletter for exclusive content!

Instagram:@AuthorNylaK

Facebook: AuthorNylaK

Join my reader group! Nyla K's Flipping Hot Readers!

Tiktok: @AuthorNylaK

Twitter: @MissNylah

Goodreads: Nyla K

BookBub: @AuthorNylaK

Made in United States
Troutdale, OR
12/31/2024

27445184R00282